Olive,
Again

Center Point
Large Print

Also by Elizabeth Strout and available from Center Point Large Print:

Anything Is Possible

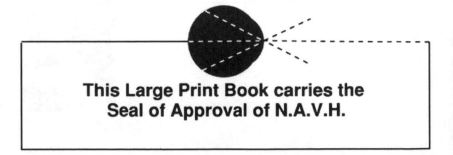

Olive, Again

Elizabeth Strout

CENTER POINT LARGE PRINT
THORNDIKE, MAINE

This Center Point Large Print edition
is published in the year 2019 by arrangement with
Random House, an imprint of Random House,
a division of Penguin Random House LLC.

"The Walk" was first published in *Night Stories:
Linden Frederick—Fifteen Paintings and the Stories
They Inspired*, copyright 2017 Forum Gallery, published
by Glitterati Arts. It was also published previously in
It Occurs to Me That I Am America, edited by
Jonathan Santlofer (New York: Touchstone, 2018).

The text of this Large Print edition is unabridged.
In other aspects, this book may vary
from the original edition.
Printed in the United States of America
on permanent paper.
Set in 16-point Times New Roman type.

ISBN: 978-1-64358-381-5

The Library of Congress has cataloged this record under
Library of Congress Control Number: 2019946710

For Zarina,
again

Contents

Arrested

I n the early afternoon on a Saturday in June, Jack Kennison put on his sunglasses, got into his sports car with the top down, strapped the seatbelt over his shoulder and across his large stomach, and drove to Portland—almost an hour away—to buy a gallon of whiskey rather than bump into Olive Kitteridge at the grocery store here in Crosby, Maine. Or even that other woman he had seen twice in the store as he stood holding his whiskey while she talked about the weather. The *weather.* That woman—he could not remember her name—was a widow as well.

As he drove, an almost-calmness came to him, and once in Portland he parked and walked down by the water. Summer had opened itself, and while it was still chilly in mid-June, the sky was blue and the gulls were flying above the docks. There were people on the sidewalks, many were young people with kids or strollers, and they all seemed to be talking to one another. This fact impressed him. How easily they took this for granted, to be with one another, to be talking! No one seemed to even glance at him, and he realized what he had known before, only now it came to him differently: He was just an old man with a sloppy belly and not anyone worth noticing. Almost, this was freeing. There had been many years of his life when he was a tall, good-looking man, no gut, strolling about the campus at Harvard, and people did look at him then, for all those years, he would see students glance at him with deference, and also women, they looked at him. At department meetings he had been intimidating; this was told to him by colleagues, and he understood it to be true, for he had meant to be that way. Now he sauntered down one of the wharfs where condos were built, and he thought perhaps he should move here, water everywhere around him, and people too. He took from his pocket his cellphone, glanced at it, and returned it to his pocket. It was his daughter he wished to speak to.

A couple emerged from the door of one apartment; they were his age, the man also had a stomach, though not as big as Jack's, and the woman looked worried, but the way they were together made him think they had been married for years. "It's over now," he heard the woman say, and the man said something, and the woman said, "No, it's over." They walked past him (not noticing him) and when he turned to glance at them a moment later, he was surprised—vaguely—to see that the woman had put her arm through the man's, as they walked down the wharf toward the small city.

Jack stood at the end of the wharf and watched the ocean; he looked one way, then the other. Small whitecaps rolled up from a breeze that he felt only now. This is where the ferry came in from Nova Scotia, he and Betsy had taken it one day. They had stayed in Nova Scotia three nights. He tried to think if Betsy had put her arm through his; she may have. So now his mind carried an image of them walking off the ferry, his wife's arm through his—

He turned to go.

"Knucklehead." He said the word out loud and saw a young boy on the wharf close by turn to look at him, startled. This meant he was an old man who was talking to himself on a wharf in Portland, Maine, and hc could not—Jack Kennison, with his two PhDs—he could not figure out how this had happened. "Wow." He said that out loud as well, past the young boy by now. There were benches, and he sat down on an empty one. He took out his phone and called his daughter; it would not yet be noontime in San Francisco, where she lived. He was surprised when she answered.

"Dad?" she said. "Are you okay?"

He looked skyward. "Oh, Cassie," he said, "I just wondered how you were doing."

"I'm okay, Dad."

"Okay, then. Good. That's good to hear."

There was silence for a moment, then she said, "Where are you?"

"Oh. I'm on the dock in Portland."

"Why?" she asked.

"I just thought I'd come to Portland. You know, get out of the house." Jack squinted out toward the water.

Another silence. Then she said, "Okay."

"Listen, Cassie," Jack said, "I just wanted to say I know I'm a shit. I know that. Just so you know. I *know* that I'm a shit."

"Daddy," she said. "Daddy, come on. What am I supposed to say?"

"Nothing," he answered agreeably. "Nothing to say to that. But I just wanted you to know I know."

There was another silence, longer this time, and he felt fear.

She said, "Is this because of how you've treated me, or because of your affair for all those years with Elaine Croft?"

He looked down at the planks of the wharf, saw his black old-man sneakers on the roughened boards. "Both," he said. "Or you can take your pick."

"Oh, Daddy," she said. "Oh, Daddy, I don't know what to do. What am I supposed to do for you?"

He shook his head. "Nothing, kid. You're not

supposed to do anything for me. I just wanted to hear your voice."

"Dad, we were on our way out."

"Yeah? Where're you going?"

"The farmers market. It's Saturday and we go to the farmers market on Saturdays."

"Okay," Jack said. "You get going. Don't worry. I'll talk to you again. Bye-bye now."

He thought he could hear her sigh. "All right," she said. "Goodbye."

And that was that! That was that.

Jack sat on the bench a long time. People walked by, or perhaps no people walked by for a while, but he kept thinking of his wife, Betsy, and he wanted to howl. He understood only this: that he deserved all of it. He deserved the fact that right now he wore a pad in his underwear because of prostate surgery, he *deserved* it; he deserved his daughter not wanting to speak to him because for years he had not wanted to speak to her—she was gay; she was a gay woman, and this still made a small wave of uneasiness move through him. Betsy, though, did not deserve to be dead. He deserved to be dead, but Betsy did not deserve that status. And yet he felt a sudden fury at his wife—"Oh, Jesus Christ Almighty," he muttered.

When his wife was dying, she was the one who was furious. She said, "I hate you." And he said, "I don't blame you." She said, "Oh, *stop* it." But

13

he had meant it—how could he blame her? He could not blame her. And the last thing she said to him was: "I hate you because I'm going to die and you're going to live."

As he glanced up at a seagull, he thought, But I'm not living, Betsy. What a terrible joke it has been.

The bar at the Regency Hotel was in the basement, the walls were dark green and the windows looked out at the sidewalks, but the sidewalks were high up in the windows, and mostly he could just see legs going by. He sat at the bar and ordered one whiskey neat. The bartender was a pleasant fellow. "Good," Jack said when the young man asked how he was today.

"Okay, then," said the bartender; his eyes were small and dark beneath his longish dark hair. As he poured the drink, Jack noticed that he was older than he had first seemed, although Jack had a hard time these days figuring out the age of people, the young especially. And then Jack thought: What if I'd had a son? He had thought this so many times in his life it surprised him that he kept wondering. And what if he had not married Betsy on the rebound, as he had? He had been on the rebound, and she had been as well, from that fellow Tom Groger she'd loved so much in college. What then? Troubled but feeling better—he was in the presence of someone, the bartender—Jack laid these thoughts out before him like a large piece of cloth. He understood that he was a seventy-four-year-old man who looks back at life and marvels that it unfolded as it did, who feels unbearable regret for all the mistakes made.

And then he thought: How does one live an honest life?

This was not the first time he had wondered this, but it felt different today, he felt distant from it, and he truly wondered.

"So what brings you to Portland?" The bartender asked this as he wiped the bar with a cloth.

Jack said, "Nothing."

The fellow glanced up at him, turning slightly to wipe the other part of the counter.

"I wanted to get out of the house," Jack said. "I live in Crosby."

"Nice town, Crosby."

"Yes, it is." Jack sipped his whiskey, put the glass down with care. "My wife died seven months ago," he said.

Now the fellow looked at Jack again, pushing his hair out of his eyes. "Sorry? Did you say—?"

"I said my wife died seven months ago."

"That's too bad," the fellow said. "That's gotta be tough."

"Well, it is. Yes, it is."

The young man's face didn't change expression as he said, "My dad died a year ago and my mom's been great, but I know it's been hard on her."

"Sure." Jack hesitated, then he said, "How's it been on you?"

"Oh, it's sad. But he was sick a while. You know."

Jack felt the inner slow burn that was familiar to him, which he felt when that widow talked about the weather in the grocery store. He wanted to say, Stop it! Tell me how it's *really* been! He sat back, pushed his glass forward. It's just the way it was, that's all. People either didn't know how they felt about something or they chose never to say how they really felt about something.

And this is why he missed Olive Kitteridge.

Okay, he said to himself. Okay now. Easy, boy.

With deliberation, he made his mind return to Betsy. And then he remembered something—how curious that he should remember this now: When he had gone in for surgery many years back, to have his gallbladder out, his wife had stood at his side in recovery, and when he woke again later a patient near him said, "Your wife was gazing at you with such love, I was struck at how she was looking at you so lovingly." Jack had believed this; it had, he remembered, made him a tiny bit uneasy, and then—years later—during an argument he brought it up and Betsy said, "I was hoping you would die."

Her directness had flabbergasted him. "You were hoping I would *die?*" In his memory he had opened his arms in astonishment as he asked her this.

And then she had said, looking uncomfortable, "It would have made things easier for me."

So there was that.

Oh, Betsy! Betsy, Betsy, Betsy, we blew it—we blew our chance. He could not really pinpoint when, maybe because there had never been a chance. After all, she was she, and he was he. On their wedding night she had given herself, but not freely, as she had in the months before. He did, of course, always remember that. And she had never really given herself freely since that night, now forty-three years ago.

"How long have you lived in Crosby?" The bartender asked him this.

"Six years." Jack switched his legs to the other side of the barstool. "I have now lived in Crosby, Maine, for six years."

The bartender nodded. A couple came in and sat down at the far end of the bar; they were young, and the woman had long hair that she smoothed over one shoulder—a confident person. The bartender walked over to them.

Now Jack allowed his mind to go to Olive Kitteridge. Tall, big; God, she was a strange woman. He had liked her quite a bit, she had an honesty—was it an honesty?—she had some-

17

thing about her. A widow, she had—it felt to him—practically saved his life. They'd gone to dinner a few times, a concert; he had kissed her on the mouth. He could laugh out loud to think about this now. Her mouth. Olive Kitteridge. Like kissing a barnacle-covered whale. She had a grandson born a couple of years ago, Jack hadn't especially cared, but she had cared because the kid was called Henry after his grandfather, Olive's dead husband. Jack had suggested she go see the little fellow Henry in New York City and she had said, Well, she didn't think so. Who knows why? Things were not good with her son, he knew that much. But things weren't good with his daughter either. They had that in common. He remembered how Olive had told him right away that her father had killed himself when she was thirty. Shot himself in his kitchen. Maybe this had something to do with how she was; it must have. And then she had come over one morning and unexpectedly lain down next to him on the bed in the guest room. Boy, he had been relieved. Relief had just flowed through him when she'd put her head on his chest. "Stay," he said finally, but she rose and said she had to get home. "I'd like it if you stayed," he said, but she did not. And she never returned. When he tried calling her, she did not answer the telephone.

He had bumped into her in the grocery store

only once—a few days after she had lain down with him; he'd been holding his jug of whiskey. "Olive!" he'd exclaimed. But she had been agitated: Her son, down in New York City, was going to have another baby any day! "I thought he just had a baby," Jack said, and she said, Well, the woman was pregnant again and they hadn't even told her until now! Olive had a grandson; why did they need more kids, there were already two the wife had brought into the marriage. Olive must have said that three times at least. He called her the next day, and the telephone just kept ringing, and he realized she didn't have her answering machine turned on. Could that be true? Anything could be true with Olive. He assumed she had probably, finally, gone to New York to see this new grandchild, because when he called again the next day, there was no answer then either. He emailed her with the subject line ?????. And then no subject. She had not answered that either. More than three weeks ago that had been.

The bartender was back in front of Jack, making the couple's drinks. Jack said, "And you? Did you grow up around here?"

"Nah," the fellow said, "I grew up right outside of Boston. I'm here 'cause of my girlfriend. She lives here." He tossed his head a bit, getting his dark hair out of his eyes.

Jack nodded, drank his whiskey. "For years my

wife and I lived in Cambridge," Jack said, "and then we came up here."

He could have sworn he saw something on the bartender's face, a smirk, before the fellow turned away and went to place the drinks before the couple.

When the fellow returned, he said to Jack, "A Harvard man? So you were a Harvard man." He pulled a rack of clean glasses from below him, and began to put them—hanging them upside down—in the rack above him.

"I cleaned toilets there," Jack said. And the idiot guy looked at him quickly, as though to see if he was joking. "No, I did not clean toilets. I taught there."

"Great. You wanted to retire up here?"

Jack had never wanted to retire. "How much do I owe you?" he asked.

Driving back, he thought of Schroeder, what a goddamn ass that man was, what a shit of a dean. When Elaine filed the lawsuit, when she actually did that, citing sexual harassment as the reason she did not get tenure, Schroeder became a terrible man. He was outlandish, would not even let Jack speak to him. It's in the hands of the lawyers, he said. And Jack was put on research leave. Three years it took for that thing to settle, for Elaine to get her significant chunk of change, and by that time Jack and Betsy had moved to

Maine; Jack had retired. They came to Maine because Betsy wanted to—she wanted to get far away, and boy they did. Crosby was a pretty coastal town she had researched online, and it was about as far away as a person could get, even though it was just a few hours up the East Coast. They moved to the town without knowing one person there. But Betsy made friends; it was her nature to do so.

Pull over.

Pull your car over.

These words were said a few times before Jack paid attention to them; they were said through a bullhorn loudspeaker, and the different sound of them, different from just the tires rumbling over the pavement, puzzled Jack, and then he was amazed when he saw the lights flashing blue and the police car right on his tail. *Pull your car over.* "Jesus," Jack said aloud, and he pulled his car over to the side of the highway. He turned the engine off and glanced down to the floor of the passenger seat at the plastic bag that had his whiskey in it, bought at a grocery store outside of Portland. He watched the young policeman who was walking over—what a puffed-up piece of crap the guy was, wearing his sunglasses—and Jack said, politely, "How may I help you?"

"Sir, your driver's license and registration."

Jack opened the glove compartment, finally found the registration, then pulled his license from his wallet and handed them to the police-man.

"Were you aware that you were going seventy in a fifty-five-mile zone?" The policeman asked him this rudely, Jack felt.

"Well, no, sir, I was not aware of that. And I'm very sorry." Sarcasm was his weak point, Betsy had always said, but this policeman was beyond hearing that.

"Were you aware that your car is uninspected?"

"No."

"It was due for inspection in March."

"Huh." Jack looked around the front seat. "Well. Here's what happened. Now that I think of it. My wife died, you see. She died." Jack peered up at the police officer. "Dead." Jack said this pointedly.

"Take your sunglasses off, sir."

"Excuse me?"

"I said, take your sunglasses off, sir. Now."

Jack removed his sunglasses and smiled in an exaggerated way at the policeman. "Now you take yours off," Jack said. "Show me yours, and I'll show you mine." He grinned up at the fellow.

After holding up Jack's license and then looking at Jack, the policeman said, "Wait here while I run these." And the policeman went back to his car, which still had the flashing blue lights zinging around. He spoke into his radio as he walked. Within moments another police car came driving up, also with blue lights flashing.

"You called for backup?" Jack yelled this after him. "Am I that dangerous?"

The second policeman got out of his car and walked up to Jack. This man was huge, and not young. He'd seen stuff, is what his walk said, what his eyes—expressionless, no sunglasses for him—said. "What's that in the bag on the floor?" the huge man asked with his big voice.

"It's liquor. Whiskey. Would you like to see?"

"Step out of the car."

Jack peered up at him. *"What?"*

The huge man stepped back. "Step out of the car now."

Jack got out of the car—slowly, because he felt winded. The huge man said, "Put your hands on the top of the car," and this made Jack laugh. He said, "There is no top. See? This is called a convertible and there is no top to the car at the moment."

The policeman said, "Put your hands on the top of the car now."

"Like this?" Jack put his hands on the window frame.

"Stay there." The man walked back to the car that had pulled Jack over and spoke to the other police officer, sitting in the front seat.

It came to Jack then how these days everything was videotaped from a policeman's car—he had read this somewhere—and he suddenly gave the finger to the two cars behind him. Then he put his hand back on the window frame. "Horseshit," he said.

Now the first policeman got out of his car and strode up to Jack, his holster strapped against his thigh. Jack, with his big belly hanging out and his hands ridiculously placed on the window frame, looked over at the guy and said, "Hey, you're packed."

"What did you say?" The policeman was pissed.

"I said nothing."

"You want to be placed under arrest?" the policeman asked. "Would you like that?"

Jack started to laugh, then bit his lip. He shook his head, looking down at the ground. And what he saw were many ants. They had been interrupted by his car tracks, and he stared down at the tiny little ants who were making their way through a crack in the pavement, piece of sand by piece of sand from the place where his tire had crushed so many of them, to—Where? A new spot?

"Turn around and put your hands up," the policeman directed, and so Jack, holding his hands up, turned around, and he was aware of the cars going by on the turnpike. What if someone recognized him? There was Jack Kennison holding his hands up like a criminal with two police cars and their flashing blue lights. "You listen to me," the policeman said. He raised his sunglasses to rub one eye, and in that brief moment Jack saw the man's eyes, and they were strange, like the eyes of a fish. The policeman pointed a finger at Jack. He kept pointing the finger but not saying anything, as though he couldn't remember what he'd been going to say.

Jack cocked his head. "Listening," he said. "All ears." He said this with as much sarcasm as he could.

Fish-Eyes walked around to the other side of Jack's car, opened the door, and brought out the bottle of whiskey in its plastic bag. "What's this?" he asked, walking back toward Jack.

Jack put his arms down and said, "I told your friend, it's whiskey. Come on, you can see that. For the love of Christ."

Fish-Eyes stepped close to Jack then, and Jack backed away, except there was nowhere to go, his car was right there. "Now you tell me again what you just said," Fish-Eyes directed.

"I *said* it's whiskey, and you can see that. And then I said something about Christ. Something about Christ and love."

"You've been drinking," Fish-Eyes said. "You have been drinking, sir." And his voice held something so ugly that Jack was sobered. Fish-Eyes dropped the bag with the whiskey onto the driver's seat of Jack's car.

"I have," Jack said. "I had a drink at the Regency bar in Portland."

From his back pocket Fish-Eyes brought something forward; it was small enough to be held in one hand, yet square-looking and gray, and Jack said, "Jesus, are you going to taser me?"

Fish-Eyes smiled, he smiled! He stepped toward Jack holding out the thing, and Jack said, "Please, come on." He held his arms against his chest; he was really frightened.

"Breathe in this," said Fish-Eyes, and a little hose appeared from the thing he was holding.

Jack put his mouth on the little hose and breathed.

"Again," said Fish-Eyes, moving closer to Jack.

Jack took another breath, then took his mouth off the hose. Fish-Eyes looked at the thing closely and said, "Well, well, you are just under the legal limit." He put the hose gadget back into his pocket and said to Jack, "He's writing you up a ticket, and after he gives it to you, I suggest you get in your car and drive straight to a place that gets this car inspected, do you understand me, sir?"

Jack said, "Yes." Then he said, "May I get back in my car now?"

Fish-Eyes leaned toward him. "Yes, you can get back in your car now."

So Jack sat himself in the driver's seat, which was low to the ground since it was a sports car, and put the whiskey onto the seat next to him, and waited for the huge man to bring him a ticket, but Fish-Eyes stood right there as though Jack might bolt.

And then—from the corner of his eye—Jack saw something he would never be sure about and would never forget. The policeman's crotch was right at Jack's eye level, and Jack thought—he *thought* but looked away quickly—that the guy might be getting a boner. There was a bulge there bigger than—Jack glanced up at the man's face, and the guy was staring down at Jack with his sunglasses on.

The huge man came over and gave Jack the ticket, and Jack said, "Thank you very much, fellows. I'll be off now." And he drove slowly away. But Fish-Eyes followed him all the way down the turnpike until Jack came to the exit for Crosby, and when Jack took that exit the guy did not follow him but headed on straight up the turnpike. Jack let out a yell: "Get yourself some tighty-whities, like every other man in this state!"

Jack took a deep breath and said, "Okay. It's okay. It's over." He drove the eight miles into Crosby, and on the way he said, "Betsy. Betsy! Wait until I tell you what happened to me. You're not going to believe this one, Betts." He allowed himself this, the conversation with her about what had just happened to him. "Thanks, Betsy," he said, and what he meant was thanks for being so nice about the prostate surgery. Which she had been; there was no doubt about that. All his life

27

Jack had been an undershorts man. Never for him those tighty-whities, but in Crosby, Maine, you couldn't buy any undershorts. This had amazed him. And Betsy had gone to Freeport for him, and bought his undershorts there. Then his prostate surgery, almost one year ago, forced him to give up the undershorts. He needed a place to put the stupid pad. How he hated it! And right now, as though on cue, he felt a squirt—not a dribble—come from him. "Oh, for Christ's sake," he said out loud. The whole state, it seemed, wore tighty-whities; just recently Jack had gone to the Walmart on the outskirts of town to buy one more package of them, and he had noticed there were no undershorts there either. Just a slab of tighty-whities sized all the way to XXX-Large for all those poor fat men, huge men, in this state. But Betsy had gone to Freeport and found him undershorts there. Oh, Betsy! Betsy!

Home, Jack had trouble believing what had happened during the day, it all seemed ridiculous and somehow—almost—incidental. He sat for a long time in his big chair, looking at the living room; it was a spacious room with a low blue couch on metal legs that stretched along a few feet from the wall facing the television, then went at a right angle along the other area of the room, with a metal-legged glass coffee table in front. Then Jack turned in his chair and stared through the windows at the field of grass and the trees beyond, their leaves bright green. He and Betsy had agreed that they liked the view of this field more than any view of the water, and as he remembered this a warmth trembled through him. Finally he rose, poured himself some whiskey, and boiled four hot dogs on the stove. He kept shaking his head while he opened a can of baked beans. "Betsy," he said out loud a few times. When he was through eating and had rinsed the dishes—he did not put them in the dishwasher, that seemed too much trouble—he had one more glass of whiskey and got to thinking of Betsy being so in love with that Tom Groger fellow. Oh, what a strange thing a life was—

But filled with a sense of goodwill—the day was almost over and the whiskey was working—Jack sat at his computer and googled the fellow, Tom Groger. He found the man; he was apparently still teaching at that private high school for girls in Connecticut; he'd be eight years younger than Jack. But only girls? Still? Jack scrolled through and saw they'd been accepting young men for about ten years. Then he found a small picture of Tom Groger; he had gray hair now, he was thin, you could see that in his face, which seemed pleasant enough, and very bland to Jack's eyes. There was an email address for him attached to the school's site. So Jack wrote to him. "My wife, Betsy (Arrow as you would have known her), died seven months ago, and I know she loved you very much in her youth. I thought you might want to know about her death." He pressed SEND.

Jack sat back and looked at the light that was changing on the trees. These long, long evenings; they were so long and beautiful, it just killed him. The field was darkening, the trees behind it were like pieces of black canvas, but the sky still sent down the sun, which sliced gently across the grass on the far end of the field. His mind went back over the day and it seemed he could make no sense of it. Had that guy *really* had a boner? It seemed impossible, yet Jack knew—in a way, he knew—the feeling of anger and power that might have produced it. If the guy had even been getting one. And then Jack thought of the ants that were still going about trying to get their sand wherever they needed it to go. They seemed almost heartbreaking to him, in their tininess and their resilience.

Two hours later, Jack checked his email, hoping his daughter might have written and hoping as well that Olive Kitteridge might have reappeared in his life. After all, she had been the one who emailed him the first time, about her son, and he had answered about his daughter. He had even told Olive one day about his affair with Elaine Croft, and Olive had not seemed to judge him. She had spoken of a schoolteacher that she herself had fallen in love with years ago—an almost-affair, she called it—and the man had died in a car accident one night.

Now as he checked his email he saw that he had forgotten (forgotten!) about Tom Groger, but there was a reply from TGroger@Whiteschool. edu. Jack squinted through his reading glasses. "I know about the death of your wife. Betsy and I were in contact for many years. I don't know if I should tell you this, or not, but she spoke to me of your own dalliance, and perhaps I should tell you—I don't know, as I said, if I should tell you or not—but there was a period of time when Betsy and I met in a hotel in Boston, and also New York. Perhaps you already know that."

Jack pushed back his chair from the desk; the wheels rumbled against the hardwood floor. He pulled the chair back in and read the message again. "Betsy," he murmured, "why, you son of a gun." He took his glasses off, wiped his arm across his face. "Holy shit," he said. In a few minutes he put his glasses back on and read the email one more time. "Dalliance?" said Jack out loud. "Who uses the word 'dalliance'? What are you, Groger, some faggot?" He pushed DELETE and the message disappeared.

Jack felt as sober as a churchmouse. He walked around his house, looking at the touches from his wife, the lamps that had that frill around

31

the bottoms, the mahogany bowl she picked up somewhere that stayed on the glass coffee table and was now filled with junk: keys, an old phone that didn't work, business cards, paper clips. He tried to think when his wife went to New York, and it was—he thought—not too far into their marriage. She had been a kindergarten teacher, and he remembered her speaking of meetings in New York she had to attend. He had paid no attention; he was busy getting tenure, and then he was just busy.

Jack sat down in his armchair and immediately stood up. He walked around the house again, stared out at the now darkened field, then went upstairs and walked around that too. His bed, their *marriage* bed, was unmade, as it was every day except when the cleaning woman came, and it seemed to him to be the mess that he was, or that they had been. "Betsy," he said out loud, "Jesus Christ, Betsy." He sat tentatively on the edge of the bed, his hand running up and down his neck. Maybe Groger was just yanking his chain, being mean for the fun of it. But no. Groger was not the sort; he was, Jack had always gathered, a serious man, he taught English, for the love of Christ, all those years at that school for little twats. Wait, was this why Betsy had said it would have "made things easier" if Jack had died during his gallbladder operation? That far back? How far back was that? Ten years into their marriage at least. "You were doing my wife?" Jack said aloud. "You little prick." He stood up and resumed his walking through the upstairs. There was another bedroom, and then the room his wife had used as her study; Jack went into them both, turning around as though looking for something. Then he went back downstairs and walked through the two guest rooms, the one with the double bed and the one with the single bed. In the kitchen he poured himself another whiskey from the jug he had bought that day. It seemed days ago he had bought it.

His own affair with Elaine Croft had not started until he'd been married for twenty-five years. The urgency he and Elaine had felt; God, it was something. It was terrible. Had Betsy felt that? Not possible, Betsy was not an urgent woman. But how did he know what kind of woman she was?

"Hey, Cassie," Jack said, "your mother was a slut."

But he knew, even as he said this, that it was not true. Cassie's mother had been—Well, she was kind of a slut, for Christ's sake, if she was off doing Groger in a hotel in Boston and in New York and Cassie was just a little kid, but Betsy had been a wonderful mother, that was the truth. Jack shook his head. Now he suddenly felt drunk. He also knew he would never, ever tell Cassie, he would let her have her mother as she had been:

a saint who put up with a homophobic father, a self-absorbed asshole.

"Okay," said Jack. "Okay."

He sat back at his computer. He retrieved the message from Trash, read it one more time, then wrote—being very careful of spelling so it would not sound drunk—Hello, Tom. Yes, I do know of your meetings with her. This is why I thought you would want to know of her death. He sent it, then he shut the computer off.

He stood up and went and sat in his armchair for a long time. He thought once again of the ants he had seen today while that awful Fish-Eyes man had him against the car, those *ants*. Just doing what they were meant to do, live until they died, so indiscriminately by Jack's car. He really could not stop thinking of them. Jack Kennison, who had studied human behavior from the medieval times, then the Austro-Hungarian times of Archduke Franz Ferdinand being killed and everyone in Europe blowing each other up as a result—Jack was thinking about those ants.

Then he thought how tomorrow was Sunday and how long a day that would be.

And then he thought—as though a kaleidoscope of colors swam past him—about his own life, as it had been and as it was now, and he said out loud, "You're not much, Jack Kennison." This surprised him, but he felt it to be true. Who had just said that, about not being much?

Olive Kitteridge. She had said it regarding some woman in town. "She's not much," Olive had said, and there was the woman, gone, dismissed.

Eventually Jack got out a piece of paper and wrote in pen, Dear Olive Kitteridge, I have missed you, and if you would see fit to call me or email me or see me, I would like that very much. He signed it and stuck it into an envelope. He didn't lick it closed. He would decide in the morning whether to mail it or not.

Labor

Two days earlier, Olive Kitteridge had delivered a baby.

She had delivered the baby in the back seat of her car; her car had been parked on the front lawn of Marlene Bonney's house. Marlene was having a baby shower for her daughter, and Olive had not wanted to park behind the other cars lined up on the dirt road. She had been afraid that someone might park behind her and she wouldn't be able to get out; Olive liked to get out. So she had parked her car on the front lawn of the house, and a good thing she had, that foolish girl—her name was Ashley and she had bright blond hair, she was a friend of Marlene's daughter—had gone into labor, and Olive knew it before anyone else did; they were all sitting around the living room on folding chairs and she had seen Ashley, who sat next to her, and who was enormously pregnant, wearing a red stretch top to accentuate this pregnancy, leave the room, and Olive just knew.

She'd gotten up and found the girl in the kitchen, leaning over the sink, saying, "Oh God, oh God," and Olive had said to her, "You're in labor," and the idiot child had said, "I think I am. But I'm not due for another week."

Stupid child.

And a stupid baby shower. Olive, thinking of this as she sat in her own living room, looking out over the water, could not, even now, *believe* what a stupid baby shower that had been. She said out loud, "Stupid, stupid, stupid, stupid." And then she got up and went into her kitchen and sat down there. "God," she said.

She rocked her foot up and down.

The big wristwatch of her dead husband, Henry, which she wore, and had worn since his stroke four years ago, said it was four o'clock. "All right then," she said. And she got her jacket—it was June, but not warm today—and her big black handbag and she went and got into her car—which had that gunky stuff still left on the back seat from that foolish girl, although Olive had tried to clean it as best she could—and she drove to Libby's, where she bought a lobster roll, and then she drove down to the Point and sat in her car there and ate the lobster roll, looking out at Halfway Rock.

A man in a pickup truck was parked nearby, and Olive waved through her window to him but he did not wave back. "Phooey to you," she said, and a small piece of lobster meat landed on her jacket. "Oh, hell's *bells*," she said, because the mayonnaise had gotten into the jacket—she could see a tiny dark spot—and would spoil the jacket if she didn't get it to hot water fast. The jacket was new, she had made it yesterday, sewing the pieces of quilted blue-and-white swirling fabric on her old machine, being sure to make it long enough to go over her hind end.

Agitation ripped through her.

The man in the pickup truck was talking on a cellphone, and he suddenly laughed; she could see him throwing his head back, could even see his teeth as he opened his mouth in his laughter. Then he started his truck and backed it up, still talking on his cellphone, and Olive was alone with the bay spread out before her, the sunlight glinting over the water, the trees on the small island standing at attention; the rocks were wet, the tide was going out. She heard the small sounds of her chewing, and a loneliness that was profound assailed her.

It was Jack Kennison. She knew this is what she had been thinking of, that horrible old rich flub-dub of a man she had seen for a number of weeks this spring. She had liked him. She had even lain down on his bed with him one day, a month ago now, right next to him, could hear his heart beating as her head lay upon his chest. And she had felt such a rush of relief—and then fear had rumbled through her. Olive did not like fear.

And so after a while she had sat up and he had said, "Stay, Olive." But she did not stay. "Call me," he had said. "I would like it if you called me." She had not called. He could call her if he wanted to. And he had not called. But she had bumped into him soon after, in the grocery store, and told him about her son who was going to have another baby any day down in New York City, and Jack had been nice about that, but he had not suggested she come see him again, and then she saw him later (he had not seen her) in the same store, talking to that stupid widow Bertha Babcock, who for all Olive knew was a Republican like Jack was, and maybe he preferred that stupid woman to Olive. Who knew? He had sent one email with a bunch of question marks in the subject line and nothing more. That was an email? Olive didn't think so.

"Phooey to you," she said now, and finished her lobster roll. She rolled up the paper it had come in and tossed it onto the back seat, where that mess still showed in a stain from that idiot girl.

"I delivered a baby today," she had told her son on the telephone.

Silence.

"Did you hear me?" Olive asked. "I said I delivered a baby today."

"Where?" His voice sounded wary.

"In my car outside Marlene Bonney's house. There was a girl—" And she told him the story.

"Huh. Well done, Mom." Then in a sardonic tone he said, "You can come here and deliver your next grandchild. Ann's having it in a pool."

"A pool?" Olive could not understand what he was saying.

Christopher spoke in a muffled tone to someone near him.

"Ann's pregnant *again?* Christopher, why didn't you tell me?"

"She's not pregnant yet. We're trying. But she'll get pregnant."

Olive said, "What do you mean, she's having it in a pool? A *swimming* pool?"

"Yeah. Sort of. A kiddie pool. The kind we had in the backyard. Only this one is bigger and obviously super clean."

"Why?"

"Why? Because it's more natural. The baby slides into the water. The midwife will be here. It's safe. It's better than safe, it's the way babies should be born."

"I see," said Olive. She didn't see at all. "*When* is she having this baby?"

"As soon as we know she's pregnant, we'll start counting. We're not telling anyone that we're even trying, because of what just happened to the last one. But I just told you. So there."

"All right then," Olive said. "Goodbye."

Christopher—she was sure of this—had made a sound of disgust before he said, "Goodbye, Mom."

Back home, Olive was pleased to see that the little spot of mayonnaise on her new jacket responded to the hot water and soap, and she hung it in the bathroom to let the spot dry. Then she went back and sat in the chair overlooking the bay. The sun slanted at an angle across it, nothing but sparkles at the moment, only a lobster buoy or two could be seen, the sun at this time of day was that bright as it cut right across the water. She could not stop thinking how stupid that baby shower had been. All women. Why only women at a baby shower? Did men have nothing to do with this business of babies? Olive thought she didn't like women.

She liked men.

She had always liked men. She had wanted five sons. And she still wished she had had them, because Christopher was—Oh, Olive felt the weight of real sadness descend now, as it had been on her ever since Henry had his stroke, four years ago, and as it had been since his death, two years ago now, she could almost feel her chest becoming heavy with it. Christopher and Ann had called their first baby together Henry, after Chris's father. Henry Kitteridge. What a wonderful name. A wonderful man. Olive had not met her grandson.

She shifted in her chair, putting her hand to her chin, and thought again about that baby shower. There had been a table with food; Olive had been able to see intermittently, from where she had sat, little sandwiches and deviled eggs and tiny pieces of cake. When Marlene's pregnant daughter went by, Olive had tugged on her smock and said, "Would you bring me some of that food?" The girl looked surprised and then said, "Oh, of course, Mrs. Kitteridge." But the girl was waylaid by her guests, and it took forever before Olive had on her lap a small paper plate with two deviled eggs and a piece of chocolate cake. No fork, no napkin, nothing. "Thank you," Olive had said.

She stuck the piece of cake into her mouth in one bite, then tucked the plate with the deviled eggs far beneath her chair. Deviled eggs made her gag.

Marlene's daughter sat down in a white wicker chair that had ribbons attached to the top, flowing down, like she was queen for a day. When everybody finally took a seat—no one took the seat next to Olive until that pregnant girl Ashley had to because there were no other seats left—when they were all seated, Olive saw the table piled high with presents, and it was then she realized: She had not brought a gift. A wave of horror passed through her.

Marlene Bonney, on her way to the front of the

43

room, stopped and said quietly, "Olive, how is Christopher?"

Olive said, "His new baby died. Heartbeat stopped a few days before it was due. Ann had to push it out dead."

"*Olive!*" Marlene's pretty eyes filled with tears.

"No reason to cry about it," Olive said. (Olive had cried. She had cried like a newborn baby when she hung up the phone from Christopher after he told her.)

"Oh, Olive, I'm so sorry to hear that." Marlene turned her head, looking over the room in a glance, then said quietly, "Best not to tell anyone here, don't you think?"

"Fine," Olive said.

Marlene squeezed Olive's hand and said, "Let me tend to these girls." Marlene stepped into the center of the room, clapping her hands, and said, "Okay, shall we get started?"

Marlene picked up a gift from the table and handed it to her daughter, who read the card and said, "Oh, this is from Ashley," and everyone turned to look at the blond pregnant girl next to Olive. Ashley gave a little wave, her face glowing. Marlene's daughter unwrapped the gift; she took the ribbons and stuck them onto a paper plate with scotch tape. Then she finally produced a little box, and in the box was a tiny sweater. "Oh, *look* at this!" she said.

From the room came many sounds of appreciation. And then, to Olive's dismay, the sweater was passed from person to person. When it reached her she said "Very nice" and handed it to Ashley, who said, "I've already seen it," and people laughed, and Ashley handed it to the person on the other side of her, who said many things about the sweater, then turned to give it to the girl on her left. This all took a long time. One girl said, "You knit this yourself?" And Ashley said she had. Someone else said that her mother-in-law knit too, but nothing as nice as this sweater. Ashley seemed to stiffen and her eyes got big. "Oh, that's nice," she said.

Finally it was time for the next gift, and Marlene walked one over to her daughter. The daughter looked at the card and said, "From Marie." A young woman waved a hand at everyone from the far end of the room. Marlene's daughter took her time attaching the ribbons from the gift onto the paper plate with tape, and then Olive understood that this would happen with each gift and in the end there would be a plate of ribbons. This confused Olive. She sat and waited, and then Marlene's daughter held up a set of plastic baby bottles with little leaves painted on them. This did not go over as well, Olive noticed. "Won't you be breastfeeding?" someone asked, and Marlene's daughter said, "Well, I'll try—" And then she said, gaily, "But I'm sure these will come in handy."

Marie said, "I just thought, you never know. So

it's best to have some bottles around even if you breastfeed."

"Of course," someone said, and the bottles were passed around too. Olive thought they would go around faster, but it seemed that every person who touched the bottles had a story to tell about breastfeeding. Olive had certainly not breast-fed Christopher—back then, no one did, except people who thought they were superior.

A third gift was presented to Marlene's daughter, and Olive distinctly felt distress. She could not imagine how long it would take this child to unwrap every goddamned gift on that table and put the ribbons so carefully on the god-damned paper plate, and then everyone had to wait—*wait*—while every gift was passed around. She thought she had never heard of such foolish-ness in her life.

Into her hands was placed a yellow pair of booties; she stared at them, then handed them to Ashley, who said, "These are gorgeous."

And then Olive suddenly thought how she had not been happy even before Henry had his stroke. Why this clarity came to her at that point she did not know. Her knowledge of this unhappiness came to her at times, but usually when she was alone.

The truth is that Olive did not understand why age had brought with it a kind of hard-heartedness toward her husband. But it was something she had seemed unable to help, as though the stone wall that had rambled along between them during the course of their long marriage—a stone wall that separated them but also provided unexpected dips of moss-covered warm spots where sunshine would flicker between them in a sudden laugh of understanding—had become tall and unyielding, and not providing flowers in its crannies but some ice storm frozen along it instead. In other words, something had come between them that seemed insurmountable. She could, on certain days, point out to herself the addition of a boulder here, a pile of rocks there (Christopher's adolescence, her feelings for that Jim O'Casey fellow so long ago who had taught school with her, Henry's ludicrous behavior with that Thibodeau girl, the horror of a crime she and Henry had endured together when, under the threat of death, unspeakable things were spoken; and there had been Christopher's divorce, and his leaving town), but she still did not understand why they should walk into old age with this high and horrible wall between them. And it was her fault. Because as her heart became more constricted, Henry's heart became needier, and when he walked up behind her in the house sometimes to slip his arms around her, it was all she could do to not visibly shudder. Stop!, she wanted to shout. (But why? What crime had he been committing, except to ask for her love?)

"It's a breast pump," Ashley said to her. Because Olive was holding a plastic contraption, turning it over, unable to figure out what it was. "Okay," Olive said, and she handed it to Ashley. Olive looked at the table of gifts and thought that not even a dent had been made in them.

A pale green baby's blanket came around. Olive liked the feel of it; she kept it on her lap, smoothing her hands over it. Someone said, "Mrs. Kitteridge, let's share," and Olive handed it to Ashley immediately. Ashley said, "Ooh, this is *nice,*" and that's when Olive saw that Ashley had drops of sweat running down the side of her face. And then Olive thought—she was quite sure—she heard the girl whisper, "Oh God." When the green blanket reached Marie at the far end of the room, Ashley stood and said, "Excuse me, bathroom break." And Marlene said, "You know where it is, right?" And Ashley said that she did.

A set of baby bath towels came around, and Ashley's chair was still empty. Olive handed them to the girl on the other side of the empty chair, and then she stood and said, "I'll be back." In the kitchen Olive found Ashley, bent over the sink, saying, "Oh God, oh God."

"Are you all right?" Olive said loudly. The girl shook her head. "You're in labor," Olive said.

The girl looked at her then, her face was wet.

"I think I am," she said. "This morning I thought maybe I'd had a contraction, but then I didn't have any more, and now—Oh *God,*" she said, and she bent over, clinging to the edge of the sink.

"Let's get you to the hospital," Olive said.

In a moment, Ashley stood straight, calmer. "I just don't want to spoil this, it's so important to her. You know"—she whispered this to Olive— "I don't know if Rick is even going to marry her."

"Who cares," Olive said. "You're about to have a baby. To hell with spoiling it for her. They won't even notice you're gone."

"Yes, they will. And then the attention will be on me. And it should be on—" Ashley's face wrinkled and she held the edge of the sink again. "Oh God, oh God," she said.

"I'm getting my bag and driving you to the hospital right now," Olive said, aware that she was using her schoolteacher's voice. She walked back into the living room and retrieved her big black bag.

People were laughing at something; loud laughter poured into Olive's ears. "Olive?" It was Marlene's voice coming to her.

Olive raised a hand above her head and went back to the kitchen, where Ashley was panting. "Help me," Ashley said; she was weeping.

"Come on," Olive said, pushing the girl toward

the door. "That's my car right there, on the lawn. Get in it."

Marlene appeared and said, "What's happening?"

"She's in labor," Olive said, "and I'm taking her to the hospital."

"But I didn't want to spoil things," Ashley said to Marlene; she stood there, confusion on her wet face.

"Now," said Olive. "Right now. In my car. On the lawn."

"Oh, Olive, let's call an ambulance. What if she has the baby while you're driving? Stay here, Olive. Let me call." Marlene reached for the phone on the wall and it seemed to take forever for someone to answer.

Olive said, "Well, I'm taking her, so you can tell whoever you get what my car looks like and they can follow me if they want."

"But what does your car look like?" Marlene seemed to wail this.

"Take a look at it," Olive commanded. Ashley had already gone through the doorway and was getting into the back seat of Olive's car. "Tell the ambulance driver to pull me over if he shows up."

As she opened the back door of her car, Olive saw the girl's face and realized: This is it. This girl was going to have her baby. "Take your pants off," Olive said to her. "Now. Take them off."

Ashley tried, but she was writhing in pain, and Olive looked through her bag, her hands shaking, and found the shears she always carried with her. "Lie back." Olive leaned into the car, but she was afraid she would poke the girl's belly with the shears, so she went around to the door on the other side and opened that, and she was able to cut the pants successfully. Then she walked back around the car again and pulled the pants off the girl. "Stay lying back," she said firmly, oh, she was a schoolteacher all right.

The girl spread her knees, and Olive stared. She was amazed. *Pudendum* went through her mind. She had never seen a young woman's—pudendum. My word! The amount of hair—and it was—well, it was wide open! There was blood and gooey stuff coming out; what a thing! Ashley was making grunting sounds, and Olive said, "Okay, okay, stay calm." She had absolutely no idea what she was supposed to do. "Stay calm!" She yelled this. She reached and touched Ashley's knees, opening them more. In a few minutes—Olive had no idea how many minutes—Ashley let out a huge sound, a large groan and screech combined. And out slipped something.

Olive thought the girl had not delivered a baby at all, but rather some lumpish thing, almost like clay. Then Olive saw the face, the eyes, the arms—"Oh my goodness," she said. "You have a baby."

She was hardly aware of the man's hand on her shoulder as he said, "All right then, let's see what we have." He was from the ambulance, she had not even heard it drive in. But when she turned and saw his face, so in charge, she felt a rush of love for him. Marlene stood on the lawn, tears streaming down her face. "Oh, Olive," she said. "Oh, my word."

Olive stood up now and walked through her house. It felt no longer a house but more a nest where a mouse lived. It had felt this way for a long time. She sat down in the small kitchen, then she got up and walked past "the bump-out room," as she and Henry had called it, now with the purple quilt spread messily on the large window seat—this is where Olive had slept since her husband's death—and then she went back to the living room, where pale water streaks from last winter's snow showed on the wallpaper near the fireplace. She sat on the big chair by the window and rocked her foot up and down. The evenings were interminable these days, and she remembered when she had loved the long evenings. Across the bay the sun twinkled, now low in the sky. A shaft of light cut over the floor-boards and onto the rug in the living room.

Olive's unease grew; she could almost not stand it. She rocked her foot higher and higher, and then when the sky had just turned dark she said out loud, "Let's get this over with." She dialed Jack Kennison's number. She had lain down beside the man almost a month ago; it still felt like she had dreamed it. Well, if Bertha Babcock answered the phone, Olive would just hang up. Or if any woman did.

Jack answered on the second ring. "Hello?" he said, sounding bored. "Is this Olive Kitteridge calling?"

"How did you know that?" she asked; a wave of terror went through her as though he could see her sitting in her house.

"Oh, I have a thing called caller ID, so I always know who's calling. And this says—hold on, let me take another look—yes, this says 'Henry Kitteridge.' And we know it can't be Henry. So I thought perhaps it was you. Hello, Olive. How are you tonight? I'm very glad you called. I was wondering if we'd ever speak again. I've missed you, Olive."

"I delivered a baby two days ago." Olive said this sitting on the edge of her chair, looking through the window at the darkened bay.

There was a moment before Jack said, "You *did?* You delivered a baby?"

She told him the story, leaning back a bit, holding the phone with one hand, then switching it to the other. Jack roared with laughter. "I love that, Olive. My God, you delivered a baby. That's wonderful!"

"Well, when I called my son and told him, he didn't think it was so wonderful. He sounded—I don't know how he sounded. Just wanted to talk about himself."

She felt she heard Jack considering this. Then he said, "Oh, Olive, that boy of yours is a great disappointment."

"Yes, he is," she said.

"Come over," Jack told her. "Get in your car and come on over to see me."

"Now? It's dark out."

"If you don't drive in the dark, I'll come pick you up," he said.

"I still drive in the dark. I'll see you soon. Goodbye," she said, and hung up. She went and got her new jacket that was hanging in the bathroom, the spot was dry.

Jack was wearing a short-sleeved shirt, and his arms looked flabby. His stomach seemed huge beneath his shirt, but Olive's stomach was big too; she knew this. At least her hind end was covered up. Jack's blue eyes twinkled slightly as he bowed and ushered her inside. "Hello, Olive."

Olive wished she had not come.

"May I take your jacket?" he asked, and she said, "Nope." She added, "It's part of my outfit."

She saw him look at her jacket, and he said, "Very nice."

"I made it yesterday," she said, and Jack said, "You made that?"

"I did."

"Well, I'm impressed. Have a seat." And Jack brought her into the living room, where the windows were dark from the outside. He nodded to an armchair and sat down in the one opposite it. "You're nervous," he said. And just as she was about to answer him what in hell did she have to be nervous about, he said, "I am too." Then he added, "But we're grown-ups, and we'll manage."

"I suppose we will," she said. She thought he could have been nicer about her new jacket. Looking around, she was disappointed at what she saw: a wooden carved duck, a lampshade with a ruffle—had this stuff been there all along? It must have been and she had not noticed it; how could she not have noticed such foolishness?

"My daughter's upset with me," Jack said. "I told you that she's a lesbian."

"Yes, you did. And I told you—"

"I know, Olive. You told me I was a beast to care. And I thought about it, and I decided you were right. So I called her a few days ago and I tried, I *tried*—in a goofy way—to tell her that I knew I was a shit. She'd have none of it. I suppose she thinks I'm just so lonely with her mother gone that now I've decided to accept her." Jack sighed; he looked tired, and he put a hand over his thinning hair.

"Is that true?" Olive asked.

"Well, I wondered. I gave it some thought. And I don't know. It could be true. But it's also true that your response got me thinking." Jack shook his head slowly, looking down at his socks, which made Olive look down at them as well, and she was surprised to see his toe sticking out of a hole in one. His toenail needed to be cut. "God, that's unattractive," he said. He covered his toe with his other foot briefly, then let it loose. "My point here is—Children. Your son. My daughter. They don't like us, Olive."

Olive considered this. "No," she finally agreed. "I don't think Christopher does like me. Why is that?"

Jack said, looking up at her, his head on one hand, "You were a crummy mother? Who knows, Olive? He could have just been born that way too."

Olive sat and looked at her hands, which she held together on her lap.

Jack said, "Wait a minute. Didn't he just have a new baby?"

"It died. She had to wait and push the baby out dead."

"Oh, Olive, that's *awful*. God, that's an awful thing." Now Jack sat up straight.

"Yup. It is." Olive whisked some lint off the knee of her black pants.

"Well, maybe that's why he didn't want to hear

56

you talking about how you delivered one." Jack gave a shrug. "I'm just saying—"

"No. You're right. Of course." The thought had not occurred to her, and she felt her face grow warm. "Anyway, she's trying to get pregnant *again* and this one will be born in a pool. A little kiddie swimming pool. That's what he told me."

Jack leaned his head back and laughed. Olive was surprised at the sound of his laughter—it was so genuine.

"Jack." She spoke sharply.

"Yes, Olive?" He said this with dry humor.

"I have to tell you how *stupid* that baby shower was. Marlene's daughter—well, the poor girl sat in a chair and put all her ribbons on a paper plate and then every single damned gift had to be passed around from one woman to the next. Every single gift! And everyone said, Oh, how lovely, and isn't that nice, and honest to good God, Jack, I thought I would die."

He watched her for a moment, then his eyes crinkled with mirth.

"Olive," he finally said, "I don't know where you've been. I tried calling you a few times, and I thought perhaps you'd gone to New York to see your grandson. You don't have an answering machine? I could have sworn you did, I've left you messages on it before."

"I've never seen my grandson," Olive said. "And of course I have an answering machine."

Then Olive said, "Oh. I turned it off one day, someone kept calling me about a vacation I'd won. Maybe I never turned it back on." She understood now that this was true; she had never turned the damned machine back on.

Jack was quiet; he studied his toenail. Then he looked up and said, "Well. Let's get you a cellphone. I will buy it for you, and I will show you how to use it. Now, why haven't you seen your grandson?"

A ripple of something went through Olive, almost a fleeting sense of unreality. This man, Jack Kennison, was going to buy her a cellphone! She said, "Because I haven't been invited. I told you how badly things went when I went to New York before."

"Yes, you did. Have you invited them to come see you?"

"No." Olive looked at the lampshade with its ruffle around the bottom.

"Why don't you do that?"

"Because they have those three kids, I told you—she had two different kids with two different men—and they have Little Henry now, and I'm sure they couldn't make the trip."

Jack opened a hand. "Maybe not. But I think it would be nice for you to invite them."

"They don't need to be invited, they can just come." Olive put both hands on the armchair's armrests, then put them back in her lap.

Jack leaned forward, his elbows on his knees. "Olive, sometimes people like to be invited. I, for example, would have loved to be invited to your house on many occasions, but you've not invited me except for that one time when I *asked* you to take me over. And so I have felt rebuffed. Do you see that?"

Olive exhaled loudly. "You could have called."

"Olive, I just told you I *did* call. I called you a couple of times, and because you turned off your friggin' answering machine, you didn't know I called." He sat back and wagged a finger at her. "Only pointing out here that people can't read your mind. And I sent you an email as well."

"Ay-yuh," Olive said. "Well, I don't call a bunch of question marks an email."

"I like you, Olive." Jack gave her half a smile, then shook his head slightly. "I'm not sure why, really. But I do."

"Ay-yuh," said Olive again, and her face felt warm again, but they talked then. They talked of their children, and after a while Jack told her about his day a few days ago, how he was stopped by the police for speeding.

"They were unbelievably rude to me, Olive. You would have thought I was wanted for murder, the way both of them spoke to me." Jack opened his hand in dismay after he said this to her.

"Probably thought you were an out-of-stater."

59

"I have Maine plates."

Olive shrugged. "Still, you're an old man running around in your zippy little sports car. They know an out-of-stater when they see one." Olive raised her eyebrows. "I'm perfectly serious, Jack. They could smell you a mile away." She glanced down at the huge watch of Henry's she was wearing. "It's late," she said, and she stood up.

"Olive, would you stay here tonight?" Jack shifted in his chair. "No, no, just listen to me. Right now I am wearing a half-diaper because of prostate surgery I had right before Betsy was diagnosed."

"What?" asked Olive.

"I'm just trying to reassure you. I'm not going to assault you. You do know what Depends are, right?"

"Depends?" asked Olive. "What do you mean—? Oh." She realized she had seen them on television ads.

"I'm telling you that I'm wearing half a Depends, a thing for people who pee their pants. Men who pee after this surgery. They say it will get better, but it hasn't yet. Olive, I'm only telling you this because—"

She waved her hand for him to stop. "Godfrey, Jack," she said. "I'd say you've been through quite a lot." But she was aware of feeling relief.

Jack said, "Why don't you stay in the guest

room, and I will stay in the guest room across the hall? I just want you here when I wake up, Olive."

"Just when you wake up? Well, I'll come back. I get up early." When he didn't answer, she added, "I don't have my nightgown or my toothbrush. And I don't think I'd sleep a wink."

Jack nodded. "I get that. About the toothbrush—we have a few new unused toothbrushes, don't ask me why. But Betsy always had extra on hand, and I can give you a T-shirt, if you care to wear it."

They were silent, and Olive understood. He wanted her there for the whole night. What was she going to do? Go home to the rat's nest she now lived in? Yes, she was. At the doorway, she turned. "Jack," she said. "Listen to me."

"I'm listening." He had remained in his chair.

She stood there, staring at the ridiculous lampshade with its ruffled business going on. "I just don't want to have to bump into you talking to that Bertha Babcock in the grocery store—"

"Bertha Babcock, that's her name. God, I couldn't remember her name." He sat back and clapped his hands once. "She talks about the weather, Olive. The *weather.* Look, Olive, I'm just saying, I would like you to stay here tonight. I promise: You get your own room, and so do I."

She came close. She did. But then she said, "I
61

will see you in the morning, if you like." It wasn't until she had pulled open the door that Jack rose and went to the door as well.

He waved his hand. "Goodbye, then."

"Good night, Jack." She waved her hand over her head.

Outside, the evening air assaulted her with the smells of the field and she heard the peepers as she walked to her car. Reaching for the handle of her car door, she thought: Olive, you fool. She pictured herself at home, sleeping on the big window seat in "the bump-out room," she thought how she would listen to the little transistor radio against her ear all night, as she had since Henry died.

She turned and walked back to Jack's door. She rang the bell, and Jack answered the door almost immediately. "All right," she said.

She used the new toothbrush that his poor dead wife had somehow bought (Olive didn't have an extra toothbrush in her house), then she closed the door of the guest room with the double bed, and pulled on a huge T-shirt he had given her. The T-shirt smelled of fresh laundry and something else—vaguely cinnamon? It did not smell like Henry. She thought: This is the stupidest thing I have ever done. And then she thought: It's no stupider than that stupid baby shower I went to. She folded her clothes and put them on the chair by the bed. She was not unhappy. Then she opened the door a crack. She could just see that he had settled himself into the single bed in the guest room across the hall. "Jack?" she called to him.

"Yes, Olive?" he called back.

"This is the stupidest thing I've ever done." She didn't know why she had said that.

"The stupidest thing you ever did was go to that baby shower," he called back, and Olive felt stunned for a moment. "Except for the baby you delivered," he called out.

She left the door partly open and got into bed and turned over on her side, away from the door. "Good night, Jack." She practically yelled the words.

"Good night, Olive."

That night!

It was as though waves swung her up and then down, tossing her high—high—and then the darkness came from below and she felt terror and struggled. Because she saw that her life—her life, what a silly foolish notion, her life—that her life was different, might possibly be very different or might not be different at all, and both ideas were unspeakably awful to her, except for when the waves took her high and she felt such gladness, but it did not last long, and she was down again, deep under the waves, and it was like that—back and forth, up and down, she was exhausted and could not sleep.

It was not until dawn broke that she drifted off.

"Good morning," Jack said. He stood, his hair messy, in the doorway of her room. He wore a bathrobe that was navy blue and stopped halfway down his calves. He was unfamiliar; she felt put off.

Olive flapped a hand from the bed. "Go away," she said. "I'm sleeping."

He roared with laughter. And what a sound it was; Olive felt a physical sensation, a thrill. At the very same time she felt terror, as though a match had been lit on her and she had been soaked in oil. The terror, the thrill of his laughter—it was nightmarish, but also as though a huge can she had been stuffed into had just opened.

"I mean it," Olive said. She turned over in the bed. "Right now. Go away, Jack," she said. She squeezed her eyes shut. *Please,* she thought. But she did not know what she meant by that. *Please,* she thought again. Please.

Cleaning

Kayley Callaghan was a young girl in the eighth grade, and she lived in a small apartment with her mother on Dyer Road in the town of Crosby, Maine; her father had died two years earlier. Her mother was a petite, anxious woman, and because her mother had not wanted to rely on her three older daughters, all with families, she had sold the big house they had lived in on Maple Avenue to an out-of-state couple who found the price to be extremely cheap and who came up on weekends to renovate it. The house on Maple Avenue was near Kayley's school, and every day she walked a block over so as to avoid going by the place where her father had died in the back room.

It was early March, and the day had been cloudy until just now; sunlight came through the windows of Kayley's English classroom. Kayley, leaning her head on her hand, was thinking about her father; he was a man without higher education, but when she was small he had told her about the famine that took place in Ireland, and the Corn Laws that made bread too expensive to buy, he had told her many things; in her mind now she envisioned people on the streets of Ireland, dying, bodies falling on the side of the road.

Mrs. Ringrose was standing in front of the class with the vocabulary book, held with both hands, on top of her protruding chest. She said, "Use it three times and it's yours," which is what she always said when they were doing vocabulary words. Mrs. Ringrose was old, with white hair and glasses that wobbled on her nose; they were gold-rimmed.

" 'Obstreperous,' " Mrs. Ringrose said. She looked over the students seated at their desks, sunlight glinting off her glasses. "Christine?" And poor Christine Labbe could not come up with anything. "Um, I don't know." Mrs. Ringrose didn't like that. "Kayley?" she asked.

Kayley sat up straight. "The dog was really obstreperous," she said.

"All right," Mrs. Ringrose said. "Two more."

Kayley knew what most people in town knew about the Ringroses: At Thanksgiving they dressed up like Pilgrims and went around the schools in the state, giving talks on the first Thanksgivings in New England; Mrs. Ringrose always took two days off from teaching to do this, the only days she ever took off.

"The children playing were being really obstreperous," said Kayley.

Mrs. Ringrose did not look pleased. "One more, Kayley, and it's yours."

Kayley also knew, because Mrs. Ringrose talked about this a lot, that one of Mrs. Ringrose's ancestors had come over on the *Mayflower* ship from England many years ago.

Kayley closed her eyes briefly, then she finally said, "My father said the English people thought the Irish were obstreperous," and Mrs. Ringrose glanced at the ceiling and snapped the vocabulary book shut. "Okay, I suppose that's good enough. You now have the word, Kayley."

Sitting in the classroom on the second floor while afternoon sun streamed through the windows, Kayley felt an emptiness in her stomach that was not hunger but a kind of vague nausea; the feeling—Kayley did not know why—had something to do with Mrs. Ringrose, whose first name was Doris.

Doris Ringrose, and her husband was named Phil. They had no children.

"See me after class," Mrs. Ringrose said to Kayley.

A week earlier Kayley had come home from cleaning the house of Bertha Babcock—which she did every Wednesday after school—and heard her eldest sister, Brenda, speaking with their mother in the kitchen. Kayley had stood by the door in the darkened hallway, the staircase she had just come up was steep and wooden and lit by only one lightbulb, her backpack with her school books was unsteady on her shoulder, and she heard Brenda say, "But, Mom, he wants it all the time, and it's kind of making me sick." And her mother replied, "Brenda, he's your husband, it's what you have to do."

Kayley hesitated, but they stopped talking then, and when she came in, Brenda stood up and said, "Hi, honey. What've you been up to?" Brenda was many years older than Kayley, and she used to be a pretty woman with her dark red hair and smooth complexion, but lately there were brown patches beneath her eyes and she had been gaining weight.

"Cleaning house for Bertha Babcock," said Kayley, slipping her backpack off. "I can't stand it." She took her coat off and added, "I can't stand *her.*"

Lighting a cigarette, Kayley's mother said, "Well, she can't stand you either, don't think otherwise. You're Irish, you're just a servant to her." She dropped the match into the saucer of her teacup and said, directing this to Brenda, "She's a Congregationalist, Bertha Babcock," and gave her a meaningful nod.

Brenda tugged on her blue cardigan, but it wouldn't meet in the middle across her stomach. "Still, it's a nice thing you're doing it." She winked at Kayley.

"Mrs. Ringrose is going to ask me to clean her house now too," Kayley said. "Mrs. Babcock recommended me."

"All right then," her mother said, as though she didn't care, and she may not have.

"Another Congregationalist?" Brenda asked this playfully, and Kayley said, "I think so."

Kayley went into her bedroom; the old wooden door never closed all the way, and as Kayley listened to the women talking—now in muted tones—she understood that this was about sex, her sister didn't want to have sex with Ed, and Kayley didn't blame her. He was okay, her brother-in-law, but he was a small man, and had bad teeth, and it made Kayley feel queer in her stomach to think that he wanted it all the time. Kayley sat down on her bed and thought she would never—ever—marry someone like Ed.

And she would never get old like Bertha Babcock, who was a widow, and whose kitchen floor was in black and white tiles, which Mrs. Babcock made Kayley clean with a toothbrush between the tiles each week; Kayley could not stand it. The Babcock house seemed to stink with a loneliness there would be no cure for.

Brenda came to the door of Kayley's bedroom; the room was small, and lit now by the overhead light that shone on Kayley's pink quilt, which lay messily on her bed, and as Brenda slipped on her coat she said to Kayley, "I have to get going, honey, the kids will need their supper." Brenda lived two towns away. Then she said, "Mom says you're still not playing the piano." Brenda asked, conspiratorially, quietly, "Should she sell it, honey?"

Kayley stood up to give her sister a hug good-bye. "No, please don't let her sell it." Kayley added, "I'll play, I promise."

It was their father who had played the piano, although after Kayley learned to play he said he would rather listen to Kayley. "I love you, and I love the piano, so the combination just sends me to heaven," their father had said, standing in the doorway of their old living room. That night Kayley sat at the piano, which was an old black upright. But she played badly because she almost never played anymore, and even the simpler sonatas of Mozart were not as easy for her as they had once been. Kayley put the lid down over the keyboard. "I'll play more," she said to her mother, who was sitting in the corner smoking a cigarette near the window she had cracked partly open, and her mother did not answer.

Kayley spent the rest of the evening in her bedroom, watching on her computer Martin Luther King, Jr., giving his "I Have a Dream" speech. This was an assignment for Social Studies class, but her father had told her about that speech as well.

• • •

The Ringrose house also had a loneliness about it. But it was a different flavor than Bertha Babcock's place, and the house was smaller— it was a Cape on River Road, and it had on the front of it a small board that said 1742—and also somehow cleaner; Kayley didn't have to work so hard. The first day she was there, Mrs. Ringrose told her she was to clean the logs in the fireplace each week with a cleaning fluid that Kayley was to put in a pail of warm water; the logs were birch, and their bark was a whitish gray. And she was to clean the wooden floors on her hands and knees, Mrs. Ringrose said, and Kayley didn't care; she was young, it wasn't the endless kitchen of the Babcock home. In the living room on a table all by itself was a wooden model of the *Mayflower*. Kayley was not to touch this, Mrs. Ringrose said that first day, holding up her finger. "Do. Not. Touch." Then she told Kayley how she was a direct descendant of Myles Standish, who had come over on this ship, and if you looked at it— Mrs. Ringrose peered down at the model—you could see where the people stayed, and Kayley murmured, "Oh yeah," although she thought of her father then, and how, when he was sick in the back room, she would watch the movie with him about Michael Collins and the green tank of the English that came into Croke Park and started shooting all the Irish people. Kayley stepped back from Mrs. Ringrose; being so close to her allowed Kayley to see the patches of pink scalp through her white hair; it gave Kayley that sense of nausea again.

But also on that first day—it was the strangest thing—Mrs. Ringrose made Kayley try on her wedding gown. The gown was yellow in places, and spread out on Mrs. Ringrose's bed. Mrs. Ringrose had a separate bedroom and bathroom from her husband. "Just try it on, Kayley. You're about the size I was when I got married, and I would like to see this gown on someone." She gave a little nod. "Come on now," she said.

Kayley looked behind her, then back at Mrs. Ringrose. Slowly she unbuttoned her blouse, and Mrs. Ringrose kept standing there watching her, so Kayley took her blouse off, and then she unzipped her jeans and took them off too, after slipping off her sneakers. She stood in her underpants and her bra in front of this woman as a milky sunlight came through the windows of the bedroom; tiny goosebumps went over her arms and legs. Mrs. Ringrose held the dress above Kayley's head, and it slipped down over her body, fitting her easily.

Mrs. Ringrose took her glasses off and wiped her eyes with her other hand. There was water still on her cheeks when she put her glasses back on.

"Now listen," Mrs. Ringrose said, touching Kayley's shoulder. "I've started a group at our church, and it's called the Silver Squares. There's already one group called the Golden Circle, but they're old, and so I have started the Silver Squares and we're going to have a fashion show in June, and I would like you to play the piano for it and wear my wedding dress."

With the woman still watching her, Kayley got into her own clothes again.

Except for Kayley's first time at the Ringroses', Mrs. Ringrose was never there. "I'll be off at the Silver Squares," she had said. Kayley got the key from under the mat and let herself in, as she had been instructed to do. A ten-dollar bill was always left on the kitchen table for her.

But the Ringroses' house really depressed Kayley in a powerful way.

For example: Mr. Ringrose's bathroom was designed to look like an outhouse. There was a dark green painted barrel around a flush toilet, so it looked like you were going to sit on a hole. Rough wooden planks were on the walls. Kayley had never spoken to Mr. Ringrose; he was not there when she cleaned, and she knew who he was only because she'd seen him around town with Mrs. Ringrose: He was tall, old, white-haired; for years he had worked in Portland at some history museum, but he had long been retired. There was no sink in his bathroom; just those barn boards with the dark green barrel in the middle. Mrs. Ringrose's bathroom was normal, white porcelain with a sink and a vanity table with her hairbrush on it and hairpins.

In the living room, the couch was small and tightly upholstered. The seat rounded up into a mound, and when Kayley sat on it she felt she might almost slip off. The chairs were the same. The upholstery was a deep rose color, and on the dark green walls were paintings of people that looked like weird dolls, they looked a little bit like grown-ups, except for how short they were, and they wore white hats and dresses that were from a different era; these pictures Kayley could not stand.

She could not stand them.

"How does she even know you play the piano?" asked Christine Labbe. She and Kayley were walking on the sidewalk, close to the center of town by the doughnut shop, and Christine was eating a doughnut that had cinnamon all over it. Christine's eyes had dark blue liner around them, and part of it was smudged.

"I don't know." Kayley turned to look at the cars going by. "Maybe she heard me playing that piano they have in the gym. I don't know how she knows."

Christine said, "She's creepy. Her husband's

74

creepy too. Dressing up like stupid Pilgrims every year and talking about that stupid fucking *Mayflower* ship her ancestors came over on. Reciting that stupid Longfellow poem 'The Courtship of Miles Standish' while kids yawn their fucking heads off."

"You should see their house," Kayley said, and she described Mr. Ringrose's bathroom.

Christine looked at her and said, "Jesus Holy Christ." Then Kayley touched her eye to show Christine that her makeup was smudged, and Christine shrugged and took another bite of her doughnut.

On Saturday afternoon Kayley rode her bicycle to the nursing home out past the bridge where Miss Minnie was. It was cold in mid-March, but there was very little snow, and Kayley's bicycle bumped over twigs that had fallen onto the sidewalk; her hands were cold because she wore no gloves. Miss Minnie used to live in the apartment above the one Kayley lived in now with her mother; Miss Minnie had lived there for years, and she was the first person Kayley had cleaned for. The old woman was tiny, with enormous dark eyes, and Kayley had been astonished at the grime, especially in the kitchen, that had built up over time. And so Kayley scrubbed and scrubbed while Miss Minnie peered into the doorway and said, "Oh, what a lovely job you're doing, Kayley!" Miss Minnie would clap her hands, she was that excited at Kayley's work, and Kayley loved her for this. Miss Minnie always gave Kayley a glass of orange juice when she was done, and Miss Minnie would sit across the table from her, leaning forward toward Kayley, and ask questions about her school and her friends; no one had asked Kayley about these things since her father died.

After Miss Minnie had her stroke last fall, Kayley went to visit her in the nursing home, even though the place was dark and smelled bad. Miss Minnie would thank her many times for coming. "It's okay," Kayley would say, "I like seeing you," and after the first few visits she gave Miss Minnie a kiss when she left, and the old lady's enormous dark eyes would glow.

Kayley locked her bike out behind the nursing home, and as she went around to the front door, Mrs. Kitteridge was just coming out. "Hello again," Mrs. Kitteridge said to her; she was a big woman, tall, and when Kayley had first met her here a month ago, she had seemed a little frightening. Now Mrs. Kitteridge held the door open for Kayley, and she said, "You're quite a kid, coming to visit someone in this place. God, I hope to hell when I get to this stage, someone just shoots me."

Kayley said, "I know. Me too. I mean I hope they shoot me too."

Mrs. Kitteridge put her sunglasses on and looked Kayley up and down and said, "Well, you won't have to worry about it for a while." She let the door close, and they stood together in the pale March sun. "Say, I did some snooping and found out you're the Callaghan girl. I had your sisters in school years ago. Your father was our postman. He was a good man, I'm sorry he died."

"Thank you," Kayley said. A sudden warmth moved through her, that this woman knew who her father had been. Kayley said, "Were you here visiting your friend?"

Mrs. Kitteridge gave a big sigh, looking through her sunglasses up at the sky. "Yes. Horrible. The whole thing. But listen," glancing back at Kayley now, "you said last time you used to clean for Miss Minnie, and I have another old woman who's looking for a house cleaner. Bertha Babcock. She's an old horror, but she'd be okay to you. I'll tell her to call you, shall I?"

"She already found me," said Kayley. "I work there on Wednesday afternoons. I started a few weeks ago."

Mrs. Kitteridge shook her head in what appeared to be sympathy.

Kayley said, "And now I have to clean for Mrs. Ringrose too. She's my English teacher."

"I know who she is. Another old horror. Well, good luck." And Mrs. Kitteridge stepped away, tossing a hand over her head.

• • •

The nursing home was dark, and it still smelled bad, of course. Miss Minnie was asleep, and so Kayley sat down on the one chair in the room. On the table by Miss Minnie's bed was a photograph of a young man in uniform, and beside this photograph was a bunch of fake violets. The same photo and the same violets had been by Miss Minnie's bed in her apartment. The photo was of Miss Minnie's brother; Kayley found this out one day when Miss Minnie picked up the photo and held it to her chest and told Kayley how he had died in the Korean War. It made Kayley sad; she would have much rathered it had been a man Miss Minnie had loved who was not related to her.

Now Kayley sat, waiting for Miss Minnie to wake up. An aide came in, a big woman in a blue uniform, and said, "She hasn't woken up all afternoon. She's depressed. She's sleeping more and more." Together Kayley and this woman looked at Miss Minnie, and then Kayley stood and said, "Okay. But can you tell her I was here? Please?"

The woman glanced at her watch. "I get off in an hour. If she wakes before then, I'll tell her."

"I'll leave her a note," Kayley said, and so the big woman went and found a piece of paper and a pencil and Kayley wrote in large letters, HI MISS MINNIE! IT'S ME, KAYLEY. I CAME

TO VISIT YOU BUT YOU WERE SLEEPING. I WILL COME BACK!

One day when Kayley's father was very sick, he had motioned to her from where he lay on his bed, and Kayley had gone and put her ear to his mouth, and he said, "You've always been my favorite child." After a moment he added, "Your mother's favorite is Brenda." His lips had a white gumminess in the corners.

"I love you, Daddy," Kayley said; with a tissue, she wiped his lips carefully, and her father looked at her with warmth in his eyes.

But she thought about this often, the fact that her father had said she was his favorite child. And she thought about her mother, who had always been a distracted woman and who worked part-time now at a dental office in town; it seemed she had little to say to Kayley in the evenings, and often Kayley's feelings were hurt by this; Kayley could actually feel a small wave of pain go through her chest at times, and she would think: This is why they say a person's feelings are hurt, because they do hurt.

The next week that Kayley worked at the Ringrose house she felt that same feeling she always got in their house, a stark feeling of dismalness. The day was tremendously sunny, the light poured through the windows of the living room, and after Kayley had washed the logs in the fireplace she sat down on the couch with the upholstery that was stiff and hard.

A strong sensual impulse suddenly went through her, as though the chasteness of the house was screaming for her. She sat there as the feeling grew, and after a moment she slowly undid the first button on her blouse and put her hand down under her bra and felt her breast and a glow went through her. She closed her eyes and undid the second button of her blouse and pulled her breast from the cup of her bra. In the stillness of the house her breast seemed vulnerable and alive to her; she touched her fingers to her mouth and then back to her breast and she kept touching her breast, filled with unbelievable sensations. She sat with her eyes closed, touching her breast, feeling the air touching it as well—it was oddly thrilling, doing this in the strangeness and silence of the Ringrose home.

A small sound made her eyes open, and in the doorway of the living room stood Mr. Ringrose. Kayley sat up straight and tried to close her blouse; her cheeks became flaming hot. The man was tall and he stood there watching her behind his glasses, not smiling. Without saying any-thing Mr. Ringrose gave the tiniest nod, and in the blurriness of the moment Kayley somehow understood he wanted her to continue. She stared at him and then said—or tried to say—"No," but he spoke first, and his voice was thick. "Go on." She shook her head, but he kept watching her, and a kind expression appeared on his face. "Go on," he said again, quietly. She stared at him, she was tremendously frightened. And he seemed to know it, because his expression of kindness grew; he tilted his head slightly down. He said quietly, "Please go on." They watched each other, and his eyes—he wore large rimless glasses—seemed kind and oddly harmless, and so in a moment she closed her eyes and touched her breast again. When she opened her eyes, he was gone.

She buttoned her blouse hurriedly and stood up; she finished her dusting with her cheeks still hot; she felt a breathlessness as she went about the place, washing the floor on her hands and knees. Her mind kept thinking: Oh my God, oh my God, oh my God.

She almost didn't see it as she was leaving, the envelope on the mat by thc front door as she left the house, and then bending down she saw that it had her last name on it. She took the envelope, and when she turned the corner she opened it and found three twenty-dollar bills.

Now Kayley felt a different fear. She stuck the money in her back pocket, still in the envelope, and rode her bicycle far out of town. "Oh my God, oh my God," she kept saying.

When she came home, her mother said, "Where were you?" Kayley said she had been riding her bike after cleaning for the Ringroses; it was such a gorgeous day. And then Kayley sat down at the piano and began to play—oh, how she played! She went through the sonatas of Mozart as though she could not dig her fingers deep enough into the fresh soil of the music; she played and played.

As they sat eating supper, her mother said, "You've barely touched that piano since your father died, and it's sitting right there taking up all that space."

Kayley said, "I'll keep playing. Please don't get rid of it."

The next week it was raining and Kayley rode her bike to the Ringrose house with her raincoat on and her hood over her head, but she was still dripping wet when she got there, and again there was no sign of either of them. She dried herself as best she could with a towel from the kitchen and went to work, getting the pail with the cleaning fluid for the logs, and as she was kneeling and running a cloth over the logs in the fireplace— there must have been a sound—she looked up; Mr. Ringrose was standing exactly where he had been standing the time before. A few raindrops were on the shoulders of his pale blue shirt, and also on his glasses, but she could still see his eyes. He simply stood there looking at her, and she did not speak. After a moment he gave her the tiniest nod, and she sat back on her heels and put her hand over her breast and he nodded the tiny nod again, and after another moment Kayley slowly stood, drying her hands on her jeans, and she went and sat back on the stiff couch, and she undid her blouse, this time watching him. For Kayley there was a sense of unreality to it as she took her blouse off slowly, then took her bra off, and the air in the room seemed to leap at her bare breasts, and the rain outside beat down on the windows. The man said in a low voice, "Thank you."

On the mat by the front door was once again the envelope filled with cash.

When Kayley was very young she had asked her mother one day if she was pretty, and her mother said, "Well, you're not going to win any beauty contests, but you're not going to be in a freak show either."

In fact, not long before her father died, Kayley—she was in the sixth grade then—was asked to be in a beauty contest. Her gym teacher called her aside and asked if she would take part in the Little Miss Moxie competition in the town of Shirley Falls; Kayley's father was furious. "No daughter of mine will be judged on how she looks!" He was really angry about it, and so Kayley told her teacher no, she couldn't do it, and Kayley didn't care about it one way or another.

Yet these days she would stare at herself in the mirror in her bedroom, turning her head one way, then another. She thought—some nights she thought this—that she might be pretty. She did not take her shirt and bra off in front of the mirror to see what Mr. Ringrose saw. That was not something she could do, but she thought about the man almost constantly.

June arrived. School would be over in two weeks.

In the activities room of the Congregational church, Kayley sat on the piano bench dressed in Mrs. Ringrose's wedding dress. It was an unseasonably hot day, and a big fan stood nearby squeaking slightly as it twirled the air around. Folded chairs were set up with an aisle between them, and the old wooden floor creaked as women walked across it, settling themselves into the chairs. Through the windows a bright blue sky could be seen, and also part of the parking lot. Every week for nine weeks now, Kayley had taken her blouse off for Mr. Ringrose—one time only he did not show up, and Kayley felt bereft—and the cash-filled envelopes, which she had stuffed in the bureau drawer beneath her underpants and socks, had become so much she had taken them and hidden them in her closet. It was odd, because sometimes there was sixty dollars, and a few times there was just a ten and a few ones, and once there were two twenties.

As Kayley sat on the piano bench, she watched Mrs. Ringrose walking around the activities room and thought: Your husband has *seen my breasts* and I'll bet you he hasn't seen yours in years! This thought made her extremely happy. Mrs. Ringrose finally gave her the nod, and Kayley began to play "Pomp and Circumstance," and the first woman who was in the Silver Squares fashion show walked down the little aisle between the folding chairs, wearing a long dress and a white cap over her gray-haired head; Mrs. Ringrose stood in the front of the room and said, "The first Pilgrims, 1620." Perhaps fifteen old women sat in the chairs that were set up for fifty, and Kayley kept playing as Mrs. Ringrose stood behind a lectern and said who each person was, and what period of time it was about whatever they were wearing.

Bertha Babcock came last; she wore an orange pantsuit. "The modern era," Mrs. Ringrose said, and they all clapped lightly.

Afterward the women sat on the folding chairs eating cookies with thin paper napkins on their laps. No one spoke to Kayley, and so in a while she went and changed out of the wedding gown and put it on the table in the front of the room, then she rode her bicycle home.

Christine Labbe stared at her from her blue-made-up eyes, then burst out laughing. "How nauseating," she said, and she laughed and laughed, coughing, bending over.

"It was," Kayley said. "It was just so stupid."

"You think?" And Christine coughed again and said, "Jesus mother of Mary, Kayley. What a stupid fucking thing. She's retiring this year, you know."

Kayley said she didn't know. She gazed at a truck parked nearby; it had a bumper sticker on it that said: REDNECKS NEEDED. FRECKLES OKAY.

"Oh yeah. The student council was getting all weepy about it, and they're going to present her with a lilac bush on the last day of school." Christine rolled her eyes.

"Who cares. I don't care, that's for sure," Kayley said.

At home these nights Kayley played the piano; she played and played, and she became good at it again. Up and down the keyboard her fingers flew.

At the nursing home, Miss Minnie sat slumped over a tray table, her head resting on her arms, her eyes closed. "Miss Minnie?" Kayley whispered, leaning toward the old woman. "Miss Minnie?" But the old woman did not respond; she did not move, or open her eyes. She had been like this— exactly like this—the last two times Kayley had ridden her bike out to the nursing home. The same aide came in, in her blue uniform, and she stood with her hands on her hips, watching Miss Minnie.

"Oh, honey," she finally said to Kayley. "She's just real old, and real depressed."

Kayley leaned down toward Miss Minnie, and she spoke quietly into her ear, feeling the woman's fine hair against her mouth. "Miss Minnie, it's me, Kayley. Listen, Miss Minnie?" And then Kayley said, "I love you." And the woman did not move.

The next time Kayley visited, Miss Minnie's room was empty—completely empty, no bed, no chair—and there were two women in it cleaning with mops. "Wait!" Kayley said, but they just kept swirling their mops, and when Kayley went to the front desk, the woman there said, "I'm sorry. We didn't have your number or we would have called."

That night, Kayley's mother only shrugged and said, "Well, it was bound to occur."

"But what happened to the picture of her brother, and her violets?"

Her mother said, "I imagine they got tossed out."

Kayley waited long enough so that her mother would not think she wanted to get away from her, but after some time passed Kayley said, "Mom, I want to go for a bike ride. The evenings are light now," and her mother looked at her suspiciously. Kayley could not ride fast enough, up Dyer Road, then down Elm Street, and then up past the school, she just could not ride her bike fast enough.

When Mr. Ringrose showed up the next week, silently as always, Kayley was dusting the legs of the couch. She turned; she was enormously glad to see him. "Hello," she whispered as she stood up. It was the first time she had spoken to him. He nodded and gave her a tiny smile, gazing at her through his rimless glasses. She unbuttoned her shirt without pause. She thought his eyes seemed even kinder than usual and she watched him steadily as she moistened her fingers and touched her breasts, the tips becoming hard almost instantly; if Mrs. Ringrose should walk in, she didn't care! This is how Kayley felt that day as she turned slightly one way, then the other, for the silent Mr. Ringrose.

She put the envelope of money inside her underwear drawer, and the next three weeks she did the same; she was astonished that one week there was a hundred-dollar bill.

School was now out, and on Wednesday mornings and Saturday mornings, Kayley worked at the doughnut shop. She poured coffee and brought out the doughnuts from the back, slipping them into the white paper bags for the customers. One Wednesday she saw Mr. Ringrose walking by the place; he was glancing down at the sidewalk and did not look up through the window. He was slightly bent over, and she almost did not recognize him at first; his white hair was sticking at odd angles from his head. She stopped in the middle of an order to watch him; he seemed to not walk in a straight line. It could not be him, she decided. But she was rattled. No, that could not have been him.

When she cleaned the Ringrose house the next week, he did not show up, and she felt terribly sad and worried.

That Saturday, as the sun was slicing through the large glass windows of the doughnut shop, Mrs. Kitteridge walked in. "Oh, Mrs. Kitteridge," Kayley said, she was surprised at how glad she was to see her. But Mrs. Kitteridge looked at her and said, "Do I know you?" And Kayley blushed.

"I'm the Callaghan—"

"Oh, *wait*. Of course. I remember you, riding your bicycle to that awful nursing home to visit that woman."

Kayley said, "Do you still visit your friend there? My friend died."

Mrs. Kitteridge looked her up and down. "I'm sorry about that," she said. Then she added, "Well, not that she's dead, who wouldn't want to be dead living in there. Damn smart of her to die. My friend is still alive."

"Oh, I'm sorry," Kayley said.

Mrs. Kitteridge ordered three plain doughnuts and two cups of coffee, and she turned to the man behind her. "Jack," she said, "say hello to the Callaghan girl." The man stepped forward; he was a big person as well, wearing aviator sunglasses and a short-sleeved shirt that showed his saggy arms, and Kayley did not really like the way he said "Hello, Callaghan girl" as though he was slightly mocking her.

"Bye now," Mrs. Kitteridge said, and they walked out, Mrs. Kitteridge waving a hand above her head.

A few evenings later, the telephone rang in their apartment, and Kayley's mother answered and said, "Yes, of course. Here she is."

Kayley had been playing the piano—ferociously she had been playing it, but she had stopped when the telephone rang—and now, when her mother said "It's for you," Kayley rose and went to the phone.

"Kayley? This is Mrs. Ringrose."

Kayley opened her mouth but no sound came out.

"I won't be needing you anymore," said Mrs. Ringrose. There was a silence after that.

"Oh, I—" Kayley started to say.

"There are a few health issues in our house, and I've retired, as I'm sure you know. So I can take care of things. Thank you, Kayley. Goodbye."

A wave of grief scooped Kayley up, and it would not let her go. She rode her bicycle through town, down along the coast, she rode and rode, thinking of Mr. Ringrose. There was no one she could tell about what had happened, and this knowledge stayed in her and made her feel almost constantly unwell. But she simply kept going, riding her bicycle, working at the doughnut shop two mornings a week, and the man who ran the place let her add another morning, Thursdays. But she was a devastated girl, and one afternoon as she knelt on Bertha Babcock's kitchen floor with the toothbrush, she felt a real dizziness. Bertha Babcock was not home, and Kayley stood up and she left the woman a note. I CAN'T WORK HERE ANYMORE. She did not even empty the pail of water, and she left the toothbrush on the floor.

The next day, her mother came into the doughnut shop and said to Kayley, "You come straight home after work." Her mother looked awful, furious and small-eyed. When Kayley got home, her mother was standing in her room. Kayley's underwear and socks had been flung onto her bed, the bureau drawer stuck open like a tongue. "Where did you get this money?" Her mother screamed the words at her, and showed her the envelopes with the twenty-dollar bills and the one envelope with the hundred-dollar bill. Her mother took the money out and let it fly around the room as she tossed it in the air. "Tell me where you got this!"

"It's my house cleaning money," Kayley said.

"No it is not! You got ten dollars to clean house for that Ringrose woman, and there's at least three hundred dollars here, where did it come from?"

"Mom, I've been cleaning for her for ages."

"Don't you lie to me!" Her mother's fury was huge, billowing through the room.

Kayley's mind worked quickly; she did the math even as her mother screamed; the other stuffed envelopes of cash were hidden in her closet, and she did not let her eyes look in that direction. Instead, she sat down on the bed and said, making her voice sound calm, "It's my house cleaning money, Mom. From Bertha Babcock, who pays me fifteen dollars, so that's twenty-five dollars a week." She added, "And I went to the bank to get a hundred-dollar bill so I could have it."

"You're lying," her mother said. "Bertha Babcock called here this morning and told me you just walked out." Kayley did not answer this. "Who taught you that you could just walk out of a job like that? Who *taught* you such a thing?"

Kayley watched as her mother screamed and screamed at her. And then a funny thing happened to Kayley. She stopped caring. Like a switch had gone off inside her. All the fear that had been escalating in her disappeared. She was done; she did not care. Her mother even slapped her across the face, which caused tears to spring to Kayley's eyes, but she did not care. It was the strangest feeling she had ever had, and the feeling—not her mother—frightened her. Her silence seemed to cause her mother's wrath to increase—"I'm calling your sister!" her mother yelled—and when it was done, when her mother had left Kayley's bedroom, Kayley looked around and thought the room seemed vandalized: A pair of her underpants had landed on a lamp that had been overturned on her small desk, socks were against the far wall, her pink quilt had been ripped.

When Brenda came over she said, "Just leave us for a bit, Mom." Sitting beside Kayley on her bed, Brenda said, "Oh, honey, what has happened?" Kayley looked at her; she wanted to cry now, yet she did not let herself. "Honey," said Brenda, taking Kayley's hand and stroking it, "honey, just tell me where you got the money, that's all, honey. Just tell me."

"If you added it up, you'd see it was my house cleaning money. And also from the doughnut shop."

Brenda nodded. "Okay, I thought so. Mom just got really, really furious because you'd quit Bertha Babcock and not told her. Mom's having a hard time, and she saw all this cash and thought maybe there were drugs involved or something."

"Oh, *please,*" said Kayley, and Brenda nodded understandingly, stroking Kayley's arm now, and said, "Oh, honey, I knew it wasn't drugs."

After a few moments Kayley said, "I kind of hate living here with her. She hardly talks to me. And—and it hurts my feelings."

"Oh, honey," said Brenda. "Now listen, honey. Mom's gotten super depressed since Dad died. And she was really too old to have had you—" Brenda leaned in and said, "But thank God she did!" Kayley looked at her sister, the dark patches beneath her eyes; she suddenly remembered how Brenda had said, "He wants it all the time, and it's kind of making me sick."

"Brenda, I love you," Kayley said quietly.

"And we all love you. Now listen to me, honey." Brenda waited and said, as though it were a secret, "Honey, you're *smart.* You know that, right? The rest of us are more like Mom," and she put her finger to her lips as though to indicate this should be kept secret. "But you're like Dad. You're smart. So, Kayley, honey, just keep on doing well in school and you will have a future. A *real* future."

"What do you mean, a real future?"

"I mean, you could be a doctor or nurse, or someone important, Kayley."

"Seriously?"

"Seriously," Brenda said.

The next day, after her mother left for work, Kayley took the many envelopes of cash from her closet, and as she walked around looking for a place to hide them, she suddenly thought of the piano. She opened the top of it, and slipped them in, and watched them fall down to the bottom behind the wires. She had no idea how she would ever get them out, but they were safe there; she had stopped playing the piano.

She now expected nothing from her mother. And so when her mother was suddenly pleasant to her on certain evenings, Kayley was surprised and she was pleasant in return. She talked to her mother about Miss Minnie one night, and her mother listened. Her mother spoke of the different patients that came into the dental office where she worked, and Kayley listened. It was a doable existence.

And this is why one Saturday when Kayley came back from the doughnut shop and stepped into the living room and saw—like a person's front tooth missing—the absence where the piano had been, she felt gutted, almost as though it was not real.

"I sold it," her mother said. "You never play

it anymore, so I sold it to a Grange Hall near Portland."

Kayley waited, but no phone call ever came about the money.

On one of the last days of summer, Mrs. Kitteridge came back into the doughnut shop. She was alone this time, and no one else was there at the moment. "Hello, child," she said, and Kayley said, "Hello, Mrs. Kitteridge."

"You still working for that Ringrose bat?" Mrs. Kitteridge asked; she had just ordered two plain doughnuts.

And Kayley said, slipping the doughnuts into a white bag, "No, she fired me."

"She fired you?" Mrs. Kitteridge's face showed surprise. Then she said, "What did you do, play with her little *Mayflower* boat?"

"No. She just called me and said I wasn't needed anymore. And that there was illness in her house or something."

"Huh." Mrs. Kitteridge seemed to be considering something. "Well, her husband's not well."

Kayley felt an odd tingling on the tip of her nose. "Is he going to die?" she asked.

Mrs. Kitteridge shook her head. "Worse than that," she said. Then she said, leaning forward, raising her hand to her cheek, "Her husband's going dopey-dope."

"Mr. Ringrose? He *is?*"

"That's what I heard. He was seen out back watering their tulip bed naked. And the tulips are long gone by."

Kayley looked at Mrs. Kitteridge. "Are you kidding me?"

Mrs. Kitteridge sighed. "Oh, it gets even worse. I've told you that much, I might as well tell you the rest. She's putting him in that nursing home where Miss Minnie was. Can you imagine that? They have to have more money than that. She could afford to put him in the Golden Bridge place, but she's sticking him out there, and *I* say—and I have always said this—" Mrs. Kitteridge rapped her hand on the counter twice. "That woman was never nice to him. Not one bit." Mrs. Kitteridge gave a severe nod to Kayley.

"Oh," said Kayley, taking this in. "Oh, that's so, so sad."

And Mrs. Kitteridge said, "I guess to God it is."

In two days, Kayley would start high school. The high school was a mile out of town, and her mother would drive her there in the morning, and she would walk back, or maybe a friend would drive her. But it was not near her old house on Maple Avenue, and today she rode her bicycle by that house, and she saw how the renovation had changed it. They had painted it a deep blue, when it had always been a white house, and there were pots of flowers on the newly made front stoop.

97

The back room where her father had died had been removed altogether, and a large porch was there instead. After she rode by it she suddenly turned at the corner and rode her bicycle out over the bridge past the mill to the old nursing home where Miss Minnie had been. She stayed on the other side of the street when she got to the place, and dismounted from her bicycle and looked at the building; it was dark green, a shingled building, and it seemed smaller than it had before. She walked her bike along the side of the road; a few cars whizzed past. She waited for the cars to go by, then crossed the street and walked her bicycle around to the back, where the employees parked. And then, not wanting to be seen by anyone, she went to the side of the building that faced the woods, and she sat down on the gravel there, her bicycle leaning against the wall of the place.

The very top of a tree had started to turn red, and Kayley looked up at it, then looked at the gravel glinting in the sun. She thought about Mrs. Ringrose, how she had started the Silver Squares, and had that fashion show, beginning with the Pilgrims. Oh my God, Kayley thought, leaning her head against the shingled wall and closing her eyes. And her *Mayflower* boat in her living room. It seemed to Kayley that the history this woman had clung to was no longer important; it would be almost washed away, just a dot left—

not just by the Irish, but by so many things that had happened since, the Civil Rights movement, the fact that the world was much smaller now, people connected in new ways Mrs. Ringrose had never imagined.

And then Kayley thought about Mr. Ringrose, who, in a way, she had never stopped thinking about, the loneliness he must have endured, and was enduring still, now just a few feet away.

Kayley shook her head, and pulled her arms up to cover her face. At the moment—only for this moment—it was all she wanted, just to be near him again.

Motherless Child

They were late.

Olive Kitteridge hated people who were late. A little after lunchtime, they had said, and Olive had the lunch things out, peanut butter and jelly for the two oldest kids, and tuna fish sandwiches for her son and his wife, Ann. About the little ones, she had no idea; the baby must not eat anything solid yet, only being six weeks old; Little Henry was over two, but what did two-year-olds eat? Olive couldn't remember what Christopher ate when he was that age. She walked into the living room, looking at everything through the eyes of her son; he would have to realize as soon as he walked in. The phone rang, and Olive moved quickly back to the kitchen to answer it. Christopher said, "Okay, Mom, we're just leaving Portland, we had to stop for lunch."

"Lunch?" said Olive. It was two o'clock in the afternoon. The late April sun was a milky sun, seen through the window over the bay, which shone with a steely lightness, no whitecaps today.

"We had to get something for the kids to eat. So we'll be there soon."

Portland was an hour away. Olive said, "Okay, then. Will you still be needing supper?"

"Supper?" asked Christopher, as though she had proposed they take a shuttle to the moon. "Sure, I guess so." In the background Olive heard a scream. Christopher said, "Annabelle, shut up! Stop it right now. Annabelle, I'm counting to three . . . Mom, I'll have to call you back," and the phone went dead.

"Oh Godfrey," Olive murmured, sitting down at the kitchen table. She had still not taken the pictures from the wall, yet the place looked remarkably different, as though—as was the case—she would be moving out of it soon. She did not think of herself as a person who had knickknacks, but there was a box of stuff in the back corner of the kitchen, and as she glanced into the living room from where she sat, that room seemed to her to be even more guilty; there was only the furniture and the two paintings on the wall. The books were gone—she had given them to the library a week ago—and the lamps, except for one, were packed into a box as well.

The phone rang again. "Sorry about that," said her son.

"Are you supposed to be talking on a cellphone and driving?" Olive asked.

"I'm not driving. Ann's driving. Anyway, we'll be there when we get there."

"All right then," Olive said. She added, "I'll be awful glad to see you."

"Me too," said her son.

Me too.

Hanging up she walked through the house, and trepidation fluttered through her. "You're doing this all wrong," she said quietly to herself. "Oh Godfrey Mighty, Olive." Almost three years it had been since she had seen her son. This did not seem natural or right to Olive. And yet when she had gone to visit him in New York City—when Ann was pregnant with Little Henry, and way before Ann had this other child, Natalie, a baby now—the visit had gone so poorly that her son had essentially asked her to leave. And she had left. And she had seen him only once since, soon after, when he had flown to Maine for his father's funeral and spoken before the whole church, tears coming down his face. "I never heard my father swear" was one thing her son had said that day.

Olive checked the bathroom, made sure there were clean towels, she knew there were clean towels, but she could not stop herself from checking again. They had said not to worry about not having a crib, but Olive did worry. Little Henry was two and a half years old, and Natalie was six weeks, how could they not have a crib?

Well, judging by how she had seen them living in New York—God, what a mess that house had been—she decided they could make do with about anything. Annabelle was almost four now, Theodore was six. What did a six-year-old boy want to do? And why did they have so many children? Ann had had Theodore with one man, Annabelle with another, and now she had spit out two more babies with Christopher. What in God's name was that about? Christopher was not a young man.

In fact, when Olive saw him stepping out of the car she could not believe—she *could* not believe—that he had gray in his hair now. Christopher! She walked toward him, but he was opening the doors of the car, and little children spilled out. "Hi, Mom." He nodded at her. There was the little dark-haired girl, dressed in a bulky pink nylon coat, also wearing a pair of knee-high rubber boots, robin's-egg blue, who turned away immediately, and the blond boy, older, who stared at Olive; Ann was taking her time getting the baby out of the car. Olive went to Christopher, her son, and she put her arms around him, and felt the awkwardness of his older man's body in her arms. She stepped back, and he stepped back, then he reached into the car and leaned over a child in an apparatus that looked like a small pilot seat for a child headed to outer space;

he brought out the kid, and said to his mother, "Here's Henry."

The child looked with large slumbering eyes at Olive, and he was placed, standing, on the ground, where he held on to his father's leg. "Hello, Henry," Olive said, and the child's eyes rolled up slightly, then he pressed his face into his father's pant legs. "Is he all right?" Olive demanded, because the sight of him, dark-haired like his mother, dark-eyed as well, caused her to think immediately: This is not Henry Kitteridge! What had she thought? She had thought she would see her husband in the little boy, but instead she saw a stranger.

"He's just waking up," Christopher said, picking the child up.

"Well, come in, come in," Olive said, realizing then that she had not spoken yet to Ann, who held the baby patiently nearby. "Hello there, Ann," Olive said, and Ann said, "Hello, Olive."

"Your boots are as blue as your hat," Olive said to the little girl, and the little girl looked puzzled and walked to her mother. "It's an expression," Olive explained—the child wore no hat.

Ann said, "We got those boots for our trip to Maine," and this confused Olive.

"Well, take them off before you come inside," Olive said.

In New York, Ann had asked if she could call Olive "Mom." Now Ann did not move toward

105

Olive, and so Olive did not walk toward Ann, but turned and walked into the house instead.

Three nights they were to stay.

Once in the kitchen, Olive watched her son carefully. His face at first seemed open, pleased as he looked around. "Jesus, Mom, you've really cleaned up. Wow." Then she saw the shadow come. "Wait, have you given away everything of Dad's? What's the story?"

"No, of course I haven't." Then she said, "Well, sure, some of it. He's been gone a while, Chris."

He looked at her. "What?"

She repeated what she had said, but she turned away as she said it. Then she said, "Theodore, would you like a drink of water?" The boy stared at her with huge eyes. Then he shook his head slightly and walked over to his mother, who, even as she was holding the baby, was shrugging her way out of a bulky black sweater. Olive could see that Ann's stomach bulged through her black stretch pants, although her arms seemed skinny in a white nylon blouse.

Ann sat down at the kitchen table and said, "I'd like a glass of water, Olive," and when Olive turned around to hand it to her, she saw a breast—just sticking out in plain view, right there in the kitchen, the nipple large and dark—and Olive felt a tiny bit ill. Ann pressed the baby to her, and Olive saw the little thing, eyes closed, clasp onto the nipple. Ann smiled up at Olive, but Olive thought it was not a real smile. "Phew," Ann said.

Christopher said nothing more about his father's possessions, and Olive took that as a good sign. "Christopher," she said. "Make yourself at home."

Then a look passed over her son's face that let her know this was not his home anymore—this is what Olive thought she saw on his face—but he sat down at the kitchen table, his long legs stretched out.

"What would you like?" Olive asked him.

"What do you mean, what would I like?" Christopher looked up at the clock, then back at her.

"I mean, would you also like a glass of water?"

"I'd like a drink."

"Okay, a drink of what?"

"A drink-drink, but I don't imagine you have anything like that."

"I do," Olive said. She opened the refrigerator. "I have some white wine. Would you like some white wine?"

"You have wine?" Christopher asked. "Yes, I would love some white wine, thank you, Mom." He stood. "Wait, I'll get it." And he took the wine bottle, which was half full, and poured the wine into a tumbler as though it was lemonade. "Thank you." He raised the glass and drank from it. "When did you start drinking wine?"

"Oh—" Olive stopped herself from saying Jack's name. "I just started to drink a little, that's all."

Christopher's grin was sardonic. "No, you didn't, Mom. Tell me the truth—when did you start drinking wine?" He sat back down at the table.

"Sometimes I'll have friends over, and they drink it." Olive had to turn away; she opened a cupboard and brought out a box of saltine crackers. "Have a cracker? I even have some cheese."

"You have friends over?" But Christopher didn't seem to require an answer, and he sat at the table with his wife, who finally stuck her breast back inside her shirt, and Christopher ate all the cheese and most of the crackers, and Ann sipped at his wine, which he drank quickly. "More?" He pushed the glass forward, and Olive, who thought he'd had enough wine, said, "Okay, then," and gave him the wine bottle, which he emptied into his glass.

Olive needed to sit down. She realized there were only two chairs at the table; how had she not realized that before? She said, "Let's go into the living room." But they did not get up, and so she stood at the counter, feeling shaky. "Tell me about the drive up," she said.

"Long," Christopher said, his mouth full of cracker, and Ann said, "Long."

Neither of Ann's children spoke a word to Olive. Not a word. Not a "thank you" or a "please"—not one word did they say. They watched her carefully, then turned away. She thought they were horrible children. She said, "Here's a peanut butter and jelly sandwich," pointing to the ones that sat on the counter, and they said nothing. "All right, fine," she said.

But Little Henry was a sweet thing in his way. In the living room—where they finally went, because Olive said again, "Let's go into the living room"—he toddled over to her and pulled his wet hand from his mouth and put it on Olive's leg where she sat on the couch, and he banged her knee a few times, and she said, "Hello, Henry!" The child said, "Hi." "Hello!" she said again, and he said, "Hi, hi." Well, that was fun.

But when Olive—only because she felt it was expected of her—asked to hold the baby, Natalie, the baby screamed her head off as soon as she was in Olive's arms. Just screamed her little head off. "Okay then, all right then," Olive said, and handed her back to her mother, who took some time getting the baby calmed down. Ann had to pull out her breast again to do this, and Olive was pretty sick of seeing her daughter-in-law's breast, it was so *naked,* the breast! All huge with milk, and a few veins running over it; honestly, Olive did not care to see it anymore.

She stood up and said, "I'll get supper started."

Christopher said, "Oh, I don't think we're hungry yet."

"No problem," Olive called over her shoulder. In the kitchen she lit the oven and put the casserole in that she had made earlier that morning, scallops and sour cream. Then she returned to the living room.

Olive had expected chaos. She had not expected the silence of these children, or even the silence of Ann, who was different than Olive remembered. "I'm tired," Ann said to her at one point, and Olive said, "I should think so." So maybe that was it.

Christopher was more talkative. Sprawled on the couch in the living room, he spoke of the traffic they had run into outside of Worcester, he spoke of their Christmas, their friends, his job as a podiatrist. She wanted to hear it all. But Ann interrupted and said, "Olive, where did you put your Christmas tree? By the front window?"

"I didn't have a Christmas tree," Olive said. She said, "Why in the world would I have a Christmas tree?"

Ann raised her eyebrows. "Because it was Christmas?"

Olive didn't care for that. "Not in this house it wasn't," she said.

• • •

After Ann had taken the older children into the study, where the couch had been turned into a bed, Olive sat with Christopher and Little Henry, who dangled from his father's lap. "Cute kid," Olive said, and Christopher said, "He really is, right?"

From the study she could hear Ann murmuring, and she could hear the higher-pitched voices— but not the words—of the children. Olive stood up and said, "Oh, Christopher, I knit Little Henry a scarf."

She went into the study—the two older kids in there just stood silently and watched her—and got the scarf she had knit, bright red, and brought it out, and she gave it to Christopher, who said, "Hey, Henry, look what your grandmother made for you," and the little boy put part of it into his mouth. "Silly thing," Christopher said to him, and pulled it gently. "You wear it to keep warm." And the child clapped his hands. Olive thought he was really a fairly amazing child.

Ann appeared in the doorway, flanked with her two kids, who were now in their pajamas. She said, "Um, Olive?" She pursed her lips a moment and then said, "Do you have anything for the other children?"

Olive felt the swiftness of dark rising up through her. It took her a moment to trust herself, then she said, "I don't know what you mean,

Ann. Are you talking about Christmas presents? I sent the children Christmas presents."

"Yeah?" Ann said slowly. "But that was, you know, Christmas?"

Olive said, "Well, I never heard a word from you, so perhaps they didn't get them."

"No, we got them," Ann said. Then she said to Theodore, "Remember that truck?"

The child shrugged one arm and turned away. And yet they stood there, that beastly mother and her two children from two different men, stood right there in the doorway, as though Olive was supposed to produce—what was she supposed to produce? She *really* had to bite her tongue not to say, I guess you didn't like that truck. Or to say to the little girl, And what about that doll? I suppose you didn't like that either? Olive had to *force* herself not to say, In my day we thanked people who sent us gifts. No, Olive really had to work not to say this, but she did not say this, and after a few minutes Ann said to the kids, "Come on, let's get you to bed. Give Daddy a kiss." And they walked to Christopher and kissed him, then walked right by Olive and that was that. Horrible, horrible children, and a horrible mother. But Little Henry suddenly wiggled out of his father's lap and dragged his new scarf across the floor to Olive. "Hi," he said. He smiled at her! "Hello," she said. "Hello, Little Henry." "Hi, hi," he said. He held the scarf toward Olive. "Gank you," he said. Well, he was a Kitteridge. He was surely a Kitteridge all right. "Oh, your grandfather would have been so proud," she said to him, and he smiled and smiled, his teeth wet with saliva.

Christopher was looking around the room. "Mom, this place looks awfully different," he said.

"You haven't been here in a while," Olive said. "Things change and your memory is different too."

Olive was happy.

Her son was talking to her alone. Little Henry had been put to bed upstairs, and his mother and his tiny baby sister were up there as well. The two older children were tucked into their couch-bed in the study. The light from the lamp in the corner spilled over her son. This was all she wanted: Just this. Chris's eyes seemed clear; his face seemed clear. The gray in his hair still surprised her, but she thought he looked good. He spoke a great deal about his podiatry practice, the young woman who worked for him, the insurance he had to pay, the insurance that his patients had, Olive didn't care what he talked about. He talked about their tenant, no longer the guy with the parrot that would screech *Praise God* anytime someone swore, but a young man with a girlfriend now, they were probably going to get married soon. On and on he talked, her son. Olive was tired, but she stifled a yawn. She would stay here forever to hear this. He could recite the alphabet to her and she would sit here and listen to it.

When he finally went to bed—"Okay, 'night, Mom," raising a hand—she sat for a while in the living room, with just the one lamp on, the water seen through the window all black, just the tiny speck of the red light out at Halfway Rock; the front deck with its wooden chairs that she had brought out only recently seemed to sit quietly and patiently in the dark. It was the first night she had not spoken to Jack in months and she missed that, but he seemed far away to her right now. And then there was a sudden shriek— *"Mama!"*—from the study. Olive's heart started to beat fast, and she got up as quickly as she could and went to the door of the study, where Annabelle stood. Annabelle looked at her, then stepped back and screamed again, "Mama!"

"Now stop that," Olive said. "Your mother is exhausted. Let her sleep."

And the little girl pushed the door shut. Olive waited for a moment, then she went upstairs to bed. But she heard the child—most likely it was Annabelle—on the stairs later, and heard her go into her parents' room, and Olive thought, Honest to God, what a brat. She heard Ann's tired voice murmuring, but Olive was on her computer, and there was an email from Jack: How's it

GOING???? I miss you, Olive. Please, please write me when you can.

And she wrote back: Oh, too much to say! I miss you too.

A part of Olive thought: Come on, Jack, I have my hands full here, I can't be there with you too! It was as though she had five hundred bees buzzing in her head.

Olive did not fall asleep for many hours that night, she kept going over her conversation with Chris like a giddy schoolgirl— oh, she had missed him!—and when she woke, she heard people in the kitchen. She got out of bed quickly; she was a very early riser, and she had not expected that Ann and Christopher—and all their children— would get out of bed earlier than she did. But they had. Every one of them was right there in the kitchen, fully dressed, when she went downstairs. Olive was not one to wear a bathrobe in front of people she felt she barely knew. "Well, hello," she said, tugging her bathrobe tightly closed. And no one said anything. The older children looked at her with open hostility—Olive felt this—and even Little Henry was silent, on his mother's lap.

Christopher said, "Mom, you didn't get Cheerios? I told you we needed Cheerios."

"You did?" Olive could not remember her son mentioning Cheerios. "Well, there's oatmeal," she said. She felt she saw Christopher and Ann exchanging a look.

"I'll go," Ann said. "Just tell me how to get there."

"No," said Christopher, "I'll go. You stay here."

And then—God, just in the nick of time—Olive said, "No, *I'll* go. Everyone just stay put."

And so Olive went back upstairs and put some clothes on and then she took her coat and her big black handbag and she walked through the kitchen as fast as she could, and drove over to Cottle's. The day was bright with sun. All she wanted was to speak to Jack. But she had walked out the door without her cellphone! And what had happened to payphones? She felt hurried and upset, knowing the kids were home waiting for their Cheerios. Jack, Jack, she called out in her head. Help me, Jack, she called. What good was the fact that Jack had bought her a cellphone when she didn't even remember to take it with her? Finally, after she had the bag with the Cheerios in it, as she was pulling out of the parking lot, she saw a payphone near the back of the lot, and she parked again and walked quickly to it, and she couldn't find a quarter at first, but then she found a quarter and she slipped it into the phone and there was no dial tone. The goddamn phone did not work. Oh, she was fit to be tied.

Olive had trouble driving home; she really had to concentrate. After she tossed the Cheerios in the paper bag onto the kitchen table, she said, "If you'll excuse me just a moment," and she went upstairs to her room, and she emailed Jack with fingers that were almost trembling. Help me, she wrote, I don't know what to do. Then she realized that he couldn't help her, he couldn't call her—they had agreed they would not speak by phone until Olive had told Chris—and so she deleted what she had just written and wrote instead, It's okay, I just miss you. Hang in there! Then she added: (More soon.)

Back down in the kitchen the silence remained. "What's the matter?" Olive asked; she heard the anger in her voice.

"There's not much milk, Mom. There was only a little. So Annabelle got it, and Theodore has to have his Cheerios plain." Christopher was leaning against the counter as he said this, one ankle crossed over the other.

"Are you serious?" Olive asked. "Well, I'll go back—"

"No, just sit, Mom." Christopher nodded at the chair that Theodore sat in. "It's okay. Theodore, give your grandmother a chair." The child, with his eyes down, slid off the chair and stood.

Ann's back was to her, and Olive could see Little Henry on one of Ann's knees, Ann was holding the baby too. "What about the rest of

117

you?" Olive asked. "What can I get for you? How about some toast?"

"It's okay, Mom," Christopher said again. "I'll make some toast. You sit, Mom."

So she sat at the table across from her daughter-in-law, who turned and smiled her phony smile at Olive. Theodore moved to his mother and whispered something into her ear. Ann rubbed his arm and said quietly, "I know, honey. But people live differently."

Christopher said, "What's up, Theodore?"

And Ann said, "He was just commenting on the paper bag the Cheerios came in, wondering why Olive didn't use a recycling bag." She looked at Olive and shrugged a shoulder. "In New York, we recycle. We bring our own bags to the store."

"Is that right?" Olive said. "Well, good for you." She turned around and opened the bottom cupboard and just about flung the recycling grocery bag onto the table. "If I hadn't been in such a hurry I would have used this."

"Oh," said Ann. "Look at that, Theodore." And the child moved away from the table, then he turned and went into the study. Ann was handing Little Henry a Cheerio. Little Henry did not seem in such a good mood this morning. "Hello, Little Henry," Olive said, and he did not look at her, just looked for a long moment at the Cheerio in his hand before putting it into his mouth.

• • •

The day was very sunny and bright; all the clouds from yesterday had gone, and the sun shone through the house. Outside—through the big living room windows—the bay was brilliant, and the lobster buoys bobbed just slightly; a lobster boat was headed out; the trees across the bay were a fine line. It was decided they would all drive out to Reid State Park to watch the surf. "The kids have never really seen the ocean," said Christopher. "The *real* ocean. They've seen the crappy stuff that floats up to New York. I'd like them to see the Maine coast. I know we've got it right here"—he nodded toward the window where the bay was sparkling—"but I'd like them to see more of it."

"Well, let's go then," Olive said.

"We'll have to take two cars," Christopher said.

"So we'll take two cars." Olive stood up and scraped the uncaten toast left by Theodore into the garbage. In her whole life, Olive would not have allowed Christopher to waste toast like this, but what did she care? Let that beastly child waste all the food he wanted.

Once outside, Olive was surprised by Christopher saying, "Mom, when did you get a Subaru?" He didn't say it pleasantly, is what she felt. She had put the car in the garage the day before; it was only out now because of her trip to the store.

"Oh," she said, "I had to get a new car, and I

119

thought, I'm an old lady on my own, I'll get a good car for the snow." She could not believe she said that. It was a lie. She had just lied to her son. The truth was, the car belonged to Jack. When her Honda had needed new brake pads, Jack had said, "Take my Subaru, Olive. We're two people with three cars, and that's ridiculous, so take the Subaru, and we'll keep my sports car because I love it."

"I can't believe you got a Subaru," her son said again, and Olive said, "Well, I did. And that's that."

The time it took to get things arranged, Olive could not believe. Christopher and Ann had to go over to the side of the parking area and have a conversation; Olive took out her sunglasses and put them on. When Christopher returned he said, "Theodore, you're going with your mother, and, Henry, we're putting your car seat in your grandmother's car." So Olive waited, chilly in her coat even though the sun was bright, while Christopher got the car seat and put it into her car, and she heard him swearing that the seatbelt wasn't working, and she said, "It's a used car, Chris," and he stuck his head out of it finally and said, "Okay, we're all set."

"You drive," she said, and he did.

Ann sat on a rock that looked out at the ocean, even though the rock must have been very cold—

it was windswept and had no moisture on it, but it still must have been cold—while Christopher ran back and forth on the beach with the kids. Olive watched this from the edge of the parking lot, her coat pulled tight around her. After a few minutes she made her way to Ann, who looked up at her, the baby asleep in her arms. "Hello, Olive," Ann said.

Olive couldn't figure out what to do. The rocks were wide, but she couldn't get herself down to a sitting position. So she stood. Finally she said, "How's your mother, Ann?"

Ann said something that got lost in the wind.

"What?" Olive said.

"I said she's dead!" Ann turned her head back to Olive, yelling this.

"She died?" Olive yelled this back. "When did she die?"

"A couple months ago," Ann yelled in the wind toward Olive.

For a number of moments Olive stood there. She had no idea what to do. But then she decided she would try and sit next to Ann, and so she bent down and placed her hands carefully on the rock and finally got herself seated.

Olive said, "So she died right before you had Natalie?"

Ann nodded.

Olive said, "What a hell of a thing."

"Thank you," said Ann.

And Olive realized that this girl, this tall, strange girl—who was a middle-aged woman—was grieving. "Did she die suddenly?" Olive asked.

Ann squinted toward the water. "I guess. Except she never took care of herself, you know. So it shouldn't have been a surprise when she had her heart attack." Ann waited a moment, then turned her face toward Olive. "Except I was surprised. I'm still surprised."

Olive nodded. "Yuh, of course you are." After a moment Olive added, "It's always a surprise, I think. Even if they're languishing for months, they still just go away. Horrible business."

Ann said, "Do you remember that song, I think it's a black spiritual—'Sometimes I feel like a motherless child'?"

" 'A long way from home,' " Olive finished.

"Yeah, that one," Ann said. Then Ann said, "But I always felt that way. And now I am."

Olive considered this. "Well, I'm very sorry," she said. Then she asked, "Where was she living when she died?"

"Outside of Cincinnati, where she always lived. Where I grew up, you know."

Olive nodded. From the corner of her eye she watched this girl—this woman—and she thought, Who are you, Ann? She knew the girl had a brother somewhere, but what was his story? She couldn't remember, she only knew they had no contact, was he on drugs? He might have been. The mother had been a drinker, Olive knew that. And her father had divorced the mother years ago; he'd been dead for a long time. She said again, "Well, awful sorry."

"Thanks." Ann stood up—remarkably easily, considering she was holding the baby—and then she walked away. She just walked away! It took Olive many moments to stand up, she had to heave herself onto one arm and roll herself a bit to get her foot under her.

"Oh, honest to God," she said. She was panting by the time she got back to the car.

On the way back, Olive said, "Chris, why didn't you tell me Ann's mother died?"

He made a sound and shrugged.

"But why wouldn't you tell me such a thing?" Through the window were the trees still bare, their limbs dark, poking toward the sky. They passed by a field that looked soggy and matted down in parts, the streaming sun showing it all.

"Oh, her mother was nuts. Whatever."

In the back seat Henry sang out, "Goggie, goggie. Train, airplane! Daddy, Mama!" Olive turned to look at him, and he smiled at her.

"He's just singing all the words he knows," Christopher said. "He likes to do that."

"But I don't understand," Olive said, after waving to Little Henry. "I just don't, Christopher.

She's my daughter-in-law, and I'd like to know what's going on in her life."

Christopher glanced at her quickly, then back at the road; he drove with one arm draped across the wheel. "I really didn't know you cared," he said. He looked over at her again. "What?" he asked.

Olive had started to ask a question. "Why—?"

"I just told you why."

And Olive nodded. Her question, which she did not ask, was: Why did you marry this woman?

They made it through another night, and one more day, and then the final night arrived. Olive was exhausted. In the entire time, except for Little Henry, the children did not speak to her. But they stared at her—with increasing boldness, she thought—because whenever she looked at them they were looking at her, and instead of glancing down as they had at first they continued to stare, Theodore with his huge blue eyes, and Annabelle with her small dark ones. Unbelievable children.

Finally they went off to bed in the study and Olive sat with Christopher and Ann and the baby while Little Henry—such a good boy!— was asleep upstairs. Olive was getting used to the breast being stuck out in the open now, she didn't like it, but she was getting used to it. And she felt sorry for Ann, who seemed to her to be diminished in her grief. So she made small talk with the woman and Ann seemed to try to do her best as well. Ann said, "Annabelle wanted those rubber boots because we were going to Maine. Isn't that sweet?" And Olive, who could not think what to say about this, nodded. Ann eventually went upstairs with the baby, and then Olive was alone with Christopher, and she realized the moment had come.

"Christopher." She forced herself to look at him, although he was looking down at his foot. "I'm getting married."

It seemed forever before he looked at her and said, with half a smile, "Wait. What did you just say?"

"I said I'm getting married. To Jack Kennison."

She saw the color leave his face; without a doubt his face became pale. He looked around the room for a moment, then turned to look at her. "Who the *fuck* is Jack Kennison?"

"He lost his wife a while ago. I've mentioned him on the phone to you, Chris." She felt as though her face was flaming hot, as though all the blood that had drained from her son's face had made its way to her face instead.

He looked at her with such genuine astonishment, she felt she would take it back immediately, the whole thing, if she could. "You're getting married?" His voice was quiet now. In a quieter voice he said, "Mommy. You're getting married?"

Olive nodded quickly. "I am, Chris."

He kept shaking his head in small gestures, slowly, just kept shaking it and shaking it. "I don't understand. I don't get this, Mom. Why are you getting married?"

"Because we're two lonely old people and we want to be together."

"Then *be* together! But why get married? Mom?"

"Chris, what difference does it make?"

He leaned forward and said—his voice sounded almost menacing—"If it doesn't make any difference, then why are you doing it?"

"I meant, to you. What difference does it make to you?" But horribly, Olive now felt a niggling of doubt. Why was she marrying Jack? What difference *did* it make?

Christopher said, "Mom, you invited us up here just to tell us that, didn't you. I can't believe it."

"I invited you up here because I wanted to see you. I haven't seen you since your father's funeral."

Christopher was looking at her hard. "You invited us up here to tell us you were getting married. Unfuckingbelievable." Then he said, "Mom, you have *never* invited us up here."

"I didn't need to invite you, Chris. You're my son. This is your home."

And then the color returned to his face. "This is not my home," he said, looking around. "Oh my

126

God." He shook his head slowly. "Oh my God." He stood up. "That's why it looks so different. You're moving out. Are you going to move into his house? Of course you are. And sell this one? Oh my God, Mom." He turned to look at her. "When are you getting married?"

"Soon," she said.

"Is there going to be a wedding?"

"No wedding," she said. "We'll go to Town Hall."

He walked to the stairs. "Good night," he said.

"Chris!"

He turned.

Olive stood up. "Your language is deplorable. You said at your father's funeral that the man never swore."

Christopher stared at her. "Mom, you're killing me," he said.

"Well, Jack is coming over in the morning to meet you before you all leave." She was suddenly furious. "Good night," she said.

She could hear—almost immediately—Christopher and Ann talking; she could not hear what they said, she was sitting in the living room, but the sound of their voices came to her steadily. Finally she rose and slowly, very quietly, went and stood by the stairs. "Always been a narcissist, Chris, you *know* that." And then Chris answered, "But Jesus Christ," and something more, and

Olive turned and went just as slowly and quietly back to her chair in the living room.

In her room later that night she kept thinking about the word "narcissist," which she knew the meaning of naturally, but did she *really* know the meaning? She looked at her computer, finding the word "narcissism" in the dictionary. "Self-admiration," it said, then, "personality disorder." She closed the computer. Olive didn't understand this, she really didn't. Self-admiration? Olive felt no admiration of herself! Personality disorder? Given the extensive and widespread array of human emotions, why was anything a personality disorder? And who came up with such a term? People like that crackpot therapist Ann and Christopher had been seeing years ago in New York. Well, that therapist had a disorder; he was crazy.

She got into bed and she did not expect to sleep, and she did not sleep. She took from her bedside drawer the little transistor radio she had held on to while she slept—or tried to—for so many nights of her later life, and she turned it on low and held it to her ear, lying with it that way. The entire night went by and she stared at the dark, turning only a few times. She watched the red digital clock, and she clung to her little transistor radio, but she heard every word that came from it and understood that she had not even dozed.

When it was light she got up and got dressed

and went downstairs. She put three bowls of Cheerios and the milk on the table. Glancing in the small mirror by the doorway she saw that she had the reddened-eye look of a prisoner.

"Hi, Mom," said Christopher, appearing in the kitchen. "What time is he coming over? Because we have a long drive."

"I'll call him right now," said Olive, and she did. "Hello, Jack," she said, "can you come over now? They have a long drive and want to get started. Wonderful. See you soon." She hung up.

"Oh, kids, look what Grandma did." Ann came in holding the baby. "She got your cereal out." The children did not look at her—Olive noticed—but sat down, Theodore and Annabelle balanced together on one chair, and ate their cereal. They made terrible smacking sounds. Little Henry put his spoon on the table and banged it hard, then smiled at Olive as milk and Cheerios sprayed through the air. "Henry," murmured Ann. And Henry said, "Airplane!" And took the spoon and rode it through the air.

As soon as Olive saw Jack's car pulling into the driveway she realized that Jack—of course—was driving his sports car, and she hoped Christopher didn't see it. When Jack knocked on the door, and she let him in, she saw that he was wearing his suede coat, and she thought he looked rich, and sly. But he had the sense not to kiss her. "Jack," she said. "Hello. Come and meet my son. And his wife," she added. And then added, "And their kids."

Jack gave a small bow in his ironical way, his eyes twinkling as they often did, and he followed her into the living room. "Hello, Christopher," he said, and he held out his hand. Christopher rose slowly from his chair and said, "Hello." He shook Jack's hand as though it was a dead fish he had been offered.

"Oh, come on now, Chris." The words were out of Olive's mouth before she realized what she had done.

Christopher looked at her with open surprise. "Come *on?*" He said this loudly. "Come *on?* Jesus, Mom. What do you mean, 'Oh, come on now, Chris'?"

"I just meant—" And Olive understood that she had been frightened of her son for years.

"Oh, stop it, Christopher! Stop it, for Christ's sake!" This was Ann's voice; she had walked into the room after Olive, and Olive, turning toward her, was amazed to see that Ann's face was red, her lips seemed bigger, her eyes seemed bigger, and she said, again, "Stop it, Chris. Just stop it! Let the woman get married. What's the matter with you? *Jesus!* You can't even be polite to him? For crying out loud, Christopher, you are *such* a baby! You think I have four little kids? I have *five* little kids!"

Then Ann turned toward Jack and Olive and said, "On behalf of my husband, I would like to apologize for his unbelievably childish behavior. He can be so childish, and this is childish, Christopher. Jesus *Christ,* is this childish of you."

Almost immediately Christopher held up his hands and said, "She's right, she's right, I am being childish, and I'm sorry. Jack, let's start again. How are you?" And Christopher put his hand out once again toward Jack, and Jack shook it. But Christopher's face was as pale as paper, and Olive felt—in her utter bewilderment—a terrible pity for him, her son, who had just been so openly yelled at by his wife.

Jack waved a hand casually and said something about it being no problem, he was sure it was a shock, and he sat down and Christopher sat down and Ann left the room, and Olive stood there. She only barely heard as her son asked Jack—who was still wearing his suede coat—what he had done for work, and she only barely heard Jack say he had taught at Harvard his whole life, his subject had been the Austro-Hungarian Empire, and Christopher nodded and said, Cool, that's cool. Ann walked back and forth with the children's things, gathering up all their belongings, the children stood in the doorway watching, sometimes going to their mother, and she shook them off. "Move!" she yelled at one of them. Little Henry stood in the doorway of the living room and began to cry.

Olive went to him. "Now, now," she said. He ran his hand over his wet eyes and looked up at her. Then—and Olive was never sure this really happened, for the rest of her life she didn't know if she imagined it—he stuck his tongue out at her. "Okay," said Olive, "okay, then," and she moved back into the living room, where Jack and Christopher were now standing, finishing their talk.

"All set?" Christopher asked Ann as she passed through the room once more with a wheelie suitcase. Then he turned to Jack. "Very nice to have met you, if you'll excuse me, I have to help my wife get our brood together."

"Oh, of course." And Jack bowed again in his ironical way. He stepped back and put his hands into the pockets of his khaki pants, and then he took them out again.

Olive was dazed as they got all their things together, their coats on, the shoes, the blue rubber boots; Ann's expression remained stony, and Christopher was obsequious in his attempts to be helpful to her. Finally they were ready to leave, and Olive put her own coat on so she could walk them to the car. Jack walked them out as well, and Olive saw her son speak to Jack once more by the passenger side—Ann was to drive—and her son seemed open-faced, and even had a smile as he spoke to Jack. The kids were all buckled in, and then Chris walked to Olive and gave her a half hug, almost not touching her, and said, "Bye, Mom," and Olive said, "Goodbye, Chris," and then Ann gave her a hug too, not much of one, and Ann said, "Thanks, Olive."

And then they drove away.

It wasn't until Olive saw the red scarf that she had knit for Little Henry lying half under the couch in the living room that she felt something close to terror. She bent down and picked it up, and she took the scarf and returned to the kitchen, where Jack was leaning forward with his arms on the tabletop. Olive opened the door and put the scarf into the garbage bin by the front door. Then she came back inside and sat down across from Jack. "Well," she said.

"Well," Jack said. He said it kindly. He placed his large, age-spotted hand over Olive's own. In a moment he added, "I guess we know who wears the pants in that family."

"Her mother died recently," Olive said. "She's grieving."

But she pulled her hand away. It came to her then with a horrible whoosh of the crescendo of truth: She had failed on a colossal level. She must have been failing for years and not realized it. She did not have a family as other people did. Other people had their children come and stay and they talked and laughed and the grandchildren sat on the laps of their grandmothers, and they went places and did things, ate meals together, kissed when they parted. Olive had images of this happening in many homes; her friend Edith, for example, before she had moved to that place for old people, her kids would come and stay. Surely they had a better time than what had just happened here. And it had not happened out of the blue. She could not understand what it was about her, but it was about her that had caused this to happen. And it had to have been there for years, maybe all of her life, how would she know? As she sat across from Jack—stunned—she felt as though she had lived her life as though blind.

"Jack?"

"Yes, Olive?"

She shook her head. What she would not tell Jack was the alarm she had felt when she saw Ann yell at her son, and what came to her as she sat here now was the fact that it had not been the first time Ann had yelled at him like that; these were openings into the darkness of a relationship one saw by mistake, as if inside a dark barn, the door had been momentarily blown off and one saw things not meant to be seen—

But it was more than that.

She had done what Ann had done. She had yelled at Henry in front of people. She could not remember who, exactly, but she had always been fierce when she felt like it. So there was this: Her son had married his mother, as all men—in some form or other—eventually do.

Jack spoke quietly. "Hey, Olive. Let's get you out of here for a while. Let's take a drive, then come to my place. You need a break from being here."

"Good idea." Olive stood and went and got her coat and her big black handbag and she let Jack walk her out to the Subaru. He helped her in, and then got in himself, and they drove away. Olive almost looked back behind her, but she closed her eyes instead: She could see it perfectly anyway. Her house, the house she and Henry had built so many years ago, the house that looked small now and would be razed to the ground by whoever bought it, the property was what mattered. But she saw behind her closed eyes the house, and inside her was a shiver that went through her bones. The house where she had raised her son—never, ever realizing that she herself had been raising a motherless child, now a long, long way from home.

Helped

It was not until the Larkin house burned to the ground that people found out Louise Larkin was not living there anymore. The newspaper said she was in the Golden Bridge Rest Home. "That means she's gone completely dopey-dope," Olive Kitteridge said to Jack Kennison as she looked up from the paper. "But my word, what a sad thing about her husband." Louise Larkin's husband had died in the fire; apparently he had lived only in the upstairs of the house, and the fire had started in the kitchen. It was drug-related, according to the newspaper that Olive was reading. The headline said: 83-Year-Old Man Dies in House Fire: Drug Users Suspected.

The next day's newspaper confirmed the part about the drug users. An arrest had been made. Two people who were drug addicts, and who had assumed the place was vacant, had broken into the house to steal things—to steal copper—and then the fire had started as a result of their cooking meth. They had both made it out of the burning house, but by the time the fire was reported, at four in the morning, there was not much the firemen could do. The place was big, but it was wooden and old, and it went like kindling. Now it sat, the charred remains, right there as you drove into the town of Crosby, Maine, and it was really a sad thing to look at.

It was autumn and the leaves had changed but were not yet falling, and the maples by the Larkin home screamed out their beautiful colors, but to be honest the place had been sad to look at for a while even before it burned almost to the ground. The grass had grown knee-high, and the bushes were no longer trimmed, covering the large, majestic windows in the front. It was no surprise that people were surprised to hear that Roger Larkin had been living upstairs there all along. But what a terrible way to die! Burned to death while two drug addicts cooked their awful stuff right below you. There was a lot of talk, naturally. The Larkins had always thought they were better than others; their son was in prison for that terrible crime; Louise had been a pretty woman, this was acknowledged by the townspeople, she had been a guidance counselor in the high school here—but she had never been right since her son stabbed that woman twenty-nine times. Where was the daughter? Nobody knew.

Jack and Olive were driving out of town, and as they went past the burned-down Larkin place, Olive said, looking out the car window, "Sad,

sad, sad." Then she craned her neck a bit and said, "Oh, someone's parked out there. Behind the tree. Whose is that?"

The car belonged to the Larkin daughter.

Suzanne had driven up from Boston the evening before, staying at the Comfort Inn on the outskirts of Crosby, making the reservation under her husband's name. This morning she had gone to the house—what remained of it—and called the only person in town she knew anymore, who in fact was the person who had called her to tell her about the situation when it happened, and this was her father's lawyer, Bernie Green. He said he would come pick her up; she couldn't remember how to get to his house.

Help me help me help me help me. Suzanne had been thinking this since she had seen the ghastly ruins of the house in the daylight this morning. Only one corner of the house remained, the rest was a pile of dark rubble and broken glass and blackened planks. A covering of low clouds swept over the sky, almost quilted in appearance. Sitting in her car, her knees bouncing, she picked at the skin near her fingernails; through the windshield she could see that the trunk of the maple tree had been charred as well. *Help me help me help me.*

As Bernie pulled into the driveway, his tires rolling over the patches of black ash, Suzanne had a sensation of floating toward his car; she had known this man since she was a child. Tall, slightly overweight, he got out and opened the door on the passenger's side, and she got in, whispering, "Bernie," while he said, "Hello, Suzanne." They drove to his house in silence; a shyness had come over her.

"You look like your mother used to," said Bernie once he was standing in his office on the second floor of his house on River Road. "Have a seat, Suzanne." He gestured toward the chair with the red velvet seat cushion. Suzanne sat. "Take your coat?" Bernie asked, and Suzanne shook her head.

"How is your mother? Does she know?" Bernie sat down heavily in his chair behind the desk.

Suzanne sat with the back of her hand to her mouth, then she leaned forward and said, "She's really *gone,* Bernie. Last night when I said I was her daughter, she told me her daughter had died."

Bernie just looked at her, his lids partway down. After a minute he asked, "How's your work, Suzanne? Are you still in the AG's office?"

"Yeah, yeah, work is good. *That* part is good," Suzanne answered, sitting back. A tiny part of her relaxed.

"What division?"

"Child protection," Suzanne said, and Bernie nodded.

Suzanne said, "It kills me, the job. I have a

case right now—" Suzanne waved a hand briefly. "Never mind. It's always like that, but I love it, my job."

Bernie watched her.

After a few moments Suzanne said, "You know, I don't think my father ever thought I was a real lawyer. You know."

"You are a real lawyer, Suzanne."

"Oh, I know, I know. But for him, you know, Mr. Investment Banker, something like working in the attorney general's office, in child protection especially—I don't know. But he was proud of me. I guess." She looked at Bernie; he was looking down now.

"I am sure he was, Suzanne."

"But did he ever say that to you? That he was proud of me?" Suzanne asked.

"Oh, Suzanne," said Bernie, raising his tired eyes. "I know he was proud of you."

Suzanne glanced over at the far window, with its long white drapes and a red valance at the top; the clouds could be seen through the drapes' opening, spreading themselves out above the river. Suzanne looked back at Bernie. "Bernie, can I tell you something?" Bernie's eyebrows rose slightly in encouragement. "When I was a little girl I used to have this stuffed dog called Snuggles. And I *loved* Snuggles, he was so soft. And when I came up here two years ago to help my father put my mother in that home, I found out—Well, I didn't even know Snuggles still existed, but my mother had become attached to it. And she was asleep when I got there last night and she was just *clinging* to Snuggles, and the people there—the aides—told me she loves that dog, sleeps with it, never lets it out of her sight." Suzanne bit the inside of her mouth, pushing her cheek with a finger.

Bernie said, "Oh, Suzanne," and let out a big sigh.

Suzanne's stomach growled; her head felt a little swimmy. She had had nothing except a cup of coffee early this morning, but she was vaguely glad to have the chattiness rise within her. Glancing about, she saw that Bernie's office was smaller than she had remembered; there was that gorgeous view of the river, which she did seem to remember. In the corner was a tall clock that was not working. Suzanne crossed her legs, kicking her foot slightly; her brown suede boot bumped against the desk. "My mother—" Suzanne paused. "I don't know if you know this—she had a little drinking problem. Honestly, I think she was always a little crazy. I think Doyle got her genes, that's what I think."

"And how is Doyle?" Bernie asked this impassively, his hands in his lap.

"Well, he's medicated." Suzanne had to wait a moment before she could continue; her brother's story was carved into her deeply; it sat quietly tucked deep beneath her ribcage all the time. "So he's okay, but he's a little bit of a zombie. Which is not bad, since he'll be there for the rest of his life. Before they got him doped up, he just cried all day long. All day long that poor boy wept."

"Oy vey," said Bernie. He shook his head, and Suzanne felt a sudden deep *deep* affection for this man she had known from such a young age. She saw that his eyes were blue, they were large eyes, watery with age. "Let's get back to your mother for just a minute, Suzanne. So she didn't know who you were yesterday? And she has no idea about the fire? She has no idea your father died? Does she know anything about Doyle anymore?"

Suzanne sat back, her foot kicking into the air, and said, "No, I don't think she has any idea about my father, and honestly?" Suzanne looked at this man across from her. "I didn't tell her."

"I understand," said Bernie. "What would be the point?"

"Well, exactly," said Suzanne. "What would be the point? My father said that when he went to visit her, she'd get really abusive—" Suzanne passed a hand through the air. "Oh, who knows. Anyway. She didn't mention Doyle, so I didn't either."

"No." Bernie shook his head, kindly. "No, no, of course not."

143

• • •

This is what Suzanne did not tell Bernie: that two years ago, on an instinct, she had driven up to visit her parents spontaneously, and when she had stepped up to the door of the house, she heard screaming inside. She had taken her key and let herself in, and in the living room her father was standing over her mother, who was sitting in a chair in a dirty nightgown, and her father was holding her mother by the wrists, lifting her and shoving her back down into the chair, lifting and shoving and yelling at her, "I can't *do* this anymore, goddammit, I *hate* you!" And her mother was screaming and trying to get away, but Suzanne's father kept her wrists in his hands. When her father turned and saw Suzanne, he sank down on the floor by the chair and began to weep, hard. Suzanne had never seen her father weep before, it had been unimaginable to her that he could. Her mother kept screaming from where she sat in the chair.

"Suzanne," her father said, his face wet, his chest heaving, "Suzanne, I can't do it anymore."

"Oh, Daddy," Suzanne said. "She's been getting so much worse, you shouldn't have to take care of her alone." Suzanne had finally gotten her mother to bed, but she had seen the bruises on her mother's wrists, and she had been shocked to find more bruises on her mother's ankles, on her upper arms too, even at the top of her chest. Her father had stayed on the living-room floor, and she sat down beside him; his red T-shirt was wet. "Dad," she said. "Dad, she's got bruises all over her." Her father said nothing, just hung his head in his hands.

She had hired round-the-clock aides to come in, meeting with each one, telling them that her mother had fallen, but she had been scared— scared to death—that they would say something to the authorities, although they never did. But in one week's time there was a sudden opening at the Golden Bridge Rest Home, and Suzanne helped her father move her mother in, and Suzanne's father retreated to the upstairs, where he had been living for a while. Her father had said to Suzanne, "Please don't come back here again, you have your life, and you must live it." He had become a shell of a man, not even recognizable to her.

Suzanne thought now that she—Suzanne—had not been quite right in the head since this had happened.

She said, "So every week, you know, I spoke on the phone with my father."

Bernie scratched the back of his head. "Tell me," he said.

"Every week I called him. Even if it was only for a few minutes. I mean, what did the man have to *say?* But we would chat, and I spoke to him the night he died. I mean, before he died, of course," and Suzanne's saying that made her think: Oh, I'm really not right in the head. She said, "I think I'm not right in my head. Not like my mother being crazy, just everything—"

Bernie raised his large hand. "I know what you're saying. You're fine. You're under stress. You're not crazy, Suzanne. Of course you feel you're not right in your head."

Oh, she loved him, this man.

Suzanne closed her eyes briefly. "Thank you," she said. And then she started to cry. She wanted to wail her head off, but her weeping came out only in little fits and starts. It was like waiting to throw up, she thought—how you could sense it but it wasn't here yet. She was surprised that he had a box of tissues—she hadn't noticed them—sitting right on his large wooden desk. He pushed them forward to her, and she pressed a tissue to her eyes. After a moment she said, "So you have people in here all ready to cry, like therapists do?" She tried to smile at him. "I mean, you're all set with the Kleenex box."

"People come here in various states of distress," Bernie said, and she realized of course that would be true.

"Well, I'm distressed," she said. She blew her nose, and scrunched the tissue up in her hand. Her crying went no further.

"Of course you're distressed. Your father, to whom you spoke each week on the telephone, has died horribly in a fire. I would think you'd be quite distressed, Suzanne."

"Oh, I am. I am. And also, I might be getting divorced."

At this news, Bernie's eyelids dropped all the way down, and he shook his head in what Suzanne thought was great sympathy. After a moment he looked up and asked, "Your sons?"

Suzanne noticed a small wastebasket under the desk, and she bent down and tossed her tissue into it. "Well, they both started college last year. One at Dartmouth, the other at Michigan. They have no idea we might be separating, thank God. But it's just—Oh, it's all awful."

Bernie nodded.

Suzanne said, "It's my fault, Bernie." She hesitated and then said the words: "I had an affair. A stupid, stupid little affair with a—oh, a kind of creepy man—and when I tell my husband I know he'll *completely* flip out and he'll want a divorce." She added, "My husband is really—" She paused, looking for the right word. "Well, he's traditional."

Bernie moved a piece of paper on his desk just slightly with his hand, and then finally he nodded one small nod.

"Why do you act like this is so normal?" Suzanne squeezed her nose with her fingers.

Bernie let out a sigh and said, "Because it is, Suzanne."

147

"Oh, man, not for me, it isn't. I feel like I've set off a bomb in my life. For years I felt like I was safe on an—I don't know, like an island. I had floated away from all those troubles that poor Doyle had, I was safe on my island with my *own* family, my husband and my boys, and now I've blown it up."

"Loss can do this," Bernie said.

"Do what?" Suzanne asked.

Bernie opened his hands upward. "Cause these . . . indiscretions."

"But when I had this *crappy* indiscretion, my father wasn't dead yet."

"But your sons have left you." Bernie pointed a finger toward the ceiling. He added, "And six years ago your brother was sent to prison for life. And, as you put it, your mother is gone. Those are huge losses, Suzanne."

These words rolled over Suzanne with a swiftness, as though something true had been said but she couldn't catch it. She gazed around his office. Oh, she wanted to stay here! A sudden crack of sunlight came through the far window, making a small strip of light across Bernie's desk, and she saw that on his desk was one small framed photograph, facing him. "Who's that?" she asked, nodding toward the frame.

He turned it around so she could see. The couple, in black-and-white, looked like they were from the olden days; the man had a full beard and a suit with a skinny tie, and the woman had a hat tight on her head. "My parents," he said.

"Really." Suzanne squinted at them. "Were they, you know, Orthodox?"

Bernie held up a hand and turned it one way, then another. "Yes, no. Eventually no."

"Eventually? I thought if you were Orthodox, you were Orthodox."

Bernie pressed his lips together, then gave a shrug. "Well. You were wrong. They died in the camps," Bernie said. "They pretended they were not Jews, but they were and so they died."

"Oh Jesus. Oh God. I'm so sorry." Suzanne's face got very hot. "I had no idea," she said.

"Why would you have any idea?" He looked at her with his eyelids half down.

"How did you end up in Maine, Bernie?"

Bernie seemed indifferent to the question. "My wife and I wanted to get away from New York, and there was—still is—a Jewish community in Shirley Falls, so we came up here, but then we got tired of it, the community, so we moved to Crosby."

She wanted to ask him how he'd come to New York after his parents had died in Europe, but she did not ask. She wanted also to ask about his faith. She wondered if he had lost his faith, if that's what he meant by being tired of the community. It would be natural—wouldn't it?— to lose your faith if you lost your parents in such a way? For many years Suzanne had had what she thought of—privately—as a faith of sorts, but this sensation had eluded her for a few years now, and she felt very bad about that. "Oh, Bernie," she said. Then she asked, "How are your kids? Grandchildren?"

"They're all fine." He looked out the window then, and after a moment he said, "Ironically, they're all living back in New York. Which is fine," he added.

"Okay," Suzanne said. She did not ask about Bernie's wife, because Suzanne had just seen his wife—they had said hello—on her way upstairs to this office. His wife looked like a melted candle, this was what had gone through Suzanne's mind. But she may have always looked like that, Suzanne could not remember.

"I wish I could stay right here," Suzanne said. Across the room was a sofa in the corner that matched the red velvet cushioned chair she sat on.

Bernie said, "In Crosby?"

"Oh God, no. No, I meant *here*. Right here in this room. I wish I could just stay here, is what I'm saying."

"Stay here as long as you like, Suzanne. There's no rush."

But they spoke then about the estate. When Bernie told her the amount of money that would come to her, Suzanne sat up straight. "*Stop* it," she said. "Bernie, that's *sickening*."

"Your father made very good investments," Bernie said.

She asked, "What did he invest in? I know he was an investment banker, but what did he invest in that made *all* this money? My God, Bernie, that's a *lot* of money."

"South Africa," Bernie said, glancing at some sheets of paper in front of him. "Way back. And also the pharmaceutical companies. Exxon, too."

"South Africa?" Suzanne asked. "Are you saying back when there was apartheid he was investing over there?" Bernie nodded, and she said, "But he didn't, Bernie. I *asked* him—when Mandela got released from prison—I asked my father if he had invested in South Africa and he said, 'No, Suzanne.' He *told* me that."

Bernie put the papers back into a folder.

"I'm giving it all away. Every penny. I don't want it." Suzanne sat back. "My *God,*" she said.

Bernie said, "Do with it whatever you like."

He told her she would have to cover the costs of cleaning the lot up—although there was insurance—and then they would put it on the market. "It should go, I think," Bernie said. "It's a great location, right there as you come into town. Someone will want it."

"Or not," said Suzanne; she was absolutely shocked about the amount of money.

"Or not." Bernie gave a small shrug.

Finally Suzanne rose, and Bernie stood up as well. She went and put her arms around him, and after a moment he put his arms around her too. She hugged him more tightly, and then she felt him pull away just slightly, so she stopped hugging him and said, "Thank you, Bernie. You've been wonderful."

As she headed for the door, he said, "Suzanne." She turned to him. "Why do you need to tell your husband about your . . . indiscretion?" He was standing with both hands loosely on his hips.

She said, "Because he's my *husband*. We can't live with this between us, it would be so, you know, so awful."

"As awful as getting divorced?"

"What are you saying, Bernie? That I should live with this lie forever?"

He turned slightly, putting one hand to his chin, and then he turned back and said, "You're the one who made the decision to have the affair. I think you should be the one who takes responsibility for it. Not your husband."

She shook her head. "We're not like that, Bernie. There have never been any secrets between us, and this would be too awful. I have to tell him."

"There are always secrets," Bernie said. "Let's go." He extended his hand toward the doorway, and she went before him down the stairs. She had forgotten that he was to drive her back.

• • •

Beneath the clouds—which were even lower now—sat the jagged part of the corner of the house that was still standing, and the gruesomeness of its remains looked exactly like what they were: remains. "Thank you," Suzanne said. She got her car key from her handbag.

"It's okay." He turned his car off, and a faint thrill went through Suzanne, that he did not want to leave her yet. After a moment Bernie said, "You know, it's not my business, but I wonder if you could see someone, a therapist. There has to be a good therapist in Boston. Just for now while you sort all these things out."

"Oh, Bernie," said Suzanne. She touched his arm briefly. "I've been to a therapist. That's who I had my stupid affair with."

Bernie closed his eyes for a long moment, then he opened them and stared straight ahead through his windshield. He said, "Suzanne, I'm sorry."

"No, it was kind of my fault. I let him come on to me."

"It was not your fault, Suzanne." He looked at her now. "It was very unprofessional, what he did. How long had you been seeing him?"

"Two years." Suzanne added, "Since my mother went into that home is when I started seeing him."

"Oy vey," said Bernie.

"But it was just the last few months—oh, it's so

153

sordid, the whole thing, and you know he's—oh, no offense, Bernie—but he's old. You know."

"Yes," said Bernie. He added, "Of course he is."

"Please don't worry. Please."

"He should be reported," Bernie said, and Suzanne said, "I'm not going to report him."

He raised a hand then and said, "Goodbye. Good luck, Suzanne. Call if you need me." Then he started his car, and she felt a terrible desolation return.

She got out, and went and sat in her car while he drove out of the driveway. A few orangey leaves had fallen onto the hood from the tree above the car. She saw on her phone that her husband had texted to see if she was okay, and she texted back that she would call him soon. She looked through the car window at the charred remains of the house where she had grown up. *Try,* she thought to herself with a kind of fury, and what she meant was: Try and have a good memory come to you.

She could not do it.

She could almost find no memories at all, just tiny fleeting images of her mother veering up from the dining-room table at night, a wineglass in her hand, her father, as though in a shadow, walking down the stairs. Doyle, always so skittish, so intense. She turned her head and squinted at the part of Main Street she could see from here, and she thought of this town, where she had spent her youth, but she had gone to a private school in Portland and so the town had never felt as real to her as it otherwise might have. As a young girl she had taken longs walks, alone, she had walked across the bridge and down by the coast; *there* was a good memory. Then she thought of Doyle sitting next to her in the car each morning, banging his knee, laughing. They'd had a real connection, because they both went to school out of town. And because she had loved him, her little brother. Most days her father drove them to school in Portland, and now Suzanne remembered him stopping at the gas station by Freeport, coming back out of the little store and tossing her a package of cellophane-wrapped doughnuts, six little ones covered in powder. "Here you go, Twinkie," her father would say, because he would also buy Twinkies for both of them, as well, to have with their lunch.

Back home, Bernie stepped into the kitchen and walked up behind his wife, who was washing dishes, and put his arms around her. She was a short woman; the back of her head was below his chin. "Oy, Eva," he said, and his wife turned to him, her hands soapy. "I know," she said. He held her to him with one arm then, and stood looking through the kitchen window at the cedar tree. "That poor girl," his wife said, and Bernie said, "Yes."

He went back upstairs to his office and sat for quite a while at his desk, turning his swivel chair to look out the window at the river. Suzanne had seemed more childlike than he would have thought from his telephone call to her with the news of her father's death; she had been calm and adult-sounding then. But he realized that faced with the image of that burned-down house, with the reality of all that had happened, she had been thrown. Still, she had surprised him with her acuity about her father; Roger Larkin had not, in fact, respected the truth that she was a lawyer, he had told Bernie a number of times that she was "really just a social worker." Bernie sat with his hands on the armrests of the chair and pictured Roger in his younger years, a dark-haired handsome man with a pretty blond wife; she had come from Philadelphia. Roger had come from poverty, in Houlton, Maine, but he was smart and went to Wharton, and then he just made money, and more money. When Roger had first come to Bernie for legal advice, it had been about investments made in South Africa; he needed a loophole, which he had already figured out, and Bernie had advised him. Bernie had said to him that day, "But I don't like this, Roger," and Roger had just smiled at him and said, "You're my legal adviser, Bernie, not my priest." This had always stayed with Bernie, because he thought that a priest also had to hear the sorts of secrets that Bernie had to hear from his clients, but a priest was—ostensibly—pure; Bernie did not feel pure. Over the years, Roger Larkin had sat on the board of the Portland Symphony, and various other boards as well. One time, many years ago, Roger had walked into this office and said, "I really need you for this one, Bernie." There had been an affair with a woman in his office, he had to have money arranged for her abortion in New York, and then she had sued him. Bernie had settled the suit quickly, and so it had not reached the papers. That part of her father Suzanne did not seem to know about.

But more unsettling to Bernie—he shifted in his chair—was the fact that two years ago Louise Larkin had made a telephone call to Bernie; it was in the evening, and Bernie happened to be in his office preparing for a case the next day, and Louise had screamed into the telephone, "He's trying to kill me! Help me, help!" And then Roger had taken the telephone away from her and spoken to Bernie in a tired voice and said that his wife had dementia and he could not take care of her anymore. Bernie had talked to Roger for quite a while, and suggested that his wife was not so demented that she didn't know how to call him, and there might be a need to investigate if Louise was calling him for help about her physical safety. Roger had said, "Well, you do what you need to do, Mr. Lawyer Man." Bernie had done nothing. But the next week he had called Roger and helped get Louise into the Golden Bridge Rest Home; she jumped the waiting line because of Roger's money. Bernie did not hear from Roger again until six months ago, when Roger came to him with an updated will.

Bernie watched the river, the clouds made the river seem gray, and then he stopped seeing the river and pictured Suzanne instead, the poor child, so pretty, like her mother had been, and so . . . so dazed. When she had tightened her hug with him before she left, he had felt—What had he felt? He had wanted to pick her up and stroke her hair and make everything bad in her life go away. He remembered her then as she had actually been as a small girl; she had played with a doll very quietly in the corner of this room while her father had done business with Bernie.

Uneasiness sat with Bernie now, and he realized it was an uneasiness he had felt on and off for years. His life had been tainted, he thought, by some of his clients, but none more than Roger Larkin had caused him to feel this way.

He went into the bathroom; he heard the telephone ring, then stop. When he came out he saw the number and recognized that it was Suzanne's; she had left no message. He called her back, but she did not pick up. And so he just sat. A tenderness flooded through him.

• • •

Suzanne was pulling into the parking lot of the Golden Bridge Rest Home. She had just left the Comfort Inn, where she had gone to pick up her bag, and the woman who worked there had frightened her; Suzanne had called Bernie; she was panicking. He had called her back as she was driving over the bridge and she hadn't answered; she had been afraid to talk on the phone and drive, she felt that swimmy in her head. Now she sat in her car and glanced at her phone, but remembering how Bernie had pulled away slightly as she hugged him she dropped the phone into her bag and sat with her eyes closed, thinking *oh help me help me help me,* and then she got out and went inside. Even though she had been there just the day before, the place still took her by surprise. Built back from the road, pleasant-looking with its black shutters, it was a world unto itself, and the smell—of cleaning fluids and also a whiff of human waste—assaulted her the moment she stepped through the double doors.

She moved past a man sitting in a wheelchair in the hallway and walked down to her mother's room. When she had come in last night, her mother had been asleep, and Suzanne had gasped at the sight of her; her mother lay with her gray hair—what was left of it—sticking out on the pillow, and she was as tiny as a person could be and still be alive. It was as though her mother had been in a science fiction movie and that her body—her essence—had been snatched. When her mother's eyes flipped open, Suzanne had said, "It's me, Mom, Suzanne," and her mother had sat up and said, "Hello." And when Suzanne repeated to her, "Mom, it's me, your daughter," her mother said pleasantly, "No, my daughter is dead." Then her mother had sung a lullaby as she rocked Snuggles, and she was still doing that when Suzanne left.

Now, as Suzanne entered the room, she had to walk by another woman seated in a wheelchair not far from her mother; the woman looked at her with filmy eyes, and when Suzanne waved her hand at the woman, there was no response.

Her mother sat serenely in her wheelchair in the corner of her room, with Snuggles on her lap. Her hair had been combed, and she wore a sweatsuit of pale off-white, on her feet were clean white sneakers. "Hello," she said to Suzanne. "You're a pretty woman. Who are you?"

"I'm your daughter, Mom. It's me, Suzanne."

Her mother said politely, "I don't have a daughter. She died. But when she was a little girl, she had this." And her mother held up Snuggles. "His name is Snuggles," her mother said.

"Mom, you remember this was Snuggles?" Suzanne leaned down toward her mother.

"I don't know who you are," her mother continued, "but my poor little daughter. She was always such a *good* girl."

Suzanne sat slowly down on the edge of her mother's bed.

"But her brother!" And her mother laughed then. "Oh, her brother was a nasty little boy. Always wanting his willie played with. Oh, he always wanted me to play with his willie, oh my, he was a bad, bad boy." She laughed again.

Chills ran down Suzanne's side, she felt them going all the way down her leg. "Doyle?" she finally asked.

Her mother's face remained uncomprehending, until suddenly it became twisted in fury. "You get out of here right now! Get out! Get out!" Spittle flew from her mouth.

And then the other woman seated in her wheelchair began to cry. It was a terrible sound—a keening, almost. Suzanne stood up and went out into the hallway. "Help me, please," she said to an aide going by. "I've upset my mother and also some woman who was in here, I guess visiting her."

The aide was a small young woman, with no expression on her face, and she said to Suzanne, "I'll be there in a minute."

"Please come in now," said Suzanne, but the aide was already going into the room next door. "Oh God," said Suzanne. She went back into her mother's room, past the woman who was crying so hard, and her mother was half standing out of her chair. She pointed her arm at Suzanne. "You! Get out of here right now!"

An hour later, Bernie still could not get Suzanne out of his mind. He kept having an image of putting her onto his lap, and holding her to him tightly. That's enough, he thought, and took out a folder of a case he had to work on.

When his telephone rang again, he saw that it was her, and he picked it up and said, "Hello, Suzanne."

He could hear that she was crying. "Oh, Bernie, I'm *so* sorry to call you, I really am, but I—"

"It's quite all right, Suzanne. I told you to call me anytime, and I meant it. If you call me again in ten minutes, I'll still mean it."

"I'm just so scared," she said. "I'm so scared!"

"I understand that. You have every reason to feel scared. But you're going to be all right." Bernie said this gently. "I've known you for years, Suzanne. And you have always been focused and smart, and you're going to be just fine. You're in the middle of a storm at the moment."

"Don't hang up," Suzanne said.

"I'm right here," Bernie answered. "You take your time."

"Where are you?" Suzanne asked. "So I can picture you."

"I'm sitting right at my desk. Alone," he added.

"Bernie," Suzanne said. "First—Now, please listen to me and tell me the truth. Do you know if my father ever had an affair? The woman who works at the Comfort Inn, when I went back to get my bag, she said she recognized my name from the credit card I had paid with, and she said she had always loved my father—she worked at that gas station in Freeport—and she said my mother used to come into that gas station with him at noontime, always so nice with her red hair, but my mother never had red hair."

There was a silence, then Bernie said, "I'm not going to answer that."

"Well, I guess you just did."

"No. I didn't." After a moment Bernie added, "You're a lawyer, and you know that privilege does not end with the death of a client."

"Okay," Suzanne said. "But just hold on, okay?"

"I'm right here, Suzanne." He added, "I'm not going anywhere." He picked up a paperclip and touched it repeatedly to his desk. He heard her weeping, and then he heard her finally stop.

"Oh, Bernie. I know my father probably had an affair, he probably had a dozen affairs, and I don't want to be like my father—"

"Suzanne." Bernie's voice was firm. He let the paperclip stay on his desk. "You are not like your father. Do you hear me? You have always been you. And you alone." Then he said, "Where are you right now?"

"At a rest stop on the turnpike. There's a mother with a little boy and they're laughing about something and it reminds me of how I used to be with my boys."

"And they're still your boys," Bernie said. "They always will be."

"But, Bernie, can I tell you one more thing?"

"Of course you can."

"I stopped to see my mother before I left town, and she told me that Doyle had always been a bad boy, that he—" Suzanne was crying again. "That he—he always wanted her to play with his willie. Oh God, Bernie. Oh Jesus."

Bernie was silent for quite a while, and then he said quietly, "Oh, Suzanne. I don't know what to say about that." He leaned forward, setting a hand to his head as he held the telephone in the other.

"But do you think—oh, Bernie, do you think she ever? Oh God, I *work* with kids like this! Even my creepy therapist told me that a guy, however nuts he is, doesn't stab a woman twenty-nine times unless he has a *lot* of aggression toward a woman. Toward, you know, I guess his mother."

"I know what you're saying," Bernie said. And then after a moment he said, "I guess we'll never know."

"No." And then Suzanne said, "But, Bernie, it makes me so *sad* for that poor boy! You know, I'm going to visit him more often. I usually go once a month to see him there in Connecticut, but now that the boys are gone and I have more time, I'm going to go much more often. I just am, oh God, Bernie, that *poor* child!"

"You go as often as you need to," Bernie said.

When Suzanne spoke next she sounded exhausted. "Bernie, my father was abusing my mother. She had bruises all over her before she went into that home."

Bernie sat up straight; a kind of jolt went through him. He said quietly, "I thought that might be true."

"You did? Why did you think it might be true?"

Bernie closed his eyes, then opened them, and said, "It's not altogether unusual in those circumstances." Then he said, "We got her into that place ahead of other people."

"How?" Suzanne asked.

"Your father had money. That's how."

"You helped him do that?"

"I did." Bernie felt himself blush. He was lying to her by not telling her how her mother had called him to say she was in danger. He opened his mouth, then closed it.

"Oh, Bernie. Well, thank you." She added, "You probably saved her life."

"I never saved anyone's life," Bernie said.

Suzanne said, "Bernie. Bernie. Do you *realize* what I came from? Do you realize that? Oh my God, those people! How did I get out alive?" Then Suzanne said, "But you did too. You got out as well." She added, "Except your parents were murdered, and mine were—well, they almost were murder*ers,* Bernie. And my brother *is* a murderer. Oh my *God.*"

Bernie said, "But you got out. Just as you said."

Suzanne asked, "How did you get out of . . . where were you born?"

"Hungary." Bernie spread his hand over his face briefly. He wanted to commend her for everything she had done with her life, to say that she had lived decently by helping those children every day through the AG's office, and by raising her boys, and by her loyalty to Doyle. But instead he answered her question. "I got out when I was a kid, because my uncle came to America and my parents wanted me to come with him, they said they would join us soon. And then they didn't."

"I didn't know you were born in Hungary. Do you remember your parents at all?"

Bernie glanced around his office before he answered her. It had been a long time since he had spoken of these things to anyone. "Well, I remember my father reading the Torah. I remember my mother setting the table. And I remember her reading to me when I was sick one time and in bed."

"Oh, Bernie." Suzanne's voice sounded stronger now. "Bernie, can I just ask you one last thing?"

"Of course, Suzanne."

"Do you have any faith? Religious faith, I mean."

Bernie felt a physical response to this, as though a small wave had just rolled through his chest. He waited and then he said, "You know, I've lived for many years as a secular Jew, and I don't believe I have any faith in that sense."

"But?" Suzanne asked. "There's a 'but'—I can hear it in your voice."

A tentative earnestness spread through Bernie now. He felt as though he had been called upon to give something of himself that was far outside his purview as a lawyer, and it was something he had never given to anyone, except his wife, vaguely, years ago. "Okay," he said. "The 'but' is this. But do I have faith? I do. The problem is, I can't describe it. But it's a faith of sorts. It is a faith."

"Can you tell me? Oh, please tell me, Bernie."

Bernie put his hand to the back of his neck. "I can't, Suzanne. Because I don't have words to describe it. It's more an understanding—I've had it most of my life—that there is something much larger than we are." He felt a sense of failure; he had failed in telling this.

Suzanne said, "I used to feel that. For *years* I would have sensations of just what you described.

But I can't really describe it either." Bernie did not answer, and Suzanne continued. "When I was a kid, and alone—I spent a lot of time alone, you know, when I wasn't at school—I would take these walks and I would get this feeling, this very deep sensation, and I understood—only the way a kid could understand these things—that it had something to do with God. But I don't mean God like some father figure, I don't even know what I mean—"

"I know what you mean," Bernie said.

"And I kept having that feeling every so often right into my adult life, I never told anybody, because what was there to tell?"

"I understand that completely," Bernie said.

"But I haven't had it for a few years, and so I wonder: Did I make it up? But I know I didn't, Bernie. I never told my husband, I never told *any*body. But whenever someone says they're an atheist, I always privately have this bad reaction, and they give all the obvious reasons, you know, kids get cancer, earthquakes kill people, all that kind of stuff. But when I hear them, I think: But you are barking up the wrong tree." She added, "But I couldn't say what the right tree is—or how to bark up it."

Sitting at his desk, Bernie felt a vague sense of disbelief; everything she was saying was entirely understandable to him.

Then Suzanne added, "I don't know why I don't

get that feeling—that sensation—anymore."

Bernie looked out at the river; it had changed, as it always did, it was now a greener color, as the cloud covering went higher up into the sky. "You will," he said.

Suzanne said, "You know what, Bernie? I've thought about this a lot. A *lot*. And here is the—well, the phrase I've come up with, I mean just for myself, but this is the phrase that goes through my head. I think our job—maybe even our *duty*—is to—" Her voice became calm, adult-like. "To bear the burden of the mystery with as much grace as we can."

Bernie was silent for a long time. He said finally, "Thank you, Suzanne."

After another moment Suzanne said, "The only other person I told about those feelings of—well, of God, or something so much bigger—well, I told that creepy therapist, after, you know, after we began—Anyway, you know what he said? He said, Don't be ridiculous, Suzanne. You were a child mystified by life, and you now think it was God you felt. You were just mystified by life, that's all. Isn't that creepy, Bernie?"

Bernie glanced at the ceiling. "Creepy? Yes. He was a very limited man, Suzanne."

"I know it," Suzanne said. Then she said, "Do you really think I shouldn't tell my husband about him? Do you think I can really live with it on my own?"

"People live with things," Bernie said. "They do. I am always amazed at what people live with." He added, "And, Suzanne, you just told me your husband doesn't know about your experience with . . . with whatever it is we've been talking about."

"You're right," Suzanne said. "Bernie, you're so smart. I love you."

Bernie said, "And, Suzanne, I love you." He wished terribly to tell her that he felt better now, that having talked to her in this way his uneasiness had been alleviated somewhat. Instead he said, "One more thing. Now listen to me."

"I'm listening," Suzanne said.

He said, "You hang up and have yourself a good cry. Have a cry like you've never had in your life. And when you're done, get yourself something to eat. I bet you haven't eaten a thing all day."

"You're right, I haven't. And I will eat something, I promise. But I don't feel like crying anymore, Bernie. I feel . . . I feel like I could practically *sing*."

"Then do that," he said.

And Suzanne, sitting in her car at the rest stop on the turnpike, did not sing. But she sat there for a long while, thinking about their conversation. She thought she would never forget it, it was as though huge windows above her had

170

been smashed—the way the firemen must have smashed the windows of her childhood home—and now, here above her and around her, was the whole wide world *right there,* available to her once again. She watched as the mother and the young boy got back into their car, laughing at something together. In front of her was a small maple tree, the leaves pink from top to bottom. "Oh, Bernie," she whispered. "Wow."

Bernie sat at his desk, staring out at the river. A kind of quiet astonishment went through him. Somehow, Suzanne had remained uncorrupted; her guilelessness in talking to him was a gift of no small proportion. She was an innocent, this came to her as naturally as breathing, and he felt right now as though her innocence had washed over him, removing some of the areas of disquiet he had gathered over the years in his profession. In a moment he would go downstairs and tell his wife that they need not worry about Suzanne. About the particularities of their conversation he would say nothing; the way Suzanne had helped him would remain his secret. Harmless enough, he thought, standing up, when you considered the variety of secrets people had been keeping to themselves for years.

Light

Cindy Coombs pulled her shopping cart out of the way of a young couple and saw the man look at her. She saw him look away, then she saw him look at her again. Somehow the man's look made her touch the zipper on her winter coat—it was a pale-blue quilted coat and the zipper was halfway open—and she walked past the two of them down the aisle even though what she needed—two cans of tomato soup— was exactly where the couple was standing. Up the next aisle she went, slowly, the shopping cart, with its wobbly wheel, making a bumping sound. In her cart there was milk and a loaf of bread. She stopped and turned toward the raisins, unzipping her coat more in order to tighten her belt. Then she kept going, not sure what to do. Tomato soup and—what was it? Butter. In her head she kept saying *butter, butter,* and tried to think where the butter was, and it was where it always was, over past the milk, many kinds of butter waited.

Where was the kind they always got? Where was it? Cindy leaned forward to get a different kind, what did it matter, and then she saw the kind they usually got, and as she leaned over to get it, she started to fall, and caught herself on the handrail of her shopping cart. She pictured her legs as two little stagnant streams, with twigs and dirt; how could they hold her up?

From behind her, a large elderly hand reached and took the butter that Cindy had been reaching for; it got tossed into her cart. Turning, she saw Mrs. Kitteridge standing there, and Mrs. Kitteridge just looked at her, straight in the eye. "Hello, Cindy," Mrs. Kitteridge finally said. "You're having a hell of a time."

Many years ago, Mrs. Kitteridge had taught Cindy in a junior high math class; Cindy had not especially liked her. Cindy said, "I am, Mrs. Kitteridge. I am having a hell of a time."

Mrs. Kitteridge nodded once, and still she stood there. "Well, let's figure out what you need, and get you out of here."

"I need two cans of tomato soup," Cindy said.

"Let's get the soup." Mrs. Kitteridge did not have a cart, just a basket, and she put the basket into Cindy's cart and took hold of the rail of the shopping cart, but she left room for Cindy to hold it as well; the sleeves of Mrs. Kitteridge's coat were bright red, and her hands around the rail of the shopping cart were puffy and old-looking. "Where *is* the damned soup? This place is such a barn these days, you can walk for miles and miles. And it's a Saturday, so a lot of people are in here." Olive Kitteridge was a big woman; she spoke almost over Cindy's head.

"Around the corner here, I think," said Cindy, and she saw with some relief that the couple who had been standing near the soup had left. Cindy put two cans of tomato soup into her cart, and Mrs. Kitteridge walked with her to the checkout. Cindy paid for her items, put them in the reusable cloth bag she had brought with her, and then she felt compelled to wait for Mrs. Kitteridge, who said, "One second there, Cindy, and I'll walk you to the car."

Together they left the place, and in the huge glass doors that slid open—right before they opened—Cindy caught her own image, and she could not believe it. The wool cap on her head did not cover its baldness, and her eyes were sunken so far in she felt the prick of awe. "I don't think I'll be coming here again," she said to Mrs. Kitteridge as she walked to her car. "I only came because Tom wanted me to."

"Ay-yuh," said Mrs. Kitteridge; the bag she carried banged against her side.

Around them a sudden gust of wind sent a few twigs swirling, and a muddy plastic bag that had been run over a number of times rose slightly, then dropped back to the ground among slushy car tracks from the old snow. Cindy opened the door to her car, got in, and realized Mrs. Kitteridge was waiting. "I'm okay now. Goodbye, Mrs. Kitteridge."

The woman nodded, and Cindy did not turn to look at her once she pulled her car out.

The drive seemed interminable, though it was less than a mile, and because it was a Saturday afternoon, it seemed to Cindy that there was more traffic than usual. When she got home she left the car in the driveway, though the door to the garage was open. The Christmas wreath was still on the front door, and she wished Tom would take it down. She must have told him a hundred times that now it was well into February, the Christmas wreath should come down. Cindy put the groceries onto the counter in their cloth bag. "Hi, honey," she called to her husband, and Tom came into the kitchen and said, "Hey, Cindy— See? You did it." He took the butter and the soup and the milk from the bag and said, "Want to watch some TV?" She shook her head and moved past him up the stairs. Too late she remembered about the Christmas wreath; she would remind him later.

Twenty years ago they had built this house. To Cindy it had seemed huge. She had been embarrassed by it as she watched the construction, the basement poured, the two-by-fours going up; she and Tom had seemed too young for such a large house. Cindy had grown up right outside of Crosby, in a house that had been very small; they had had almost no money, she and her mother and her two sisters. Her father had left the family years earlier, and Cindy's mother worked night shifts at the hospital as a nurse's aide; it had not been easy. But Cindy had been lucky; she had gone to the university, paying her way and borrowing money. And there she had met her husband, who went on to work in the accounting office at the ironworks where he had been ever since. Only later did Cindy realize that this house they had built was a regular-size house, with three bedrooms upstairs and a living room and dining room and kitchen downstairs. A few years later they built the garage, attached to the house, and instead of that making the place look bigger, somehow it caused the house to seem smaller. A perfect-size house; for years she had thought that. But as the boys reached adolescence, she started to think that the house looked ordinary, and she asked Tom if it could be painted a robin's-egg blue. The boys had objected; she let it go, and the house had remained white all these years.

Cindy lay down on the bed and looked through the window at the tops of the trees, the limbs bare, and yet there was that funny little soft sun that sneaks around on a cloud-filled afternoon in February—what was it? The bare branches seemed to reach out, reach out, the opposite of shrinking.

When she saw Tom standing in the doorway of the bedroom, his face open, looking to please, absolutely helpless, she said, "You know what I've been thinking lately?"

"What, sweetheart?" Tom came into the room and reached for her hand. "What have you been thinking?"

"How I wanted to paint this house blue, and we never did it, because the boys—and you—said no, you didn't want to."

Tom's big face seemed in her eyes to get slightly bigger, and he said, "Well, let's do it now, sweetheart. We can have the house painted any color you want. Let's do that!"

Cindy shook her head.

"No, I mean it." Tom bent his head down toward her. "It would be fun, sweetie heart. Let's paint the house."

"No." She shook her head again and turned her face away from him.

"Sweetheart—"

"Oh, Tom. Stop. Please. I said no. We are not going to paint the house now." She waited a moment, then said, "Honey, can you please take down the wreath that's still on the front door?"

"Right now," he said, nodding. "Sweetie heart, consider the wreath gone."

178

· · ·

Before her illness, Cindy had worked as a librarian at the local library. She loved books, oh, did she love books. She loved the feel of them, and the smell of them, and she had loved the semi-quiet of the library, as well as the old people who came sometimes for the whole morning, just to have a place to go. She had liked helping them get online with a computer, or finding the magazine they wanted to read. Most of all, she had loved checking out books, mentioning to people the books she liked; these people would come back and talk to her about the books they had read at her suggestion. Cindy used to read everything, and even now there were books piled on the table beside the bed, books were piled up on the windowsill, and some on the floor as well. She almost had no preference for any kind of book, and she had sometimes thought that odd; she had read Shakespeare and the thrillers of Sharon McDonald, and biographies of Samuel Johnson and different playwrights, silly romance novels, and also—the poets. She thought, privately, that poets just about sat on the right hand of God.

When she was young, Cindy had thought about being a poet—what a silly idea. But as a child she had liked poetry; her third-grade teacher had given her a copy of Edna St. Vincent Millay's *Poems Selected for Young People*, and when her little sister colored all over it in red crayon, Cindy hit her. Always this memory caused Cindy deep pain, because of what had happened later to her little sister. But Cindy had memorized all the poems in the book before they were colored over in red, and she felt—somehow—that it had ushered her into a world far away from her tiny home. This was partly because her teacher had told her that Edna St. Vincent Millay had grown up in Maine too, only an hour away; and that the poet, as a young girl, had been raised in poverty. The teacher had been kind in how she said that, and it was not until years later that Cindy realized it was to help her, Cindy, with her own circumstances of need. Cindy had written some poetry, but only for herself; she knew nothing about it, really. Andrea L'Rieux, who was two years younger than Cindy, had become the Poet Laureate of the United States a year ago, and Cindy felt a vast and secret pride that this person from Crosby, Maine, had accomplished such a thing. In truth, Cindy did not always understand the poetry that Andrea wrote. But it was brave; Cindy knew that. The poetry was a lot about Andrea's life, and Cindy understood, reading it, that she, Cindy, could never have done what Andrea did. She could never have written about her mother in such a way, could never have written down the revulsion she felt at the sight of her mother's cheeks drawing in as she smoked, nor even could she have written anything about herself.

What she would have written about was the light in February. How it changed the way the world looked. People complained about February; it was cold and snowy and oftentimes wet and damp, and people were ready for spring. But for Cindy the light of the month had always been like a secret, and it remained a secret even now. Because in February the days were really getting longer and you could see it, if you really looked. You could see how at the end of each day the world seemed cracked open and the extra light made its way across the stark trees, and promised. It *promised,* that light, and what a thing that was. As Cindy lay on her bed she could see this even now, the gold of the last light opening the world.

The next day, Sunday, after lunch, Cindy returned to bed, and Tom came upstairs with her, trying to be helpful, arranging the pillows, straightening the quilt.

A car could be heard coming up the driveway, and Tom pulled back the curtain and looked out. "Oh Christ," he said. "It's that old bag. Olive Kitteridge. What in hell is she doing here?"

"Let her in," Cindy said, her voice muffled in the pillows.

"What, sweetheart?"

Cindy sat up. "I said, let her in. Please, Tom."

"Are you crazy?" Tom asked.

"Yes. Let her come in."

And so Tom went down the stairs and Cindy heard him open the front door, which they never used, and in a moment Mrs. Kitteridge came up the stairway, followed by Tom, and she stood in the doorway of the bedroom. She wore her red coat, which was rather puffy, the way winter coats can be.

"Hi, Mrs. Kitteridge," Cindy said. She sat up in the bed, putting the pillows behind her back. "Tom, can you take her coat?" And so Mrs. Kitteridge took off her coat and handed it to Tom, who said, "Cindy? You want me to stay?" Cindy shook her head at him, and he went back downstairs with the coat of Mrs. Kitteridge.

Mrs. Kitteridge was wearing black slacks and a jacket-type thing that went halfway down her thighs; its print was of bright reds and orange swirls. She placed her black leather bag on the floor. "Call me Olive. If you can. I know sometimes a person can't when I've been Mrs. Kitteridge all their life."

Cindy looked up at this woman before her; she saw in her eyes a distinct light. "I can call you Olive. Hello, Olive." Cindy looked around and said, "Here, pull up that chair."

Olive pulled the chair over toward the bed, it was a straight-back chair, and Cindy hoped that she could fit on it comfortably. But with her coat off, Olive didn't look quite as large, and she sat on the chair and folded her hands in her lap. "I thought if I called you might say I shouldn't come over." Olive waited. Then she said, "And I thought, hell's bells, I want to go over and see that girl. So I just got in the car and came."

"It's fine," Cindy said. "I'm glad you did. How are you, Olive?"

"The question is you. You're not okay."

"No, I'm not."

"Any chance you will be?"

"Fifty percent. Is what they say." Then Cindy added, "I have my last treatment next week."

Mrs. Kitteridge looked straight at Cindy. "I see," she said. Then she looked around the room—at the white bureau, and the clothes hanging over another chair in the corner, and all the books stacked on the windowsill—before looking back at Cindy. "So you feel crappy? What do you do all day? Do you read?"

"It's a problem," Cindy acknowledged. "Because I do feel crappy. And I don't read as much as I used to. I can't really concentrate."

Olive nodded, as though considering this. "Yuh," she said. Then she added, "Hell of a mess to be in."

"Well, it is kind of."

"I should say so." The woman sat there, her hands still folded in her lap. It didn't appear she had anything else to say.

And so Cindy blurted out, "Oh, Mrs. Kitteridge. Olive. Oh, Olive, I'm so—I'm so *angry*."

Olive nodded. "I should think to God you would be."

"I want to feel peaceful, I want to accept this, but I am so angry, I'm just angry every minute, and when I saw you in the store, people had been looking at me. I don't want to go out, people look at me and they get afraid."

"Yuh," Olive said. Then she added, "Well, I'm not afraid."

"I know that. I mean, I appreciate it."

"How's Tom?"

"Oh, *Tom*." Cindy sat up, and the bedclothes seemed to her almost soiled, although they had been changed the day before, but there was that faint odor of something like metal that she had smelled for months now. "Olive, he keeps talking like I'll get better. I can't believe it, I just can't believe it, it makes me so lonely, oh dear God, I am so lonely."

Olive made a grimace of sympathy. "God, Cindy. That sucks. As the kids used to say. That really sucks."

"It does." Cindy lay back on her pillow, watching this woman who had come over uninvited. "There's a nurse who comes in twice a week, and she told me Tom was acting like every man she's ever seen in these situations. That men just can't *deal* with it. But it's terrible, Olive.

184

He's my husband and we've loved each other now for many years, and this is awful."

Olive sat looking at Cindy, then looking at the foot of the bed. "I don't know," she said. "I don't know if it's a male thing or not. The truth is, Cindy, I wasn't very good to my husband during his last years."

Cindy said, "Yes, you were. Everyone knew—you went to the nursing home every day to see him."

Olive shook her head. "Before that."

"He was sick before that?"

"I don't know," Olive said thoughtfully. "He may have been and I just didn't know it. He became very needy. And I wasn't—I just wasn't very nice to him. It's something I think about a lot these days, and it bugs me like hell."

Cindy waited a moment. "Well, if you didn't know he was sick—"

Olive heaved a deep sigh. "I know, I know. But I'm just saying, I wasn't especially good to him, and it hurts me now. It *really* does. At times these days—rarely, very rarely, but at times—I feel like I've become, oh, just a tiny—tiny—bit better as a person, and it makes me sick that Henry didn't get any of that from me." Olive shook her head. "Here I go, talking about myself again. I've been trying not to talk about myself so much these days."

Cindy said, "Talk about anything you want. I don't care."

"Take a turn," Olive said, raising a hand briefly. "I'm sure I'll get back to myself."

Cindy said, "One time, it was on Christmas Day, I just began to cry. I cried and cried, and my sons were both here and so was Tom, and I stood on the stairs, just wailing, and then I noticed that they had all left, they walked away from me until I stopped crying."

Olive's eyes closed briefly. "Oh Godfrey," she murmured.

"I scared them."

"Yuh."

"And now they will always think of that, every Christmas to come, my sons will remember that."

"Probably."

"I did that to them."

Olive sat forward and said, "Cindy Coombs, there's not one goddamn person in this world who doesn't have a bad memory or two to take with them through life." She sat back and crossed her feet at her ankles.

"But I'm scared!"

"Oh, I know, I know, of course you are. Everyone is scared to die."

"Everyone? Is that true, Mrs. Kitteridge? Are you scared to die?"

"I am scared to death to die, is the truth." Olive adjusted herself on the chair.

Cindy thought about this. "I've heard of people who make peace with it," she said.

"I guess that can happen. I don't know how they do it, but I think it can happen."

They were quiet. Cindy felt—she almost felt normal. "Well," she said finally. "It's just that I'm so alone. I don't want to be so alone."

"'Course you don't."

"You're scared to die, even at your age?"

Olive nodded. "Oh Godfrey, there were days I'd have liked to have been dead. But I'm still scared of dying." Then Olive said, "You know, Cindy, if you *should* be dying, if you do die, the truth is—we're all just a few steps behind you. Twenty minutes behind you, and that's the truth."

Cindy had not thought of that. She had thought that Tom, and her sons, and—people—that they would go on living forever and ever, without her. But Olive was right: They were all headed where she was going. If she was going.

"Thank you," Cindy said. "And thank you for coming over."

Olive Kitteridge stood up. "Bye now," she said.

When Cindy's mother was dying—she had been fifty-two and Cindy had been thirty-two—her mother had screamed and wept and cursed Cindy's father for abandoning them years before. In truth, Cindy's mother had frequently, during Cindy's lifetime, screamed and wept; the poor woman had been so tired. But when her mother was dying it scared Cindy terrifically, how her mother carried

187

on, and she had thought to herself: I will not die that way. And this is why she felt so bad that she had done that to her sons by crying hard on the stairs on Christmas Day. Cindy had not, during her sons' lives, screamed and wept. Cindy had cared for them every single second, it seemed like this to her, and she had hugged them and held them when they were small and needed comfort.

She thought about this a great deal, and she thought about it a few nights later as she sat next to Tom on the couch, a blanket pulled up to her throat, watching television with him. She said, during a television commercial, "Honey, I feel so bad about that day I cried on the stairs with you and the boys here. I told Mrs. Kitteridge. I forgot to tell her it reminds me of my mother."

Tom pulled back and looked at her quickly. "Mrs. Kitteridge? Why would you tell that old bag anything so personal?"

"Well—" Cindy began.

"Did you hear she got married to Jack Kennison?"

"She *did?*" Cindy started to sit up straight.

"Yes, she did. Can you imagine anyone marrying that old bag, except for her poor first husband, Henry?"

After that, Cindy didn't say much.

A few days later the weather turned bad. It rained and was also sleeting, and as Tom was getting things ready for her—her lunch was in the refrigerator, the phone was near her bed, another cellphone was in bed with her—as he was doing these things before he went to work at the ironworks, she found that he was irritating her. "It's okay, honey, just go," she said.

"Are you sure?" he asked, and she said that she was sure, just please go now.

And so off he went, calling once more from down the stairs, "Goodbye, sweetie heart!" And she called back to him, and then he was finally gone.

Cindy dozed, and when she woke she was annoyed that Tom hadn't left any lights on in the house. He was too cheap, is what she thought; it was depressing with no lights on, and so she got herself out of bed and went about the bedroom, turning on the lamp on the bureau and the one beside her bed, although through the bedroom door the hallway remained gray.

Her phone whistled. There was a text from her sister-in-law Anita, asking, Can I call? Cindy sat on the edge of the bed and texted back Yes.

"You doing okay?" asked Anita. And Cindy said, yeah, it was the same as usual.

"Sorry I haven't been by this week, I'll come soon." And Anita started to speak of her problems at home, which Cindy felt bad for—Anita's kids were all kind of crazy; they were in high school. Cindy got up to walk into the hallway to turn more lights on, and she heard a car in the driveway, and going over to look out the window she saw Mrs. Kitteridge getting out of her car.

"Anita," Cindy said, "Mrs. Kitteridge just drove up. I told you how she came to visit me. Well, she's here again."

Anita laughed. "Well, have a good time. Like I said, I always kind of liked that woman, myself."

The rain was coming down hard, and Mrs. Kitteridge did not have an umbrella. Cindy rapped on the window, and Mrs. Kitteridge looked up. Cindy waved her arm for Mrs. Kitteridge to come in, then she pointed to the side door, and in a few minutes the side door had opened and closed and there was Mrs. Kitteridge standing in her coat at the bedroom door.

"Take off your coat," Cindy said. "I'm sorry you got wet. Just throw it on the floor. Unless you want it hung up. If you want it hung up, then—" But Mrs. Kitteridge tossed her coat, the same red puffy one, onto the rug and she sat down in the straight-backed chair once again. Her hair was plastered to her head from the rain. Drops landed on her collar and she stood up and said to Cindy, "Where's the bathroom?" And Cindy indicated where it was, and in a moment Olive came back with a pink-and-white-striped hand towel and she sat down again and toweled her hair; Cindy kind of couldn't believe it.

Cindy said, "Mrs. Kitteridge, did you get

married? Tom said he heard you married Jack Kennison, but I thought, That can't be right."

Olive Kitteridge held the towel above her head and looked at the wall. She said, "Yes, it's true. I have married Jack Kennison."

Cindy stared at her. "Well, congratulations. I guess. Is it weird?"

"Oh, it's weird." Olive looked at her and nodded. "It is weird, yessiree." Olive hesitated, and then, starting to dry her hair again, she added, "But we're both old enough to know things now, and that's good."

"What things?"

"When to shut up, mainly."

"What things do you shut up about?" Cindy asked, and Olive seemed to think about it, and then she said, "Well, for example, when he has his breakfast, I don't say to him, Jack, why the *hell* do you have to scrape your bowl so hard."

Cindy asked, "How long have you been married?"

"Coming up to almost two years, I guess. Imagine at my age, starting over again." Olive put the towel in her lap and raised one opened hand slightly. "But it's never starting over, Cindy, it's just continuing on."

For quite a while they sat in silence, and the rain could be heard on the roof. And then Olive said, "I don't imagine you want to think of Tom starting over."

Cindy let out a great sigh. "Oh, Mrs. Kitteridge, I can't stand to think of him alone. I can't stand it, really, I can't. He'd be just a—Oh, he'd be like a big huge baby all alone, and that breaks my heart. But that he might *be* with someone, it breaks my heart more."

Olive nodded as though she understood this. "You know, Cindy, you and Tom grew up together. Henry and I were like that. Eighteen when we met, twenty-one when we married, and the truth is—that's who you lived with, that never ever goes away." Olive gave a shrug. "It just doesn't."

"Do you talk about Henry to Jack Kennison?"

Olive looked at her. "Oh, yes. When Jack and I first met, we talked about his wife and my husband nonstop. Nonstop."

"Was that uncomfortable?"

"God, no. It was wonderful."

Cindy lay silent for a while. "I don't know that I want to be talked about."

Olive shrugged. "Not much you can do about it, if it comes to that. But I'll tell you this, you will be sainted. You will become an absolute saint."

Cindy laughed. She laughed! And Olive, after a moment, laughed as well.

Then Cindy said, "Your son. Does he like this Jack Kennison?"

Olive said nothing for a moment. Then she said, "No, he does not. But I don't think he likes me much either. Even before I married Jack."

"Oh, Olive, I'm sorry."

Olive's foot was bobbing up and down. "Ay-yuh," she said. "Nothing to do about it at this point."

Cindy hesitated, and then she asked, "Were things always bad with your son?"

Olive tilted her head as though thinking about this, and then she said, "I really don't know. I don't think so. Not for a while. Maybe things started with his first wife."

After a minute, Cindy—who'd turned her gaze toward the window, and saw the grayness of the sleet that was splattering against it—said, "Well, I'm sure you didn't scream and yell a lot like my mother did. She was difficult, Olive. But then, she had a difficult life." She turned her face back to Olive.

And Olive said, "Oh, I think I did scream and yell a lot."

Cindy opened her mouth, but Olive continued. "I can't honestly remember, but I think I did. I was pretty awful when I felt like it. My son probably thinks I'm a difficult woman, like you think your mother was."

"Well, I still loved her," Cindy said.

"Yuh. And I suppose Christopher loves me." Olive shook her head slowly. The two women were silent for a few minutes. Olive held the towel in her lap.

Then Olive leaned forward and said quietly, "I will tell you this, Cindy. There are times I miss Henry so much I feel that I can't breathe." She sat back, and Cindy thought there might be tears in her eyes. Olive blinked, then she finally said, "I miss him so much, Cindy, right out of the blue—and it's not because Jack isn't good to me, he is, mostly—but something will happen and I will think *Henry.*"

"I'm awfully glad you came over," Cindy said. "You wouldn't believe the people who don't come over to see me."

"Yes, I would. Believe it."

"But why don't they come see me? I mean, Olive. Old *friends* don't even come see me."

"They're scared."

"Well, too bad!"

"Oh, I agree. I agree with you about that."

"But you're not scared."

"Nope."

"Even though you're scared of dying."

"That's right," Olive said.

The weather remained nasty; the wind whistled through the windows and it rained and then snowed briefly and then rained again. To Cindy it seemed like this went on for days. In the mail during this time she received a card from the librarians she had worked with. It had a flower on it, and inside it said, Get Well Soon! And everyone had signed their names. Cindy threw it into the wastebasket. The nurse came and changed the bed, and Cindy was glad to see her; they spoke briefly and companionably. But when the nurse finally left, Cindy got back into bed and pulled the covers up almost over her head. She listened to Pandora on her phone, with her earplugs in, which was something she did more and more. There was no sense today that she could read a book; she did not want to read a book. And she did not want to watch any movie on the iPad that Tom had bought her for that purpose.

Then she took her phone and texted her sons, who were both at the university. One more to go, she wrote, I love you both!! And in a few minutes, they had both texted back, We love you too, Mom. Her older boy texted again and said, Good luck with the last one! And she wrote back, Thank you honey!, and sent him a kiss emoticon. She wanted to write more, to say, But I really really REALLY love you! But there was no point in that. There were so many things that could not be said, and this had occurred to Cindy with more frequency and it made her heart ache. But she was very tired, and in a way that helped her, for she gave herself over to it, listening to her music on her phone. When she dozed, she did not feel herself fall asleep, and so she was surprised when she woke up.

Toward the end of the day, Anita stopped by on her way home from work, and Cindy sat at the kitchen table with her. Anita's husband—Tom's brother—might be losing his job, and Cindy said, "Anita, you have a lot of stuff going on," and Anita said, "I do. And so do you," and then Anita laughed; she had a burble of a laugh, and she pushed her glasses up her nose, and Cindy put her hand over Anita's. "And Maria with those tattoos," Anita said. "Up and down each arm, and I told her, Well, you just wait till that arm gets flabby. And she said, I'm getting them on my butt too—" Tom came through the door then, and Cindy asked if Anita wanted to stay for supper, and Anita said, "God, I would *love* to stay for supper." And she got up and put her coat on. "But I got to feed that freakin' family of mine."

The next day the sun came out. It shone brightly as Cindy walked across the driveway to the car with Tom, who had taken the morning off to go with her for her last treatment, and she noticed the sun but almost nothing else, and she didn't say much to Tom as he drove her to the hospital. Once there she sat as she had before, for more than an hour while the stuff was dripped into her, then Tom helped her get back into the car and he said, "I'm going to stay right with you, Cindy. All day." Back at the house, Cindy got into bed, and pretty soon Tom came up the stairs and sat on the bed next to her. He was eating an apple, and Cindy could not stand the sound of it. He crunched the apple, and there were slurping sounds too, and she finally said, "Tom, can you finish that apple somewhere else?" And he looked hurt, and said, "Okay," and went back downstairs.

Exactly a week after Cindy's final treatment, Olive Kitteridge showed up, and she said, "Congratulations. What's next?"

"A scan in three months. So we wait."

"Okay, then." After a moment, Olive said, "Jack and I had a fight. Boy, it was a whopper."

Cindy said, "Oh, Olive, I'm sorry to hear that."

"Yuh, well, I'm sorry to report it. It had to do with our friends. Our social life, as Jack put it."

Cindy lay back on her cushions and watched Olive. Her face seemed to be moving; she was distressed. "You want to tell me?" Cindy asked.

"Well, he has these friends from his former life, the Rutledges, and I said the other night after we'd had dinner with them, There's nothing wrong with Marianne Rutledge that a pin wouldn't fix." Here Olive raised her hand, fingers together, and made a jabbing motion in the air. "So stuffed up on herself, that woman, honest to good God. And he took offense! He took offense, and *then* he said, Well, Olive, your friends are rather provincial. He said that. He said that they never asked him about himself—God, what a male thing to say!—and that he found them to be pro-vin-ci-al. And I told him what was provincial was the fact that he cared that his daughter is gay—that he should be ashamed about calling anyone provincial when he feels that way, I said it's more than provincial, Mr. Harvard Smarty Pants, it puts you right back in the Dark Ages. I got so furious that I got into the car and drove, and do you know where I thought I was driving to? Home! I thought I was going to drive back to where I used to live with Henry, and it took me a few minutes to realize that that house isn't even there anymore. So I drove out to the Point, and I sat in the car, and I bawled like a baby, and then I drove back to Jack's house, well, our house, I suppose, and—Here's the thing. He was waiting for me, and he felt terrible. He felt *awful* that he had said those things.

"And I had been thinking about it on the drive back to the house, and I realized I'm a peasant and Jack is not. I mean, it's a class thing. So when I got back and saw that he was so sorry, I told him that, the business about this being a class thing, very calmly, and do you know? We must have talked for two hours straight, we just talked and talked, and he said he was kind of a peasant too, and that's why he was so sensitive about people being provincial, because all his life he had deep down felt provincial, and he didn't want to be. He said, I'm a snob, Olive, and I'm not proud of that. His father was a doctor, you know, outside of Wilkes-Barre, Pennsylvania, and I thought that was hardly being a peasant, but his father was a general practitioner with an office in the back of their rather small house, and Jack said he felt like he never fit into the school there, and then his first wife, Betsy, well, she *was* to the manor born, she was from Philadelphia, a Bryn Mawr girl—"

Olive stopped talking. Then she said, "Well, we had a wonderful talk, is what happened."

"I'm glad," Cindy said. "But, Olive, what do you mean, you're a peasant?"

"Well, I mean, I am not all la-di-da. My father never graduated from high school, though my mother was a teacher. But we were small-time people, and I'm proud of it. Now you better tell *me* something," Olive said.

So Cindy told Olive that her hair should start coming back within a month. It would look like fuzz for a while, but then it would come back, and Olive looked at her with interest, nodding slightly.

Then Olive said, "Say, I've been meaning to ask. What about your sisters, Cindy? What happened to them? Didn't you have a sister? Or two?"

Cindy was surprised that Olive remembered. She said, "Yes. One of them lives in Florida.

She's a waitress. And my little sister died many years ago—" Cindy hesitated, then said, "Of a drug overdose." She added, "She'd had issues for years."

Olive Kitteridge looked at her, and after a moment she gave a small shake of her head. "Godfrey," she said. She crossed her ankles, turning her rump slightly on the chair. "Well, then I guess they don't come and see you."

"My sister-in-law comes. Anita. Honestly, Olive? She's the only person other than you who has come to see me consistently."

"Anita Coombs," Olive said. "Sure, I know who she is. Works in the town clerk's office."

"That's right."

"Nice person. She always seemed that to me."

"Oh, she's wonderful," said Cindy. "Boy, she has some problems. But who doesn't?" And then Cindy sat up straighter, and she said, "Olive, did you tell me about that fight you had with Jack Kennison because you think I'm going to die?"

Olive looked at her with what seemed to be genuine surprise. After a moment she said, crossing her ankles the other way, "No, I told you because I'm an old woman who likes to talk about herself, and there was really no one else I felt comfortable telling."

"Okay," said Cindy. "I thought maybe you figured I was a safe person to tell because you thought I'm going to die, so why not tell her."

Olive said, "I don't know if you're going to die."

They were silent, and then Olive said, "I saw you had your Christmas wreath still up. Some people do that, I never knew why."

Cindy said, "Oh, I *hate* that. I've told Tom so many times. Why can't he remember to take it down?"

Olive flapped a hand through the air. "He's upset, Cindy. He can't concentrate on anything these days."

And it was strange, but Cindy saw then that Olive was right. Such a simple statement, but it was completely true. Oh, poor Tom!, Cindy thought, Tom, I haven't been fair to you—

But Olive had turned to gaze out the window. "Would you look at that," Olive said.

Cindy turned to look. The sunlight was magnificent, it shone a glorious yellow from the pale blue sky, and through the bare branches of the trees, with the open-throated look that came toward the end of the day's light.

But here is what happened next—

Here is the thing that Cindy, for the rest of her life, would never forget: Olive Kitteridge said, "My God, but I have always loved the light in February." Olive shook her head slowly. "My God," she repeated, with awe in her voice. "Just look at that February light."

The Walk

About his children, something was wrong. This came to Denny Pelletier as he walked alone on the road one night in December in the town of Crosby, Maine. It was a chilly night, and he was not dressed for it, having only a coat over his T-shirt, with his pair of old jeans. He had not intended to walk, but after dinner he felt the need in him arise, and then later, as his wife readied herself for bed, he said to her, "I have to walk." He was sixty-nine years old and in good shape, though there were mornings when he felt very stiff.

As he walked, he thought again: Something was wrong. And he meant about his children. He had three children; they were all married. They had all married young, by the age of twenty, just as he and his wife had married young; his wife had been eighteen. At the time of his children's weddings, Denny did not think about how young they were, even though now, walking, he realized that it had been unusual during that time for kids to marry so young. Now his mind went over the classmates of his children, and he realized that many had waited until they were twenty-five, or twenty-eight, or even—like the really handsome Woodcock boy—thirty-two years old when he married his pretty yellow-haired bride.

The cold was distracting, and Denny walked faster in order to warm up. Christmas was coming soon, yet no snow had fallen for three weeks. This struck Denny as strange—as it did many people—because he could remember his childhood in this very town in Maine, and by Christmastime there would be snow so high he and his friends would build forts inside the snow banks. But tonight, as he walked, the only sound was the quiet crunching of leaves beneath his sneakers.

The moon was full. It shone down on the river as he walked past the mills, their windows lined up and dark. One of the mills, the Washburn mill, Denny had worked in starting when he was eighteen; it had closed thirty years ago, and then he had worked in a clothing store that sold, among other things, rain slickers and rubber boots to the fishermen, and to the tourists, as well. The mill seemed more vivid to him than the store, the memories of it, though he had worked there not nearly as long as he had at the store. But he could remember with surprising clarity the machines that went on all night, the loom room he worked in; his father had worked as a loom mender there at the time, and when Denny began

204

he had been lucky enough to go from sweeping the floors for three months to becoming a weaver and then, not long after, a loom mender as his father had been. The ear-splitting noise of the place, the frightening scoot a shuttle could take if it got out of place, whipping across the cloth and chipping pieces of metal; what a thing it had been! And yet it was no more. He thought of Snuffy, who had never learned to read or write, and who had taken his teeth out and washed them in the water trough, and then a sign had been put up: No Washing Teeth Here! And the jokes about Snuffy not being able to read the sign. Snuffy had died a few years ago. Many—most— of the men he had worked with at the mill were now dead. Somehow, tonight, Denny felt a quiet astonishment at that fact.

And then his mind returned to his children. They were quiet, he thought. Too quiet. Were they angry with him? All three had gone to college; his sons had moved to Massachusetts, his daughter to New Hampshire; there had seemed to be no jobs for them here. His grandchildren were okay; they all did well in school. It was his children he wondered about as he walked.

Last year, around the time of Denny's fiftieth high school reunion, he had shown his eldest boy his yearbook, and his son had said, "Dad! They called you *Frenchie?*" Oh sure, Denny said, with a chuckle. "It's not funny," his son had said, adding, "Mrs. Kitteridge, way back in seventh grade, she told us this country was supposed to be a melting pot, but it never melted, and she was right," and he had gotten up and walked away, leaving Denny with his yearbook open on the kitchen table.

Mrs. Kitteridge was wrong. Times changed.

But Denny, who had turned to walk along the river, now saw his son's point: To be called "Frenchie" was no longer acceptable. What Denny's son had not understood was that Denny had never had his feelings hurt by being called "Frenchie." As Denny kept walking, digging his hands deeper into his pockets, he began to wonder if this was true. He realized: What was true was that he, Denny, had *accepted* it.

To accept it meant to accept much: that Denny would go to work in the mills as soon as he could, it meant that he did not expect to go on to school, to pay attention to his studies. Did it mean these things? As Denny approached the river, and could see in the moonlight how the river was moving quickly, he felt as though his life had been a piece of bark on that river, just going along, not thinking at all. Headed toward the waterfall.

The moon was slightly to the right of him, and it seemed to become brighter as he stopped to look at it. Is this why he suddenly thought of Dorothy Paige?

Dorie Paige had been a beautiful girl—oh, she was a beauty! She had walked the halls of the high school with her long blond hair over her shoulders; she was tall and wore her height well. Her eyes were large, and she had a tentative smile always on her face. She had shown up at the end of their sophomore year, and she was the reason Denny had stayed in school. He just wanted to see her, just wanted to look at her. Otherwise he had been planning on quitting school and going to work in the mill. His locker was not far from Dorie's, but they shared no classes, because Dorie, along with her astonishing looks, had brains as well. She was, according to teachers, and even students said this, the smartest student to have come through in a long time. Her father was a doctor. One day she said "Hi" as they were at their lockers, and Denny felt dizzy. "Hi there," he said. After that, they were sort of friends. Dorie hung around with a few other kids who were smart, and those were her real friends, but she and Denny had become friends too. "Tell me about yourself," she said one day after school. They were alone in the hallway. "Tell me everything." And she laughed.

"Nothing to tell," Denny said, and he meant it.

"That's not true, it can't be true. Do you have brothers and sisters?" She was almost as tall as he was, and she waited there for him while he fumbled with his books.

"Yeah. I'm the oldest. I have three sisters and two brothers." Denny finally had his books, and now he stood and looked at her. It was like looking at the sun.

"Oh wow," Dorie said, "is that wonderful? It sounds wonderful. I only have one brother and so the house is quiet. I bet your house isn't quiet."

"No," said Denny. "It's not too quiet." He was already going out with Marie Levesque, and he worried that she would show up. He walked down the hall away from the gym, where Marie was practicing—she was a cheerleader—and Dorie followed him. So at the other end of the school, near the band room, they talked. He could not now remember all they said that day, or the other days, when she would suddenly appear and they headed toward the band room and stood outside it and talked. He did remember that she never said he should go to college, she must have known—of course, "Frenchie"—that he did not have the grades, or the money, to go; she would have known because of the classes they were not in together, just as he knew she would go to college.

For two years they did this, talked maybe once a week. They talked more often during the basketball season, when Marie was practicing in the gym. Dorie never asked Denny about Marie, though she'd have seen him in the halls with her. He saw Dorie with different guys, always a different fellow seemed to be following Dorie, and she'd laugh with whoever it was, and call out, "Hi, Denny!" He had really loved her. The girl was so beautiful. She was just a thing of beauty.

"I'm going to Vassar," she said to him the spring of their senior year, and he didn't know what she meant. After a moment she added, "It's a college in upstate New York."

"That's great," he said. "I hope it's a really good college, you're awfully smart, Dorie."

"It's okay," she said. "Yeah, it's a good college."

He could never remember the last time they spoke. He did remember that during the graduation ceremony, when her name was called, there had been some catcalls, whistles, things of that sort. He was married within a year, and he never saw Dorie again. But he remembered where he was—right outside the main grocery store here in town—when he found out that she had finished Vassar and then killed herself. It was Trish Bibber who told him, a girl they had been in school with, and when Denny said, *"Why?,"* Trish had looked at the ground and then she said, "Denny, you guys were friendly, so I don't know if you knew. But there was sexual abuse in her house."

"What do you mean?" Denny asked, and he asked because his mind was having trouble understanding this.

"Her father," said Trish. And she stood with

209

him for a few moments while he took this in. She looked at him kindly and said, "I'm sorry, Denny." He always remembered that too: Trish's look of kindness as she told him this.

So that was the story of Dorie Paige.

Denny headed back to his house; he went up Main Street. A sudden sense of uneasiness came over him, as though he was not safe; in fact, the town had changed so much over these last few years that people no longer strolled around at night, as he was doing. But he had not thought of Dorie for quite a while; he used to think of her a great deal. Above him the moon shone down; its brightness continued, as though the memory of Dorie—or Dorie herself—had made it so. "I bet your house isn't quiet," she had said.

And suddenly it came to Denny: His house was quiet now. It had been getting quieter for years. After the kids got married and moved away, then, gradually, his house became quiet. Marie, who had worked as an ed tech at the local school, had retired a few years ago, and she no longer had as much to say about her days. And then he had retired from the store, and he didn't have that much to say either.

Denny walked along, passing the benches near the bandstand. A few leaves scuttled in front of him in the harsh breeze. Where his mind went he could not have said, or how long he had walked.

But he suddenly saw ahead of him a heavy man bent over the back of a bench. Almost, Denny turned around. But the large body was just draped over the back of the bench—such an unusual thing—and appeared not to be moving. Slowly Denny approached. He cleared his throat loudly. The fellow did not move. "Hello?" Denny said. The man's jeans were slightly tugged down because of the way he was hanging over the bench, and in the moonlight Denny could see the beginning of the crack of his ass. The fellow's hands were in front of him, as though pressed down on the seat of the bench. "Hello?" Denny said this much more loudly, and still there was no response. He could see the fellow's hair, longish, pale brown, draped across his cheek. Denny reached and touched the man's arm, and the man moaned.

Stepping back, Denny brought out his phone and called 911. He told the woman who answered where he was and what he was looking at, and the dispatcher said, "We'll have someone right there, sir. Stay on the line with me." He could hear her speaking—into another phone?—and he could hear static and clicks and he waited. "Okay, sir. Do you know if the man is alive?"

"He moaned," Denny said.

"Okay, sir."

And then very shortly—it seemed to Denny—a police car with its blue lights flashing drove right up, and two cops got out of the car. They were calm, Denny noticed, and they spoke to him briefly, then went to the man who was draped across the back of the bench. "Drugs," said one of the policemen, and the other said, "Yep."

One of the policemen reached into his pocket and brought out a syringe, and he steadily, quickly, pulled up the sleeve of the man's jacket and injected the man, in his arm, in the crook of his elbow, and very soon the man stood up. He looked around.

It was the Woodcock boy.

Denny would not have recognized him, except that his eyes, deep-set on a handsome face, looked at Denny and said, "Hey, hi." Then his eyes rolled up for a moment, and the policemen had him sit down on the bench. He was not a boy any longer—he was a middle-aged man—yet Denny could think of him only as a kid in his daughter's class years ago. How had he turned into this person? Large—fat—with his longish hair and all doped up? Denny stayed where he was, looking at the back of the fellow's head, and then an ambulance drove up, siren screaming and lights flashing, and within moments two EMT men jumped out and spoke to the policemen, one of the policemen saying, Yes, he had injected him with Naloxone right away. The two EMT men took the Woodcock boy's arms and walked him into the ambulance; the door shut.

As the ambulance drove away, one of the policemen said to Denny, "Well, you saved a life tonight," and the other policeman said, getting into the car, "For now."

Denny walked home quickly, and he thought: It was not his children at all. This seemed to come to him clearly. His children had been safe in their childhood home, not like poor Dorie. His children were not on drugs. It was himself about which something was wrong. He had been saddened by the waning of his life, and yet it was not over.

Hurriedly he went up the steps to his house, tossing his coat off, and in the bedroom Marie was awake, reading. Her face brightened when she saw him. She put her book down on the bed and waved her hand at him. "Hi there," she said.

Pedicure

It was November.

No snow had fallen yet in Crosby, Maine, and because the sun was out on this particular Wednesday there was a kind of horrifying beauty to the world: The oak trees held their leaves, golden and shriveled, and the evergreens stood at attention as though cold, but the other trees were bare and dark-limbed, stretching into the sky with dwindling spikiness, and the roads were bare, and the fields were swept clean-looking, everything sort of ghastly and absolutely gorgeous with the sunlight that fell at an angle, never reaching the top of the sky. The sky was a darkish blue.

Jack Kennison suggested to Olive Kitteridge that they take a ride in the car. "Oh, I love rides," she said, and he said he knew that, he was suggesting a ride to make her happy. "I'm happy," she said, and he said he was too. So they got into their new Subaru—Olive didn't care for his sports car—and off they went; they decided to head for Shirley Falls, an hour away, where Olive had gone to high school, and where her first husband, Henry, had come from.

Jack and Olive had been together now for five years; Jack was seventy-nine and Olive seventy-eight. The first months, they had slept holding each other. Neither one of them had held another person in bed all night for years. When Jack had been able to be away with Elaine, they sort of held each other at night in whatever hotel they were in, but it was not the same as what he and Olive did their first months together. Olive would put her leg over both of his, she would put her head on his chest, and during the night they would shift, but always they were holding each other, and Jack thought of their large old bodies, shipwrecked, thrown up upon the shore—and how they held on for dear life!

He would never have imagined it. The Olive-ness of her, the neediness of himself; never in his life would he have imagined that he would spend his final years with such a woman in such a way.

It's that he could be himself with her. This is what he thought during those first number of months with a sleeping, slightly snoring Olive in his arms; this is what he still thought.

She irritated him.

She would not have breakfast, but would get going right away, as if she had things to do. "Olive, you don't have anything to do," he would say. And she thumbed her nose at him. Thumbed her nose. God.

It was not until after they married that he began to understand that her anxiety level was high. She rocked her foot constantly as she sat in her chair, she would suddenly leave the house, saying she had to buy some fabric at the Joann fabric store, and she would be gone within moments. But she still clung to him at night, and he still clung to her. And then after another year they did not cling to each other at night but shared the bed and argued about who had taken the blankets during the night; they were really a married couple. And she had grown increasingly less anxious; quietly, this made Jack feel wonderful.

But a couple of years ago they had gone to Miami and Olive hated it. "What are we supposed to do, just sit in the sun?" she had demanded, and Jack took her point; they came home. Last year they had gone to Norway on a cruise around the fjords and they had liked that a great deal better. These days taking a drive was what they both enjoyed. "Like a couple of old farts," Jack had said during their last drive, and Olive said, "Jack, you know I *hate* that word."

They drove along now, leaving the town of Crosby, Maine, behind; they drove past the little field with the stone wall and the rocks that showed through the pale grass. "Well," Olive said. "Edith fell off the pot and broke her arm, so they had to take her away."

"Take her away?" Jack asked; he glanced over at her.

"Oh, you know." Olive wiggled her hand through the air. "Off to rehab, or wherever."

"Is she going to be all right?"

"Dunno. Suspect so." Olive looked out her window; they were entering the town of Bellfield Corners. "God," she said, "is this town sad." Jack agreed that the town was sad. Only one diner was open on Main Street, and there was a credit union, and a gas station. Everything else was closed down. Even the mill, which you used to see when you first came into town, had been torn down in the last ten years; Olive told this to Jack.

"I've never been to Shirley Falls," Jack said as they drove out of the town of Bellfield Corners onto the open road once more.

Olive moved so that her back was almost against the car door, and she looked at Jack. "Are you kidding me?" she said. "You have never been to Shirley Falls?"

"Why would I have been to Shirley Falls?" Jack asked. "What's in Shirley Falls these days? Oh, I know it was important, way back in the day, but what's there now?"

"Somalis," said Olive, turning forward once more.

"Oh, right," Jack said. "I forgot about them." Then he said, "Okay, I didn't *forget* about them,

218

I just haven't thought about them for a while."

"Ay-yuh," Olive said.

"How did Edith fall off the pot?" Jack asked after a few moments.

"How? I suspect she just . . . fell. How do I know?"

Jack laughed; he loved this woman. "Well, you know she fell. You know lots of things, Olive."

"Say, do you know what Bunny Newton told me the other day? Apparently her husband used to know this man who lost his wife, and this man liked this other woman for ten years—even while his wife was still alive—and this other woman, on her birthday, went out and sat down in the middle of the turnpike and got hit and killed. Just sat herself down. Did you ever hear of such a thing? Now the man is mourning her far more than he mourned his wife."

"So she killed herself?"

"Sounds like that to me. Godfrey, what a way to go."

"And how old was this woman?"

"Sixty-nine. Oh, and she weighed eighty-seven pounds. So Bunny says. I think it sounds a little crazy to me."

"It sounds like some piece of information is missing," Jack said.

"I'm just reporting," Olive answered. "Oh," she said, "the woman was filing for divorce. Maybe that's important, who knows. Crazy."

"It's not one of your better stories," Jack conceded.

"No, it's not." After a few minutes Olive said, "I really liked my pedicure, Jack."

"I'm glad, Olive. You can have another one."

"I plan on it," she said.

A few days earlier, Jack had come upon Olive in the bedroom, and she had tiny tears coming from her eyes. It was because she couldn't cut her toenails anymore, not the way she used to be able to, she was too big and too old to get her feet close enough to her, and she hated, she said, she just *hated* having her toenails so awful-looking. And so Jack had said, "Well, let's get you a pedicure," and Olive acted like she barely knew such a thing was possible. "Come on, come on," Jack said, and he got her in the car and drove her out to Cook's Corner, where there was a nail salon. "Come on," he said as she hung back, and so she followed him into the place, and Jack said, "This woman would like a pedicure," and the small Asian woman said, Yes, yes, okay, this way. Jack said, "I'll be back," and waved at Olive, who looked bewildered, but when he went back and picked her up, what a smile she had on her face.

"Jack," she said, almost breathless, once they were in the car. "Jack, they have one jug of water for one foot, and another jug for the other, well, they're like little tiny bathtubs, and you just stick your feet in, and the woman, oh, she did a wonderful job—!"

"You're an easy woman to please," he had said to her.

And she had said, "You may be the first person to think that."

Now Olive said, "She rubbed my calves, oh, it felt good. Massaged, that's the word. She massaged my calves. Lovely." After another moment she added, "You know that writer who writes all those spooky books—what's her name—Sharon McDonald—well, she's just a Bellfield Corners girl, is all she is."

"What do you mean?" Jack asked.

"I mean, years ago, when she was starting out, she started out her life in Bellfield Corners. That's all she is, really. Just a Bellfield Corners girl."

Jack considered this. "Well, maybe that's why she can write about horror so well."

"I didn't know she wrote anything well," Olive said.

"Boy, are you a snob," Jack said.

And Olive said, "And you're a nitwit, if you read her junk."

"I've never read her junk," Jack said. He did not say that his dead wife, Betsy, used to read everything the woman wrote, there was no point in telling Olive that. They were driving along the river now, and there was a beauty to it, the starkness, the gray ribbon of it right next to the road. "I'm glad we're taking this drive," Jack said.

"Oh, me too," Olive said. Then she said, "*Say,* I have a story for you. Bunny and her husband were at Applebee's the other night, and they were sitting toward the back and there was only one other couple, just as fat as can be, and then the man began to cough, and then he began to throw up—"

"God, Olive."

"No, listen to this. He kept vomiting, and the woman pulled out these plastic bags and kept apologizing to Bunny while she held these plastic bags for the man to keep puking into."

"They should have called an ambulance," Jack said, and Olive said, "That's what Bunny suggested. But it turned out the man had a medical condition called, oh, what was it called, Zanker's? Zenker's diverticu—something, according to the wife, so Bunny and Bill paid their bill, and this poor fat couple sat while he finished throwing up."

"God," Jack said. "My God, Olive."

"Just reporting." She shrugged.

They were only now entering Shirley Falls, through the back way. The buildings became much closer to one another, and the high wooden houses, built years ago for the millworkers, were there as well, almost on top of one another, with their wooden staircases down the backs of them. Jack peered through the car window and saw a few black women wearing hijabs and long robes walking along the sidewalk. "Jesus," he said, because the sight surprised him.

"My mother, back in the day," Olive said, "oh, she hated hearing people speaking French on the city buses here. And of course many of them were speaking French, they had come from Quebec to work in the mills, but, oh, how Mother hated that. Well, times change." Olive said this cheerfully. "*Look* at these people," she added.

"It's kind of weird, Olive." Jack said this, peering to the right and left. "You have to admit. Jesus. It's like we drove into a nest of them."

"Did you just say a nest of them?" Olive asked.

"I did."

"That's offensive, Jack."

"I'm sure it is." But he felt slightly ashamed, and he said, "Okay, I shouldn't have put it that way."

They drove through the town, which seemed to Jack to be very bleak, and then they drove across the river and up a long hill where there were houses in neighborhoods. "Turn, turn, right there," Olive demanded, so Jack turned right and they drove down the street and she showed him the house that Henry had grown up in.

"Nice," Jack said. He didn't really care where Holy Henry had grown up. But he made himself look, and consider, and it seemed the right place for Henry to have been raised. The house was a small two-story, dark-green, with a huge maple tree on its front lawn.

"Henry planted that tree when he was four years old," Olive said. "He did." She nodded. "He found this tiny sapling and he decided to stick it in the ground, and his mother—old horror—apparently helped him water it when it was tiny, and now there it is."

"Very nice," said Jack.

"You don't care," Olive said. "Well, never mind, let's go."

Jack made himself look around the little neighborhood, and he said, "I care, Olive. Where do you want to go now?"

And she said out to West Annett, where she had grown up, so he drove the car while she directed him, and they went along a narrow road, past many fields that were still oddly green for November, and the sun slanted across them with that horrifying gorgeousness. They drove and drove, and Olive told him about the one-room schoolhouse her mother had taught in, how her mother had had to come early to get the fire started in the winter, she told him about the Finnish woman who used to watch her—watch Olive—when Olive was too small to go to school, she told him about her Uncle George, who was a drunk and who had married a young wife and the young wife fell in love with a neighbor—"Right there, that house right there"—and then the neighbor, well, Olive didn't know what went on with him, but the young wife had hanged herself at the bottom of her cellar stairs.

"Jesus," Jack said.

"Yup," said Olive. "I was scared to go down to that cellar when I was a kid, someone would send me down to get potatoes or something and, oh, I hated going down there."

"God," said Jack.

And then Olive said that her Uncle George had remarried, but ten years after his first wife died, he hanged himself in the same spot.

"My *God*," Jack said.

So it was like that, they drove around many back roads and they talked. Jack talked about his own childhood, which he had already done, but seeing Olive's childhood home made him think of his childhood home outside of Wilkes-Barre, Pennsylvania, and he spoke of it again now, the sense of its smallness to him, even when he was young, though it was not as small as Olive's house had been, but he had felt *cramped,* he said now. Olive listened, and said, "Ay-yuh."

Then she said, "Would you look at that," because Jack had turned a corner and before them was the November sinking sun against the darkening blue sky. Along the horizon was a spread of yellow. And the bare trees stuck their bare dark limbs into the sky. "That's kind of amazing," Jack said.

Up and down the car went, up one small hill and down another, around a long curve, around a short bend, the car dipped and rose over the road as the sun set around them.

Jack said, "Let's try that new restaurant in Shirley Falls. I heard Marianne Rutledge mention something about it the other day. It's supposed to be the only nice restaurant in the town. What's it called—some funny name."

"Gasoline," said Olive.

He glanced over at her. "That's right. How did you know about the fancy restaurant in Shirley Falls called Gasoline, Olive? You surprise me."

"And you surprise me. Don't you read anything? There was an article about it in the paper a few months ago. Imagine calling a restaurant Gasoline. I never heard of such a thing."

Jack parked on the street a block away from the restaurant, which had its name in neon lights outside, and as he locked the car he looked around. It had been dark for well over an hour, and the darkness at this time of year always seemed to Jack to be *really* dark; he didn't like it and he didn't want his car stolen or broken into. Olive stood on the sidewalk. "Oh, come on, Jack," she said, as though she could read his thoughts—to Jack it sometimes seemed she could—"for heaven's sake, the car is fine."

"I know that," he said.

The place seemed cavernous at first glance when they stepped inside. High-ceilinged, with a bar where the glasses twinkled and the liquor bottles were all lined up in front of a huge mirror; beyond the bar were the tables. Two more large mirrors hung on opposite walls, and on each table was a tiny flickering cup. The hostess ushered them to a table in the center of the place, there were few people here at the moment, and so they sat down and Olive shook out her napkin and said, "I hope they have steak. I want a steak." And Jack said he was sure they had steak. "My treat," he added, winking at her.

The waitress brought Jack a whiskey and Olive a glass of white wine, and eventually they ordered; Olive ordered a steak and Jack got the scallops, and after a while the waitress brought the food over; Olive and Jack were talking so much they had to lean back and let the waitress place the food down, and then they continued talking. Olive was telling Jack about the Somalis, who had moved here more than fifteen years ago, how it had caused a ruckus at first, Maine being such a white, white state. "And old," Olive added. But the Somalis were very entrepreneurial, according to Olive, and had started a bunch of businesses in town.

"Well, that's great," Jack said, and he meant it, although he didn't care a whole lot. But she was making it interesting, as interesting as it could be to Jack, because she was Olive, and he knew they would start talking about something else soon; he was waiting.

The big heavy door of the restaurant opened and a couple came in. Jack, glancing toward the door, saw the woman first and he thought: That almost looks like—And then he heard her voice. She turned and spoke to the man, who had come in right behind her, and it was her voice that was unmistakable. Jack could hear her say, "Oh, I know that, I know that, yes, I know that," and he—Jack—said quietly, "No."

"No what?" Olive asked. She was about to bite into her steak, which she had just cut a piece of.

"Nothing," Jack said. "I thought I saw someone I knew, but it's not."

But it was.

And he could not believe it. He really could not believe it. It was not unlike falling off his bicycle so many years ago when he was a child, the slow sense of something terrible happening, and the knowledge that there was nothing he could do about it. Watching the pavement come up to meet his cheek.

He sat without moving while he saw them walk

farther into the place, he watched the hostess greet them, he watched as they walked toward him. She was wearing a gold-colored sheepskin coat with a brown scarf around her neck, the gold-colored coat almost matched the color of her hair, and she seemed slightly larger than he would have thought, maybe it was the coat, and very pretty as she always had been; she was wearing clunky gold earrings that seemed big to him, and then he saw her look at him. He saw in her face a flicker of confusion, then saw her look away, and then she looked back at him and she stopped walking right by his chair. "Jack?" she said. "Jack *Kennison?*" A faint scent of perfume reached him; it was the same scent she had always worn, and Jack felt an odd tingling along his jaw.

"Hello, Elaine." He rearranged his napkin on his lap.

Elaine stared down at him, her earrings like two punctuation marks on the side of her face, and Jack wondered if he should stand up, and so he did, and then he saw—he saw this distinctly—her green eyes go from his face involuntarily down his body and back up. He sat down, his belly hitting the table's edge. The fellow she was with had stopped as well.

Her face was older—naturally—but it was surprisingly the same. Slightly bigger, her face seemed; she had put on a bit of weight. Her makeup was perfect, her green eyes were lined with black and they looked very green, and her hair was a little longer than when he had known her. "Jack, what are you *doing* here?"

"I'm having my dinner."

He watched her eyes move to Olive, who right then said, sticking out her hand, "Hello. I'm Jack's wife, Olive," and he saw Elaine's silent amazement. Elaine shook Olive's hand. "Elaine Croft," she said. And then she put her hand on the arm of the fellow she was with and said, "This is Gary Taylor." So Gary shook Olive's hand, and then Jack's hand, and Jack thought the guy looked like an imbecile, with his round glasses and his one earring (an earring, for Christ's sake, a tiny gold hoop!) and his hair down to almost his shoulders.

Elaine turned back to Jack, and he saw how she wanted to ask, and so he said, "Betsy died, by the way. Just so you know."

"She died?" Her eyes widened in a way that pleased him; she was that surprised.

"She did." Jack picked up his fork.

"When—"

"Six years ago, now."

"Do you—do you *live* here, Jack?" He was aware of her slightly lowering herself, as though to see him more clearly.

"We do not live in Shirley Falls, no. But tell me, Mizz Croft." He put his fork back onto his plate and gazed up at her. "What is it that brings you to the town of Shirley Falls?"

She looked at him, her face becoming cold; the "Mizz Croft" had been received. "Clitorectomies, Dr. Kennison, is what brings me here."

"I see." Jack almost laughed.

"There's a Somalian population that lives here," Elaine said.

"Yes, I am aware of that," Jack answered.

Olive held up a finger. "Somali." Olive said this with a thrust of her finger. "Not 'Somalian.' People make that mistake all the time. But it's *Somali* population, just so you know."

Elaine's face got a prissy look, even colder. She said, "Yes, I know that, Mrs. Kennison. And I said 'Somali.' "

"No, I heard you say—" Olive widened her eyes, gave a small shrug, then cut another piece of steak.

Jack said, "And how are you researching clitorectomies, Elaine? Are you knocking on the doors of *Somalians* and saying, Hello, I'm Elaine Croft, I teach at Smith College, and we're trying to find out: Do you have women in your household who have had a clitorectomy?"

Elaine looked down at him; on one side of her mouth was a tiny half smile, fury, he knew from the past. "Goodbye, Jack," she said, and she nodded toward her bozo friend and they walked away and Jack saw her speak to the waitress and they went to a table as far away from Jack and Olive as the space allowed.

"Who was that?" Olive asked, eating her steak, and Jack said she was just a woman he had known years ago at Harvard. He almost said, "She's a nut," but he didn't.

"Well, she didn't seem very nice. Full of herself, I'd say. What does she mean she's here to investigate—what did she say?"

"She said clitorectomies, Olive. The woman has apparently come to town to study female circumcision."

Olive said, "Oh, for God's sake, oh, for heaven's sake, I never heard of such a thing, Jack."

"Well, now you have." He ate his scallops with no notice of them being anything at all except food that he was eating: fuel. He still had the sensation of falling off his bicycle, but he was not sure that he had landed yet.

"You know, it's just sad what the Somali population has been accused of—"

"Let's drop it, Olive," he said, and Olive said, "Fine with me." After a few moments she asked how his scallops were, and he said that they were very good. "Well, this steak is just wonderful," she said; she was halfway through it.

From the corner of his eye he could see Elaine and her—whatever he was—leaning across the table and talking, and he understood that she would be telling the fellow who Jack was. Jack wanted to throw his napkin onto the table and go over and say, "But that's *not* the story!" He felt that his vision was affected as he looked at his food. In truth, he only wanted to get home. And then in his mind's eye he saw again what he had thought was astonishment in Elaine's response to Olive saying she was his wife. Betsy had been a quietly pretty woman, Elaine had met her a few times at faculty parties. And he thought again how her green eyes had gone down his body when he stood up, noticing his large stomach, of course.

It was endless as Olive finished her steak, commenting on it yet again, then saying, "Shall we have dessert?" And Jack said no. He could see her surprise, and he said, "I'm sorry, Olive, I'm just not feeling that well."

"Why didn't you tell me?" Olive demanded. "How long have you not been feeling well?" And he said, Only recently, and she said, Well, this was a waste of money, then, coming to such a restaurant that ends up making you not *feel* well. And then she was silent. Jack, aware of Elaine, aware that she could very well be watching them, touched Olive's arm and leaned into her and said, "Oh, Olive, who cares, it's just money." Olive only looked at him.

As they left the restaurant, Jack did not glance over at Elaine's table.

• • •

Her feet had been beautiful. They had been the sweetest feet Jack had ever seen in his life, and Elaine had been surprised; she claimed she had not known that about her feet, and perhaps she had not. But she had high arches and small ankles, and her toes—which were always polished a bright red color, or sometimes a tangerine, "I have a pedicure every week," she laughingly told him their first time—were the loveliest toes Jack felt had ever existed anywhere. "You're killing me from the feet up," she would laugh in her bed, and he began to call her Socrates, after the man who had claimed he was dying from the feet up. Jack often started with her feet, once he had discovered them; she would laugh and laugh because she was ticklish, and she asked him if he had a foot fetish, but in fact Jack did not have a foot fetish, only a fetish for her feet. Her stomach had been dimpled, and her backside was not small. She had been a beauty, in the eyes of Jack; he had never seen anyone as beautiful, understanding that it was because he loved her.

God, he had loved her. He had missed a class once because of a fight they'd had, it was too painful for him to leave her, even as he could not now remember what the fight had been about, most likely whether he would stay with Betsy, even though Elaine had always, from the start, said, "I don't want you leaving your wife, Jack, I don't want that responsibility." They were in a hotel in Cambridge, which was risky as they both lived in Cambridge, but it had not felt as risky as being seen coming from her house so many times. And in their hotel room that day, perhaps she said something about Betsy, and he missed his class—the only class he missed his entire teaching career, except when he'd had his gallbladder out many years earlier—to be with her. And this is what he remembered: When they were done, had made up, she said something about having to go meet with Schroeder, the dean, she had been stepping out of the shower, having asked him to hand her the towel, and then she had said she had to get to a meeting with the dean, while Jack had missed his class! And something in Jack had clicked, though he never—even to this day—could have said why. But something in him that day realized: She is a careerist.

And of course she had been. Everyone at that school was a careerist. But it was not until she came up for tenure and Jack voted against her because everyone else on the committee had voted against her—and also, he had privately never thought her work was that strong—that she decided to file a lawsuit against Jack citing sexual harassment. And when Schroeder called him into his office that day, Schroeder told him she had recordings of Jack's late-night drunken calls to her—calls Jack had made over the course of the last year as he felt her affections slipping—and she had emails from him as well, and Schroeder said to Jack, "Just take a research leave until we get this settled."

A research leave.

And then Schroeder would not talk to him again. Three years later, Elaine Croft walked away with a settlement of three hundred thousand dollars. By that time Jack had left; he and Betsy had come up to live in Crosby, Maine.

Jack himself had been a careerist. But that had been many years before he met Elaine. By the time he met her, he was sick of being on that faculty; but she was young, and she was out to make it and she did.

Only not at Harvard.

He should never have mentioned Smith tonight. It gave away the fact that he had googled her—which he had a few years ago—and learned that she had gotten a tenured job at Smith and he had thought: Perfect.

Jack unlocked the car from a distance, holding up the key and pressing on it; the lights flickered once and the ping sound occurred, and then as he walked toward the car he saw in the streetlight that someone had run something against the car—most likely a key—and made a long, long scratch along the driver's-side door. "I don't believe it," he said. "I just don't believe this." Olive stood peering at it as well, and then she said "But who would *do* such a thing?" and walked around to her side of the car.

Jack said, "I'll tell you who would do such a thing. Some young fellow who doesn't like the look of a new Subaru." He added, "Goddamn them to hell." Inside the car now, he said, *"Jesus."*

"Well, it seems a foolish thing for someone to do," Olive said, strapping on her seatbelt. And then she said, "But it's just a car." And somehow this made Jack even more furious.

He said, "Well, it's the last car I will ever buy," which was a thought he had had when he had bought the car.

He pulled up to the stop sign at the end of the street and braked the car hard, then pulled ahead suddenly; he could see Olive being slightly thrown against the back of her seat. "Oh, my, my, my," she said quietly, as though to playfully chastise him.

But as they headed out of town, onto the open road now, Olive was silent in the seat next to him. And Jack had nothing to say to her, he still felt the sense of the bicycle overturning. But as he drove along the river without seeing anything except the white line in the road, it returned to him, the fact that Olive was his wife, and that they had had a day together of happiness before seeing Elaine tonight. But it did not feel like happiness that he had experienced with Olive, it felt far away from him now.

And so the day they had had together folded over on itself, was done with, gone.

In the silence of the dark car Jack was aware of Olive—his wife—aware of her presence in a way that felt insurmountable. A pocket of air rose up his chest and he opened his mouth and belched; it was a long and loud sound. Olive said, "Good God, Jack, you might excuse yourself." Jack kept staring straight ahead at the black road before him and the pale white line running down its middle.

Olive said, "I guess Gasoline knows what they're talking about naming it that foolish name. Why don't they just shorten it to Gas?"

Jack said, "At least I didn't *fart*," and he was aware that he had fired a salvo—really without meaning to—and Olive did not respond.

As they finally entered the dismal town of Bellfield Corners, Olive said quietly, "I know who she was, Jack." He glanced over at her. He could just see her profile in the dim light, and she looked straight ahead.

"And who was she?" Jack asked dryly.

"She's that woman who got you fired from Harvard."

"I didn't get fired," Jack said; this made him really angry.

"She was the reason." Olive said this, still quietly. And then, turning her face toward him, she said, and it seemed her voice almost trembled, "I have to tell you, Jack. The only thing that upsets me about her is your taste in women, I think she is a dreadful, dreadful woman."

When Jack did not answer, Olive continued, "At least that foolish Thibodeau girl that Henry was in love with way back when, she was mousy, but she was decent. An innocent girl. And that fellow, Jim O'Casey, that I had my almost-affair with a hundred years ago, at least he was a lovely man."

Jack drove past the sign for the credit union; the whole town was dark except for the gas station, which seemed eerily alone with its lights.

"Oh, stop it," Jack said. "Honest to God, Olive. Some man with six kids and a wife who says to his fellow schoolteacher, Will you leave Henry and go off with me?, then ends up drunk and wrapped around a tree, is not a *lovely* man, Olive. Jesus Christ."

"You have no idea," Olive said. "You have no idea what you're talking about, and I would appreciate it if you left your stupid—stupid—opinions to yourself. He was a lovely man, and that snot-wot is a creep. That dreadful woman you bedded down all those years."

"That's enough, Olive."

"No, I'm not through. She was supercilious. She was just *crap,* Jack."

"Olive, I'm asking you to stop this. Okay, she was crap. Who cares?"

"I care," Olive said. "I care because it says something about *you.* When you're attracted to crap, it says something about you."

"It was many years ago, Olive." He thought the ride was unbelievably long; he was aware of the miles to go before they got home. He drove around a curve too quickly.

"And so was my almost-affair with that man who was lovely. You never met him, you don't know. But he was a lovely man, Jack, and you telling me that he wasn't, it's just horrible of you. And now I know why you would say that. Because of this woman you were so drawn to yourself." She paused, then said, "It makes me *sick.*"

He almost yelled at her. He almost shouted at her to shut up, to stop it; he came so close he could feel the words in his mouth; in a way, he almost thought he had yelled these things, but he had not. And she said no more. When they got home, she got out of the car and slammed the door.

"Enjoy your whiskey," Olive said to him as she went up the stairs; he heard her go into their bedroom. He hated her then.

• • •

Jack drank his whiskey quickly, sitting in his chair, because he was so frightened. What frightened him was how much of his life he had lived without knowing who he was or what he was doing. It caused him to feel an inner trembling, and he could not quite find the words—for himself—to even put it exactly as he sensed it. But he sensed that he had lived his life in a way that he had not known. This meant there had been a large blindspot directly in front of his eyes. It meant that he did not understand, not really at all, how others had perceived him. And it meant that he did not know how to perceive himself.

He got up to get more whiskey, pouring it into the tumbler he had just emptied, and then he went into the bathroom, where he splashed his pee like an old man. Turning to leave, he saw his face in the mirror. He *was* an old man: He was half-bald, his nose seemed to have become bigger, there was no connecting this man in the mirror to who he had been when he knew Elaine. He went back and sat in his chair and sipped his whiskey. But who had he been back then? A person much older than she was, someone who thought she was beautiful, who loved her intelligence, who loved her youth, but how in the world did that make it different from any other stupid sordid story of its kind? It didn't. There was nothing different about the story—except that it was his. And that it ended the way it did. It still amazed him, that Elaine had managed that. She must have been using him all along. Which is what Betsy had said immediately when he first told her the story, as he stood in the kitchen of their Cambridge home shaking visibly.

Elaine's face tonight, he realized, had a coldness to it that had surprised him. Her makeup was too perfect, there was something cold about that. And then he realized: I was cold. So he probably had been attracted to, without recognizing it, this coldness in her. Betsy had not been cold—except to him. But her nature had not been a cold one. She was friendly and people liked her.

Oh, Betsy—!

Betsy, who read all those books by Sharon McDonald. Oh, how he wanted right now for Betsy to be back with him, he did not care how dull he had found her, how careless she had been of him, he did not *care,* he only wanted her back. Betsy, he cried inside himself, Betsy, Betsy, Betsy, you don't know how much I miss you!

And he did. And it was not just tonight. There had been nights—a few—while Olive lay snoring in their bed, that he had sat on the front porch and—half-drunk—wept, because he wanted to be with Betsy instead. It seemed to him at such times that Olive talked only of herself—he knew that that was not (completely) true, but she was

242

fascinated by herself in a way that was tiresome for Jack on those nights, and was this because he wanted to talk about himself instead? Yes. He was not stupid, Jack. He understood that he had as many qualities as Olive had in that way. And he also knew, even tonight in his grief, that his marriage to Olive had been surprisingly wonderful in many ways, to go into old age with this woman who was so—so Olive.

But in his memory, now, he thought of Betsy, her quiet prettiness, her simplicity of self, yet she was not simple at all. She had, without blinking an eye, accepted the fact that Cassie was a lesbian, she had had an affair (oh, Betsy!)—no, there was nothing simple about Betsy. And on this night, he wished she was alive and with him. And this baffled him and yet did not. It baffled him because of their whole life squandered— only not really their whole lives, they had had many laughs, many sweet moments, and these came to him fleetingly tonight. He pictured how he made crêpes on the weekends, and they, all three of them—Betsy and Cassie and himself— ate them at the kitchen table; in his mind, they were laughing. He pictured his wife later, as she came to bed, her face lowered, but then the sudden open smile she might give him, and his heart felt a horrifying rush then, because he really had loved her in his way, and she was gone. But they had still squandered what they had, because they had not known.

When he thought of Betsy's affair with that Tom Groger he did not know what to think. But it had obviously begun way before his own. And sitting in his chair now, looking out over the dark, dark night, so dark he was not even able to see the trees and the field, he tucked his elbows into his stomach and said out loud, quietly, "Oh, Betsy, I wish you had not done that, I wish you had not done that!"

But Betsy was dead. And he was not.

Jack almost slept downstairs. But in the end he climbed the stairs and got into the bed next to Olive; he had no idea if she was awake or not.

That night he dreamed of Betsy and Cassie: His child was young, and she was holding her mother's hand, their backs were to him. But then they turned and waved at him, and he felt joy— *joy*—and he walked to them quickly, but then it was only Cassie, and then even she disappeared, and in the dream Jack found himself on a large, large rock; it curved downward as though it was the earth itself, or the moon—because it felt that isolated—and he was alone on this rock and the panic he felt was estimable. He woke, crying out, and even then he did not know where he was.

Olive spoke his name, "Jack," she said, she was sitting up in bed. When he said, "Olive,

I don't know where I am!," she said, calmly, "Okay, Jack, come with me," and she walked him through the house, she took him downstairs into the living room to show him the house he lived in, and even with her showing him this he was deeply confused and frightened, even as he heard Olive's voice speak to him—"Jack, this is your home, this is the living room, and now we're back in the bedroom"—even as he heard this, he understood that he was alone with his nighttime dream.

As people always are, with these things.

Exiles

Jim and Helen Burgess flew from New York City to Maine in July with their eldest grandson, Ernie—he was seven years old—to take him to summer camp. They rented a car in Portland, and after dropping the boy off Helen wept a little bit in the car and kept telling Jim she thought the boy was too young to be going away for a month, and Jim said the kid would be all right. They were now on their way to Crosby, where Jim's brother, Bob, lived with his second wife, Margaret. Helen had met Margaret only once before, a number of years ago when Bob brought Margaret to New York, and Helen had been aware— it was hard to miss—that Margaret had not liked the city at all, she had been afraid— afraid!—and after that, Bob came on his own to New York to visit; he came maybe once a year.

Helen had not been in the state of Maine for almost a decade, and she looked around with interest as they entered the town of Crosby. They had driven along the coast briefly; the spruce trees were standing skinny and straight on the islands, and the water sparkled like crazy, and now they were passing a few white clapboard houses and also brick houses. The sun was bright, and there was a display of some kind taking place on Main Street; there were booths and different people strolling around. "This is really pretty," she said, and Jim said, Yeah, he guessed it was.

Bob's house was not difficult to find; it was right off Main Street and was a large old brick house, four stories high. Now it was divided into condos, and as Helen stood on the steps in the afternoon sunshine she felt very glad to be there. But when she saw Margaret she could have just about fallen over; Margaret's hair—which used to be a streaky blond and piled up sort of messily on her head—was all gray now, and cut right below her ears.

Margaret said "Hello!," and Helen reached up to kiss her cheek, leaving a lipstick stain, which Helen then tried to rub out with her finger. "Whoopsie," Helen said, but Margaret said "Oh, don't worry," and Helen and Jim followed her up a really steep set of stairs while Margaret was saying that Bob had gone to buy some wine, he'd be back in a minute. The carpet on the stairs was gray, and filthy—Helen was surprised—and then Helen, as she followed Margaret through the door to their apartment, was just as surprised at the place: It was small, only two rooms, a kitchen in one of them, and there was the oddest furniture in that room, a couch right in the kitchen area and two chairs matching, all very old-appearing, and the upholstery had big yellow areas on a red background, and then there was the small living room; apparently their bedroom was upstairs one more flight, there was a stairway in the living room, but Margaret didn't say and Helen didn't ask. "What a lovely place," Helen said as she walked through it, because Jim had said nothing as he shook off his jacket and sat on the couch in the living room. "It's okay," said Margaret, and she shrugged, putting her hands forward in a gesture of welcome. "It's ours."

Helen thought she would go absolutely batty if she had to live in two rooms like this, although the windows were long, almost to the floor, and the view was quite nice, really, it looked right down on the park where the trees stood with their huge sprays of green leaves and a few children could be seen kicking a ball. "Oh, it's so cozy," Helen said, sitting down in a rocking chair whose upholstery had split open.

The door in the kitchen room squeaked, and then there was Bob, walking now into the living room. Jim rose and slapped his brother on the shoulder. "Slob-dog, how are you?" He asked this with an open-faced grin. "Looking good, kid," Jim said to Bob, and Bob said, "You too," even though Helen knew that Jim—always in good shape, and always a handsome man—had gained ten pounds during the last year, and she thought it made his eyes seem smallish. "Oh, Bobby," Helen said, and after kissing him she touched her hand to his cheek. "Hel*lo,* Bobby," she said. And Bob said, beaming, "Hello, Helen, welcome to Crosby, Maine."

"It's just lovely," Helen said.

A number of years earlier, Bob Burgess had asked his wife—they had been married for five years at that time; Bob had moved up from New York City, where he had lived his entire adult life—if she would mind if they moved out of the town of Shirley Falls and went and lived in Crosby instead, an hour away, and as soon as he asked her this, he could see that she was crestfallen. He said immediately, "No, never mind," but she asked him why he wanted to, and he answered her honestly: Shirley Falls just made him too sad. They were sitting in their living room at the time, and the ceiling was low, and the room received little natural light even in late June, which it was at the time of this conversation, and he looked around the room and said, "I'm sorry."

Whenever he thought of that evening he felt a great love for this woman, his second wife, Margaret, the Unitarian minister, because she had continued to question him, and it turned out that what made him sad was not just that the place was so decimated as a town these days, all its Main Street shops closed for years now except for those that the Somalis had; it was not just this—the quiet sense of horror Bob felt at being in a city that had once been vibrant and filled with life—it was that it reminded him on some level all the time of his childhood there, and the car accident that had killed his father when Bob was only four years old. He had been surprised to realize that this was the source of his discomfort, but Margaret had not seemed surprised at all. "It makes sense, because you spent your whole life thinking you were the one who killed him," she said, uncrossing her legs and crossing them again the other way. "And maybe I did," said Bob. Margaret shrugged, and said almost hopefully, "And maybe you did." This had always been the understanding in the family, that Bob had been responsible for the death of his father. But in fact Jim, four years older than Bob, had confessed to Bob a decade before that he—Jim— had been the one playing with the clutch when the car rolled down their driveway and struck their father, who had been checking the mailbox there. And, because Jim, Bob, and Susan— Bob's twin sister—had grown up in northern New England, in a culture and during a time when no one mentioned these sorts of things, they had— accordingly—never spoken of the accident since it had happened. Until the day when Jim, in his fifties, had told Bob that he—Jim—had done it. And so Bob, as a result, had felt that he had lost something profound. His identity had been taken from him. This was Margaret's idea, and he had seen immediately that she was right. In any case, she had agreed that day that they would move to the town of Crosby, about an hour away.

A coastal town, and pretty.

It was one o'clock, and the four of them decided they would go for a quick walk. The inn where Helen and Jim were staying that night was just two blocks away, so they all went to check them in; they would bring the bags later. The sidewalk was wide enough only for two people, and Jim walked with Margaret, Bob and Helen walking behind them. Helen said, "Bobby, the last time you came to New York, you were on your way to see Pam before you caught the train. I always meant to ask you, how did that go?" Pam was Bob's first wife; they had remained friendly, much to Helen's bafflement, and Bob said now, "Oh, she's doing great. Yeah, it was great to see her."

The inn had a large wraparound porch that a few people were sitting on in white rocking chairs, and Helen waved to them and they nodded back. The woman who checked them in was a pretty woman with glossy hair, and when she said she came from New York City originally, Helen was thrilled. "Do you like it up here?" Helen asked, and the woman said she did, she and her family loved it. The woman showed them their room; it was two rooms, really, with a small sitting room and two wingback chairs, then the bedroom. "Oh, how nice!" Helen said. After that, they walked for two more blocks, up Dyer Road, where the trees lined both sides of the street, then walked the back way to Main Street. Helen said, "What a *sweet* town, Bobby," as they went up those awful filthy stairs to the apartment.

The plan was this: Jim and Bob were going to go to Shirley Falls, and they would be back for dinner. Their sister, Susan, still lived there—she had never left—and because Susan and Helen didn't especially get along, it had been decided—before the trip, Margaret had offered this—that Helen and Margaret would stay in Crosby and walk through the art display that was being featured on the sidewalks of the town this weekend and then the brothers would meet up with them in a few hours. "Bye, bye," said Helen, and she gave both men a kiss; Margaret just waved a hand.

Anyway, Helen and Margaret sat in the living room for a few minutes; Helen fingered her gold earring and said "So, how *are* you?" and Margaret said that she and Bob were both just fine. "How are *you?*" Margaret asked, and Helen said she was worried about little Ernie; then Helen brought out her phone and showed Margaret pictures of her grandchildren, Margaret putting on the pair of glasses she wore attached to a black string over her large bosom, peering at the phone and saying, Oh, they were just adorable, weren't they. "I'll probably talk about them too much," Helen said, and Margaret took her glasses off and said, "Oh, no worries," so Helen showed her two more pictures, then she put her phone away and said, "Shall we go?" And Margaret got her handbag and off they went.

As soon as they were out of Crosby and driving on the back roads to Shirley Falls, Bob felt a happiness rise in him—it overtook the apprehension he had been feeling earlier—and now he was just happy. His brother drove. "Jimmy, it's so good to see you up here," Bob said, and his brother turned and smiled at him laconically. "You're all right, right?" Bob asked then, because he was suddenly aware of something slightly different about his brother—he couldn't put his finger on it—but it was as though Jim was not *quite* there.

"I'm fine," Jim said. "Tell me what you're up to."

So Bob told him—which Jim already knew—that he still drove to Shirley Falls three days a week to work arraignments, and Jim asked if he had many Somali clients, and Bob said a few but not many. The Somalis had moved to Maine almost twenty years earlier, settling in Shirley

Falls because they thought it was safe. Bob had recently had a case where a Somali woman was accused of welfare fraud, and Jim seemed interested in this.

Jim, who had gone to Harvard Law School on a full scholarship, who had been famous at the height of his career for successfully defending the singer Wally Packer after Wally was accused of killing his girlfriend, these days did only a few small defense cases, and when Bob asked him about them now, Jim just waved a hand dismissively. Instead, Jim asked, "What did you think of Helen? You think she looks okay?"

"She looks great," Bob said. "She's always looked great. She looks smaller, but not much older."

"She looks smaller because I've gotten bigger," Jim said. "Nice of you not to say anything."

"You look pretty good, Jimmy."

After a moment Jim said, "What's with Margaret's hair?"

"Oh." Bob let out a sigh. "She said she was tired of worrying about it, so she let it go natural and cut it off."

Jim glanced over at Bob. "Okay." Then Jim said, "Did you think I was going to say she looks like a lesbo?"

Bob answered honestly. "I figured that's the first thing you were going to say to me when we were alone."

"Nah, she looks fine. Who cares. I've mellowed out. So, Susan's okay?" Jim asked.

"She's great. You'll see. She looks great. I mean, you know, for Susan."

"Can't believe her mental son is getting married," Jim said. "Jesus, he seemed practically normal when he came to New York last year."

"Right?" Bob glanced out the window at the field they were passing with the rocks in it; the grass was a vivid green, and the sun poured over the whole thing. "Everything worked out, Jimmy." He looked over at his brother.

Jim looked at the road in front of him. "Okay," he said.

Helen became tired as they went down the street and stopped at every display of art. Booth after booth of white canvas sporting a variety of artwork: watercolors and oil paintings. Helen thought it all terribly amateurish—many of the paintings were of the sea, and also white clap-board houses, the corners of them, often with a rosebush painted in. "Look at all this," she said to Margaret. "It's lovely!"

Margaret said that it was.

It kept bothering Helen, the way Margaret looked. She had forgotten that Margaret had such large breasts. They seemed positively huge to Helen, and Margaret wore a long loose dress of dark blue and they still poured forth beneath it.

And her hair! Why would anyone wear her hair in such a way? Just chopped off like that. Oh dear, Helen thought, glancing at Margaret through her sunglasses. Oh, Bobby, what a change you made! Pam had been very stylish—if not a little overdone, in Helen's view—but Bob had now lived with this other wife for almost a decade. Well. What could you do about it? Nothing.

"Hey, hi there," said a woman to Margaret, and Margaret said, "Well, hello." And she stopped and talked to the woman, who seemed about Margaret's age, who even had hair not unlike Margaret's, they chatted about the woman's sister, how she was doing much better, and then Margaret said, "Oh, this is my sister-in-law, Helen," and Helen stuck out her hand and the woman seemed surprised, and she shook it, and then they walked their separate ways. This happened a number of times: people stopping Margaret to talk. They all seemed glad to see her. Margaret asked about their kids, and jobs, and someone's mother, but she didn't say again "This is my sister-in-law, Helen," and Helen just stood there trying to look interested. So at one point, when Margaret was talking to a man, Helen said, "Hi, I'm Helen, I'm Margaret's sister-in-law," and she stuck her hand out, and the man—it was a big man this time that Margaret was talking to—brought his hand out of his pocket to shake Helen's hand with little vigor.

"You're very popular," Helen said to Margaret as they continued down the street, and Margaret said, "I'm a minister. When we moved here a few years ago, I was lucky to get a part-time job with the UU church."

"The what church?" asked Helen.

"Unitarian," said Margaret.

And Helen said, after a moment, "Well, you're still popular." Margaret looked at Helen through her sunglasses and laughed, and so Helen laughed as well. They were moving past a café that had its doors open. Helen stopped and brought out a straw hat from her bag, the hat could be rolled up, and now she unrolled it and put it on her head.

"You look like a tourist," Margaret said to her, and Helen said, "Well, I am a tourist."

Another man walked by, he had a gray beard, and Helen saw that he was wearing a skirt. Helen looked away, then looked back at him. It was a kilt, she realized, though it didn't seem as long as a kilt usually was. It was brown, and the man wore a gray T-shirt and brown walking shoes. "Hello, Fergie," said Margaret, and the man said, "Hello, Margaret."

When they were past him, Helen said, "Why was he wearing that?"

"I guess he likes it," Margaret said.

"I've lived in New York for fifty years, and I have never seen a man walking down the street in a skirt," said Helen. "A kilt," she added. Margaret turned her sunglasses toward Helen, and Helen said, raising a finger, "Whoops, that's not true. There used to be a man who went jogging on Third Avenue in a black negligee. Which is still not a skirt."

"Well, I guess you win," said Margaret. "Far as I know we have no men jogging about in black negligees."

"He was old, too. The man in the black negligee," Helen said.

Margaret kept walking.

"It was kind of weird," Helen said. "You know."

And Margaret didn't say anything; she just stopped at the next booth of art.

Helen was becoming hot, even with her hat stopping the sun from hitting her straight on her head, and she said to Margaret as she stepped up behind her, "I didn't know it got so warm in Maine."

Margaret said, "Well, it does."

And then Helen decided she would buy a piece of art. That's what she decided to do so that Margaret wouldn't think she was a snob, because maybe Margaret was thinking that Helen was a snob. "Hold on," she said, touching Margaret lightly on the arm. "Let me look at these paintings." They were seascapes, a lot of purple waves and foaming spray. Helen found one, a smaller piece stuck up high on the white canvas:

It was a painting of a rock with water swirling around it. "Oh, I'll take that," Helen said, and she brought out her credit card and the fellow seemed very pleased to sell it to her. "I'll just take it, no need to wrap it in anything," Helen said, because the fellow was ready to put it in brown wrapping paper.

As Helen took the painting and turned to go, she bumped into a tall big old woman who was saying loudly to the man she was with, "God, have I seen enough of this crap! Come on, Jack."

Margaret said, "Oh, hello, Olive."

The woman looked surprised and she said, "Hello, Margaret." Then she looked Helen up and down through her sunglasses; Helen could see the woman's head move slightly as she took Helen in. "Who are you?" the woman asked.

"I'm Margaret's sister-in-law," Helen said, and the woman kept looking at her and Helen added, "My husband is Bob's brother, and we came up from New York to drop our grandson off at camp."

The woman said, "Well." She pointed a finger at the painting Helen held. "You enjoy that," and she turned around, waving a hand over her head as she and the man walked past the two of them.

"She's got me all stuffed up on antidepressants," Jim was saying. He shrugged, and gave his lopsided grin to his brother and sister. "What can I do?"

"Are you depressed, Jimmy?" Susan sat down at the kitchen table across from her brother. Susan was an optometrist, and she had taken the afternoon off to be with both of them. Sunlight fell through the window, making a square on the table and across Susan's arm.

"Well, not now." And Jim laughed.

Susan and Bob did not laugh, and Susan said, "But were you before?"

Jim placed his hands together on the table and looked off to the side. "I don't know." He looked around the kitchen some more; it was a small kitchen, but Susan's house was a small house. There were orange curtains at the kitchen windows, one was just slightly lifting in the breeze from the open window; the room was warm. "But she seems to think I'm easier to live with when I'm on them, so—I am. On them." Jim looked at Bob and smiled. "Maximum dose, so I don't drink. Which is okay. But I'll tell you, Helen's taken up the sauce. She enjoys her nightly wine, I have noticed that."

Susan glanced at Bob, and they both said nothing for a few moments. Then Susan said, "But you're okay, though. Right?"

"Sure," Jim said, looking from one to the other. To Bob it seemed as though he was looking at Jim through a pane of glass; he understood now what was different about Jim. His edge was gone. It's not that he had mellowed, it's that he was medicated. Bob felt a slight tightening of his chest, and he sat up straight.

Jim added, "Got that huge house now, all done up spiffy." His face glistened just slightly.

"You don't like it?" Susan asked, plucking at the front of her blue-and-white-striped blouse, and Jim looked serious.

"You know," Jim said, as though he was just realizing this now, "I really don't. I miss the old way it was, it was a pretty great house, and now it's like . . ." He looked around Susan's kitchen as though the answer was there.

"A palace," Bob said. "It looks like a modern palace."

"Yeah," Jim said slowly, looking at Bob, nodding.

"Well, maybe it was your penance for having those affairs," Susan said, and Jim said immediately, "Oh, it *was,* there's no doubt about that."

Jim and Helen lived in a brownstone in Park Slope, and a few years earlier they had renovated the entire place. When Bob first stepped inside after the renovation, he could not believe it was the same house. All the old original woodwork, the horsehair wallpaper, all of that was gone, and the house seemed as sleek as a palace. "What do you think?" Helen asked, eagerly, almost breathlessly, and Bob said it was amazing. "Really something," he said.

"You don't like it," Helen answered, and Bob had said that wasn't true at all, but it was true.

Susan got up to turn off the teakettle, and as she made tea—three mugs with a tea bag in each—Jim said, "I miss Maine."

Bob said, "What?" And Jim repeated what he had said.

"Do you? I've been thinking about Mommy a lot," Susan said, turning her head toward Jim.

"That's funny," Jim said, "because I have too."

"What have you been thinking?" Susan asked. She brought two mugs to the table and turned back to get the third.

"I don't know. What a hard life she had." Jim said, "You know what else I've been thinking about recently? We were really poor growing up."

Susan said, "You just now figured that out?" She laughed abruptly. "Jimmy, my goodness, of course we were poor."

Jim looked at Bob. "Did you know that?"

Bob said, "Ah—yes. I did know that, Jim."

"You know, I've been rich so long—I mean, I've lived like a rich person for so long—that I kind of forgot that when we grew up we were really pretty poor."

"Well, we were, Jimmy," Susan said. "I can't

believe you forgot that. We had newspapers stuffed into all the windows to keep the cold out."

"I didn't *forget* it. I'm just saying I haven't *thought* about it."

Susan sat down. "But we weren't unhappy, really." She looked from one brother to the other. "Were we?"

"Nah," Bob said, just as Jim said, "Yes."

"Jimmy, you were unhappy?" Susan, who had picked up her mug, now put it back down.

"Of course I was unhappy. I thought I had killed Dad, and every day I thought about that. And about how I let Bob take the blame. Every *day* I thought of that."

Susan shook her head slowly. "Oh, Jimmy," she said. "I'm so sorry."

Bob said, "Jim, just let that go. We were kids. We'll never know what really happened."

Jim looked at him. "Well," Jim finally said, "it's okay to tell me to let it go now, but it was with me every day of my life." He looked around, crossed one leg over the other. "Every single day."

"Look," Bob said—and he was sort of quoting Margaret—"if it had happened today we probably would have all gone to therapy and talked about it. But it happened more than fifty years ago, and nobody ever mentioned anything back then, not up here in Shirley Falls—*anything.* And you got caught in the middle of it." He added, "I'm really sorry, Jimmy."

Jim looked at him with seriousness. "No, I'm the one who's sorry, Bobby."

Susan reached and put her hand over Jim's hand that held his mug of tea. "Oh, Jimmy," she said. "Well, we're all here, we all made it through."

A look of sadness came over Jim's face, and Bob tried to think of something to say to dispel it, but Susan was asking Bob about Pam. "How's she doing?" Susan asked. "You know, I think one of the funnest summers was when she lived with us in that house. She was pretty great. Not everyone would have wanted to spend their summer from college living with us in that *tiny* house, but she did. I guess she came from a small place too. Jim, you were gone . . ." And Jim nodded. "Anyway, I think of her. She's okay?"

The last time Bob had been to New York, he had called his ex-wife, Pam, and they had met at a café near where she lived on the Upper East Side. "Bobby!" she said, and threw her arms around him. She looked the same, only older, and he told her this, and she laughed and said, "Well, you look *great*."

"I've missed you," he said, and this was true.

"Oh, Bobby, I've missed you so much," she said, flicking her hair back; it was shoulder-length hair, dyed a nice reddish color. "I just keep thinking, are you okay up there in that awful state of Maine? Oh, I don't mean to say it's awful—it just seems so . . ."

"Awful," he said, and they laughed. "I'm fine, Pam. It's all just fine."

As Bob remembered this now, he felt a surge of love for Pam; they had married right out of college, just kids. And they had stayed married for almost fifteen years. In Bob's mind, Pam had left him when she found out—when they found out—that Bob couldn't father children. And it had broken Bob's heart. Only later did he realize it had broken Pam's heart as well, but she found a man, and had her two boys—boys that Bob had met over the years, great kids they were—and her husband seemed fine. She never complained about him; he was a top manager of a pharmaceutical company, and Pam had tons of money now, but whenever she and Bobby got together, they were just like kids again. Only older, and they both said this every time they met.

"She's great," Bob said to Susan.

Margaret had not liked New York. This had been evident to Bob on their one visit there together: He saw her fear as they walked down the stairs to the subway, and even though he tried to reassure her, and she tried—he could see this—to take it all in stride, it had not really gone that well, because Bob could not stop himself from sensing her discomfort, and it had made him sad, because he loved New York, where he had lived for thirty years before meeting Margaret in Maine.

"Will you tell Pam I was asking about her?" Susan said, and Bob said of course he would.

Jim said, "You're better off with Margaret," and Susan said, "Why do you say that?"

But Bob said, "Susan, tell us how Zach is. Jim said he seemed pretty good when he came to New York."

"Oh, Zach." Susan ran her hand through her hair, which was gray and wavy and cut just above her shoulders. "Jim, he's doing so well. Into computer programming, as I'm sure he told you, and he's going to marry that girlfriend he met down in Massachusetts."

"Do you like her?" Jim asked. He raised his tea mug, took a sip, returned it to the table.

"I do."

"Well, there we are." Jim looked around now as though a restlessness had come over him. "You know, you guys, I'd like to come back up here more. I miss it. I miss Shirley Falls, and I miss you both."

Bob and Susan looked at each other, Susan widening her eyes slightly. "Well, *do,*" she said. "Boy, we would love that."

"I gained ten pounds this year," Jim said. "Can you tell?"

"Nah," said Bob. He was lying.

"Bob, you still boozing it up?" Jim squinted at his brother.

"No. Maybe one glass a night at most.

And I haven't had a cigarette since I married Margaret."

Jim shook his head slowly. "Amazing." Then he asked Susan, "How's the eye business?"

"Booming," Susan said. "I could retire, but I don't feel like it. I like my job."

"Look at you two," Jim said.

Back in the small apartment, Helen said, "How about a glass of wine?"

Margaret looked surprised—to Helen she looked that way—and she said, "Okay," and she got out the bottle of white wine that Bob had put in the refrigerator earlier and opened it and poured a small amount into a mason jar. She handed it to Helen.

"Lovely," Helen said, and decided she would not make a joke about the wineglass. "You're not having any?" Margaret shook her head, sitting down in the rocking chair that had the split upholstery; Helen sat on the couch. Helen crossed her legs and swung a foot. "So," she said.

"So," Margaret said.

"Oh, let me show you just a few more pics of my grandkids," and Helen brought out her phone. "I just keep thinking about little Ernie. I'm just not sure he's *old* enough to be at camp all by himself, but his parents wanted him to, and even Ernie seemed keen on it, but the cabin he was in seemed—well, terribly rustic." When Margaret didn't respond, Helen found some pictures on her phone and had Margaret look at many pictures of her three grandchildren. She told Margaret how little Sarah was talking already—almost full sentences and she was barely two, could you believe it? "No," said Margaret, peering at the phone through the glasses she wore on the string that fell over her chest. Then Margaret sat back and sighed.

Helen rose and went into the kitchen, returning with the bottle of wine. She poured more into her glass and then said, looking at her phone again, presenting it to Margaret, "And look at Karen! She's three, and she's so different from her brother, he's all confident and outgoing, and Karen—don't you like that name, Karen? it's so straightforward—and she is just the *sweetest* little thing—" Helen looked up at Margaret and said, "I'm talking about my grandchildren too much."

Margaret said, "Yes. You are."

Helen felt a sense of disbelief, and her face got hot immediately. She put her phone into her handbag, and when she looked back at Margaret, she saw that Margaret's cheeks were pink as well. "I'm sorry," Helen said. "I'm very sorry. I know you and Bobby never—"

"No, having no children makes us different. We feel fine about it, but it does get tiresome to hear—" Margaret waved a hand and stopped. "I apologize. I'm sure your grandchildren are all just wonderful."

Helen took two big swallows of the wine and felt the warmth of it spread through her chest. "I wonder when the boys will be back," said Helen, looking around the place; she was mad at Margaret now, just plain mad. She stood up. "If you'll excuse me, I'm going to use your bathroom."

"Of course," Margaret said.

Helen took her wine with her and finished the glass as soon as she closed the bathroom door. But then she realized that if she called Jim, everything could be overheard, so she sat on the toilet and texted him. Jimmy, she texted, where are you? M is making me NUTS. She waited, and there was no response. Then she texted, I think she is GRUESOME. Oh, come on, Jimmy, she thought, and then she worried that Margaret would not hear her peeing—because Helen had not needed to—and so she tried, and then she made a small gaseous sound, which was very upsetting, Margaret was right out there listening! After a moment she stood up and washed her hands carefully—the towel looked a little grimy—and then she returned to where Margaret was still sitting in the rocking chair as though she hadn't moved at all.

Helen poured herself more wine.

"I really am awfully sorry," Margaret said to her.

"No, no, that's fine." Helen drank the wine.

On the drive back to Crosby, Jim said, "You know, Bobby, here's the truth: I've loved Helen even more since she redid the house." He glanced over at Bob, who sat without moving. "You know why?"

"No," said Bob.

"Because she actually thought it would help. She thought if she changed the house it would eradicate everything that had gone on in it, meaning that last year when I fell apart and screwed those dopes, and Helen really thought, If we change things, it will be different."

Jim looked again at Bob, then back at the road in front of him. "But of course it doesn't change anything, and now we're living in a whole new house, which used to be our old house where many wonderful things happened. And when I realized that's why she was doing it, making that godawful renovation, it made me love her more, Bobby. I think it made her more human to me, or something. I love her more than I did before, and that's the truth."

"Okay," said Bob. "I get it."

After another minute Jim said, "Helen didn't make me go on this stuff. I did it myself."

They drove in silence for a moment after that;

Bob understood what Jim had said, but the information seemed to stay outside him. "She didn't make you?" Bob asked. "Then why did you?"

And then Jim said, "I'm scared." Jim looked straight ahead as he said this.

"Of what, Jimmy?"

"Of dying." Jim looked over at Bob, gave him his wry half-smile. "I'm scared to death of dying. I really am. I can feel it coming so fast—whoosh! Jesus, it all goes so fast these days. But you know what?"

"What?"

"I don't really care, either. I mean, about dying. It's so *strange,* Bobby. Because on one hand I have these moments—or I *had* these moments before I got all doped up—of just sheer terror. *Terror.* And at the very same time, I kind of feel like, Yeah, okay, let's go, I'm ready." Jim was silent for a moment, glancing in the rearview mirror; he let a car pass him. "But I'm scared. Or I was. Before the medication."

And now Bob felt frightened. Jimmy, he wanted to say, you can't get scared, you're my leader! But he knew—a part of him knew, and oh God it made him sad—that Jim was not his leader anymore. Then he said, "If Helen isn't making you take the stuff, why did you tell Susan it was Helen who insisted on it?"

Jim looked as though he was considering this. He said, "Because I know Susan doesn't like

Helen, so I blamed Helen for it." He turned to look at his brother, and his eyes widened. "Listen to me, Bobby, wow, am I an asshole."

Bob said, and he was surprised to hear the level of irritation in his voice, "You know what, Jim? Will you stop that? You did one stupid thing ten years ago when Zach got in all that trouble, for crying out loud, and it brought up all the guilt you'd been feeling, and so you—you acted out. You had an affair. Or a couple of them, I don't know. That doesn't make you an asshole, Jim. It makes you a human being. Jesus, will you stop this?"

Jim said immediately, "You're right, you're right. Sorry. I really am sorry. God—I sound so melodramatic. I'm sorry about that, Bobby."

And Bob felt a swift swoop of desolation; he could not remember ever speaking to his brother like that, or having Jim respond with an apology as he just had.

Helen held her mason jar of wine and rocked her foot. "A year ago, Jimmy and I were on our cruise to Alaska," Helen said. She didn't know why she said this.

"Yes," said Margaret. "So I heard."

"It rained every day. When we got to the glacier place, Glacier Bay, we were supposed to take a helicopter up to see the glaciers, but it was too foggy."

273

"That's a shame," said Margaret.

"No, it's not. Who cares?"

Margaret looked at Helen. "I should think you would have cared. You'd paid all that money to go see the place."

"Well, I didn't care," said Helen. She took two more large swallows of wine. After a moment she said, and she could feel her cheeks flushing slightly, "I'll tell you what I cared about: the Indonesians who worked on the cruise ship. Everyone working on that boat was from Indonesia, and we got talking to one fellow one night and he worked ten months a year on that boat and went home to Bali for two months. And I bet you *anything*," she pointed a finger at Margaret, "that those guys are stacked up on top of each other in the bottom of that ship with no windows, and once I realized that—well, I couldn't really enjoy myself anymore. I mean, we were taking this trip on the backs of these people."

Margaret said nothing, although she had opened her mouth as though she were about to.

"What are you thinking?" Helen asked her.

"I was thinking, How liberal of you."

After a moment, Helen, who had some trouble taking this in, said, "Why, Margaret, you hate me."

"Don't be ridiculous."

But now Helen felt sad. She thought ministers

were supposed to be nice people. She made a raspberry sound with her lips. "I'm sad," she said, and Margaret said, "I think you may be a little drunk."

Helen felt her face flush again. She took the bottle of wine and poured more into the stupid mason jar. "Bottoms up," she said.

And then the men could be heard on the stairs, and after a minute the door squeaked open and closed and there they were, standing in the living room. "Oh, *boys,*" said Helen. "Boy, am I glad to see you two." She squinted up at them. "Are you guys okay?"

She couldn't see Jim's eyes, but something in the way the men stood made her feel they were not okay. "Look," she said, "I bought a piece of crap." She pointed to the small painting, which was on the floor next to the couch.

Bob picked it up, and Jim stepped behind him to look. "God, Helen," Jim asked, "why did you buy that?" And Bob said, "It's not so bad."

"It's awful," Helen said. "I just bought it—to be nice. Who was that woman?" Helen looked with confusion at Margaret. "That pickle person. You know—" She tried to snap her fingers, but her fingers slipped. "That person, what—you know, what's like a pickle?"

"Olive." Margaret said this coldly.

"Olive." Helen nodded.

"Olive Kitteridge," Margaret said.

"Well, she said this was crap."

"Olive thinks everything is crap," said Bob. "That's just who she is."

Margaret stood up and said, "I think we'd better go to dinner. Helen needs some food."

It wasn't until Helen herself stood up that she realized how drunk she might be. "Whoopsie," she said, quietly. She looked around. "Where did Jimmy go?"

"He's in the bathroom," Bob said. "We'll go in just a minute."

And then Helen saw the staircase that went upstairs from the living room. "Bobby, is that where you sleep? Up there?"

Bob said that it was.

And Helen climbed the stairs. "I'm just going to peek," she called out. She put her hand on the wall to steady herself. These stairs were steep as well, and they turned a corner partway up. She stood on the landing and turned around. There was a plant on the landing, and its leaves spread far up and down the steps. "Boy, that would give me the creeps," Helen said, and then as she started up the rest of the stairs she fell backward, and what she was aware of was how long the fall was taking, how her body was bumping and bumping down these stairs, it was taking forever, and it was shocking. And then she stopped.

Margaret yelled, "Don't move her!"

· · ·

Jim went in the ambulance with Helen, and Margaret and Bob followed in their car. Margaret said, "Oh, Bob. Bob. This was all my fault." He looked over at her. Her eyes seemed bald-looking to him, and they were red-rimmed. "No, it was," she said. "It was all my fault. Bob, I couldn't *stand* her. And she knew it. And it was terrible of me, I didn't even really try with her. Oh, Bob. And she knew! She knew, because people always know these things, and so she got drunk."

"Margaret—"

"No, Bob. I feel terrible. She just drove me crazy, and there was no reason that she should have, but she's—Oh, Bob, she's just so *rich*."

"Well, she is rich. That's true. But what does that have to do with it?"

Margaret looked over at him. "It makes her self-centered, Bob. She never even asked about me once."

"She's shy, Margaret. She's nervous."

Margaret said, "That woman is not shy. She's *rich*. And I just couldn't stand her from the very beginning. You know, her hair done so nicely, and her gold earrings. Oh, Bob. And then when she got out her foolish straw hat I thought I'd die."

"Her straw hat? Margaret, what are you saying?"

277

"I'm saying I couldn't stand her and she knew it, Bob. And I feel terrible."

Bob said nothing. He could think of nothing to say. But a quiet sense of almost-unreality seemed to come to him, and he thought the word "prejudice," and he understood that he needed to drive carefully, and so he did, and then they reached the hospital.

It was midnight by the time Helen was released. She had broken an arm, and two ribs, and her face had been badly bruised; one eye was purplish and swollen. Now she sat silently, with her arm in a white cast that bent by the elbow, while Jim—whom Margaret had driven back to their place to get his car—went around and opened her car door and then helped her into the car. There had been a CAT scan done of her head, and there was no damage, and she had had a number of X-rays to check for internal injuries. Now Bob got into the back seat, and he texted Margaret that Helen was okay, Margaret should go to bed.

Jim said over his shoulder, "You have to sleep sitting up when you break any ribs."

"Oh, Helen," said Bob, reaching to touch the back of Helen's head. "I'm so sorry."

Jim said, "Hellie, we'll drive back tomorrow. I'm going to rent an SUV, and we'll just drive straight back. You'll be more comfortable that way, I think." And Bob could see Helen nod slightly.

At the inn, Bob helped his brother get Helen seated in the wingback chair—once she was in her pajamas, her cast sticking out at an angle, and her robe pulled over her—in the sitting-room part of their room, and then he said he would be back.

When he went up the stairs to his own bedroom, he was surprised to see that Margaret was fast asleep. There was a small light on by the bed, and he watched this woman, who seemed almost a stranger to him at this moment. He recognized now the smallness of her response to a world she did not know or understand; it was not unlike the response his sister had had to Helen. And he knew that had he not lived in New York for so many years—if his brother, whom he had loved as God, had not lived there as well, rich and famous for all those years—then he might have felt as Margaret did. But he did not feel as she did. He turned the light off and walked down the stairs and back to the inn.

The door of the room was unlocked, and he entered it quietly. Jim lay snoring on the bed, and Helen sat, as though asleep, in the chair. On her feet now were thin pink slippers with fluffy pompoms on their ends.

Inside Bob moved a sadness he had not felt in years. He had missed his brother—his brother!—

and his brother had missed Maine. But his brother was married to a woman who hated Maine, and Bob understood that they would not come up here again. Jim would live the rest of his life as an exile, in New York City. And Bob would live the rest of his life as an exile in Maine. He would always miss Pam, he would always miss New York, even though he would continue to make his yearly visits there. He was exiled here. And the weirdness of this—how life had turned out, for himself, and Jim, and even Pam—made him feel an ocean of sadness sway through him.

A sound came from the chair, and he saw that Helen was awake, and she was weeping quietly. "Ah, Helen," he said, and he went to her. He turned and found a box of tissues on the table, then he put a tissue over her nose and said softly, "Blow," and this made Helen laugh a little, and Bob squatted next to her chair. He put his hand on her hair, drawing it back from her face. "Ah, you're going to be all right, Helen," he said. "Don't you worry. Jim's going to drive you straight home tomorrow, and you will never have to come back to this awful state."

She looked at him in the duskiness of the room, her one eye almost swollen shut, the other eye looking at him searchingly. "But you live here," she said. "It's not awful for you, is it, Bobby?"

He paused, then whispered, "Sometimes," and he winked at her and so she laughed again.

"Bobby?"

"What, Helen?"

"I've always loved you."

"I know that. And I've always loved you too."

Helen nodded just slightly. "Okay," she said, "I'm sleepy."

"You rest. I'm right here, and Jim is in the next room."

"Is he snoring?"

"Yes."

"Okay, Bobby."

And Bob sat back on his heels, and after Helen's eyes had remained closed for a while he moved back quietly to sit in the chair opposite her. He ached, as though he had walked far longer than his body could walk, his whole entire body ached, and he thought: My soul is aching.

And it came to him then that it should never be taken lightly, the essential loneliness of people, that the choices they made to keep themselves from that gaping darkness were choices that required respect: This was true for Jim and Helen, and for Margaret and himself, as well.

"Bobby?" Helen whispered this.

"What is it, Helen?" He got up and went to her.

"Nothing. I just wanted to know if you're here."

"I'm right here." He stayed by her for a moment, then went back and sat in his chair. "Not going anywhere," he said.

The Poet

On a Tuesday morning in the middle of September, Olive Kitteridge drove carefully into the parking lot of the marina. It was early— she drove only in the early hours now—and there were not many cars there, as she had expected there would not be. She nosed her car into a space and got out slowly; she was eighty-two years old, and thought of herself as absolutely ancient. For three weeks now she had been using a cane, and she made her way across the rocky pathway, not glancing up so as to be able to watch her footing, but she could feel the early-morning sun and sensed the beauty of the leaves that were turned already to a bright red at the tops of the trees.

Once inside, she sat at a booth that had a view of the ocean and ordered a muffin and scrambled eggs from the girl with the huge hind end. The girl was not a friendly girl; she hadn't been friendly in the year she'd worked here. Olive stared out at the water. It was low tide, and the seaweed lay like combed rough hair, all in one direction. The boats that remained in the bay sat graciously, their thin masts pointing to the heavens like tiny steeples. Far past them was Eagle Island and also Puckerbrush Island with the evergreens spread across them both, nothing more than a faint line seen from here. When the girl—who practically slung the plate of eggs with the muffin onto the table—said, hands on her hips, "Anything else?," Olive just gave a tiny shake of her head and the girl walked away, one haunch of white pants moving up then coming down as the other haunch moved up; up and down, huge slabs of hind end. In a patch of sunlight on the table Olive's rings twinkled on her hand, which sight—lit in such a way—gave her the faintest reverberation of surprise. Wrinkled, puffy: This was her hand. And then, minutes later, just as she had put another bite of scrambled egg onto her fork, Olive spotted her: Andrea L'Rieux. For a moment Olive couldn't believe it was the girl—not a girl, she was a middle-aged woman, but at Olive's age they were all girls—and then she thought, Why not? Why wouldn't it be Andrea?

The girl, Andrea, sat at a booth by herself; it was a few booths away from Olive, and she faced Olive, but she sat staring out at the water with tinted glasses halfway down her nose. Olive placed her fork on her plate, and after a few moments she rose slowly and walked up to Andrea's booth and she said, "Hello, Andrea. I know who you are."

The girl-woman turned and stared at her, and

for a moment Olive felt she had been mistaken. But then the girl-woman took off her tinted glasses and there she was, Andrea, middle-aged. There was a long moment of silence—it seemed long to Olive—before Olive said, "So. You're famous now."

Andrea kept staring at Olive with eyes that were large, her dark hair was pulled back loosely in a ponytail. Finally she said, "Mrs. Kitteridge?" Her voice was deep, throaty.

"It's me," Olive said. "It is I. And I've become an old lady." She sat down across from Andrea, in spite of thinking that she saw in the girl's face a wish not to be disturbed. But Olive was old, she had buried two husbands, what did she care; she did not care.

"You've gotten smaller," Andrea said.

"Probably." Olive folded her hands on the table, then put them onto her lap. "My husband died four months ago, and I don't eat as much. I still have an appetite, but I'm not eating as much, and when you get old, you shrink anyway."

Andrea said, after a moment, "You do?"

"Shrink? Of course you do. Your spine gets crunched up, your belly pops out—and down you go. I can't be the first person you've seen get old."

"You're not," Andrea agreed.

"Well, then. So you know."

"Bring your plate over," said Andrea, looking

285

past Olive to where Olive had been sitting. "Wait, I'll get it for you." And she scooted from her seat and in a moment returned with Olive's plate of eggs, and the muffin, and also Olive's cane. She was shorter than Olive had thought: childlike, almost.

"Thank you," Olive said. "I only started with the cane three weeks ago. I had a little car accident, is what happened. I was in the parking lot near Chewie's. And I stepped on the gas pedal instead of the brake."

Andrea opened her hand slightly and said with a friendly half-grimace, "That's fair."

"Not if you're eighty-two years old. Then everyone seems ready to take away your license. Although I must say, the policeman was very nice. I wept. Can you imagine? I still can't believe I did. But I stood there and I wept. Awfully nice man, the policeman. And the ambulance people, they were nice too."

"Were you hurt?"

"Cracked my sternum."

"God," Andrea said.

"It's fine." Olive pulled her jacket closed. "I move more slowly, and now I just drive in the early morning. Try to, anyway. I totaled two cars in the parking lot that day."

"Two?"

"Two. That's right. Well, three, if you count mine. I had to get my friend Edith's husband,

Buzzy Stevens, to help me get another car when the insurance check came in. I don't think Buzzy cared much for that, but there we are. No one was hurt. Just me. Shook me up, I will say."

"Well, of course," Andrea said in her deep voice.

"I saw on Facebook you were just in Oslo," said Olive. She ate some of her egg.

"You follow me on Facebook? Are you serious?"

"Of course I'm serious. You just had a whole Scandinavian tour doing poetry readings. I went to Oslo with my second husband, I've had two husbands," Olive said. "And with my second husband we went to Oslo and took a boat—a cruise, I guess it was—around the fjords. They were beautiful, they were. My word. But then Jack got sad, and then I got sad, and we both said, It's beautiful here, but not as pretty as home. We felt better once we'd figured that out." Olive wiped her nose with a paper napkin that was on the table. She felt as though she was panting.

The girl was watching her carefully.

"I don't know what you thought about the fjords, but that's what we thought." Olive said this, and sat back.

"I never saw the fjords."

"You never saw the fjords?"

"No." Andrea sat up straight. "I gave a reading and hung around with my publisher, and then I had to move on. I wanted to move on. I guess I really don't care about the fjords."

"Huh," Olive said.

"I get lonely when I travel," Andrea said.

Olive wasn't sure she'd heard this right, but she decided she had, and she thought about it. "Well," she said, "you were probably always lonely."

Andrea looked at her then, gave her a look that confused Olive somewhat; the girl's eyes were brown but almost a little bit hazel too, and they seemed to break into a tenderness around their corners as she looked at Olive. The girl said nothing.

If there was one student Olive had had over her vast years as a seventh-grade math teacher, if there was one student who was not going to be famous, it was Andrea L'Rieux. The only reason Olive even remembered her was because she used to see the girl out walking alone, and so sad-looking. Such a sad-looking face that girl had. But she had been no student; nope, she had certainly not been that. Not even in English class, because when the girl began to rise to prominence, when she became Poet Laureate of the United States (!) a number of years ago, even her high school English teacher had told a reporter that Andrea had not been much of a student. Horrible old Irene White, stupid as a stick and wouldn't have known talent if she'd seen it, but still—

"Irene White is dead," Olive told Andrea, and Andrea nodded and shrugged a slight shrug.

"She seemed old when I had her," Andrea said. "I remember rouge would get stuck in the wrinkles of her cheeks."

"Well, she sure wasn't very generous about you," Olive said, and when the girl looked at her with surprise, Olive realized that Andrea had not seen the article.

And then Andrea said, "I don't read anything about myself."

"Good idea," Olive said. "Anyway, when they came snooping to me, I said nothing."

She'd have had nothing to say. She wasn't going to say the girl had been sad-faced, that she came from a family with God knows how many siblings, let others say that. And they did! But not the sad-faced part; apparently no one but Olive had seen the girl walking the roads of Crosby, Maine, thirty years ago. *The sun went down on the apple trees / and held the dark red seemingly forever.* This was the only line of Andrea's poetry that Olive could remember. Maybe because it was the only line she liked. She had read a great deal of Andrea's poetry. Everyone in town seemed to have read Andrea's poetry. Her books were always center on display at the bookstore. People said they loved her work. Andrea L'Rieux had been hailed as all sorts of things: feminist, postmodernist, political mixing with the natural.

She was a "confessional poet," and Olive thought there were some things a person need not confess. (There were *"angry vaginas"* in one poem, Olive remembered now.)

"Thank you," Andrea said. "For not talking to any reporter," she added. And then she shook her head and said, almost to herself, "I just hate it all."

"Oh, come on now," Olive said. "It has to be fun. You got to meet the president."

Andrea nodded. "I did."

"It's not everyone from Crosby, Maine, who gets to rub shoulders with the president." Olive added, "What was he like?"

"I think he just shook my hand." Now her eyes held mirth as she looked at Olive.

Olive said, "And his wife? Did you shake hands with her as well?"

"I did."

"So what are they like?" Olive loved this president. She thought he was smart, and his wife was smart, and what a hell of a job he had, with Congress being so horrible to him. She would be sorry to see him go.

"He was kind of arrogant. His wife was very nice. She said she read my poetry and loved it, blah-fucking-blah-blah." Andrea tugged a stray piece of hair back behind her ear.

Olive finished her egg. She thought surely a poet could find words other than the phrase

Andrea had just used. "Use your words," Olive had told her son, Christopher, when he was small. "Stop whining and use your words." Now Olive said to Andrea, "My husband—Jack, my second husband—he would have agreed with you about the arrogance." When the girl made no response to this, Olive asked, "What are you doing up here?"

Andrea exhaled a long sigh. "My father got sick. So—"

"My father killed himself," Olive said. She started in on her muffin, which she always kept until last.

"Your father did? He committed suicide?"

"That's right."

After a moment, Andrea asked, "How?"

"How? Gun."

"Really," Andrea said. "I had no idea." She put both hands on her ponytail and smoothed it over her shoulder. "How old were you?"

"Thirty. Why would you have any idea? I assume your father is not going to kill himself."

"I think it's unusual for a woman to use a gun," Andrea said, picking up the saltshaker and looking at it. "Men, yes, that's what they do. But women—usually I think it's pills with women." She sent the saltshaker spinning just slightly across the table.

"I wouldn't know."

"No." Andrea pulled her fingers through her

291

hair that was just above the ponytail. After a few moments, she said, "My father wouldn't know how to kill himself. He's, you know, not right in the head anymore. He never was right in the head. But you know what I mean."

"You mean he's demented. But what do you mean he was never right in the head?"

"I dunno." Andrea seemed deflated now. She shrugged. "He was just always—he was just always so *mean*."

Olive knew from Andrea's poetry that the girl had never liked her father, but Olive could not now seem to remember any particular reason for this, he was not a drunk, she'd have remembered that—Olive said, "So now he's going to die?"

"Supposedly."

"And your mother is dead." Olive knew this; the girl's poetry had been about that.

"Oh, she passed twenty years ago. She'd had eight kids. I mean, come *on*."

"You don't have any kids, am I right?" Olive glanced up as she pulled apart her muffin.

"No. I had enough of babies growing up."

"Never mind. Kids are just a needle in your heart." Olive drummed her fingers on the table-top, then put the muffin piece into her mouth. After she swallowed, she repeated, "Just a needle in your goddamn heart."

"How many do you have?"

"Oh, I have just the one. A son. That's enough.

292

I have a stepdaughter too. She's lovely. Lovely girl." Olive nodded. "A lesbian."

"Does she like you?"

This question surprised Olive. "I think she does," she said. "Yes, she does."

"So you have that."

"It's not the same. I met her when she was a grown-up, and she lives in California. It's not like your own kid."

"Why is your son a needle in your heart?" The girl asked this with hesitancy, as she tore at the orange peel that had garnished her plate.

"Who knows? Born that way, I guess." Olive wiped her fingers on a napkin. "You can put that in a poem. All yours."

The girl said nothing, only looked up through the window at the bay.

It was then that Olive noticed the girl's sweater, a navy-blue thing with a zipper up the front. But the cuffs were grimy, old-looking. Surely the girl could afford some nice clothes. Olive moved her eyes away quickly, as though she'd seen something she ought not to have seen. She said, "Well, it was good of you to let me join you. I'll be on my way."

The girl looked at her, startled. "Oh—" she said. "Oh, Mrs. Kitteridge, please don't go. Have some more coffee. Oh, you're not drinking coffee. Do you want a cup of coffee?"

"I don't drink coffee anymore," Olive said. "It

doesn't seem to agree with my bowels. But have some more if you'd like. I'll wait with you while you have some." She turned to find the girl who worked here, and the girl came right over and was very pleasant to Andrea. "There you go," the girl said, smiling—smiling!—at Andrea, and poured her a cup of coffee. "When you get old," Olive told Andrea after the girl had walked away, "you become invisible. It's just the truth. And yet it's freeing in a way."

Andrea looked at her searchingly. "Tell me how it's freeing."

"Well." Olive was slightly taken aback; she didn't know how to explain it. "It's just that you don't *count* anymore, and there is something freeing about that."

"I don't understand," the girl said. And what shot through Olive's mind was the thought: You're honest.

Olive said, "I don't think I can explain this well. But you go through life and you think you're something. Not in a good way, and not in a bad way. But you think you are something. And then you see"—and Olive shrugged in the direction of the girl who had served the coffee—"that you no longer are anything. To a waitress with a *huge* hind end, you've become invisible. And it's freeing." She watched Andrea's face and saw that it was struggling with something.

Finally the girl said, "Well, I envy you." And she laughed, and Olive saw that her teeth were bad; she wondered briefly why she had not seen this in photos of the girl. "I envy you for ever thinking you were something," Andrea said, her voice throaty.

"Oh, now stop it, Andrea. Last I heard you were Poet Laureate of this country a few years back."

"Yeah," said Andrea. "I was."

As they walked toward Olive's car, Olive going faster than she would have on her own, the girl rummaged in her coat pocket and the next thing Olive knew a plume of cigarette smoke was going over her. Olive felt a deep tremor of disappointment, and she thought: Well, she's just a L'Rieux. That's all she is. Famous or not.

Andrea said, as they stood by Olive's car, lifting her hand with the cigarette held between two fingers, "It's all about class now, smoking. It's like shooting heroin, but that's not really a class thing anymore." And then—and this surprised Olive like hell—the girl wrapped her arms around Olive and said, "It was so nice to see you, Mrs. Kitteridge." Olive thought her hair might catch on fire from the cigarette in the girl's hand.

"You too," said Olive, and she got into her car and started it, and backed away slowly, not looking out the window in the direction of the girl—it was a job to back a car up these days. All the way home she told Jack about what had happened; it was Jack, her second husband, whom she seemed to want to tell this to.

When she spoke on the telephone that night to her son, Christopher, who lived in New York City, she mentioned seeing the girl, and he said, "Who's Andrea L'Rieux? You mean one of the million L'Rieuxs in that family out on East Point Road?"

"Yes," Olive said, "the one who became Poet Laureate."

"Became what?" Christopher asked, not especially nicely, and Olive understood that Christopher did not follow Poets Laureate or anyone with whom he had grown up, though Andrea was younger than he was. "She became the Poet Laureate of the United States of America," Olive said, and Christopher said, "Well, whoopdee-do."

When she told her stepdaughter, Cassie, on the telephone, the child was far more appreciative. "Oh, Olive, how nice! Wow."

And when she told the owner of the bookstore—Olive walked in the next day with the sole purpose of telling him this—he said, "Hey, that's very, very cool. Andrea L'Rieux, man, she's just *amazing*."

"Yup," Olive said. "We had a nice chat. We had breakfast together. She was quite nice. Seemed very ordinary."

She called her friend Edith, whose husband, Buzzy, had helped her buy the car; they lived in the assisted-living place out by Littlehale's Farm; and Edith was pretty excited for her as well. "Olive, you're the kind of person people want to talk to."

"I don't know about that," Olive said, but then she thought that what Edith said was true. "She seemed a lonely child," Olive said. "As though all her fame and whatnot has meant nothing to her. Sad child. Ratty clothes, smoking her head off. Really, Edith, she was a lonely thing."

For a couple of weeks Olive waited to hear from Andrea. Each morning when she checked the mail, she realized she was waiting for a card, an old-fashioned, handwritten card that said, How lovely it was to see you, Mrs. Kitteridge. Let's stay in touch! The girl could get her address from the Internet. But no card came, and after a while Olive stopped waiting for it. When she saw in the newspaper that Severin L'Rieux had died, she wondered if Andrea was still in town, most likely she had come back for the funeral, which according to the paper would be held at St. John's, and that made sense to Olive; made her shudder a tiny bit too. All those French-Canadian Catholics, well—goodbye to Severin L'Rieux.

• • •

For their trip to Oslo, Jack had bought them first-class tickets for the plane. Olive was furious. "I don't fly first-class," she had said.

Jack had laughed. "You don't fly anywhere," he said, and that made her angrier.

"I'm not flying first-class. It's obscene."

"Obscene?" Jack sat down at the kitchen table and watched her, still with amusement in his face. "I like obscene." When she didn't answer him he said, "You know what, Olive? You're a snob."

"I am the opposite of a snob."

Jack laughed a long time. "You think being a reverse snob is not being a snob? Olive, you're a snob." Then he leaned forward and said, "Oh, come on, Olive. For Christ's sake. I'm seventy-eight years old, I have money, you have money—though, yes, I have a lot more money than you do—and if not now, when?"

"Never," she said.

So she had flown coach while he sat up front in first class. She could not believe he would do that, but he did. "Bye now," he said, waving his hand once, and she was left on her own to find her seat; it was the bulkhead. She sat in the aisle next to a large man—Olive was large herself—and by the window was the man's girlfriend, an Asian girl probably twenty years younger, but how could you tell with Asians. Before they had even taken off, she hated them both. She was ready to cry when the flight attendant took her bag from her and put it in the overhead bin. "I want my bag," Olive said, and the woman told her she could get it as soon as they were airborne.

The big man next to her kept turning toward his girlfriend, so his fat back was in Olive's space. She heard their conversation in bits and pieces, and she recognized early on that the man was a bully, he was bullying his young girlfriend. She thought they were disgusting. "This is what you should be listening to," the man said, and he repeated that many times. As though the girl had poor taste in music. And then the man whispered in his girlfriend's ear, and the girl leaned forward slightly to look at Olive. They were talking about her! She, with her knees bent up, unable to straighten her legs, an old woman—What in the world did they have to say about her? The Asian girl gave a little shrug and Olive heard her say, "Well, that's her life." Whose life? What did that girl know about Olive's life? Oh, she was fit to be tied, and she did not sleep a wink the whole flight over. At one point Jack stepped through the curtain dividing the cabin and said to her, "Well, hello, Olive! How's it going?"

"I want my bag," she told him. "If you could please get me my bag."

He got her bag from the overhead bin, placed it in her lap, whispered in her ear, "There, there, little miss."

"Go away, Jack," she said. And she saw the big man beside her watching her. She closed her eyes, and kept them closed; the flight was absolutely endless.

But as they went through customs Jack was kind to her. He said, "Let's get you to the hotel and get you some sleep." He kept his eye on her as they moved through the line. At the hotel she fell asleep immediately, and they boarded the boat the next day.

When he became sad a few days later, she felt terrible—and frightened. She thought he missed his wife (even though Olive was his wife). She thought she was all wrong for him. Finally, she said, "Jack, I think I'm not a good wife for you—" He looked at her with surprise; she could see his surprise at what she said. "Olive, you're actually the perfect wife for me. You really are." He smiled and reached for her hand. "I'm just homesick," he said. "All this goddamn beauty—" Tossing his head toward the window of their cabin. "It makes me miss the coast of Maine."

"I miss the coast of Maine too," she said. And after that they were fine. They had a wonderful time.

The last night on the boat, he said, "Oh, Olive, I got you a first-class ticket for the way home. Hope you don't mind." He winked at her.

And she could not believe the flight home. She

had her own seat that stretched backward and forward. It was like she was an astronaut, in her own little cubbyhole. There was a kit, with socks and a mask and a toothbrush, all for her! She ate a roast beef sandwich and had ice cream for dessert, and she could not stop looking across the aisle at Jack. He made a kissing sound and said, "Now, don't disturb me." And drank his glass of wine.

The second week of October, Olive went to get her hair cut by Janice Tucker, a woman who worked from her home. Olive always had the first appointment of the day, at eight o'clock, and as she settled into her chair, Janice wrapped the plastic apron around her and said, "I heard you had breakfast with Andrea L'Rieux."

"I did," said Olive. "I certainly did."

"Then you must feel terrible about her accident."

"What did you say?" Olive turned her head.

"In the paper just yesterday. I thought you'd have seen it. Wait, I'll get it for you." Janice turned around and went through a pile of newspapers on the table in the waiting area. She brought back the paper and said, "Here. Look at this. Oh, Olive, I thought you knew."

The small headline read: Former Poet Laureate Struck by Bus, Survives. And a small paragraph said that Andrea L'Rieux had been hit by a bus on a street in Boston, that she was in stable condition with a broken pelvis and internal injuries. A complete recovery was expected.

Olive felt a secretion from the back corners of her mouth. She put the paper on the counter and sat back and said nothing, while Janice got her little scissors and began to snip at Olive's hair. "So sad, right?" Janice asked, and Olive nodded. She felt awful. As the woman snipped tenderly at her hair, Olive felt worse and worse. And then realizing she had no Jack—or Henry, her first husband—to go home and tell this to, she said suddenly, "Janice, I think the girl was trying to kill herself."

Janice stood back, the scissors near her chest. "Olive, stop."

"No, I think she was. I've been sitting here thinking about it, and she talked about suicide to me. She said how men use guns and women tend not to use guns, they mostly use pills, and I should have known, I should have realized—"

"Now, Olive. Don't you think that. Do not even think that. I'm sure it's not true. She was hit by a bus, it happens, Olive."

"Janice, you didn't see her. She looked like hell. She wore a ratty little sweater, and she was smoking. She hated her father, and then he died. And that can make a person messed up too."

Janice seemed to think about this. And then she said, "Olive, I just don't believe that she tried to kill herself. I don't want to believe it, and so I'm not going to."

"Fine," said Olive. "Fine, fine, fine."

She did not tip Janice, as she usually did, and then she left, waving one hand above her shoulder as she went down the steps with her cane.

It was a glorious autumn. The leaves clung to the trees and were more vivid than they had been in years. People said this to one another, and it was true. And the sun shone down on all of it, day after day. It rained mostly at night, and the nights were cold, and the days were not too cold, but they were not warm. The world sparkled, and the yellows and reds, and orange and pale pinks, were just splendid for anyone driving down the road out to the bay. Olive could see this without driving; from her front door she saw the woods, and every morning when she opened the door she was aware of the beauty of the world.

This surprised her. When her first husband had died, she had not been aware of anything. This is what she thought. But here was the world, screeching its beauty at her day after day, and she felt grateful for it. Inside the front closet, Jack's coats and sweaters remained. And this was different too. She had gotten rid of Henry's clothes quickly, once he died. She had even started getting rid of them while he was still in the nursing home, the new pair of shoes he had on the day of his stroke, that he would never wear again—she had gotten rid of those quick as a flash. Camel-hair-colored suede shoes, the laces not yet dirty a bit.

But Jack's clothes she held on to, and the smell of them still arrived faintly when she opened the closet. There was the dark green cardigan with the leather elbow patches he wore when they went to dinner the first time, and the blue gabled one from when they'd had their first real fight and he had said, "God, Olive, you're a *difficult* woman. You are such a goddamn difficult woman, and fuck all, I love you. So if you don't mind, Olive, maybe you could be a little less Olive with me, even if it means being a little more Olive with others. Because I love you, and we don't have much time."

She'd heard him.

And then he'd said, sitting on the bed, "Let's get married, Olive. Sell the house you had with Henry and move in here. Please marry me, Olive."

"Why?" she had asked.

His slight smile, with one corner of his mouth turned up. "Because I love you," he said. "I just plain goddamn love you."

"Why?" she asked.

"Because you're Olive."

"You just said I was too much Olive."

"Olive. Shut up. Shut *up,* and marry me."

304

When he died in his sleep beside her, oceans of terror rolled over her. Day after day she was terrified. Come back, she kept thinking, oh please please please come back! Eight years they'd had together, as quickly over as an avalanche, and yet—horrible—she thought of him at times as her real husband. Henry had been her first, and then Jack had been her real one. Horrible thought, and it could not be true.

How quickly now darkness fell!

For Olive this meant a change in the way she lived. She did not drive when it was dark, and so by four o'clock she was in bed, watching her television set. She dozed a little bit, and would wake frightened. And then it would subside. She watched the news, and she was interested. What a hell of a mess this country was in. Then she ate her dinner, and had a glass of wine. The wine had arrived in her life with Jack. Before then Olive had never once imbibed. "Oh, for Christ's sake, Olive, would you have a glass of wine?" he said to her once, before they were married. "If anyone could use a glass of wine it's you." He himself had whiskey, and no small amount of it. But she had never seen him drunk. Still, she had bristled when he said that, about her needing a glass of wine. And yet he had been right. Because when she had one a few nights later, she felt like she was—She just felt all right.

And alone, without Jack, the wine still helped her. She never had more than one glass, but she thought it still helped her.

Winter came.

It snowed as though it would not stop, white swirling stuff, or white gritty stuff, every few days a new storm hit. For Olive, these were days of torture. She could not believe how long time was—how long the afternoons were—she could not believe it! And yet she should have known, she must have known, because of when Henry had his stroke. But she was always going to the nursing home then, it seemed she had been busy. Had she been? Well, she was not busy now. She had the newspaper delivered because there were days she could not drive with all the snow. And one day she saw a small article about Andrea L'Rieux. The bus driver who had hit her had been drunk; the investigation had just closed. Really? Olive read through it again, and tossed the paper aside. Well, so Janice Tucker had been right. Andrea had not been trying to kill herself after all. "Fine," Olive said out loud. "Fine, fine, fine."

She looked at the clock and it was only two.

And then May finally arrived.

Olive opened the door to step outside, only wanting to see the view of the woods that spread out beyond the curved driveway. From the front door one could see the long, large field, but Olive liked this view too, she supposed because it reminded her of the woods by the house with Henry. Turning to go back inside, she saw in her mailbox a magazine; it was sticking partway out as though to get her attention, and she was surprised, the mail would not be here for hours. It said *American Poetry Review*, and then she saw there was a Post-it someone had put near the front as though to mark a page. Taking it, she went inside and closed the door, and before she had even left the foyer, she saw on the cover that it said: New Poetry by Andrea L'Rieux.

Seated now at the breakfast nook, she opened it to the page that had the Post-it and read: *Accosted.* Olive did not understand why that had been marked, until slowly, as she read the poem, it came to her, like she was moving—very, very slowly—under water. *Who taught me math thirty-four years ago / terrified me and is now terrified herself / sat before me at the breakfast counter / white whiskered / told me I had always been lonely / no idea she was speaking of herself.* Olive read on. It was all there, her father's suicide, her son being a needle in her heart; the poem's theme, pounded home again and again, was that she—Olive—was the lonely, terrified one. It finished, *Use it for a poem, she said / All yours.*

Olive stood unsteadily and walked to the

307

garbage and put the magazine in it. Then she sat down again and looked out at the field. She tried to understand what had happened, all the while knowing—but not believing—what had happened. And then she realized that someone in town had dropped the magazine off at night, had driven up to her house and put that damned magazine in her mailbox, having stuck that Post-it to the page so that Olive would be sure to see it, and this stung her even more deeply than the poem had. She recalled how years and years ago her mother had opened the door one morning and a basket of cow flaps had sat there on the step, with a note that said, For Olive. She never knew who had brought the cow flaps, and she could not think who would have brought this magazine.

After a few minutes, or maybe an hour—Olive did not know how much time went by, how long she sat immobile at her table—she went and got the magazine from the garbage and read the poem again. This time she spoke out loud: "Andrea, this poem *stinks*." But her cheeks became very warm; she could not remember her cheeks ever becoming as warm as they did while she sat there looking at the poem. She started to rise to put the magazine in the garbage again, but she did not want it even in the house, and so she found her cane and walked to her car and drove out past Juniper Bay, where she found a garbage can for the public, and there was no one around, and so Olive, taking the Post-it from it, threw the magazine in there.

When she got back to the house she telephoned Edith. Edith said, "Olive, how are you?"

"What do you mean, how am I? I'm fine. Why wouldn't I be fine?" She thought she heard in Edith's voice some knowledge of the poem.

"Well, I don't know," Edith said. "I don't know how you are, that's why I'm asking."

"How's Buzzy these days?" Olive asked.

"Oh, Buzzy's fine. You know, he's Buzzy. Gets up at the crack of dawn, goes out and gets our coffee and brings it back, same as always."

"Well, you're lucky he's around," Olive said.

"Oh yes, my word. I am lucky." Edith said this with more feeling than Olive thought she needed to.

"Goodbye," Olive said.

She walked around the house that day and thought about Buzzy getting up early, driving to get their coffee. But where in the world would Buzzy get a copy of *American Poetry Review*? Buzzy wouldn't have known poetry if it walked up and introduced itself to him. Buzzy had built houses for a living. But still, Edith had asked her how she was. Christopher had said to her one time, "You're paranoid, Mom." She hadn't liked that a bit, and she didn't like it now, thinking of it.

• • •

That night, Olive soiled herself while she was asleep, and she woke immediately with the warmth of her excrement seeping from her. "Horrors," she whispered to herself. This had happened twice before, since Jack died, and Olive would not tell her doctor, or anyone. As she changed the sheet and showered—it was one in the morning—she thought about Andrea. And she thought how she, Olive, had always held it against Andrea that she was French-Canadian. She had. Almost without knowing it, she'd held it against all the L'Rieuxs. And against the Labbes and the Pelletiers, although once in a while a kid surprised her, like the Galarneau girl who had light in her face and was so smart, Olive had liked her. Was this the truth? It was the truth. Olive sat down on the edge of her bed. *It's a class thing, like shooting heroin. Only that's not so much lower-class anymore.*

Jack's voice: "You're a snob, Olive. You think being a reverse snob is not being a snob? Well, you're a snob, my dear."

Olive had approached Andrea L'Rieux that day at the marina because the girl was famous. That's why she had sat herself down and talked to her like she knew her. If Andrea L'Rieux had never become the Poet Laureate of the United States, if she had just been what Olive would have expected of her—another woman with children and sort of happy and mostly unhappy (her sad-faced walks)—then Olive would never have approached her. She hadn't even liked the girl's poetry, except for the line about the darkness and the red leaves. But she had sat down across from her because she was famous. And also because she, Olive, was—Andrea was right—lonely. She, Olive Kitteridge, who would not have thought this about herself at all. She said fiercely, out loud, "You remember this, Olive, you fool, you remember this."

In the semi-dark of the bedroom, Olive got out her small computer, and she went to Andrea's Facebook page. She had never written a comment before, and she at first couldn't figure out how to do it. But then she did, and she wrote, "Saw your new work. Good for you." She sat looking out the window at the darkness of the field; only one streetlamp, far away, could be seen from here. She went back to the computer and added a line: "Glad you're not dead."

For a long time, Olive sat on the bed; she was just looking through the glass at the dark field. It seemed to her she had never before completely understood how far apart human experience was. She had no idea who Andrea L'Rieux was, and Andrea had no idea who Olive was, either. And yet. And yet. Andrea had gotten it better than she had, the experience of being another. How funny. How interesting. She, who always thought that she knew everything that others did not. It just wasn't true. *Henry.* This word went through Olive's mind as she gazed through the window at the darkness. And then: *Jack.* Who were they, who had they been? And who—who in the world—was she? Olive put one hand to her mouth as she contemplated this.

Then Olive put the computer away and got back into bed. She spoke the words softly out loud: "Yup, Andrea. Good for you. Glad you're not dead."

The End of the Civil War Days

The MacPhersons lived in a large old house on the outskirts of Crosby, Maine. They had been married for forty-two years, and for the last thirty-five they had barely spoken to each other. But they still shared the house. In his youth, Mr. MacPherson—his name was Fergus—had had an affair with a neighbor; back then there was no forgiveness and no divorce. So they were stuck together in their house. For a while their younger daughter, Laurie, had come back home briefly, her marriage had broken up and she and her six-year-old son came to live with them— both Fergus and his wife had been gladdened by their arrival, in spite of its cause—but very soon Laurie said that "their continued arrangement," as she put it, was too unhealthy for her child, and so she left, moving to a small apartment near Portland.

Their arrangement was this: They lived with strips of yellow duct tape separating the living room in half; it ran over the wooden floor and right up against the rug that Ethel MacPherson had put on her side of the room; and in the dining room the tape was there as well, running over the dining room table, dividing it in half exactly, running down into the air and then onto the floor. Each night Ethel made dinner and placed her plate on one side of the taped table, and placed her husband's plate on the other side. They ate in silence, and when Ethel was done eating she put her plate on her husband's side of the table and then she left the room; he did the dishes. The kitchen had been taped too, years earlier, but because of the sink and the cupboards, which both MacPhersons needed access to, especially in the morning, they had let the tape become peeled in places and they mostly ignored it. As they ignored each other. Their bedrooms were on separate floors, so that was not an issue.

The main issue, naturally, was the televisions in their living room. On either side of the duct tape sat a television; Fergus's was the bigger of the two, and Ethel's was older. For years they sat there in the evenings—Fergus drawing his fingers through his beard; Ethel, who in the early years might have had her curlers in, but eventually she cut her hair short and dyed it an orangey-yellow; she still was often knitting—watching separate shows on their televisions, each turning up the volume to drown out the other. But then a few years ago Fergus—right before he retired from the ironworks, where he had been a draftsman—went and got a fancy set of earphones that were attached to something like an old-fashioned telephone cord that he stuck into his television, and so he sat in his lounge chair with his earphones on, and Ethel could keep her television down to almost a regular sound.

In any event, their older daughter, Lisa, was coming home in a week for her annual visit from New York City, where she had moved eighteen years earlier. There was something about her that Fergus could never quite put his finger on: She was a pretty thing, but she never mentioned a boyfriend except for once in a very great while. Now she was close to forty, and the fact that she would probably not have children saddened him. Fergus had a special place for Lisa in his heart that he did not have for her younger sister, Laurie, though he loved Laurie as well. Lisa had a job as the administrative assistant to a program at the New School. "So you're a secretary," Fergus had said, and she had said, Yeah, well, basically she was.

Now—it was a Friday evening in early August—Fergus said out loud to his television, "Goddammit," and this caused his wife to begin to sing. "La-la-lahhh-la, deedly-dee-dum," she sang out loudly because she hated when he swore, but he had his earphones on and probably couldn't hear, so she gave it up. Fergus had sworn because his daughter's visit was going to coincide with the Civil War Days in the park next week, which Fergus always took part in, dressing up like a Union soldier and marching back and forth on Saturday and shooting a rifle—they were blanks, of course—and then he slept in his little canvas pup tent in the park with the other soldiers, and they cooked their meals on tiny makeshift stoves like the kind that were used in the Civil War days. It was Fergus's job to beat the drum, along with one other man, a nasty old codger named Ed Moody from down the coast who—when he joined a few years ago—seemed to think that he was the drummer; there had been trouble about that, but the regiment had finally said that both men could beat a drum. In truth, Fergus's enthusiasm for this entire thing had been waning, but he knew his wife laughed at him for partaking in it, and so he continued to do so. He had, when he thought about it, always preferred the St. Andrews group—the Highland Games when men of Scottish ancestry all wore their kilts and marched about the fairgrounds, bagpipes whining; Fergus played the drum for them as well, as he marched in his kilt of the MacPherson plaid.

The dog, who had been lying in the corner of the room, a small—now old—cocker spaniel named Teddy, rose and walked over to Fergus and wagged his tail. Fergus took his earphones off. Ethel said, "I hope your father plans on taking you out, I don't feel like it tonight," and Fergus said, "Tell your mother to hush up." Fergus rose, and as he was leaving with the dog he said, "Teddy, I guess we'll go to the grocery store," and his wife said, "I hope to heck Fergus doesn't forget the milk." In this way, they communicated.

For years Ethel had worked in the town clerk's office, giving out fishing licenses and dog licenses and things of that sort to people who came in. So she was friendly with Anita Coombs, who still worked there, and tonight at the grocery store Anita was in line when Fergus walked up with the milk and his cans of baked beans and his hot dogs. "Hello, Fergus," said Anita, her face widening in pleasure. She was a short woman with glasses, who had sorrows of her own; Fergus knew this from listening to his wife on the telephone. Fergus gave her a nod. "How's everyone?" Anita asked. And Fergus said everyone was just fine. In his pocket his hand went around the roll of bills he always carried. Years ago, his wife had said to the girls that their father was so cheap he'd hang up the used toilet paper to dry if he could, and he had been stung by that; ever since, he carried around a roll of cash as if that made it not true.

"Getting ready for those Civil War Days?"

Anita asked as she took out her credit card and stuck it in the slot for credit cards. Fergus said he was. Anita squinted at the card in the machine, then turned to Fergus and said, touching the edge of her eyeglasses, "I heard that you folks may not be spending the night in the park this year. Too many druggies out at night now."

Fergus felt a splinter of alarm go through him. "Don't know," he said. "Guess we're considering all angles."

Anita took back her card, then took her recycling bag of groceries and hoisted it over her shoulder. "You say hi to Ethel," she said, and he said he'd do that, and she said, "Awful nice to see you, Fergie," and she left the store.

In his car in the parking lot of the grocery store, Fergus took out his phone and saw a text from Bob Sturdges, who was the captain of their little Civil War army. It said: Got some problems, give me a call when you can. So Fergus called him from the car and found out that what Anita had said was partly true: They were not going to be spending the night in the park. But Anita had been wrong about the druggies. It was because there was too much political stuff happening around the country these days, too many people upset about things; they had already stopped having Confederate soldiers in their unit, but you never knew. And also, the men were getting old. These were the reasons Bob Sturdges gave to Fergus about why they would not be spending the night in the park; Fergus felt disappointment and then, when he hung up, some relief. So they would go pitch their tents on Saturday and that would be that.

Lisa had telephoned to say she'd be late; she'd flown to Portland and rented a car, and she'd told her parents—who each held a telephone receiver in their hand—that she was going to visit her sister on her way up. Traditionally, the girls had never been especially close; both Fergus and Ethel noted to themselves that it was curious that Lisa would stop and pay Laurie a visit rather than wait for Laurie to come to the house with her son, which is what Laurie had always done in the past.

But now Lisa's car could be heard turning in to the driveway, and her mother went to the door and waved and called out, "Hello, Lisa! Hello!" And Lisa got out of the car and said, "Hi, Mom," and they sort of hugged each other, which is what they always did, a sort of half a hug. "Let me help you," said her mother, and Lisa said, "No worries, Mom, I've got it." Lisa's dark hair was pulled back in a low ponytail, longer than it was last year, and her dark eyes—always large—shone with light. Ethel watched her daughter bring in her little suitcase, and then Ethel said, "You're in love." It's because of how Lisa looked that her mother said this; there was an extra layer of beauty to her face.

"Oh, Mom," said Lisa, closing the door behind her.

A few years back, Fergus had had a fling with a woman at the Civil War Days. Her name was Charlene Bibber, and she was one of the women who dressed up in a hoop skirt and a shawl and a small cap over her head with the handful of other women there who were dressed like that—most of them wives of the so-called soldiers—and that night Fergus had some whiskey and he found himself at the edge of the park—it was a glorious night—and there was Charlene, whose husband had been a soldier until he'd died the year before, and Fergus said, "You're a pretty thing tonight," and she had giggled. In fact, Charlene had graying hair and was plump, but that night she seemed to exude something that Fergus wanted. He took her around the waist and then messed around with her a bit while she kept saying, "Fergie, you naughty boy, you!" Laughing as she said it, and then up by the bandstand they had done it; the surprise of this, and the hustling of getting that damned hoop skirt up, had made it seem exciting at the time. But when he woke in his pup tent the next morning he thought, Oh holy Christ, and he found her and whispered an apology to her, and she acted as though nothing had happened, which he thought extremely rude.

"Listen, you guys," Lisa said. She had kissed her father, who had stood up to greet her and who was now sitting back down in his lounge chair, and Lisa sat down in a chair across from her mother, next to her mother's television, but then she got up and moved the chair so that it was directly on the strip of yellow duct tape; she looked back and forth between her parents. She touched the long bangs that fell onto her face, moving them slightly aside. "I stopped and saw Laurie on the way up—"

Fergus said, "We know, Lisa. That was good of you."

Lisa glanced at him and said, "And I told her something, and she said I had to tell you guys, that if I didn't she would—so I have to tell you." The dog sat at Lisa's feet, and he suddenly whined and wagged his tail, poking at Lisa's jeaned legs with his nose.

"So tell us," said Ethel. Ethel took a glimpse at her husband; he was looking at Lisa impassively.

Lisa smoothed her long brown ponytail over her shoulder, and her eyes were very bright. "There's a documentary that's been made." She said this and raised her eyebrows. "And it stars me." Then she turned to the dog, patting him, and making kissing sounds toward him.

Fergus said, "What do you mean, a documentary?"

"What I said," Lisa answered.

Fergus sat up straight in his chair. "Now, hold on," he said. "You're starring in a documentary? I didn't know documentaries had stars."

"Tell your father to hush up," Ethel said. "And then tell me about this documentary. What do you mean, you're starring in it? Honey, this is so exciting."

Lisa nodded. "Well, it is, frankly. Very exciting."

A few times during the summer months, after the Highland Games in June, Fergus would put on his kilt—not the one with the MacPherson plaid, but a different one of plain color; he had gained weight and bought the last one at a store for only twenty-one dollars and ninety-nine cents, the price had pleased him—and he walked the streets of Crosby. He enjoyed this; people were pleasant, and he liked the feel of the kilt; he wore it with a gray T-shirt that matched his gray beard, and he wore his brown walking shoes with it as well. People, often summer people, would stop and talk to him, and they spoke of their own Scottish pasts, if they had one, and he was always surprised—and pleased—at how many people were proud of their ancestry this way. Years earlier there had been a pack of boys up near High Street that would call out, "What does a Scottish man wear under his kilt? A wang, a wang," and they would convulse with laughter. He had felt like throwing stones at them, but of course he did not, and he noticed as the years went by that this sort of thing happened much less frequently and so he had his own private theory that people were becoming more tolerant—about a man wearing a kilt, anyway, if not more tolerant about the mess in the country—and this pleased him.

"About your work?" Ethel was asking Lisa. "Or is this a documentary about someone who comes from a small town and lives in New York City?"

Lisa closed her eyes, and opened them. "About my work," she said. She stood up. "Oh, you guys, we'll talk about this later. Let me get unpacked."

Fergus said, "No, tell us now, Lisa. Spit it out, kid. Not everyone stars in a documentary."

Lisa looked at him. "Well. Okay. Now, listen, you guys. I'm a dominatrix," she said.

Fergus couldn't sleep. He stared at the dark above his head. Then he closed his eyes and immediately felt afraid and so he kept his eyes open, but he couldn't sleep that way. After almost two hours he got out of bed and went down the hall and listened, and he heard Lisa moving about her room, so he knocked lightly on the door.

"Dad?" She stepped back and let him in. She

was dressed in her pajamas; they were pink silky-looking things, the bottoms long.

"You know, Lisa," he said. He put his hand to the back of his head. "You know, if it's money you need, honest to God, just say the word. I never should have assumed you could have made it on your own down there—"

"Dad, it's not the money. Well, it kind of is, I guess, but that's not the point." Lisa put her hand to her hair, which was out of its ponytail now, and she smoothed it over her shoulder; it looked glossy to Fergus, like a television ad.

He sat down on her bed; his legs felt weak. "What is the point?" he said.

"Oh, Dad." She looked at him with such great sadness on her face that he had to look away.

Earlier—that afternoon, after a great deal of confusion, especially from Ethel, who did not understand what a dominatrix was and who kept saying, "I just don't understand what you mean, Lisa"—Lisa, after explaining to her mother what she did as a dominatrix, that she dressed up and had men play out their sexual fantasies, had said to her parents, "People need to be educated."

"Why?" Ethel and Fergus had said this at the same time.

"So *they* can *understand*," Lisa said. "Just like how Mom doesn't even know what we do."

Fergus had unwittingly walked across the tape to his wife's side of the living room. "People don't need to understand that kind of behavior. Good God, Lisa." He tugged on his beard, walking about. Then he said, "You're only excited because some damn person, some goddamn nimrod, decided to make a movie about this."

"A documentary," Lisa said. She said, almost with exasperation, "It isn't about sex, Dad. I'm not a *prostitute,* Dad." She added, looking up at him, "I don't have sex with any of these men, you know."

"I don't understand," Ethel said, moving her hand through her hair; she stood up and looked around and then sat right back down. "I really don't understand any of this."

Fergus felt puzzled but—only slightly—relieved to hear that she didn't have sex with anyone, but he said, "What do you mean it's not about sex? Of course it's about sex, Lisa. Come on."

"It's about playacting. Dressing up." Lisa's voice sounded like she was trying to be patient. "If you watched it, you might learn something. Laurie watched it."

"You have it?" Fergus asked.

"Yeah, I have a DVD. I'm not suggesting you watch it, I'm just saying if you *did*—"

Now, late at night, Lisa only said, still with the sadness in her face, "Go to sleep, Dad. I never should have told you. It was a mistake. But you know, you might have found out, because it will go public, and I thought you should know."

"You don't have sex with these men?" Fergus asked.

"I don't, Dad. No."

Fergus backed out of the room. "Good night," he said.

"Sweet dreams," Lisa called to him.

And Fergus could not believe she said that.

In the morning, Fergus overslept—he had not fallen asleep for ages—and when he woke he could hear Lisa and her mother in the kitchen. He knelt and got out his Civil War uniform from the trunk beneath his bed; the hat seemed squashed, and he punched it a few times. The whole uniform looked wrinkled; he had not taken it to the cleaners to have it pressed as he had in the past. "Oh, for Christ's sake," he murmured to himself. He put it on, got out the small brush for his mustache, which he tried curling at the ends, then went into the bathroom and sprayed hairspray on it, which got into his eyes and stung like hell.

In the kitchen, while sunlight was streaming through the window, he said to Lisa, "Good morning," and she smiled at him—"Hi, Dad"—and he poured himself a bowl of cereal and took it into the dining room, and then he did something he never did, which was to sit on Ethel's side of the yellow duct tape, and he did that so he could hear better what they were saying. But they were talking about dish towels. Dish towels! Lisa was saying that she'd like to go to that store out by Cook's Corner where they have nice dish towels, and Ethel was murmuring something that sounded like Okay, they could do that. Fergus finished his cereal and went back to the kitchen, rinsed the bowl, and told Lisa that he was going off and would see her tonight. "Have a good time," Lisa said. And then his wife said, "Tell your father to enjoy his day," which kind of surprised him, and he said to Lisa to tell her mother thank you.

But he did not have a good day. Taking it from the garage, he put his pup tent into the back of his truck, and when he got to the park everyone was already there; in fact, he heard the gunshots before he even pulled up. It seemed a motley crew this time, not as many men were there as usual, and he got out his tent and walked over to Bob Sturdges, who greeted him and said, "Over there," pointing to a place near the pup tents that Fergus was to use for his own, and Fergus was already too hot in his uniform as he put the damned thing up. He could not stop thinking about Lisa. He thought of her as a young girl, home from school at the end of the day: She'd always been a cheerful sort, not like Laurie, who was prone to sulking.

One of the men nearby—Fergus could not remember his name—was cooking something on a tiny grill placed over a little fire, and Fergus took his coffee—he had cheated and ground the beans earlier—and his tin cup and went and sat with this man, who said, "Hello, Fergus!" And Fergus made his coffee, feeling like a fool, and sat and drank it with this man, whose name finally came to him, Mark Wilton. "Not so many folks today," said Mark, and Fergus said no, there weren't.

From above them the sun came down sharply; they were in a tiny spot of shade from an oak tree, but much of the park was in full sunlight. The oaks and maples caused a dappling of the brightness, and Fergus suddenly remembered the park when he had been a kid here; there were elms in those days, and their leaves were so full, so thick, that the park had felt like it was garlanded. The grass in his memory had been greener as well, and in fact these days there was a whole section of the park that was just dirt, caused by the farmers market that showed up twice a week, the carts ruining the grass below.

Turning, Fergus saw a woman walking toward them in a long dress, skirt puffed out, bright blue, and she was carrying a little blue parasol against the sun. He could see her face, and what struck him was the look of almost-smugness on it. But it wasn't smugness, he realized, as much as a suppressed joy for being able to wear such a dress today. She was a big woman to begin with, and the dress made her appear even bigger. "Hello, Fergus," she said as she got closer to him, and God Almighty if it wasn't Charlene Bibber.

"Hello, Charlene, that's quite a dress you've got on today." Fergus gave her a nod.

"Yes, it is," said Mark Wilton. "Look at you."

"Well, thank you, boys. I made this dress myself by *hand*." Charlene stood there, a few beads of sweat lining her upper lip. "I thought to myself, no sewing machines back in those days, so off we go, Charlene, you can do this, and so I did."

Fergus stood up and said, If they would excuse him, he'd forgotten something back at his house.

"What'd you forget?" asked Charlene, and he just shook his head. As he got into his truck he saw that she was still watching him.

In the driveway, he was surprised to see Laurie's car, and even more surprised when he saw his grandson, Teddy—named after the dog—sitting in the back seat of the car. "Teddy Bear," said Fergus, opening the car door. "What are you doing sitting here all alone?"

The boy looked at him with serious eyes. "Mom said I couldn't come in, that the conversation was something I couldn't hear."

"Uh-oh," said Fergus. He loved this kid like the devil. "Aren't you kind of hot?"

The boy nodded. "But I got the windows down. She said she wouldn't be long."

"How long has she been in there?"

The boy shrugged. "I don't know. Not very long, I guess. I just wish—" He looked around miserably. "I just wish I didn't have to sit here." Then he said, quizzically, "Grandpa, you've got your uniform on. It looks different."

"Come sit on the porch, at least," said Fergus. "Come on, I'll take the blame if you get in trouble for just sitting on the porch. Come on, Bear." And so Teddy got out of the car with a book, and he sat down on the first step of the porch.

"Why does your uniform look different?" Teddy asked.

"Oh, it's not pressed."

"Pressed?" Teddy asked, squinting up at his grandfather.

"It's not ironed. Probably why it looks different." Fergus glanced down at his pants, and was struck by how rumpled they were.

Through the open window came sudden hollering.

Teddy looked up at Fergus with alarm in his eyes, and Fergus said, "Okay, back in the car, kid. I'll come get you soon. I promise." And so the boy returned to the car, and said, "It's going to be okay, right?" And Fergus said, "You bet it

330

is," and he thought the boy's face relaxed some, and this pleased Fergus unduly.

"Did she tell you?" Laurie flung these words at her father when he walked into the house. "Did she?"

"She did," Fergus said. "Just calm down."

"That she sticks pins in men's penises? Did she tell you that?"

Fergus had to sit down. "For Christ's sake, Laurie. Stop it." His scrotum seemed to shrivel as he said this.

"You're telling me to stop it? I can't believe you're telling me to stop it. I'm the normal one in the family! Oh my God, your daughter is a *prostitute* and you're telling *me* to calm down." Laurie's neck stuck forward a bit as she said this.

"Yes, I am," Fergus said. "I am asking you to calm down right now, Laurie MacPherson. This is not helping matters one bit."

Laurie turned to her mother. "Mom. Help me out here. Please."

But Ethel, who had been standing behind her chair, now sat down in it and she said only, "Oh, Laurie." She added, "But she's not a prostitute, Laurie. I think."

"Oh my God," said Laurie. She dropped her pocketbook onto the floor and put both hands on her hips.

"It's just that I don't know what to say," Ethel said. "Can't you understand that? I just don't know what to *say*. The whole thing has been—it's just been awful."

"You *think?*" Laurie gave a little dramatic head toss as she said this.

Fergus said, "Laurie, for Christ's sake, calm the hell down. Now."

Laurie pressed her lips together, then reached down and picked up her pocketbook. She said quietly, "This is the sickest family that ever lived on God's earth." She turned and walked through the door, slamming it so hard that a pan on the other side of the kitchen fell from a shelf it was on.

Fergus rose and went after her. "Teddy Bear," he said to his grandson, bending down to speak to him through the car window, "let's you and I see each other soon. Your mother's mad at the moment, but she'll get over it, and then you and I can go fishing."

"Fishing," said Laurie, as she strapped her seatbelt on. "You can go effing fishing all right." And she drove out of the driveway with her tires squealing while her poor son looked down at his lap as Fergus waved to him.

In the living room, Lisa seemed serene. She was wearing a white T-shirt and jeans, and she looked young. She was speaking to her mother, and she turned her body slightly to include her father as he came in and sat in his chair. A glance at Ethel made Fergus actually feel sorry for his wife; she seemed frightened, and smaller physically. Lisa was saying, "You know, I just want to say, Mrs. Kitteridge told us, years ago in that math class—I will never forget it—one day she just stopped a math problem she was doing on the board and she turned around and she said to the class, 'You all know who you are. If you just look at yourself and listen to yourself, you know exactly who you are. And don't forget it.' And I never did forget it. It kind of gave me courage over the years because she was right; I did know who I was."

"You knew you were a—a dominatrix?" Fergus asked. "Is that what you're saying?"

"Kind of, yes, that is what I'm saying. I knew, I always knew I loved to dress up, and I like to tell people what to do, I *like* people, Dad, and these people have certain needs and I get to fulfill them, and that's a pretty great thing."

Ethel said, "I'm just not understanding this. I am not understanding this at all." Her eyes seemed like they were turning in different directions; this is the image Fergus got when he glanced at her again. He also noticed that the roots of her hair were dark and the yellow parts were sticking out; she must have been running her hand through it—yes, there, she did it, ran her hand through her hair. "Honey, I'm trying," Ethel said. "Lisa, I am trying, but I just don't *get* it."

Lisa nodded patiently. Her dark eyes shone and

her face had that glow that it had when she had first walked into the house. "And this is exactly why we're doing the documentary. Because people don't have to feel so—so, so, you know, marginalized anymore if they are into this stuff. It's all just human behavior, and that's what we're trying to say." She smoothed her hair over her shoulder; she had a confidence that was notable.

Fergus cleared his throat, and sat forward with his elbows on his knees. "If putting needles into some man's penis is acceptable human behavior, then something's very, very wrong." He tugged on his beard. "*God,* Lisa." He stood and turned to leave the room, then turned back and said, "Human behavior? For Christ's sake, the concentration camps run by the Nazis were human behavior. What's this defending-human-behavior crap? Honestly, Lisa!"

And then the tears came. Buckets of them. Lisa wept and wept, her eyes becoming smudged and causing black stuff to roll down her cheeks. How could he say she was a *Nazi?* How could he *say* that? And then, after minutes of sobbing noisily, she said it was because of ignorance. She stood up; there was a smudge of black eye makeup on her white T-shirt. "I love you, Dad," she said. "But you are ignorant."

By the side of the road stood Anita Coombs, next to a low blue car with a bent fender. Fergus pulled his truck over and got out. There were no other cars around, it was on the road out toward the Point, and all one could see were fields. The sun beat down and made Anita's fender glint. "Oh, Fergie," she said as he approached. "Boy, am I glad to see you. This damn car broke down."

Fergus put his hand out, and she handed him the key. Squashed into the driver's seat, he tried to start the car and nothing happened. He tried a few more times, then got out and said, "It's dead. Did you call anyone?"

"Yeah." Anita gave a great sigh and looked at her watch. "They said they'd be here in fifteen minutes, and that was half an hour ago."

"Let me call them," said Fergus, and he took Anita's phone and called the tow people and spoke to them brusquely. He gave her back the phone. "Okay," he said. "They're on their way." He leaned against her car and folded his arms. "I'll wait with you," he added.

"Thanks, Fergie." Anita seemed tired. She put her hands into the front pockets of her jeans and shook her head slowly. Then she said, "Where're you headed?"

"Nowhere," said Fergus, and Anita nodded.

It was Sunday afternoon. Fergus had gone back to the park in the dark last night and found his pup tent, standing by itself—he had been vaguely surprised to see that it was still there—and he had packed it up and put it into the back of his truck.

Also in the back of his truck now, in a garbage bag, was his Civil War uniform, with the boots and the cap. This morning after breakfast—she had seemed calm again, never mentioning her foolish documentary—Lisa said, "I'm going to call Laurie. I don't like that she's so mad at me." Fergus almost said, "I'm mad at you too," but he didn't; he just took the dishes and washed them while Ethel remained at the dining-room table, drumming her fingers on it. They could both hear, from Lisa's room, her voice, but could not make out the words. But Lisa talked and talked and talked, and after a while Ethel said, "Come on, Teddy," and took the dog out for a walk. When she came back she asked, "Still talking?" And after a moment Fergus said, "Yes." Then he said, "Teddy, tell your mother I'm going for a drive," and he had gone out in his truck with the intention of taking his Civil War uniform to the garbage can out near the Point and dumping it in there. In the truck he had said out loud a few times, "Creag Dhubh!" which was the war cry of the MacPherson clan, and then he stopped it; he thought of the Highland Games and wondered if that was foolishness too: standing there every summer in his kilt yelling that with the rest of the clan.

Now he said to Anita, "What do you think of Olive Kitteridge?"

"Olive?" said Anita. "Oh, I've always liked her

myself. She's not everyone's cup of tea, but I like her." After a moment she said "Why do you ask?" and Fergus just shook his head. Anita gave a small laugh. "She was the one—did Ethel tell you this?—who suggested to us when we were filling out those fishing licenses and they asked for the weight of the person, Olive said, 'Why don't you ask them what they think a game warden would say about how much they weighed?' It was kind of brilliant. You know, you get these fatties in there and you don't want to just say, Hey, how much do you weigh? So we started doing that."

"Anita," Fergus said, turning to her. "This is a hell of a world we live in."

"Oh, I know," Anita said casually. She nodded. "Yuh, I know." She added, "Always has been, I suspect."

"Do you think so?" Fergus asked. He looked at her through his sunglasses. "Do you think it has always been this bad, really? It seems to me like things are getting crazier."

Anita shrugged. "I think they've always been crazy. That's my view."

And so Fergus thought about this.

After another few moments he said, "Things all right with you, Anita?"

She gave a sigh that made her cheeks expand for a moment. "Nah." She looked both ways on the road and said, "Gary's been a mess since he got laid off, and that was a few years ago, and my kids are crazy." She looked at Fergus and made a circle around her ear with her forefinger. She said, "I mean, they are really crazy." She shook her head. "You know what my oldest son is into? He watches some Japanese reality show on his computer where the contestants sniff each other's butts."

Fergus looked over at her. *"God,"* he said. Then he said, "Come on, Anita, the world has certainly gotten crazier."

"Oh, maybe a little, who knows." Anita shrugged slightly.

Fergus finally said, looking at the ground, "Well, kids. What can you do."

"Nothing," said Anita. "How are your girls?"

"Oh, they're crazy too. Batty as can be." He saw the tow truck across the field and motioned toward it and Anita said, "Oh, good."

"You're going to need cash for the tow," Fergus said. "You got it?"

"No, just my credit card."

Fergus reached into his pocket and gave Anita his roll of cash. He waited until the tow truck was driving away, Anita sitting in the front seat of it, waving to him, and then he got back into his truck and drove to the Point and threw his uniform into the garbage, pushing the bag all the way down into the bin. He wondered about Anita's children, how crazy they were, or were not. Watching people sniff each other's butts?

Jesus *God.* That was pretty goddamn crazy stuff.

Back home, he was surprised once again to see Laurie's car in the driveway, but no Teddy sat in it, and when he walked into the house he heard his television on. He knew it was his, and not Ethel's, because of the kind of sound it made. He went straight into the living room and found Ethel and his daughters all sitting on his lounge chair, Ethel on the front edge of it, and one girl on each arm, and he was about to open his mouth and say What the hell when he saw that on the television screen was—it was Lisa—and she was dressed in leather and holding a whip, and she cracked the whip and a man moaned; his face was on the floor, turned to its side, and the image pixelated his face, but his buttocks were bare, and again this woman—Lisa—whipped him and again he moaned.

"Turn that off," Fergus said. "Turn that off right now." His wife pressed a button on a remote control, and the screen went a blank blue except for the DVD sign. "And who said you could use my TV?" Fergus added.

Lisa said, "We had to, Dad, because Mom's is too old to take a DVD and she said she was ready to try and watch this, and so did Laurie—"

"Dad," Laurie said. "You won't believe this. She had one guy that she made roll around in like a hundred squished-up bananas and then—oh God, Dad, she took a *dump* on him!"

Fergus looked at Laurie hard. "And what changed your mind about this filth?"

Laurie said, "Well, Lisa and I had a really long talk and I began to think about it, and I think maybe she's right, people should be educated, so I came here to watch it with Mom. And Mom said she would give it a try, because, you know, it's Lisa, it's her daughter—"

"Where's Teddy?" Fergus looked around.

"He's at his father's. It's Sunday."

Fergus had an odd sensation of not fully knowing where he himself was. He said to Lisa, "You took a shit on a man?"

Lisa looked down. "That's his thing, Dad."

Fergus walked to the television set, and then he was aware of a different strange feeling, his eyes became blurry very quickly, and without any sense of warning that his body would do this he went crashing to the floor, hitting his head on the corner of his television; briefly he saw stars. When he came to, he heard the loud talking of women, this would be his family, and they were trying to sit him up, and they did, and then he was standing and they were pushing him into the car.

All Fergus wanted to do was curl up, this kept going through his head, just curl up, curl up, curl up, and when they got him to the hospital he did that, he curled up on the floor of the emergency room, and very quickly a nurse came and got him standing again, and then he was on a thin bed and he curled up on the bed. When someone tried to straighten out his legs, he curled them right back up, almost to his chest, and his head was down there too. All he wanted was to stay curled up with his eyes closed.

Eventually he heard someone say "sedative," and he thought Yes, give me that, and they must have, because he slept deeply, and when he woke he felt frightened and did not know where he was.

"Dad?" It was Lisa, lowering her head, speaking to him quietly. "Oh, Daddy, guess what? You're okay! Oh God, Daddy, you scared us so much, but you're okay. They're going to keep you here tonight, but you're okay, Daddy."

She held his hand, and he squeezed it.

Then Laurie was there, and she said, "Oh, Dad, we were so scared," and he nodded.

Then he was alone, and he fell asleep again. When he woke, he knew right away that he was in the hospital and it was nighttime, a small light was on above his hospital bed. He closed his eyes again.

As he lay there he became aware of someone stroking his arm, very slowly, rhythmically, back and forth went the hand on his arm. He kept his eyes closed so it would continue, and it did. After many minutes went by—who knew how many minutes?—he turned his head and opened his eyes and saw that it was his wife. She stopped when she saw him watching her and put her hand into her lap.

"Ethel," he said. "What have we done?"

"Done about what?" she asked quietly. "You mean our life, or our children?"

He said, "I don't know what I mean." After a moment he said, "You have to tell me about Anita's kids. Not right now, but someday soon."

"Oh," Ethel said. "They're looney tunes."

"Not like ours," he said.

Ethel said, "Not like ours."

And then he nodded toward his arm, a small nod, but old marrieds that they were she understood. She began to stroke his arm again.

Heart

Olive Kitteridge opened her eyes.

She had just been somewhere—it had been absolutely lovely—and now where was she? Someone seemed to be saying her name. Then she heard beeping sounds. "Mrs. Kitteridge? Do you know where you are?" Wherever she had been was very sunny and there was no sun here, just lights on above her. "Mrs. Kitteridge?"

"Huh," she said. She tried to turn her head, but it wouldn't turn. A face appeared right near hers. "Hello," she said. "Who are you? Are you Christopher?"

A man's voice said, "I'm Dr. Rabolinski. I'm a cardiologist."

"Is that right," said Olive, and she moved her eyes to looking back up at the lights.

"Do you know where you are?" the man's voice said.

Olive closed her eyes.

"Do you know where you are, Mrs. Kitteridge?" The voice was getting annoying. "Mrs. Kitteridge, you're in the hospital."

Olive opened her eyes. "Oh," she said. She considered this. "Well, hell's bells," she said. The beeping sound continued. "Phooey to you."

Now a woman leaned down. "Hello? Mrs. Kitteridge?"

Olive said, "It was awful nice. Just awful nice."

"What was nice, Mrs. Kitteridge?"

"Wherever I was," said Olive. "Where was I?"

"You were dead." This was the man's voice.

Olive kept looking up at the lights. "Did you say I was dead?" she asked.

"That's right. You had no pulse."

Olive considered this. "Petunias," she said, "are such a nuisance." She said this because she thought the word "deadhead." To deadhead petunias was a constant job. "Godfrey," she said, thinking of lavender petunias. "All the time," she said.

"All the time, what? Mrs. Kitteridge?" This was the woman, who kept appearing and then disappearing.

"Petunias," said Olive.

And then the voices lessened, they were chatting among themselves, and the beeping sound continued. "Can't you get that to stop?" Olive asked the ceiling.

The woman's face, a plain face, came back into view. "Get what to stop?"

"That beep-beep-beep-beep." Olive tried to

figure out who this woman was; there was something familiar about her.

"That's the heart monitor, Mrs. Kitteridge. That lets us know your heart is beating."

"Well, turn it off," said Olive. "Who gives a damn?"

"We do, Mrs. Kitteridge."

Olive thought through everything that had happened so far. "Oh," she said. And then she said, "Oh, *shit*. Honest to Christ," she said. "For fuck's sake." The woman's face went away. "Yoo-hoo," said Olive. "Hey, yoo-hoo. Excuse me, I have no idea why I said 'shit.' I never say 'shit.' I hate the word 'shit.'" No one seemed to hear this, though she could hear voices nearby. "All right," said Olive, "I'm going back now." She closed her eyes, but the beeping continued. "Oh, for heaven's sake," she said.

The man's face returned. Olive liked the man better than the woman. He said, "What is the last thing you remember?"

Olive thought about this. "Well," she said, "I can't say. What should I say?"

"You're doing fine," the man said.

What a nice man. "Thank you," Olive said. Then she said, "I would like to go back now, please."

The man said, "I'm afraid you won't be going home for a while, Mrs. Kitteridge. You've had a heart attack. Do you understand?"

• • •

When she woke up next, a different man was there; he seemed almost a boy. "Hello," she said. "What's your name?"

"Jeff," said the fellow. "I'm a nurse."

"Hello, Jeff," said Olive. "Now tell me why I'm here."

"You had a heart attack." The fellow shook his head sympathetically. "I'm sorry."

Olive moved her eyes to look around. There were many machines, and many little lights, and still that beeping noise. Then she looked at her arm and saw there were things attached to it. Her throat felt funny, kind of achy. She looked back at the boy. "Uh-oh," she said.

"Yeah," he said, with a shrug. "I'm so sorry."

Olive pondered this a while. "Well, it's not your fault," she said. The boy had brown eyes, and long eyelashes. A lovely young man.

"Oh, I know," he said.

"What's your name again?"

"Jeff."

"Jeff. Okay, Jeff. How long do you think I'll be in here?"

"I really don't know. I don't even think the doctor knows." Jeff was sitting in a chair, she realized, that was pulled up right next to the bed she was lying on.

She looked around, without raising her head. "Am I alone?" she asked.

"No. You have two roommates. You're in the ICU."

"Oh *hell*." After a moment Olive said, "Who are the roommates? Are they men?"

"No. Women."

"Can they hear me?"

Jeff turned his head, as though to look at someone. He turned back and said, "Dunno."

Olive closed her eyes. "I'm very tired," she said. She heard the chair being pushed back. Don't go, she wanted to say, but she was too tired to say it.

When she next woke, her son, Christopher, was sitting by her bed. "Christopher?" she said.

"Mom." He put his hands in front of his face. "Oh, Mommy," he said, "you scared me to death."

This was more confusing to Olive than anything that had happened so far. "Are you real?" she asked.

Her son's hands came away from his face. "Oh, Mommy, say something else. Oh *please* don't have lost your mind!"

For a few moments Olive was silent; she had to gather her thoughts. Then she said, "Hello, Chris. I haven't lost my mind at all. I've—apparently—had a heart attack, and you have—apparently—come to see me." When he didn't say anything, she demanded, "Well? Did I get it right?"

Her son nodded. "But you scared me, Mom. They said you were swearing. And I thought, Oh God, she was swearing? Then she's gone absolutely dippy, and I thought, I'd rather she be dead than dippy."

"I was swearing?" Olive asked. "What kind of swearing?"

"I don't know, Mom. But they got a kick out of it. When I asked, they just laughed and wouldn't tell me, just that you were really angry."

Olive considered this. Her son's face seemed quite old to her. She said, "Well, never mind. I was someplace gorgeous, Chris, and then they brought me back here and I guess I was mad, I don't remember, but ask me anything and I'll show you I'm not dippy. God, I hope to hell I'm not dippy."

"No, you sound better. You sound like yourself. Mom, they said you were *dead.*"

"Isn't that interesting," Olive said. "I think that's awful interesting."

Dr. Rabolinski held her hand when he spoke to her; she did not remember that he had done that before. But his hand was smooth and yet a man's hand, and he held her hand in both of his, or sometimes just one of his hands would hold one of hers as he spoke to her. He had glasses that were fairly thick, yet she could see his eyes behind them; dark and penetrating, they looked at her as he spoke, holding her hand. She was a strong woman, he said, and gave her hand a little squeeze. She'd had a stent put into her artery, he said. She had been intubated; Olive did not know what that meant, and she did not ask. He told her again that she had had a heart attack in the driveway of the woman who cut her hair. She had fallen forward onto her car horn, so the woman came right out and called 911 immediately, and this was why Olive was alive, even though she had had no pulse when they came to get her. But they had brought her back to life.

Looking into Dr. Rabolinski's eyes while he held her hand, Olive said thoughtfully, "Well, I don't know if that was such a good idea."

The man sighed. He shook his head slowly. "What can I say," he said, sadly.

"Nothing," she said. "Nothing to say to that."

She had fallen in love with him.

Olive stayed on in the ICU unit; pneumonia arrived because of the intubation. These were days when she knew very little of what was happening to her, she had the sense that she was a huge chunk of smelly cheese and every so often someone seemed to mop her up, turning her one way, then the other. She drifted in and out of sleep, and then she seemed to not be able to sleep at all. A deep sadness gripped her, and she could only stare at the ceiling, or try to talk to Christopher—who showed up, she thought, quite a lot—sitting by her bed, talking to her, sometimes looking so anxious that she wanted to say, "Please go now," but she didn't say it, she was old and tired and her son was there to be with her. It seemed to her to be one of the few times in her life when she didn't say what she thought. But when he wasn't there her sadness deepened, and she understood after a while that she was probably not going to die, but that her life would be very different.

She said this quietly to Dr. Rabolinski when he came to see her and sat on the bed and held her hand. "Your life is going to be very much what it used to be," he said to her. "You just need to recover, and you will."

"Ay-yuh," she said, and she pulled her hand away.

But he stayed seated. Oh, what a nice man he was. She flopped her hand back over to where he could hold it again if he wanted to, but he didn't, and in her foggy state she understood that she had made it impossible for him to do so.

"Hold my hand," she said. "I like it when you hold my hand." And so he held her hand again, and told her that she was being given intravenous antibiotics and they were helping and soon she would be out of here.

• • •

And then she was out of there, and into a regular hospital room. She stayed in the hospital room for a few days, later she found out it had been seven days, and when she thought of it she thought it had seemed longer than that, and also shorter. In other words, time had become something different. She was moved to a room where her bed looked out a window onto the trees—it was autumn and she watched the maple leaves fall off one by one, sometimes two or three of them would flutter downward— and she liked that. She didn't like the woman she shared the room with, and she asked that the curtain be drawn between the two beds, and someone did that for her, and Olive said, "Now let it *stay* that way."

At night it seemed to her she did not sleep and yet she did not seem to care, or perhaps she did sleep; Christopher had brought her little transistor radio to the hospital for her and she clung to it, held it to her cheek, like it was a stuffed animal and she was a child. In the early mornings, she watched it get light through the window and the sky was astonishing as it changed from pale gray to rose to blue; it backlit the treetops and then penetrated them; Olive really felt astonished by this. Beautiful! And then—so early the sun had barely come up—Dr. Rabolinski appeared, saying, "Hello, Olive, how's my favorite patient today?"

"Oh hell," she answered, "I want to go home."
Except she didn't want to, because she was in
love with this man. Privately the shame of this
seared her. But she could do nothing about it.

When he asked if she had moved her bowels,
she almost died. "No," she said, looking away.
When he asked if she had broken wind, she
said, "Don't know." And he said, Okay, but let
him know when this happened. He sat down
on the bed and took her hand. He said she was
doing very well, that she could go home in a few
days.

"I'm an eighty-three-year-old woman," she
said, looking at him. His eyes behind his thick
glasses looked back at her.

And he shrugged and said, "In my world, that's
a baby."

But when they brought in the breakfast trays
and the hospital day started she would become
querulous and want to go home. Christopher—
who had returned briefly to his home in New
York City but was now back—showed up, sometimes while she was poking at her scrambled
eggs, or sometimes later, but he looked tired,
and she worried about him. "I've arranged for
home healthcare," he said to her. "Someone will
be with you around the clock for the first two
weeks."

"I don't need that," Olive told him. "Phooey."

But truthfully, the idea of being alone in her house made her afraid.

In the afternoon, the nurse Jeff came to see her before he started his duty in the ICU. "Hello, hello," she told him. "I've been walking around the halls, I'm ready to go home."

"You're amazing," he said. And one time he took her arm as she walked the halls with him, her cane in her other hand.

"So are you," she said.

Dr. Rabolinski asked her again if she had moved her bowels, and she considered lying about it, but she did not. "Nope," she said.

"Don't worry," he said. "You will."

And then that afternoon—oh ye gods! Olive broke wind, and broke it some more, and then she began to leak from her back end. She didn't understand at first what was happening, but as she raised herself from the bed, she stared at the mess that was there. She rang for the nurse. The nurse did not come. She rang again. The nurse finally arrived and said, "Oh dear." And that made Olive feel worse.

"I should say so," Olive said. "This is horrible."

"Don't worry," the nurse said. "It happens."

"It does?" Olive demanded, and the nurse said, Yes, sometimes it did, it was the antibiotics she'd been on for her pneumonia, let's get you into the shower and she'd change the bed, and when Olive came out of the shower the bed was changed and on the bed was a huge papery diaper.

When Dr. Rabolinski showed up the next morning, Olive waited to see if he had heard of her horror, and when he did not mention it, she finally said, "My bowels moved with a frightful ferocity." She made herself look at him when she said that. He said, "It's the antibiotics," and gave a small shrug. So she relaxed a tiny bit and asked when she could go home, and he said, Any day now. He sat on the bed after that, without saying anything, and Olive gazed out the window. For a few moments she felt something close to bliss, but it was more as though time had stopped—just for these few moments time had stopped—and there was only the doctor and life, and it sat with her in the morning sunshine that fell over the bed. She put her hand on his briefly, and still looking out the window she said, quietly, "Thank you," and he said, quietly, "You're welcome."

Back home, Olive felt awful. She couldn't understand how she had lived in this house—Jack's house—for so many years, it seemed very different to her, and she worried that it would always feel that way. It was chilly, and she turned the heat up high, which she had never done before. The living room seemed huge, she felt she could barely walk across it, and she slept in the guest room downstairs. But Betty showed up—the first home healthcare aide—and she was a big person. Not fat, just big. Her maroon cotton pants were tight on her, her shirt barely closed; she was probably fifty years old. She sat down immediately in a chair. "What's up?" she asked Olive, and Olive didn't care for that.

"I've had a heart attack and apparently you're supposed to babysit me."

"Don't know that I'd call it that," Betty said. "I'm a nurse's aide."

"Fine," said Olive. "Call yourself whatever you want. You're still here to babysit me."

When Olive, walking to the kitchen a few minutes later, looked out the window at the truck that Betty had driven over in and saw on the back of it a bumper sticker for that horrible orange-haired man who was president, she almost died. She took a deep breath and walked back to where Betty sat, and she said to Betty, loudly, "Listen to me. We will not talk about politics. Do you hear me?" And Betty shrugged and said, "Okay, whatever." Olive shuddered every time she thought about that bumper sticker.

But after a few days of Betty, Olive sort of got used to her. It turned out that Olive had had the woman years ago in Olive's seventh-grade math class; she had forgotten until Betty reminded her. "You sent me to the principal's office a lot," Betty said.

"Why?" Olive asked. "What could you have done?"

"I wouldn't stop talking in class. I was mouthy."

"And I sent you to the principal's office?"

Betty nodded. "I'd do it on purpose. I had such a crush on him."

Olive watched her from across the room.

"Oh, did I have a crush on that man," Betty said. "Mr. Skyler. Whoa."

"Jerry Skyler," said Olive. "He was a nice man, I liked him myself. He'd always say to people, 'You're doin' excellent.' He'd been a coach."

Betty laughed. "You're right! He'd always say that. Well, I *really* liked him. You know, I was skinny back then," and she ran her hand down in front of herself. "And kind of cute. And I think he thought I was kind of cute. Who knows. But, boy, I was crazy about that guy." Betty shook her head slowly, then pointed a finger at Olive and said, "You're doin' excellent."

At four o'clock a different woman would show up; her name was Jane, and she was pleasant but Olive found her bland. Jane made dinner for her, and Olive told her she would like to be alone, so Jane went upstairs. And then when Olive woke up in the morning yet another woman was there, but she left soon and Betty came back.

A few days later, around four o'clock—when it was time for Jane to show up—Betty answered the door, and Olive heard her say "Hello," but she heard something different in Betty's voice, it was not as pleasant as it usually was. Olive got up and walked out into the hallway, and standing there was a young dark-skinned woman wearing a brilliant peach-colored headscarf, and a long robelike dress that was a deeper peach color. "Well, hello, hello," said Olive. "Look at you! You look like a butterfly, come on in."

The young woman smiled, a row of brilliant white teeth showing across her face. "Hello, Mrs. Kitteridge," she said. "My name is Halima."

"Well, just come right on in. Very nice to meet you," Olive said, and the woman came into the living room and looked around and she said, "A big house."

"Too big," Olive said. "Make yourself comfortable."

Betty left, without saying a word, and Olive was disgusted by that. But Halima took right over; she got to work in the kitchen, asking Olive what she ate, and then she made the bed in the guest room, even though it was five o'clock, while Olive sat in the living room.

"Come sit," Olive finally called to the woman, and so the woman came in and sat down and Olive thought again that she looked beautiful. "I'm going to call you Butterfly," Olive said, and the woman smiled with those bright white teeth and shrugged and said, "Okay, but my name is Halima."

"Now tell me, Ms. Halima Butterfly, you must come from Shirley Falls."

And Halima said that was right; she had gone to Central Maine Community College and earned her nurse's aide degree and—she shrugged, raising her arms slightly, her robe flapping like gentle wings—here she was, she said.

"You were born here?" Olive asked.

"I was born in Nashville. Then my mother moved here fifteen years ago."

"Was she in one of those camps in Kenya?" Olive asked her.

And the woman's face brightened. "You know about the camps?" she asked.

"Of course I do. Do you think I'm an ignorant fool?"

"No, I don't think that." Halima leaned back in the chair. "My mother was in the camp for eight years, and then she was able to come over here."

"Do you like it here?" Olive asked.

Halima only smiled at her, and then said, "Let's get you something to eat. You're too skinny," and this made Olive laugh. "I have never been skinny in my life, Ms. Halima Butterfly," she said, and Halima went into the kitchen.

"Don't just sit here and watch me eat," Olive said to her after Halima had put out a slab of meatloaf and a baked potato done in the micro-wave. "If you're not going to eat anything, get out of here." So Halima swept herself away, then returned to the kitchen just as Olive was finishing with her meal.

"Why do you wear that stuff?" Olive asked.

Halima was washing the dishes, and she turned to smile at Olive over her shoulder. "It is who I am." After a minute, Halima turned the water off and said, "Why do you wear *that* stuff?"

"Okay," said Olive. "I was just asking."

The next day Olive said, "Now you listen to me, Betty Boop."

Betty sat down in the chair across from Olive.

"I saw how you treated that woman yesterday, and we'll have none of that in this house." Betty's face—Olive could suddenly see this distinctly—looked as though she was twelve years old again and sulking. "And stop sulking," Olive said. "Honest to God, it's time you grew up."

Betty shifted her rump on the chair and said, "You told me we weren't going to discuss politics."

"Damn right," said Olive. "And that woman is not politics. She's a person, and she has every right to be here."

"Well, I don't like the way she looks, that stuff she wears, it gives me the creeps. And it *is* politics," Betty added.

Olive thought about this, and finally she sighed and said, "Well, in my house you are to be nice to her, do you understand?" And Betty got up and started to do some laundry.

At the end of that first week, Betty drove Olive to her appointment with Dr. Rabolinski. Olive had put lipstick on, and she sat next to Big Betty in her car; it was Olive's car that Betty drove, Olive would honestly rather have died than be seen in a truck with that bumper sticker. Olive was silent, frightened to think of seeing this man again. In the waiting room of his office they sat for almost an hour, Betty flipping through magazines, sighing, and Olive just sitting quietly with her hands in her lap. Finally, the nurse called Olive in. Olive put the paper gown on and sat down on the examining table, and the nurse came back in and stuck things on her chest and did an EKG, then took the metal things off her and left Olive alone. Olive sat up. A mirror across from her caused her to look at herself and she was aghast. She thought she looked like a man in drag. The lipstick was so bright on her pale face! How had she not noticed this at home? She looked around for a tissue, urgent to get the foolish lipstick off, when Dr. Rabolinski walked in and closed the door behind him. "Hello, Olive," he said. "How are you?"

"Hellish," she said.

"Oh dear." The man sat on a stool and wheeled it toward her. He sat gazing at her through his thick glasses. "Your EKG was just fine. Tell me why you feel hellish," he said.

And Olive felt then that she was in the first grade, only she had become Squirrelly Sawyer, the boy who sat in front of her in that grade. Squirrelly Sawyer, that she would remember him now. He came from a very poor family and he never understood what the teacher wanted from him, and his state of confusion—and his constant silence—now came back to Olive with a rush of force. She herself could not speak as the doctor waited for her reply.

After a moment the doctor took his stethoscope and deftly slipped it through the opening of her gown to listen to Olive's heart. Then he put the stethoscope on her back and told her to take deep breaths. "Again," he said, and she breathed in deeply. "Again." He sat back on the stool and said, "I like everything I hear." He held her wrist and she realized he was taking her pulse, and she did not look at him. "Good," he said, and wrote something down. He put the band of Velcro around her arm and pumped it up for her blood pressure and said "Good" again, and wrote that down as well. Then he sat on the stool once more, and she could tell he was looking at her and he said, "Now try and tell me why you feel hellish."

And tears—*tears,* dear God!—slipped down her face and over her lips with that foolish lipstick; she felt them tremble. She could not speak, and she would not look at him. He handed her a tissue and she took it and wiped her eyes and her mouth, watching the streak of color come off on the tissue. He said, "Don't worry, Olive. It's natural. Don't forget what I told you—after a heart attack it is common to feel depressed. You are going to feel better, I promise you that."

Still, she wouldn't look at him.

"Okay?" he said, and she nodded. "Come back and see me in a week," he said.

He got up and left the room. And then she wept and wept, and finally cleaned off the lipstick and wiped her eyes and got dressed, and when she went out Betty looked up at her with some surprise, and Olive flapped a hand at her to indicate she should shut up. They drove home in silence.

When they were inside the house, Betty said, "Now just tell me, are you okay?"

Olive sat down in the chair that used to be Jack's. "I'm fine," she said. "Just damn sick of it all."

"You're doing really well, though," Betty said, heaving herself down in the chair across from the one Olive sat in. "Believe me, I've had patients who couldn't take a shower for weeks by themselves, and the first day you got home, you went right in and washed your hair and came right out." Betty pointed at her and said, "You're doin' excellent!"

Olive looked at her. "They couldn't take a shower? After a heart attack?"

"Sure," Betty said.

"So what did you do?"

"I *helped* them," Betty said. "But I haven't had to help you a bit. I haven't even taken your arm, for criminy's sake."

Olive considered this. "Well, I'm still sick of it," she finally said.

When Halima Butterfly showed up, Betty said with exaggeration, "Hello there!" Olive could have killed her.

"She's an idiot," Olive said to Halima once Betty had gone. Halima looked at Olive and said, "You mean her bumper sticker?"

"Yes," Olive said, "that is exactly what I mean."

Halima said, looking down, running a finger across the table that a lamp sat on, "Do you know when my little brother heard that man became president, he started to cry." Halima looked up at Olive. "He cried and said, Now we'll have to go back, and my mother explained to him that he was born here and he didn't have to leave."

"Oh Godfrey," said Olive; briefly she closed her eyes. Then Olive said, "Tell me what it's like to be you." Halima looked around the room. Today she wore a dark red robe and a dark headscarf. "By the way," Olive added, "that peach-colored thing you had on the other day was just lovely."

Halima smiled slightly and said, "You don't like this?"

"Not as much," Olive said. "Too dark."

Halima told Olive that she had four sisters and two little brothers, and that two of the sisters and one brother lived in Minneapolis. "Why?" Olive asked. And Halima said they liked it there. Then she stood up and said she was going to get started on Olive's dinner.

When Halima Butterfly did not show up the next day—it was Jane again—Olive felt very bad. She asked Jane where the Somali girl was, and Jane said that she didn't know.

Olive kept thinking about this, she kept going over in her head why the girl had not shown up; she just hadn't liked Olive was what Olive thought, and this hurt her feelings and also made her angry.

The next morning when Betty was out doing some errands for her, Olive called the home healthcare place and asked why Halima had not shown up. The woman on the phone said she had no idea, scheduling was not what she did. "Fine," Olive said, and hung up.

The next week's visit to Dr. Rabolinski, Olive drove the car herself, but she had Betty with her. Earlier, she had taken a practice drive into town and then back home—also with Betty. "See?" Betty said. "You're all good."

This time Olive had prepared herself. She looked as good as she could for a baggy old woman with a heart attack under her belt; she wore a blue and white jacket she'd discovered in her closet, and when she saw the doctor, she felt almost no attachment to him. This surprised her; and she noticed too—or thought she did—that he was not as nice to her as he had been before. "You're doing fine," he said, then shrugged. "What can I say? You are good to go."

"Ay-yuh," she said.

"I'll see you in a month," he told her. And then, as he was going out the door, he stopped and said, "You must have been a very good mother, Olive."

She could not have heard him right. "Why in the world do you think that?" she asked as she stuck her legs down over the table.

"Because your son was so often in attendance at the hospital, and he's called me twice to make sure you're all right." The doctor cocked his head slightly. "So you must have been a very good mother."

Olive was baffled by this. "I don't know if that's true," she said slowly.

"Get dressed and see me in my office," Dr. Rabolinski said.

In his office, he simply repeated that she was doing fine. And Olive got up and left.

As she drove home, with Big Betty next to her,

Olive wondered if her initial feelings for the man had been because she thought he had saved her life. Maybe you fall in love with people who save your life, even when you think it's not worth saving.

But in Jack's house—because now it was Jack's house once more, and not hers, Olive had felt this increasingly since she had first come home from the hospital—she felt unsteady. She did not feel as she had. She kept thinking: I'm different. After the last day that Betty, and the others, worked for her (Betty had tried to hug her, though Olive only stood there), she felt especially bereft; she felt unwell and tired. But when she told Dr. Rabolinski this the next time she saw him, he said, "You're doing just fine, Olive. There is no reason you can't live alone and drive your car. You're fine now."

"Ay-yuh," she said.

At times she could name it. It was almost panic that she felt. "Damn man," she said, and she meant the doctor, who was still young and had no idea—he had no idea—what it was like to be old and alone. But other days she felt okay. Not wonderful. But she could drive and get her groceries, and she visited her friend Edith at that awful old folks' home she lived in called Maple Tree Apartments. Then when she came home she was glad to be there, although she could not shake the feeling that it was Jack's house. She sat in Jack's chair these days so that she wouldn't have to look at it gapingly empty. And sometimes as she sat there a deep sadness trembled through her, because she wanted to be living in the house she had built with Henry; that house had been torn down, and she couldn't even stand to go by the spot. But what a nice house it had been! What a nice man Henry had been! And the sadness would deepen as she looked around this house she lived in—had lived in for almost eight years—and she would think: Honest to God. To sit in the middle of this field when I could still be by the water.

She thought about Jack's expression the night he died in bed next to her. He had said, "Good night, Olive," and reached to turn the light off, but first giving her a fleeting smile, which now in her memory seemed to be a smile he gave when he was far away from her. She had lived with him just long enough to begin to recognize these things, the changes in expression—so brief—that indicated he was somewhere else. And she thought he was like that when he said his last words, "Good night, Olive."

To hell with you, she thought, but she was really hurt by this recognition. He was not with her when he died. Oh, he was with her, he was lying next to her, but only because this was his home—his home with his wife Betsy—and Olive felt (now) that it was not her home, and she felt unsteady in it.

Then one afternoon she fell.

It was the middle of an afternoon in April, and a storm came in. Olive watched while the clouds moved above the field and then she heard the raindrops landing on the porch, hitting the windows. She rose and went out to the porch. She was only going to take in the cushions from the chairs she had put out recently, and she did not put on a coat or take her cane, but she walked out onto the porch, and as she bent to pick up a blue cushion from the wooden chair, she peered closer and saw that right there on the boards of the porch was a cigarette butt. Olive kept looking at this, she could not figure out where in the world it would have come from. She was really puzzled—and alarmed. But there it was, and it did not look like it had been there that long—certainly not for weeks, the white part of the cigarette was still white, but just flattened. Right next to the chair. Had someone been sitting in this chair smoking while she was away? How could that be?

Olive bent down—she couldn't figure out later how she fell, but she did. She fell right over, almost on her head, but then she rolled onto her side, between the house and the back of the chair, and she was so surprised by this that her head seemed a little different for a moment; it was just surprise. And then she couldn't get up. She could not get up.

"Olive, get up," she said quietly, aloud. "Olive, get up." She tried and tried, but she did not have the strength in her arm to push herself up. "Get up," she kept saying, over and over. "Olive, get up—you damned fool. Get *up*." The wind shifted slightly, and the rain began to come on her straight as though aimed at her. It was a cold rain, and she felt the drops pelting her face, her arm, her legs. My God, she thought, I'm going to die out here. She had spoken to Christopher the night before on the phone, he wouldn't think to call her for at least a few more days. And if other people called her—who, Edith?—and got no answer, they would think nothing of it. "Olive, get up, you get up right now," she said again and again.

It was that she would die of—what would she die of? Exposure? No, it wasn't cold enough, though she was very cold with this rain beating down on her. She would die of starvation. No, she would die of dehydration, and how long would that take? Three days. She would lie here like this for three days. "Olive, you get up right now." You heard about this kind of thing happening. Marilyn Thompson, who fell in her garage and lay there for two days; Bertha Babcock, who fell down her cellar stairs and lay there for days before being discovered, dead.

"You get up right now, you damned fool." But she couldn't. She kept trying, but she could only roll slightly more onto her side, and her arms did not have the strength. She spied the spigot there sticking out from the house. Jack had not wanted the spigot there, he thought it looked stupid coming out of the house straight to the porch, but he had said his wife had wanted it to make watering her plants easier. "Damn right, Betsy," Olive said. Her teeth were chattering now. Inch by half inch, Olive was able to move her body by thrusting it again and again until she could reach the spigot. She kept trying to reach it and she kept falling short, but then she finally got her hand around it, and by God if it didn't help. It stayed steady, the spigot, and she was able, by holding it, to get herself to a sitting position, and then she turned and knelt, and then she put her hands on the arms of the chair and she finally stood. She was so shaky that she placed a hand on the shingled wall as she moved slowly back into the house. Once inside, she sat for many minutes, wet, in the wooden chair by the table, and then she finally felt strong enough to shower.

But that had really been something. Sitting on the bed, holding a towel to her hair, Olive looked around. Who in the world had been having a cigarette on her porch? Who could it *be?* Olive kept picturing a man, sinister, smoking on her porch while he waited for her to return, some horrible man who knew she lived out here in the middle of nowhere all alone.

For the next week Olive could not stop feeling dread. She felt it when she went to bed, she felt it as soon as she woke. She felt dread in the afternoon when she sat and read her book. It did not abate, it got worse. And then she understood that it was true terror she felt, a different sort of terror than when Jack had died, or Henry. In those cases she had been *filled* with terror, but now terror sat next to her. It sat down across from her in the breakfast nook, it sat on the bathtub while she washed her face, it sat near her by the window as she read, it sat there on the foot of her bed.

And she began to walk around this home she had shared with Jack, and she said, "I hate it, I hate it, I *hate* this place."

Loneliness. Oh, the loneliness!

It blistered Olive.

She had not known such a feeling her entire life; this is what she thought as she moved about the house. It may have been the terror finally wearing off and giving way for this gaping bright universe of loneliness that she faced, but it bewildered her to feel this. She realized it was as though she had—all her life—four big wheels beneath her, without even knowing it, of course, and now they were, all four of them, wobbling and about to come off. She did not know who she was, or what would happen to her.

One day she sat in the big chair that Jack used to sit in and she thought she had become pathetic. If there was one thing Olive hated, it was pathetic people. And now she was one of them.

She heard a car drive into the driveway, and she got up slowly and went to the door, peeking out of the curtain that covered the door's window. Well, by God, if it wasn't Halima Butterfly! Olive opened the door, and Halima sailed through it and said, "Hello, Mrs. Kitteridge."

"What are you doing here?" Olive asked, closing the door behind her.

"I'm visiting you," said Halima. She wore the same peach outfit Olive had first seen her in. "I was in the area, and I thought, I'll go see Mrs. Kitteridge. How are you?"

"Ghastly," Olive said. Then she said, "Why didn't you come back?"

Halima said, "I don't like to drive all the way to Crosby from Shirley Falls, so when I can have a client nearer to me I take them instead." She shrugged her robed shoulders. Then she smiled her amazing smile of bright white teeth. "But I'm here now."

"All right then," Olive said.

Seated in the living room, Olive told Halima about her fall and the cigarette butt. Halima looked concerned. "I don't like that," she said. "You should not be living alone."

Olive made a noise of disgust, waving her hand to indicate that this was a stupid thing to say. But Halima sat forward, pointing a finger at Olive. "In my culture," she said, "you would never be alone."

Olive didn't care for that. "Well, in my culture," Olive said, pointing her own finger toward the woman, "sons get married, go away, and never come back."

The Maple Tree Apartments had a waiting period of twelve months. But on the telephone one night, Christopher said he had figured out how to get her in there in just four months. "Mom," he said, "I signed you up after your heart attack just in case. So you're on the waiting list." Then Christopher said, "But, Mom, listen to me carefully. You're going to have to sell that house. We need you to live in assisted living, but you can live in the independent living part of it. You can't live alone in that house anymore."

Olive was very tired. "Okay," she said.

And so that was that. As spring broke through, Olive noticed it and felt glad. The forsythia bushes first, and also the snowdrops by the house. But then it snowed lightly one night, and in the morning the forsythia looked like scrambled eggs. Then the daffodils came out, and eventually the lilac trees. She noticed these on the road to the Maple Tree Apartments, where she went these days with more frequency to visit her friend Edith, whose husband, Buzzy, had recently died. Edith kept going on about what a wonderful man he had been; Olive had never particularly liked him, but she sat while Edith told her once more how he had taken a fall and been sent "over the bridge," as Edith said it was called, the place across an actual little bridge where people went when they had strokes and things, and then how he had died so suddenly. . . . Oh, it was tiresome to listen to. But Edith said she was glad that Olive would soon live there as well, although she said it only once and Olive would have liked to hear it more.

Whenever she entered and left the Maple Tree Apartments, Olive looked—naturally—at the whole thing with different eyes. The people seemed so *old*. Godfrey, there were men shuffling along, and women all bent over. People with walkers that had little seats in them. Well, this was to be her future. But in truth, it did not feel real to her.

And then one day when she was sitting in Jack's chair she heard a car drive into the driveway and she said out loud, "Who the hell is that," and she got her cane—suddenly hoping that it was Halima

Butterfly again—and went to the door, and it was Betty getting out of her truck. As Olive opened the door, Betty said "Hi, Olive!" in a voice that Olive thought was false in its cheerfulness.

"Come in," said Olive.

Betty sat right down in the chair she had always sat in, and she dropped her pocketbook onto the floor beside her. "How are you?" Betty asked.

And Olive told her. She told her she was moving to the Maple Tree Apartments at the end of the summer, and she told her how she had fallen and almost died (this is how she put it to Betty), and then she told her how it was over a cigarette butt that she had found by the chairs on the porch.

"Oh," said Betty. "That was probably mine. Sorry."

Olive had to take a minute to allow this to register. "What do you mean?" she asked.

Betty said, "I came over here one day and you weren't home so I sat out there and had a cigarette."

"You *smoke?*" Olive said. "Are you kidding me?"

Betty looked down at her feet, she had on sneakers with no shoelaces. "Only when I'm really upset. And I was upset that day." She looked up at Olive then and said, "Jerry Skyler died."

Olive said nothing, just watched her. She

was amazed to see tears come into Betty's eyes.

"Yup," said Betty, brushing them away with the back of her hand. "I googled him one day and found out he died. He was only sixty-eight. A heart attack, though maybe I shouldn't tell you that part. He died raking leaves in the back of his house north of Bangor."

Olive had been ready to yell at her, this woman who had had a cigarette on her porch, who had scared her to death—to the point of *moving!*—But Olive did not yell. She watched Betty's face, she saw the tears slipping down over her mouth, the very same way tears had slipped down Olive's mouth when she had put lipstick on for the doctor she had been in love with. And Olive thought about this: the way people can love those they barely know, and how abiding that love can be, and also how deep that love can be, even when—as in her own case—it was temporary. She thought of Betty and her stupid bumper sticker, and the child who had been so frightened that Halima Butterfly had told her about, and yet to tell any of this right now to Betty, who was genuinely suffering—as Olive had suffered—seemed cruel, and she kept silent.

After a moment Olive heaved herself out of her chair and brought a Kleenex to Betty, dropping it onto her lap, and then she returned to her seat. Betty blew her nose, wiped at her eyes. "Thanks," she said.

After a while, Olive asked, "What is your life like, Betty?"

Betty looked at her. "My *life?*" she said. More tears came over her face. "Oh, you know." She waved the tissue through the air slightly. "It sucks," she said, trying to smile.

Olive said, "Well, tell me about it. I'd like to hear."

Betty was still weeping, but she was smiling more too, and she said, "Oh, it's just a life, Olive."

Olive thought about this. She said, "Well, it's your life. It matters."

And so Betty told her then about her two marriages that had both gone wrong, three children who desperately needed money, about her son who had developed strep throat when he was twelve and it had affected his brain and he was now always talking about how crazy he felt, her own job for a while delivering newspapers at four o'clock in the morning, how she eventually got herself to school to become a nurse's aide. Olive listened, sinking into this woman's life, and she thought that her own life had been remarkably easy compared to things this girl had gone through.

When Betty got done talking, Olive was silent.

For Betty to have carried in her heart this love for Jerry Skyler, what did that mean? It was to be taken seriously, Olive saw this. All love was to be taken seriously, including her own brief love for her doctor. But Betty had kept this love close to her heart for years and years; she had needed it that much.

Olive finally said, leaning forward in her chair, "Here's what I think, young lady. I think you're doin' excellent." Then she sat back.

What a thing love was.

Olive felt it for Betty, even with that bumper sticker on her truck.

Friend

On a morning in early December, Olive Kitteridge clambered onto the small van that took residents from the Maple Tree Apartments into town to go to the grocery store; it had snowed lightly the night before, a white glistening everywhere. She grabbed hold of the railing that went up the small steps to where the driver waited—a sullen young man with tattoos on his neck—and she sat down in the third seat next to the window. She was the first person to board the van, and this was her first time on it. Olive still had her car, but she had decided to take the van into town today because her friend Edith, who had lived at Maple Tree for a few years, had recently told Olive that she needed to be friendlier to the people who lived here. "Ay-yuh," Olive had said. "Well, I think they need to be friendlier to me."

She watched now as the other old people—Godfrey, some of them were positively ancient—climbed on, and then a woman who looked a little younger than most of them got on and sat down next to Olive. "Hello!" the woman said to Olive, settling herself in with a variety of recycling bags and also a big red handbag. She was a pretty woman, with very blue eyes and white hair that was a bit longer than Olive thought it needed to be. "Hello there," Olive said, and the van pulled out, bumping over the speed bumps until they were on the main road away from the place. The woman's name was Barbara Paznik, she told Olive, and she asked how long Olive had lived at Maple Tree. Olive told her, three months. Well, Barbara said, shifting her weight a tiny bit to look Olive more in the face, *she* had moved in one month ago, and she thought it was the *most* wonderful place, didn't Olive think so? Olive asked, "Where did you come from?" And the woman said she came from New York City, but she had gone to camp in Maine when she was a girl and she and her husband had vacationed here for years, and now here they were, and they *just* loved it. Loved, loved, loved it. They were early risers and they took a walk on the path through the trees each morning. After a moment the woman said, "Where do you come from?" But Olive turned to look out the window; the woman's breath smelled.

They were driving past the Congregational church, where Olive's first husband, Henry, had had his funeral, and then the van drove down Appleton Avenue past the small houses there; a child and his mother had just come out the door

380

of one. The child was a boy, he wore no hat, and his mother, Olive noted, looked tired. She was wearing sneakers in this snow.

"I come from here," Olive said, turning to the woman. But Barbara Paznik was talking to the woman across the aisle from her now, the back of her tweed coat was almost all Olive could see. After a moment, Olive took her finger and poked the tweed coat hard, and Barbara turned with surprise on her face. "I said I come from here," Olive said, and Barbara said, "Oh, I see," and then went back to speaking with the woman across the aisle.

In the parking lot of the big grocery store, the van pulled to a stop, and people got off—slowly. Olive bought toothpaste and laundry soap and some crackers and oatmeal, then she was ready to go. For a few minutes, she sat on a bench inside the store, by the front door, holding her recycling bag with the stuff in it; she had gone to this grocery store most of her life, and she had never sat on this bench by the door; this fact now made her feel strangely—and particularly—sad. She got up and went back out to the van. The driver opened the folding door; he kept looking down at his cellphone. She tapped the snow from the tip of her cane and sat down in the seat by the window that she had been sitting in before; she was the first person back on the van. Silence surrounded her as she waited.

Watching while the others finally got into the van, Olive noticed that a few of the old women were apparently wearing those Depends things, those awful diapers for old people. She could see them bulk up the women's hind ends if their coat didn't go below their waist, and one woman, as she bent to get something she had dropped onto the floor of the bus, just about exposed this fact to everyone. It made Olive shudder.

Barbara Paznik did not even look at Olive when she got on; she simply went behind Olive and sat with someone else. No one sat in the seat next to Olive. And everyone seemed to be yakking to somebody. Then, as the van wound its way up the street and around the corner—Olive could not believe this—they all started to sing. "The wheels on the bus go round and round, round and round. . . ." Women looked at her with laughter on their ancient faces as they sang, even the few old men were laughing. Olive had to look out of the window, her cheeks getting warm. "God, Jack," she thought, "you're missing a hell of a time." She felt enormously angry at him for dying. And then she thought: He wasn't so much, that Jack.

To Olive, it felt that a screen had been lowered over her, the type of thing that went over a cake on a summer picnic table to keep the flies out. In other words, she was trapped, and her vision of the world had become smaller. Every morning, she drove to the local doughnut shop and bought two doughnuts and a cup of coffee to go, and then she drove out to Juniper Point and watched the water while she ate her doughnuts; the tides, the seaweed, the spruce trees on the little island, these things reminded her of her life with Henry. She would get out and throw her coffee cup in the garbage can there. And then reluctantly she drove back to the Maple Tree Apartments.

Her apartment, which was one room with a kitchenette and a bedroom and a large bathroom, faced north, and therefore got no direct sunlight. This bothered Olive tremendously. She loved the sun. Was she to live without sun? She had told this to Christopher on the telephone when she had first arrived, and he said, "Mom, we were lucky to get you in there at all."

She had brought with her the single bed from the guest room of the house she had lived in with her second husband, Jack, and a wooden table that she had had with her first husband, Henry. And a small hutch that she had with Henry as well. It had been Jack who had suggested storing those pieces of furniture in the basement of their house, and now she was very glad she had done so. It meant there were pieces of Henry here. "Thank you, Jack," she had said, after the movers had left. And then she said, "And thank you, Henry."

On the hutch she had placed a photograph of Henry and also a smaller photograph of Jack.

Every evening a group of residents gathered in the lounge area, where there were small wooden tables and a group of chairs, dark green with armrests. Here these people had their wine, and Olive kept trying to join them. The evening after that horrific van ride, she went and stood near the group of people in the lounge, holding a glass of white wine, but these people—she thought—made it clear that she was not one of them. They were wealthy, Olive had come to understand, and they were snobs. This evening a woman, who was tall and wore dark blue slacks with a white blouse, was talking about Harvard. Harvard this, and Harvard that. Olive said to her, "My second husband taught at Harvard. He went to Yale, and then he was the youngest person to get tenure at Harvard."

The woman looked at her. Just looked at her. "I see," she said, and walked away.

"Well, hell's bells to all of you," Olive said, putting her wineglass down on a small tabletop, and in her mind she meant Jack as well. In fact, when she got back to her apartment, she put away the one photograph of Jack, and just had Henry's photo there on the hutch by itself.

A few of the people were local; her friend Edith, for example, who had lived in this place for years, but Edith had a full life here. When Olive, on her very first night, went into the dining room for supper—it was a large room with foolish white latticework on the top half of the walls—Edith was sitting at a table for four, with three other people, and she gave Olive a little wave, and that was that, and Olive sat alone at a table for two. She hadn't known what to do with her face as she ate the stupid salad from the salad bar, and then the skimpy piece of salmon and yellow rice.

But Bernie Green was living here. Olive remembered him, because when Henry had to sell his pharmacy to that huge chain, Bernie had handled the legal aspects for him, and Henry had always spoken highly of him. And here he was, looking old as the hills, and where was his wife? His wife was over the bridge, it turned out; she had developed Alzheimer's very soon after they had moved here together, and so Bernie went every morning—over the little walking bridge that went to the Alzheimer's unit—and he sat by her bed even as she became more and more out of it. Whenever Olive saw him he had tears in his eyes, and sometimes they were just coming straight down his face. What was that all about? She asked Christopher this on the phone, and he said, "Well, Mom, he's probably sad about his wife," and Olive had said, "But, Chris, he walks around weeping!" And Christopher had said it was cultural. "Cultural?" Olive demanded.

"What in hell does that mean?" Christopher said it meant the guy was Jewish, and Jewish men weren't ashamed to cry.

Olive hung up disgusted with them both.

Ethel MacPherson had lived here for six months—she had moved in after her husband, Fergus, died—and she seemed to know everything about everyone; she was the one who told Olive about Bernie's wife going over the bridge. Ethel said, "Oh, I couldn't stand being in that big old house after Fergie died! Oh, how I miss him!"

"Wasn't he the fellow that used to walk around Crosby in his kilt?" Olive asked.

Ethel said, Yes—that was her husband.

"What was that all about?" Olive asked. "I never quite understood that myself."

Ethel seemed insulted by that. "Well, if you had Scottish ancestry you might think differently" is what Ethel said.

And Olive said, "I do have Scottish ancestry!"

"Well, maybe it doesn't mean to you what it did to Fergie," Ethel said, and she moved away, waving at someone across the dining room.

Phooey to you, Olive thought. But she felt awful; nobody was talking to her, and after a few minutes she went back to her little apartment.

As soon as it got dark she tucked herself into her little single bed and watched television. The news was amazing to her. And this helped her.

The country was in terrible disarray, and Olive found this interesting. At times she thought fascism might be knocking on the door of the country, but then she would think, Oh, I'll die soon, who cares. Sometimes she thought of Christopher and all his kids and she felt worried about their future, but then she would think: There's nothing I can do about it, everything is going to hell.

Eventually Olive found the Chipmans; they had lived an hour away in Saco, and he was a retired engineer and his wife was a retired nurse. Both were Democrats, thank God, so they could talk about the mess of the world, and they ate their supper together, the three of them at a table for four. This helped Olive; it gave her a place. The fact that she thought they were both a bit dull was not something she dwelled on, but often enough after eating with them she would roll her eyes on the way back to her room.

This is how she lived.

A few days after Christmas, her son, Christopher, and his wife and all four of their children came to visit. And here was a surprise! Christopher's oldest son, Theodore, who had been fathered by a different man and who had never, in Olive's memory, spoken to her, stepped into her apartment, a young adolescent now, and said, "I'm sorry you got sick. With your heart and stuff."

"Well," Olive said, "it happens."

And then the boy said tentatively, "Maybe things will get better here."

"Maybe," said Olive.

Olive's granddaughter Natalie was eight by now, and she would talk to Olive, but then would turn and cling to her mother, who rolled her eyes at Olive and said, "She's going through a stage."

"Aren't we all," Olive said.

But Little Henry, Olive's grandson who was ten, had memorized all the presidents of the United States. "Good for you!" Olive told him, but she was extremely bored as he recited them, and when he got to the current president, Olive made a noise of disgust, and the boy said, seriously, "I know."

After Christopher's family left, she was bereft, and she ate in her apartment for two days before she went back out and joined the Chipmans.

It was April when Olive first spotted the woman—she lived two doors down and across the hall from her—and Olive thought she looked mousy, and Olive had never cared for that mousy look. Olive kept on walking to the dining room, and after Olive seated herself at the table, waiting for the Chipmans to come in, she noticed that the mousy woman, who wore a big pair of glasses on her small face and had a cane with four prongs on the end of it, had also come into the dining room, and that she was looking around with uncertainty. Olive reached for her own cane and waved it in the air, and the woman looked at her then, and Olive indicated that she should sit with her. "Godfrey," Olive murmured, because it was taking Mousy Pants some time to make her way around the tables, and she still looked tentative, as though Olive had not meant to have her sit with her.

"Sit!" Olive said when the woman finally got to the table, and Mousy Pants sat and said, "My name is Isabelle Daignault, and thank you for inviting me to sit with you."

"Olive," said Olive. (She thought to herself "Frenchie" because this woman had that last name.)

But then the Chipmans came in, and Olive introduced the couple to her. "Isabelle." And they all began to eat and talk, and Mousy Pants said very little, and Olive thought, Oh, honest to God. When they had finished eating, Mousy Pants stood up and waited with some uncertainty, and Olive said to her, "You going back?" And Mousy Pants said that she was, so they walked out of the dining room together and back down the hallway.

Mousy Pants said, "I've only just moved in here, just two days ago."

"Is that right?" Olive said. Then Olive added, "It takes some getting used to, I'll tell you that.

The Chipmans are okay. The rest of the people are snot-wots mostly." Mousy Pants looked at her with confusion on her face. "Bye now," Olive said. And she left the woman at her door.

Spring had really arrived now, and Olive decided she wanted a typewriter. She had started to type things up—memories—on her computer, but the printer stopped working and she became so frustrated she shook; her hands were shaking. She called up Christopher and said, "I need a typewriter." Then she added, "And a rosebush." And by God if that boy didn't drive up from New York City the next week with a typewriter and two rosebushes; he brought Little Henry with him.

As Christopher carried in the electric type-writer, he said, "These are hard to come by now, you know," but she thought he did not say it meanly.

"Well, I appreciate it," Olive told him. He had brought five cartridges of ink and he showed her how to insert them. And then he planted the rosebushes as she directed, right outside her little back doorway in the patch of ground before the sidewalk; the man who ran the place had said she could garden out there. Christopher dug the holes deep, like she asked him to, and he watered the rosebushes right away as she told him to do as well. "Hi, Grandma," Little Henry kept saying;

she was busy with the rosebushes. But afterward, when Christopher came inside and had washed his hands, Little Henry looked at his father, who nodded at him. "Want to see a picture I made for you?" the child asked, and Olive said, "Yes, I would." And the boy carefully unfolded a piece of paper with a watercolor done of a skeletal-looking person and a big house. Olive thought it was very unimpressive. "Who is that?" she asked, and he said, "Me, and that's my house," and Olive said, "Well, well."

"Want to put it on your refrigerator?" Little Henry asked with great seriousness, and then he said, "That's what Mommy does with our drawings," and Olive said, "I'll stick it up there later."

About the typewriter, Olive felt almost happy. She liked the sound it made, she liked the fact that she could slip in a piece of paper and have it come out—without that damned blinking printer!—and she liked stacking the papers up. Some days she read over the things she had written, and some days she didn't. But the pile grew slowly. It was the only time she felt that sense of the screen she lived inside of lifting, when she was typing up her memories.

One day a memory came to her. But it could not be true. She was a little girl, asking her mother why she had no brothers or sisters like other people did, and her mother looked down at her and said, "After you? We didn't dare have another child after you." But this memory could not be true, and Olive did not type it up.

She did type her memory of how in the months before they discovered her mother's brain tumor her mother had behaved oddly—and one of the odd things had been that her mother would go and stroke her car as though it had been a horse from her childhood farm. When Olive thought of this now, she understood. She had never understood it before, but because her car gave her the only freedom she had, Olive saw that her mother had loved her car as well, as though it had been the pony from her youth and would get her out, from one place to another.

"Henry believed in God," Olive typed one day. Then she added, "So did I because of the frogs we dissected in biology class." She remembered how in college she had thought one day, looking at the inside of a frog: There must be a God who made all these things. Now she considered this, and then typed, "I was young then."

Mousy Pants continued to eat with Olive and the Chipmans, and then one day, as they walked back from the dining room, Mousy Pants asked Olive if she would like to come in and visit. Only recently had Olive found out that Mousy Pants came from Shirley Falls—that's how mousy she was, not to have mentioned it earlier—and so Olive said, "All right," and she went into Mousy Pants's apartment and was surprised by all the little knickknacks the woman had, a figurine in lederhosen and another in a Swiss dress, and many different photographs spread out on the surfaces of tables. Olive sat down. "Well, at least you have some sun," she said.

She saw how Mousy Pants's ankles were very swollen, and her wrists—which Olive had noticed before—were also swollen, and Mousy Pants said to her now, "I have rheumatoid arthritis."

"Horrible," said Olive, and the woman agreed that it was difficult.

Mousy Pants spoke quietly, and Olive asked her if she could speak up. "I can't hear you," Olive said, leaning forward in her chair.

Mousy Pants said, "Yes, I'm sorry."

And Olive said, "Oh, for God's sakes, there's no reason to be sorry, I'm just asking if you can *speak up*."

Mousy Pants sat forward herself then, and she began to talk. She talked without stopping, and Olive found herself becoming extremely interested in everything she said. The woman said this: She said her name had originally been Isabelle Goodrow, and as a girl she had become pregnant by her father's best friend. This was not long after her father had died. She was an only child, and she had been very protected, and she had known—she said this looking at Olive directly—nothing about sex at all. And so this happened. The man was married and lived in California with his family, and he had come back to the small town in New Hampshire where Isabelle and her mother were living to visit. And when he left she was pregnant. Her mother had taken her to the Congregational minister, who had said that God's love worked in mysterious ways, and so Isabelle, who graduated from high school just about this time, had the baby and stayed home with her mother, and she took some courses at the university but her mother died, and then she was alone with the baby. And she felt very ashamed. "Back then, people did," Isabelle said. "I mean, people such as myself. Very ashamed." She sat back.

Olive said, "Go on."

After a moment Isabelle sat forward again and said that she had packed everything up one day and driven up the coast to Shirley Falls, Maine.

"I told you I went to high school in Shirley Falls," Olive interrupted. "I came from the little town of West Annett and I went to high school there, and so did my husband." Isabelle waited, her swollen fingers draped over the top of her cane. Olive said, "Okay, keep going. I won't stop you again."

Well, said Isabelle, she knew no one in that town when she first arrived, and she guessed that was the point. But she was very lonely. She found a babysitter for her little girl, and she got a job working in the office room of a shoe factory, she was the secretary to the man who ran that department, and the room was filled with women. "I thought I was better than they were," Isabelle said. "I really did. For years, I worked with these women, and I thought, Well, my grades in high school were very good, I would have been a teacher if I'd not had Amy, and these women could never be teachers. I would think things like that," she said, and she looked directly at Olive again.

Olive thought: By God, she's honest.

The women in the office room, though, turned out to be real friends. When Amy was sixteen years old, there was a crisis. Isabelle found out that Amy had been having a relationship with her math teacher. "A sexual one," Isabelle said. Isabelle had become furious. "Do you know what I did?" She looked at Olive, and Olive saw that the woman's eyes were smaller and becoming red.

"Tell me," Olive said.

"Amy had always had beautiful hair. Long, wavy yellow hair, her father's hair, not mine, and when I found out about that math teacher—Olive, I walked into that girl's bedroom with a pair of shears—and—and I cut her hair off." Isabelle looked away and took her glasses off and drew a hand across her eyes.

"Huh." Olive considered this. "Well, I guess I can understand," she said.

"Can you?" Isabelle looked at her, putting her glasses back on. "I can't. Oh, I mean I *did* it, so I should understand it, but, oh, the memory haunts me, what a thing to do to that child!"

"Does she like you now?" Olive asked.

And Isabelle's face broke into gladness. "Oh, she loves me. I don't understand how she can, I really was not a good mother, I was so quiet and she had no friends, but yes, she lives in Des Moines now, and she has one son who is thirty-five and living in California doing computer stuff. But yes, Amy does love me, and she's the reason I can afford this place."

Olive asked to see a photograph of the girl, and Isabelle pointed behind Olive, and Olive turned around and saw a whole array of photos. The girl was much older than Olive would have pictured, but then she remembered how young Isabelle was when she had her. Amy wore her grayish hair short now, but her face was full and had a sweetness to it. "Huh," Olive said. She looked at the photos carefully.

"Well, I wasn't a good mother either," Olive said, turning back to face Isabelle. "But my son loves me. Now. After I had my heart attack he seemed to grow up." She said, "What does Amy do?"

Isabelle said, "She's a doctor. She's an oncologist."

"My word," Olive said. "Well, that's something. Working with cancer patients all day, my goodness."

"Oh, I think it has to be very hard, but she seems to find it fascinating. You know, her first little boy, he died when he was eighteen months old. Not of cancer. SIDS. And she was in nursing school, and then she just kept right on going. She's married to a doctor as well. He's a pediatrician."

Somehow Olive found this astonishing. She said, "Well, my son is also a doctor, in New York City."

"New York!" Isabelle said, and asked what kind of doctor he was.

"A podiatrist," said Olive. Adding, "People walk a lot in New York. He has a blazing practice." She looked over at the many little figurines that were on a shelf by the window.

"Those were my mother's," Isabelle said.

"So when did you marry?" Olive asked, looking back at her.

"Oh, I married a wonderful man, he was a pharmacist—"

"*I* married a pharmacist!" Olive almost yelled this. "My husband's pharmacy was right here in

Crosby, and he was a *lovely,* lovely man. Henry was made of love."

"So was my husband," Isabelle said. "I married him right about the time Amy went to college. He died last year, and our house was just too much for me, and so Amy got me into this place."

"Well," said Olive. "Well, well, well. We *both* married pharmacists."

Isabelle said, "My husband's name was Frank."

"And he was a Franco," said Olive. "What we used to call a Frenchie." And Isabelle said yes, and wasn't that funny, because back when she worked in that shoe factory, thinking she was superior to the women who worked there, she would never have thought she'd marry a Franco. But she did. And he was wonderful. He'd had a wife who'd died very young, before they'd had any children, and what this man did after his wife died, every day in the spring and summer and fall, was to go home after work—he and this young wife had had a house outside of Shirley Falls with fields all around—and he would get on his mower and he just mowed those fields. Mowed and mowed and mowed. And then he met Isabelle.

"Did he stop mowing?" Olive asked.

Isabelle said, "He didn't mow as much."

Olive felt a warmth move through her; she

stuck her cane onto the ground and pushed herself out of the chair. "Well, I like the sunlight you get here," she said.

Then something happened that made Olive far more concerned than the lack of sun in her apartment. Olive's bowels began to leak. She had first had this occur at night, it had woken her each time with a terrific sense of dread, and then one day on her way out of the dining room, she thought: I'd better hurry back to the bathroom, but she didn't get there quite in time. For Olive, this was absolutely appalling.

She rose at six in the morning the next day and got into her car—she passed Barbara Paznik and her husband, who were out walking, and Barbara waved with enthusiasm—and Olive drove to the Walmart far out of town. Walking as quickly as she could with her cane, she bought a box of those atrocious diapers for old people, and she brought them back and put them in the top of her bathroom closet. She wondered when she should put one on. She never knew when these episodes would occur.

A few nights later after supper, as she and Isabelle walked down the hallway, she felt the urge, and when Isabelle said, "Do you want to come in?," Olive said, "Yes, and hurry," and she walked directly into Isabelle's bathroom. "Whew," she said, and as she was straightening herself out a few minutes later, she glanced up and saw—a box of Depends!

Olive came out and sat down and said, "Isabelle Goodrow Daignault. You wear those foolish diapers for old people," and Isabelle's face became pink. Olive said, "Well, so do I! Or at least I'd better start occasionally wearing them."

Isabelle pushed her glasses up her nose with the back of her swollen wrist and said, "My bladder can't seem to control itself, so I had to start wearing them. Not always, but at night I do."

Olive said, "Well, my back end leaks, I'd say that was far worse."

Isabelle's mouth opened in dismay. "Oh, good heavens, Olive. That *is* worse."

"I guess to God it is. And I think after I eat is when this happens. Honest to good God, Isabelle. I'm going to have to make sure I have my foolish *poopie panties* on. Even my granddaughter's outgrown them—years ago!"

Isabelle seemed to enjoy that; she laughed until tears came from her eyes. Then she told Olive how she was always embarrassed to buy them when she took the van to the store with the other old people (she did not have a car); she always tried to sneak off and get them, and Olive said, "Hell, I'll buy all you want, I go to Walmart when it opens at six in the morning is what I do."

"Olive." Isabelle let out a sigh. "I'm awful glad I met you."

• • •

When Olive returned to her apartment she didn't write up any memories; she just sat in the chair and watched her birds at the feeder outside her window and thought that she was not unhappy.

And so the year went by. At Christmas, Olive met Amy Goodrow and her husband, who was Asian—Olive already knew this from the photographs—and she was surprised by Amy in person; there was something at once kind about her, but also cool. Olive didn't know what to make of her, but she told Isabelle after they had left—they had flown into town for three days—that she was a nice girl. "Oh, she is *wonderful,*" Isabelle said, and Olive thought about that, how much Isabelle adored this girl.

Olive's own family stayed in New York for Christmas. "They have all those little kids and the tree and all that foolishness," Olive told Isabelle. And Isabelle said, "Of course they do."

Another spring slowly arrived.

One evening Olive noticed that Bernie Green had some guests with him at supper. She watched from the doorway as she entered. They were a couple, maybe in their fifties, but as she watched she suddenly realized: Why, that's the Larkin girl! So Olive walked over to their table, and she said, "Hello, are you the Larkin girl?"

401

And the woman looked up at her, closing her dark red cardigan with one hand, and said, tentatively, "Yes?"

Olive said, "I thought so. You look like your mother. I'm Olive Kitteridge. She used to be a guidance counselor at the school where I worked."

The woman said, "Well, I'm Suzanne, and this is my husband." The man nodded at Olive pleasantly. Olive thought Suzanne was a pretty thing, though she seemed to Olive to have a pulse of sadness going through her.

"Do you know—oh, this was years ago now—" Olive sat down at the empty chair at the table. "Your mother called me a cunt."

Suzanne Larkin's hand went to her throat, and she looked at her husband, and then at Bernie. Bernie started to chuckle.

"Oh, I deserved it," Olive said. "I went to see her after my first husband died, and I went there because I thought her problems were worse than my own, and she knew that was why I was there, it was extraordinary, really, I never forgot it. But my word, what a word to use."

Suzanne Larkin looked at Olive, and then a sudden kindness came to her face. "I'm so sorry about that," she said.

And Olive said there was no reason to be sorry at all.

"She just passed away this week," the girl said.

"Oh Godfrey," Olive said. Then she said, "Well, I'm sorry. For you."

And the girl reached to touch Olive's hand lightly. "No reason to be sorry." She leaned in toward Olive. "At all."

Mostly, Olive and Isabelle spoke of their husbands, and also a little bit of their childhoods; Olive had told Isabelle right away that her father had killed himself in the kitchen of his house when Olive was thirty years old, and Isabelle's face had shown genuine sorrow. This was important to Olive; had the woman appeared judgmental, Olive thought they might have stopped being friends. Only seldom did they mention their grandchildren, and one day Olive asked Isabelle why she didn't talk more about her grandson, the fellow in California doing computer stuff. Isabelle put her hand to her chin as though thinking about this. "Well, talking about grandchildren can be boring for others, and also—" Here Isabelle sighed and looked around Olive's living room—they traded off their places to visit—and said, "And also, I don't really know him very well. The truth is, Olive, Amy is good to me, but she does live in Iowa, and I sometimes think when a child moves that far away they're really trying to get *away* from something, and in this case I suspect it's me."

Only then—in a certain way—did Olive fully

understand why Christopher lived in New York City. "I guess you're right," she said slowly, the pain of this a reticulation spreading through her. And then she thought about Amy. That's what her slight coolness had been: Amy loved her mother, but she was not close to her. The things that happen in childhood do not go away.

"I love my grandson," Isabelle was saying. "Oh, I do, but he's not really a part of my life."

Olive swung her foot up and down. After a minute she told Isabelle how she had written a letter to Little Henry and one to his older brother, who had suddenly been nice to Olive, and they had both written back, and then she got a call from Christopher saying, "Mom, you need to write the girls as well." And Olive had been stung by that, so she wrote the girls, and never heard a thing back from them.

Isabelle listened, and shook her head slowly. "I don't know, Olive," she said.

And Olive said, "I don't either."

And then one day Isabelle did not show up for supper. Olive went and banged on her door, and Isabelle came to the door—though it took her a long time—and she had bruises up and down her arm, which she showed to Olive as soon as Olive got inside. "Oh, Olive," she said. "I fell." And she told Olive how she had been getting into the shower when she fell and for a few moments it seemed she wouldn't be able to get up, but she did, and now she was very scared. Tears glistened behind her glasses. "I'm scared they'll move me over the bridge," she said. And Olive understood.

That day they each gave the other an extra key to their apartments, and it was decided that every morning and every evening one of them would slip the key into the other's door and make sure the other was okay, and then just walk out. Olive was surprised at the amount of safety she felt the first time—that night—when she heard her door open at eight o'clock and saw Isabelle walking into her bedroom. Olive waved, and Isabelle waved, and then Isabelle walked out. So it got like that. Olive checked on Isabelle at eight in the morning, and Isabelle checked on her at eight every night. During these times they seldom spoke, just gave a wave, and they both agreed it worked out well.

One day Olive opened the door to Isabelle's apartment—it was a little earlier than usual, Olive had been up for hours—and just as she was about to holler "It's only me," she heard Isabelle talking, and so she almost walked out, thinking Isabelle had a friend over.

But then Olive heard this: Isabelle, speaking in a baby voice, said, "Mommy, do you think I'm a good girl?"

And then Isabelle's voice changed to a calm, adult voice, and she said, "Yes, honey. I think you're an awfully good girl. I really do."

Isabelle's baby voice again: "Okay, Mommy, that makes me happy. I try to be a good girl."

Isabelle's adult calm voice: "And you succeed. You're a very good girl."

Baby voice: "Mommy, I need to take a shower."

Adult voice: "Okay, honey. You can do that."

Baby voice: "I can? Because sometimes I get scared. That I'll fall or something, Mommy."

Adult voice: "Oh, I understand that, honey. But you'll be okay. You can do it."

Baby voice: "Okay, Mommy. Thank you, Mommy. You're awfully good to me."

And then Olive saw Isabelle start moving toward the bathroom, and very quietly, so quietly that Olive felt the tension ripple right down her back, Olive closed the door, hearing it click, and she waited outside the door of Isabelle's apartment, and after a few moments she heard the shower running, and so Olive went back down the hall to her room.

Sitting in her wingback chair by the window, Olive kept hearing Isabelle talking to herself in those two different voices; a chill kept going down her arms. Was the woman schizoid? Olive could not stop herself from feeling a deep fear. Maybe Isabelle was going dopey-dope. Another chill ran down Olive's leg.

· · ·

That afternoon, Olive said to Isabelle, as they sat in Olive's apartment, "I've been thinking about my mother a lot."

Isabelle looked pleasantly at Olive. "Have you?" she said. When Olive didn't answer, Isabelle said, "What is it you've been thinking, Olive?"

And Olive said, with a small shrug, "I don't think my mother ever really liked me. I guess she loved me, but I don't know if she liked me."

Isabelle said, "Oh, Olive, that's sad."

So Olive just took the bull by the horns and said, "What about your mother, Isabelle? Tell me more what she was like."

And Isabelle did not change her expression; she just said, "Oh, she loved me. But you know, Olive, I disappointed her. With my pregnancy so early on, that was very hard on my mother. And then she died. And it was very sad, Olive, it's made me sad all these years, because I would have liked her to live long enough to see that Amy—oh, that Amy is a doctor, and so smart, and I would have liked her to know about my marriage to Frank. She would have felt so much better."

"Yes," Olive said. "Well, that's life. Nothing you can do about it."

"No." Isabelle shook her head appreciatively. "That's true. But I miss her these days. Somehow especially these days. Sometimes I talk to her—I even have her talk to me. The way she always would when I was little." Isabelle shook her head slowly; light reflected off her glasses as she looked at Olive. "It comforts me. And it gets mixed up with my being a mother to Amy, because I don't think I was such a good mother to her. You know, I've told you that before."

Olive had to think about this once Isabelle went home. Apparently, Isabelle was not schizoid, nor was she going dopey-dope. She missed her mother and was calling upon her in her own voice. Or in her mother's voice. For a long time, Olive sat in her chair by the window. A hummingbird came to the trellis, and then a titmouse. Olive, after many minutes of thinking about what Isabelle had told her, said tentatively, "Mother?" And it sounded foolish. Her own voice, an eighty-six-year-old woman's, saying the word. And she could not answer in her mother's voice. Nope, it was not going to happen.

And so, in a way, Olive felt a different layer of bereavement now; Isabelle still had her mother, in some form, and Olive did not. Olive sat, pondering this. After a moment, she stood up and said, "Well, phooey to you," but she didn't know who she meant.

It was June now.

One week earlier, as Olive had driven out of

the parking lot on her way to Walmart, she had seen Barbara Paznik and her husband out taking their morning walk, and Barbara had smiled and waved vigorously. And then apparently (Olive learned this later), Barbara had keeled over soon after; she had had a stroke, and two days later she was dead. Olive was amazed by this, and she was amazed at how distressed she felt.

She sat now in the early afternoon on one of the chairs set up in the meeting room for Barbara's memorial service; she had put on a pair of poopie panties just in case. Isabelle had not come because she had not known the woman, and she said she didn't feel right attending. About twenty people sat in a room that could hold three times that many. No one was weeping; they sat quietly while Barbara's daughter spoke about her mother always being so upbeat, and then a nephew spoke about Aunt Barbara always being so fun, and then— essentially—that was that. Olive started back to her apartment, then turned and went back toward the meeting room, and she found Barbara's husband, talking to two women. She waited until he had stopped, then she said, "Barbara tried to be nice to me one day and I wasn't very pleasant to her. I'm sorry she's gone. Sorry for you," she added.

And the man was so nice! He took her hand and he thanked her, he even called her Olive, and said that she mustn't worry about how she had treated

Barbara; his wife had never said anything to him about it. And then he leaned in and kissed Olive on the cheek. She could not believe it.

And she could not believe how sad she felt.

For the entire afternoon she sat by her window in her wingback chair and pondered many things. She had not been nice to Barbara Paznik because the woman came from New York. Then she thought how Barbara Paznik had been younger than Olive, and full of energy, and she was gone now. Dead. Olive kept picturing the woman's vibrant, pretty face. And somehow Olive, in spite of her two husbands having died, now understood that this had to do with her, with Olive. *She* was going to die. It seemed extraordinary to her, amazing. She had never really believed it before.

But it was almost over, after all, her life. It swelled behind her like a sardine fishing net, all sorts of useless seaweed and broken bits of shells and the tiny, shining fish—all those hundreds of students she had taught, the girls and boys in high school she had passed in the corridor when she was a high school girl herself (many—most— would be dead by now), the billion streaks of emotion she'd had as she'd looked at sunrises, sunsets, the different hands of waitresses who had placed before her cups of coffee—All of it gone, or about to go.

Olive shifted slightly in her seat, wearing her poopie panties beneath her black trousers and flowery top. She kept thinking: Barbara Paznik was alive, and now she is dead. And then, her mind twirling around, Olive suddenly remembered catching grasshoppers as a child, putting them in a jar with the top on, and her father had said, "Let them out, Ollie, they'll die."

She thought then about Henry, the kindness in his eyes as a young man, and the kindness still there when he was blind from his stroke, the pleasant expression on his face as he sat in that wheelchair, staring. She thought about Jack, his sly smile, and she thought about Christopher. She had been lucky, she supposed. She had been loved by two men, and that had been a lucky thing; without luck, why would they have loved her? But they had. And her son seemed to have come around.

It was herself, she realized, that did not please her. She moved slightly in her chair.

But it was too late to be thinking that—

And so she sat, watching the sky, the clouds high up there, and she looked down then at the roses, which were pretty amazing after just one year. She leaned forward and peered at the rosebush—why, there was another bud coming right behind that bloom! Boy, did that make her happy, the sight of that new fresh rosebud. And then she sat back and thought about her death, and the sense of wonder and trepidation returned to her.

It would come.

"Yup, yup," she said. And for many more minutes she sat there, not even really knowing what she thought.

Finally Olive stood up slowly, leaning on her cane, and moved to her table. She sat down in her chair, put her glasses on, and put a new sheet of paper into the typewriter. Leaning forward, poking at the keys, she typed one sentence. Then she typed one more. She pulled the sheet of paper out and placed it carefully on top of her pile of memories; the words she had just written reverberated in her head.

I do not have a clue who I have been. Truthfully, I do not understand a thing.

Olive stuck her cane to the ground and hoisted herself up. It was time to go get Isabelle for supper.

Acknowledgments

I would like to thank the following people for their help with this book: Jim Tierney, Kathy Chamberlain, and Jeannie Crocker, my childhood friend who reassured me about the cultural differences between New York City and Maine; Ellen Crosby, my college roommate, whose support through the years has been significant and meaningful, and who has provided for my readers the name of the town of Crosby; Susan Kamil, Molly Friedrich, Lucy Carson, Dr. Harvey Goldberg, and—always—Benjamin Dreyer.

About the Author

ELIZABETH STROUT is the #1 *New York Times* bestselling author of *Olive Kitteridge*, winner of the Pulitzer Prize; *Anything Is Possible*, winner of the Story Prize; *My Name Is Lucy Barton*, longlisted for the Man Booker Prize; *The Burgess Boys*, named one of the best books of the year by *The Washington Post* and NPR; *Abide with Me*, a national bestseller; and *Amy and Isabelle*, winner of the *Los Angeles Times* Art Seidenbaum Award for First Fiction and the *Chicago Tribune* Heartland Prize. She has also been a finalist for the National Book Critics Circle Award, the PEN/Faulkner Award for Fiction, the International Dublin Literary Award, and the Orange Prize. Her short stories have been published in a number of magazines, including *The New Yorker*. Elizabeth Strout lives in New York City.

elizabethstrout.com
Facebook.com/elizabethstroutfans
Twitter: @LizStrout
To inquire about booking Elizabeth Strout for a speaking engagement, please contact the Penguin Random House Speakers Bureau at speakers@penguinrandomhouse.com.

WITHDRAWN

Center Point Large Print
600 Brooks Road / PO Box 1
Thorndike, ME 04986-0001 USA

(207) 568-3717

US & Canada:
1 800 929-9108
www.centerpointlargeprint.com